THE GILDED HEIRESS

A NOVEL

JOANNA SHUPE

AVON

An Imprint of HarperCollins*Publishers*

HarperCollins books may be purchased for educational, business, or sales promotional use. For information, please email the Special Markets Department at SPsales@harpercollins.com.

Avon, Avon & logo, and Avon Books & logo are registered trademarks of HarperCollins Publishers in the United States of America and other countries.

hc.com

FIRST EDITION

Interior text design by Diahann Sturge-Campbell

Title page illustration © CaptainMCity/Stock.Adobe.com

Library of Congress Cataloging-in-Publication Data has been applied for.

ISBN 978-0-06-331031-5

25 26 27 28 29 LBC 5 4 3 2 1

THE GILDED HEIRESS

For Rich, who is the best other half I could ever ask for

THE
GILDED
HEIRESS

Chapter One

New York City
October 1878

L ater the police would ask, Why hadn't anyone heard?

The Fifth Avenue mansion was full of revelry that night. The guests celebrated in elaborate costumes, while toasting with champagne and eating bluepoints next to dripping ice sculptures. More than three hundred of society's finest were in attendance, along with a seventy-five-piece orchestra.

The hosts were none other than the Pendeltons, who possessed a dizzying kind of wealth, the kind that had been unimaginable before the war. Acceptance into high society hadn't come easy, yet Mrs. Pendelton was determined to see it through. Her daughter, Joséphine—named after an empress, naturally—was twenty-two months old, her two-year-old birthday coming soon in December, and Mrs. Pendelton would not allow the girl to be slighted in the years to come.

Tonight changed the social hierarchy. The coveted invitation had been the talk of the city for the last three months, with everyone angling to get on the list. The mansion, the size of a full city block, was the draw, but Mrs. Pendelton knew this was a sign of good things to come.

In the end the evening was a smashing success, with the sun just peeking over the horizon as the last guest departed. Mr. Pendelton still planned to get in a full day's work, so he retired immediately. Before seeking her bed, Mrs. Pendelton decided to go up to see her precious little girl for a few moments.

The nursery was empty, however.

She quickly rang for the sleeping nursemaids, who claimed no knowledge of the baby's whereabouts. Alarmed, Mrs. Pendelton awoke the entire household to begin a search for Joséphine. Lights were switched on, closets and empty rooms thoroughly investigated.

That was when they discovered the ladder outside the nursery's window.

An army of blue-coated Metropolitan Police officers swarmed the mansion. There were illustrators and photographers, roundsmen and detectives. Even several of the police commissioners stopped by. They tromped along the perimeter of the mansion, through the gardens, and around the ladder. Their muddy footprints soiled the Persian carpets and Italian marble floors as the staff was questioned again and again.

Why hadn't anyone seen or heard anything? The staff explained the noise and coal smoke outside required them to keep their windows closed. Furthermore, most of the maids and footmen had enjoyed extra champagne and food downstairs as the party wound down, while those not involved, like the nursemaids, were already asleep.

Little Joséphine could not be found.

Hysterical, Mrs. Pendelton took to her bed, while Mr. Pendelton awaited a ransom message. He telephoned the bank and readied his assets. Whatever these kidnappers demanded, he would pay it.

Except the telephone never rang. A cable never arrived.

It was unbelievable. Unprecedented. As the days wore on, the detectives remained flummoxed, the press agog. Politicians gave stump speeches that promised to eliminate crime. The public's appetite for information on the missing baby only seemed to grow. Headlines updated the city twice a day, until after a few weeks when the story moved from the front page to the inside.

Three months later the story was buried with the adverts and notices in the back.

At this point Mrs. Pendelton demanded that her husband offer up the largest reward in history to get her baby returned.

One hundred thousand dollars for any information regarding the whereabouts of little Joséphine Pendelton.

The incentive brought out the worst criminal element imaginable. Every charlatan, confidence man, and huckster presented themselves at the Pendelton residence with their "evidence," but none were credible. As the years wore on, the possibility that Joséphine would be found dwindled to almost nothing. Even Mr. Pendelton gave up hope.

But Mrs. Pendelton knew her little girl was out there somewhere. She could feel it.

And one day they would be reunited . . .

Chapter Two

Boston
May 1896

LEO

It was true that a fool and his money are soon parted—most often because of someone like me.

Money was in the forefront of my mind all day, every day. Specifically, who had it and how could I get my hands on it?

This afternoon was no different. I stood at the edge of a promising gathering in Post Office Square, my eyes sizing up the crowd. At least one fool with deep pockets lurked in every crowd. I merely had to lure him over.

"Find the red queen!" I called out to no one and everyone. "It's easy, folks! Three cards and all you have to do to win is to keep your eye on the pretty lady." Except it was impossible to win. Thanks to my sleight of hand abilities and some clever misdirection, the mark would never find the red queen. No one said I played fair.

Cards weren't my preferred game—it was a lot of work in the hot sun for three or five bucks—but my other plans came up short this month. I needed money, fast. My mother and five sisters depended on me to keep the family afloat.

After twenty minutes I was forced to admit defeat. No one was biting. The crowd's attention was locked onto a lady singing in the square instead. I decided to find another location. After all, the day was still young.

As I packed up my case, I heard her voice lingering in the

afternoon air. She was good. Very good, actually. Each note was delivered perfectly in a pleasing husky rasp. Who was this woman? Why was she singing here instead of on a stage?

I had to find out.

I picked my way through the crush, lifting a pocket watch and a billfold along the way, until I reached the front. It was there that I got my first peek at her. I let out a low whistle. She was a looker, with blond hair piled under a smart straw hat and green eyes that sparkled in the afternoon sun. Her simple shirtwaist and skirt were the same variety worn by just about every woman in town, though I could tell her clothing wasn't new.

It was clear she didn't have much stage presence. She stared far off into the distance, a remote statue, rather than working the crowd. Was she a struggling actor? An unemployed singer?

I elbowed the gent next to me. "Any idea who she is?"

The man shook his head. "Nah, but I've seen her out here fairly regular for the last few weeks."

Captivated, I continued to stand there, unable to look away as one song blended into the next. She really was something, combining both talent and beauty. Finally, she finished and everyone applauded. People moved forward to toss coins into her collection jar.

"Thank you. I appreciate your support," she said to the crowd, her voice threaded with the sounds of the Boston streets. She gestured to the jar. "I'm just beginning my career, but someday I'm going to be bigger than Lillian Russell and Enrico Caruso combined!"

I nearly rolled my eyes. I admired the girl's ambition—I had a bit of it myself—but if she wanted to be a famous singer, street corners were a waste of time. She had to meet the right people at the right places, get auditions with the best theater producers. I had no experience in that business, but even I knew how it was done.

Just then, someone paid her a compliment and she smiled.

I paused, mesmerized. From the curve of her jaw to her straight aristocratic nose, not to mention that beautiful mouth . . . There was something more, something unique about her. With her proud bearing and delicate features, she could've been at home in any Beacon Street drawing room. Any Fifth Avenue drawing room, for that matter.

"Hey! You!"

That voice . . . My head snapped over and I saw a familiar patrolman headed in my direction. Shit! It was O'Toole.

In a blink, I took off in the opposite direction, weaving between the bodies in the square as best I could while carrying my large case. I didn't need to check to know that O'Toole was following. I could hear him shoving people out of the way and yelling for everyone to move.

I was no stranger to the Boston Police Department. They didn't take kindly to a man trying to earn a dishonest living on the street, unfortunately. Most of the officers left me alone, but O'Toole wasn't one of them—which might've had something to do with how I'd conned his brother last year with a fake stock racket.

I ran faster, determined to lose him in the streets. "Look out!" I called to a lady standing in my way. She stepped aside, but it slowed me down. The crowd on the walk was too thick here, so I edged into the street. It was more visible, but I could run faster. I hurried toward the alleys, where I knew I could hide.

"Stop, Hardy! You're only making it worse on yourself!"

The soles of my worn leather shoes slapped on the cobblestones as I kept going, ignoring O'Toole. I knew these streets better than almost anyone else, not to mention I had more friends in this town than the coppers. It was time to put that knowledge to use.

I ducked between some buildings and found a familiar door, which I shoved open. Though the interior was dark, I could hear voices inside. I let the door close behind me and hurried toward the sound.

A cloud of blue silk and brown hair moved toward me the instant I reached the front hall.

"Leo! My darling!" Rebecca owned this establishment and oversaw the girls who worked here. "It has been ages."

"Hello, Becca." I took her elbow and began leading her deeper into the well-appointed salon. A handful of girls were gathered around, chatting and entertaining customers. "Ladies." I tipped my hat, then said quietly to Rebecca, "I need to hide out for a few minutes."

"Are you in trouble, darling?"

"Aren't I always?" I gave her my most charming smile.

She shook her head at me, though her eyes were sparkling. "Let's get rid of this, then." She took my case and hid it behind the lining of the tall windows. "Now, come with me. Sadie, Frannie, you come along as well."

As the four of us started up the main staircase, a knock boomed on the front door. Rebecca winked at me. "Girls, show Mr. Hardy up to a room. It needs to look believable. I'll handle the front door."

The girls took my elbows and we raced to an empty room. The three of us undressed me as quick as a wink, my clothes tossed casually on a chair, then I fell down on the bed. The girls crawled on top of me, sandwiching me between the two of them.

"You haven't been to see us in a while," Sadie said with a pout as she unlaced the front of her gown.

Frannie was already kissing her way down my chest. "Yeah, Leo. What gives?"

"Now, girls," I said, closing my eyes as a bolt of lust rushed through my veins. "It's nothing personal. Just a temporary fiscal deficit."

Sadie's bare breasts pressed against my side as her mouth met mine. The kiss deepened as our tongues intertwined—and I lost my train of thought when Frannie reached her target. Wet heat surrounded my semihard cock, and I groaned into Sadie's mouth.

"I think he likes it, Frannie," Sadie pulled back to say.

"Hell yes, he does." I yanked Sadie back for another kiss while Frannie worked magic between my legs. Her head bobbed under the coverlet as she gave my cock long pulls of her sweet lips. I palmed Sadie's breast and rolled her nipple between my fingers.

"I know he's up here!" a booming voice echoed in the hall. *O'Toole.*

I didn't stop what I was doing and neither did the girls.

"Officer, really. This is an egregious infringement upon my rights." Rebecca sounded calm and confident. "I haven't any idea for whom you are searching, but why don't we return to the sitting area and you may tell me all about it?"

"I ain't got time for that, madam," O'Toole snapped. "A man ran in here. Where did he go? Hidin' up in one of these rooms, is he?"

Rebecca chuckled. "There isn't a man hiding anywhere in here—unless you count one hiding from his wife!"

"Balderdash," O'Toole said. "I saw him enter with my own eyes. Where is he?"

Somewhere nearby a door opened, followed by shouts. "Officer!" Rebecca said sharply. "You may not scare my customers."

When another series of shouts followed, Sadie rose up and straddled my head. She lifted her skirts and I understood immediately. "Bless you, sweetheart," I said before grabbing her hips.

Sadie dropped the layers of cloth, covering my head, and lowered her pussy right onto my face. I inhaled her tangy scent and let her juices coat my tongue as I licked her slick flesh. Goddamn, that was nice.

The door opened, but I barely heard it. I was too invested in what I was doing and the way Frannie was tasting my cock like a delicious treat. All three of us were moaning and grunting, the room filled with the scent of sex. I could already feel an orgasm building in my balls.

"Dear god!" I heard O'Toole exclaim as he took in our debauched scene.

"I tried to warn you," Rebecca said. "As you can see, all my customers have been here for quite some time. Now, let's leave them to their vices, shall we?"

"But, but . . . I didn't think such a thing was possible," O'Toole was saying as the door closed.

"We must educate you, then." Rebecca's fading voice was husky and alluring, the perfect businesswoman. "I would love to offer you a whiskey on the house and explain these things. We do adore our local patrolmen."

"I'm married," O'Toole said, as if this were pertinent information. "Wouldn't be proper for me to stay."

"Oh, honey," Rebecca said from far away. "Almost everyone here is married."

Twenty minutes later O'Toole went upstairs with one of the girls. When the coast was clear I kissed Sadie and Frannie goodbye, gave Rebecca a few bills to cover their services, then slipped into the alley. I found myself grinning like a madman the whole way home.

Christ, I fucking loved this city.

CHAOS GREETED ME the moment I stepped inside the small house on Tremont Street.

This wasn't unusual. The Hardy household was a lively and loud one on the best of days. I have five sisters and they were an energetic bunch in tight quarters.

Molly met me at the door. One of the fifteen-year-old twins, she was the quirkiest of my sisters. She was obsessed with old copies of the *National Police Gazette* she'd found, and she idolized the female criminals and thugs mentioned in the pages. Currently, she was pretending to be Gallus Mag, a fierce woman who kept the peace—as well as the ears of unruly patrons—at a dockside saloon in New York City. "Hand over your entry fee or I'll cut you," she said, blocking my entrance.

"Move it, Gallus."

I tried to edge by, but she wasn't having it. Darting around me, she slapped her hand on my chest. "Two cents or you'll be sorry."

Shaking my head, I reached into my pocket and found two coins. "There. May I come in now?"

Molly took the money and stepped aside. "Yes, but mind your manners or I'll be forced to toss you."

I stripped off my coat and hung it by the door. The comforting sights and smells of home assaulted me and my shoulders relaxed. This was the only place in Boston where I could be myself.

Three of my sisters were in the front room of our tiny place, each of them with sewing on their lap. My mother took in mending and laundry from the neighborhood to supplement what I earned. We were determined to keep the Hardy girls out of the factories and brothels. It hadn't been easy.

Hattie, the middle child at nineteen, paused in her stitching to look me up and down. "What's with the fancy suit again today?"

"None of your concern," I said back. "Where's Flora?" At twenty-two, Flora was the wildest of the bunch. I didn't like that she wasn't here.

No one spoke, so I glared at Carolyn. She could never lie to me, a trait I exploited whenever I needed to know what was going on.

Carolyn sighed. "She went out about an hour ago."

"Where?"

"She didn't say," Molly/Gallus answered.

I arched a brow at Carolyn. I could see her brown eyes were conflicted. "Do you know?"

She shook her head. "I suspect, but I don't know for sure."

Christ, I didn't have the energy for this today. Grabbing an apple off the table, I tilted my head toward the door. "Caro, with me."

Wrinkling her nose, Carolyn put down her mending and followed me out the front door. We stood on the stoop, with her avoiding my eye. I took a bite of my apple. "Tell me where?"

"Leo—"

"Now, Caro. I don't have time for this."

She huffed and studied her shoes. "There's this man she's been seeing. He's filling her head full of stuff, dreams of a better life."

Anger and panic flared behind my sternum. I'd dreaded something like this happening for the last few years. "What man? Give me a name."

"I don't know his name," Carolyn said. "But he hangs out with the McLaughlin boys."

Shit. The McLaughlins were one of the Southie street gangs. Flora was out of her depth. "Does Ma know?"

"No. Flora said she was going to see a friend."

"Good. Let's keep it that way. Thanks, kid." I ruffled the hair on the top of her head and she shoved me away.

"Leo, stop it. You can't do that to me anymore. I'm a lady now."

"A lady, huh? You might be twenty, but you'll always be a kid to me." I reached for the doorknob. "Not a word of this to anyone. I'll talk to Flora when she comes home."

We went back inside and I headed for the kitchen. My mother was kneading bread on the counter. Tess, the other twin, was chopping potatoes nearby. I strolled over and kissed my mother's cheek. "Afternoon, ladies."

She looked me up and down as I leaned against the far wall, then her expression softened. "You look so handsome. Just like your father."

I didn't want to hear about Steven Hardy. He died a long time ago, a brokenhearted drunk, and I was too busy trying to keep us all afloat to miss him. "How was your day?"

"Fine. And yours?"

"Awful. Got run out of Post Office Square today." Her eyebrows knitted, so I rushed to add, "Don't worry. I'll make up for it tomorrow."

"Good, because the man was here about the rent again today. We're three months behind and he said he can't carry us anymore."

"I'll talk to him." *Add it to my list of things to do.*

"What will you tell him?"

"Ma, please. I'll handle it. We'll give him what we were saving for the electric and make up the rest later."

My mother looked over at Tess. "Sweetie, give me a moment with your brother."

Thanks to a lifetime of respiratory issues, Tess wasn't much of a talker. She merely nodded at the request and left the kitchen. When we were alone, my mother asked, "Where is Flora?"

"Out with a friend, I'm told. Why?"

"She's out more and more during the day." She flipped the dough over and continued kneading. "I'm worried it's a man."

"I'll speak to her. I'm sure it's nothing to worry about." It was definitely something to worry about.

"Thank you. She doesn't listen to me. Never did, even as a baby. I feel as though I failed with that one."

"Ma, don't beat yourself up over it. You had your hands full with all of us, living in a tiny one-bedroom apartment on the west side of Manhattan."

"Those were the good times," my mother said, working the dough with her knobby knuckles. Every year her hands grew stiffer and more painful. "I miss the days when your father worked for the Pendeltons."

The Pendeltons.

My fingers strangled the apple in my hand as bitterness clogged my throat. For twenty years my father worked for the richest family in the country—the last eight as their head gardener—yet they cast him off one day like he had typhoid. Sacked without warning two years after the Pendelton baby went missing. No one would hire him after that, not without a reference, so we moved to Boston, where my father proceeded to drown his sorrows in a bottle of whiskey.

The Pendeltons ruined my father's life and my family's future. I'd never forgive it. And someday, I'd find a way to even the score.

"You know how I feel about them," I said, taking another bite of apple.

"It wasn't all bad. And you should pity them. They never did find their kidnapped little girl."

"Well, I don't pity them. Not after what they did to Papa."

She sighed heavily and shook her head. "Try to remember the good times in life, Leo. You'll be happier that way. Like how much you loved trailing your father around on that estate."

It was true. To a ten-year-old boy the Pendeltons appeared to have the perfect life. What was it like to be born so rich? I was especially fascinated by Mrs. Pendelton, who always seemed happy and smiling—

Wait a moment.

The singer from the square, the one with the gorgeous smile? That smile, if memory served, reminded me a bit of Mrs. Pendelton. Combined with the blond hair and her stiff demeanor? Put the girl in a fancy gown and she could pass for a relative . . .

Pass for a *daughter*, perhaps?

I paused, midchew. The idea was pure madness, which was likely why it appealed to me. And it wasn't so far-fetched. No one would know what this long-lost daughter looks like as a grown woman.

The wheels in my brain started turning.

She needed some polish. And there was the issue of getting her to New York and in front of the Pendeltons, not to mention clothes and traveling money. But she wanted to sing professionally, which meant—

A tiny piece of dough hit my chest. "Leo!" my mother asked. "What are you dreaming up?"

"Did you throw food at me?"

"When you ignored me? Yes, I did. I was asking if you plan to go out and find Flora, but you didn't hear me."

"Is there still a reward for the missing Pendelton daughter?"

"Yes, last I heard. It's never been claimed, though many have tried. Why?"

Many may have tried, but none of them were *me*. I knew the family, the estate better than any other huckster. "Nothing. Just an idea."

Molly poked her head inside the kitchen. "There's a policeman knocking on the door. Should we answer it?"

"NO!" my mother and I both said at the same time.

"Jesus Christ, calm down. That's why I came to tell you."

My mother began wiping her hands on a towel. "Do not use that language in this house, Molly Hardy."

"I'm Gallus Mag," Molly complained.

"I don't care who you are. No blasphemy in this family."

Molly grumbled as she left the kitchen. My mother tried to tame her hair, which was a bit sweaty from her kneading. "Dare I ask why an officer is at the door again?"

"Don't answer it. He'll go away eventually."

"Leo, I'll not have an officer loitering on our stoop. Better for me to tell him you aren't here and then he'll go away." She untied her apron and placed it on the counter. "But afterward you will tell me why he's here, young man."

"It's nothing to worry about. They don't have anything on me." Not enough to prove, anyway.

"I hope not. I can't lose you, too."

My mother didn't approve of how I earned a living, but she tolerated it. We didn't have much of a choice, considering our situation. An honest job wouldn't pay enough. At least my line of work let me keep my own hours and the profits were decent.

She walked out of the kitchen and went to the front door. I edged into the hall, close to the door but out of sight. Thankfully, my sisters were quiet in the front room. No doubt they were listening in as well.

The latch clicked as my mother opened the door. "Hello? May I help you?"

"I'm looking for a Mr. Leo Hardy. He live here?"

Yep, it was O'Toole all right.

"That is my son, but he doesn't reside here any longer."

Bless my mother. I grinned at the ceiling.

"You sure? This was the last known address we had for him."

"I believe I would know if my son lived under my roof, Officer. Might I inquire as to what this is regarding?"

"It's regarding the chase he led me on today out in Post Office Square."

"You must be mistaken, Officer. My son has a job with a newspaper over on Boylston."

O'Toole snorted. "Ma'am, I hate to be the one to tell ya, but your boy is nothing but a—"

"If you have come here," my mother said, cutting him off, "to besmirch the reputation of my son, you are wasting your time. He's a good man. Now, if that is all, there is bread I am kneading."

O'Toole grumbled something under his breath, but I couldn't make it out.

"If I see him, I will pass that message along," my mother said. "I wish you a pleasant evening, Officer."

The door closed and I exhaled. Fucking O'Toole.

My mother walked by me on her way to the kitchen. She didn't say anything, so I trailed after her. "Nicely done. I couldn't have lied better myself."

"It's not a point of pride, Leo. You know I don't like lying."

"Regardless, you were brilliant." I leaned against the counter and watched her set to work on the dough again. "What did he say at the end under his breath?"

"He said to tell you he's not finished with you."

I crossed my arms across my chest and studied the faded wallpaper on the other side of the room. O'Toole was a problem, but not my most pressing at the moment. As usual, money was my dilemma. Maybe this Pendelton heiress scheme was worth considering . . .

The more I thought about the idea, the more I liked it. God knew the Pendeltons deserved the swindle—I'd been dreaming of revenge for years—and they could well afford it. The money was a drop in the bucket to people like them. The real baby was long gone, but this girl was close enough to pass—at least close enough for me to collect a reward and disappear.

If I pulled this off, my mother and sisters would be set for life. No more kneading dough, sewing, or laundry. They could dine on lobster and tenderloin every night, move to a big house up on Beacon Hill. Find decent husbands who weren't in Southie gangs.

By the time the Pendeltons realized they'd been swindled, I'd be off in Paris or Rome. Somewhere no one could find me—not even the Boston police.

First, I'd need to convince this young woman to trust me enough to travel to New York. A theatrical manager scheme might work. I could pull in a few favors, get her enough meetings to prove I was legit, then take her off to Broadway. It didn't have to be perfect, merely plausible.

If I knew one thing, it was that people saw what they wanted to see. Present them with a shiny enough bauble and they never noticed it was glass. The Pendeltons would never know the difference and all my problems would be solved.

I could almost smell the stacks of cash.

Chapter Three

JOSIE

The last notes floated away on the breeze and the crowd broke out into applause. I smiled and closed my eyes, soaking in the approval like a patch of dry grass in the rain.

I couldn't get enough.

Singing was my obsession, but it was about more than earning money. It was how I expressed what I was feeling. There was too much happening inside my head and I didn't know any other way to get it out than through song. I would die if I couldn't sing.

It was also my only talent, the single thing I could do to make me stand out in this dashed world. I planned to use it to my advantage, just as soon as I figured out how.

The applause died down and I thanked the crowd. As the people wandered away I gathered my things. It had been a good day thus far. Soon Pip and I would be able to afford a better neighborhood. Pippa Devlin, my closest friend and roommate, grew up with me at the Boston Children's Asylum, and she worked as a barmaid in the saloon where I sometimes performed. We didn't have it easy, but we were used to hardship, thanks to our upbringing at the asylum.

I capped the jar, sealing all that beautiful money in tight. Thieves and miscreants were everywhere in this city, and I couldn't risk having my earnings stolen. I slipped the jar into my carpetbag and hefted it over my shoulder.

"Miss!"

Walking quickly, I ignored the deep voice. It wasn't uncommon for a man to approach me after a performance. Some assumed I did more than sing on the street for money, which couldn't be further from the truth.

I had no time for men in any capacity. I was going to be famous and everyone knew that women in love made terrible decisions, always putting themselves second. Well, I would never do that. My career came first.

He shouted again, closer this time, and I sighed. There would be no outrunning him, so I slowly turned. A man hurried toward me, his lithe frame clad in a smart dark suit. A derby covered oiled chestnut-colored hair, and startling blue eyes peeked out from under the brim of his hat. His wide smile showed off even white teeth, and I blinked. Most people undoubtedly found his handsome demeanor reassuring, but I was instantly on edge. What did a man who looked like this—and dressed like this— want with me?

Nothing good. That was what.

Folding my hands, I waited. "Yeah?"

He tipped his hat. "That was quite a rousing performance, miss. Your voice is magnificent."

"Thanks."

I spun and started to hurry away, but he suddenly appeared before me, blocking my path. "I was here the day before yesterday to watch you. Maybe you remember me?"

Was he serious? There were far too many people in the square to remember one, even if he was such a handsome specimen. "Nope, I don't."

I tried to edge around him, but he wouldn't budge. "Wait, don't rush off. Perhaps I could buy you an ice cream. There's a saloon around the corner."

Ice cream? That was a new one. "No thanks. I need to be on my way." When I tried to leave, he danced ahead of me again. Huffing, I said, "You better move, mister, or I'm punching you."

"Wait. Don't hit me. The name's Leo. Leo Hardy."

He waited for me to introduce myself, but I didn't bother. "As I said, you'd better move, Mr. Hardy."

He put up his palms. "I'm not a masher, I swear it."

"Exactly what a masher would say. Now, move."

A chuckle emerged as he grinned at me. Sakes alive, he was pretty. Heat bloomed in the pit of my stomach, but I shoved the unwanted feeling away. This was hardly the time to start swooning after a handsome face.

"I admire your spirit, miss," he said. "A young woman can never be too cautious in this city. But I merely wish to speak with you regarding your singing career."

Now that got my attention. "What about it?"

"No can do. I never discuss business on the street. It's ice cream or bust, Miss . . . ?"

"Smith."

The little lines around his eyes deepened as he smiled down at me. "Miss Smith. What do you say?"

Was I honestly considering this? I was hungry and he looked like he could afford a treat or two. Was there harm in hearing what he had to say while I ate, then set about my business? "All right, but just ice cream."

Relief coasted over his features. "Excellent. This way."

We walked side by side toward the far end of the square. I held tight to my carpetbag, using it as a buffer between us. It could also be used as a weapon, if necessary.

"How long have you been singing?" he asked.

"As far back as I can remember. The director of the place where I grew up always encouraged it."

"And where was that?"

"The Boston Children's Asylum." I wasn't ashamed of my upbringing. Most of the nuns at the asylum had been kind to me, and I came to love many of the girls there. I hardly ever wondered about my real family anymore. "What about you? Where did you grow up?"

"Not far from you, actually. Tremont Street. I live there with my mom and five sisters."

A thin thread of jealousy twisted around my heart. "Must be nice to have such a big family."

"I suppose. It can be overwhelming, too."

We dodged a few carriages and carts to cross the busy street. "Overwhelming, how?" I asked.

"Our father died a long time ago and it's been my responsibility to care for the family ever since."

"The man of the house. That must be tough. How old were you when your father died?"

"Fifteen."

At that age I'd already accepted that I wouldn't have a family. Most girls were adopted by age nine or ten, so my eleventh, twelfth, and thirteenth birthdays had been sad ones. Then Pip and I made a pact to stick together, no matter what. We'd never let anyone come between us, and we'd travel the world together when I became famous.

I dodged a pack of boys playing hoops and sticks on the walk, then came back to Leo's side. "You don't talk like you grew up on Tremont Street. And you dress like you're from Beacon Hill."

"I confess to a sartorial fixation. As for my speech, I strove to purge the Boston from my voice."

"Why?"

"Because it seemed judicious to blend in, not stick out."

Hmm. That made sense, I supposed, but everyone I knew talked like I did. Instead, Leo used fancy words and proper pronunciation, like a politician.

Leo opened the door to the ice cream parlor and I stepped inside. I'd walked by this place before, but never entered. Pip and I bought our ices from a cart on the street when we had money to spare. Which was almost never. Ice cream saloons were for wealthy folks.

So I took my time looking around. The walls were painted in

bright yellows and blues, with small round tables and iron chairs spread along the tile floor. Jars and containers lined the marble counter, each filled with various colorful sweets. It was as if happiness had exploded over every inch of this place.

"Over here," Leo called, gesturing to an empty table.

He held out a chair and I sat, careful to place my carpetbag on the floor beneath my feet. I arranged my skirts to hide it, then lifted a menu. I pretended to study it while actually looking at Leo instead. He seemed to be a few years older than me, so perhaps twenty-six or twenty-seven. Clean-shaven, no scars. His clothing was pristine, with a white collar and gold studs. A sapphire winked out from his tie, a watch chain dangling from his vest.

"Do I pass inspection?" he asked, not looking up from his menu.

I could feel my cheeks heating. "You're quite handsome, which I'm sure you must know."

The edge of his mouth kicked up. "Still is nice to hear, especially from a striking young woman."

"No need to flatter me. I've got no interest in you that way."

"And what way is that?"

"Like a man." I peered at him closely, not bothering to hide my inspection this time. "Are you rich?"

His lips twitched like he was fighting a smile, his expression considering. "Are you a woman who says whatever pops into her mind?"

Unfortunately, yes. Though god knew the nuns at the asylum did their best to curb my runaway mouth.

Ladies do not interrupt when a person is speaking, Josie.

Ladies do not argue, Josie.

Ladies should never discuss matters of which they have no knowledge, Josie.

Except I couldn't seem to stop from blurting out the thoughts in my head. "Are you one of those gents who thinks women should be seen and not heard?"

"Are you one to always answer a question with another question?"

"Yes, when you never answer mine."

"No, I'm not rich."

"Good."

That got his attention. He frowned at me from over his menu. "Why is that good?"

I lifted one shoulder. "Because I trust rich men even less than poor men."

Thankfully, the waiter arrived at that moment and took our order. I hadn't looked much at the menu, so I ordered a vanilla ice cream. Leo ordered strawberry.

"Vanilla?" he asked when we were alone.

"Why not vanilla?"

"I mean no offense, but there was a whole list of flavors from which to choose. Yet you selected the safest one."

I didn't know anything about ice cream or the flavors. But I disliked someone making me feel stupid for it even more. I went on the attack. "Maybe I like vanilla and don't care what anyone else thinks about it."

"Fair enough, miss, but maybe you should think bigger."

"Bigger than vanilla? What does that mean?"

"I meant your voice." He leaned back and settled in his chair. The full weight of his stare, sharp and bright, rested on my face. "Have you given thought as to what you'd like to do with your ability?"

That was easy. "Become famous and travel the world."

He nodded as if he liked my answer. "A fine aim, yet how do you plan to accomplish such a feat?"

I pointed to the street beyond the window. "By singing."

"And? Anything else?"

The back of my neck prickled. He was trying to make me feel small and stupid again. Like the nuns at the asylum when I spoke out of turn. "If you've got something to say, spit it out. I don't like guessing games."

He put up his hands. "Fair enough. I'm offering to assist you in becoming a famous singer."

I snorted. Oh, indeed. This handsome man had suddenly dropped out of the sky with the answer to all my problems. "And how do you plan to do that?"

"I'm acquainted with a few theater owners in town. I can procure you some dates as practice. Then we travel to New York."

"New York?" I squeaked in surprise and my knee bumped the table. The water glasses nearly toppled over.

Leo took his napkin and calmly blotted the spilled drops of water on the marble tabletop. "New York has Broadway, the Metropolitan Opera House. Carnegie Hall. Careers are made there, Miss Smith."

It sounded incredible, like a giant leap toward everything I'd ever wanted. But any offer this good had to have a catch. "And what's in it for you?"

"You're right. I never do anything purely for altruistic reasons. I'd be doing this for money," he said. "As your manager I would receive twenty percent of all your earnings."

Twenty percent? That sounded high. "For how long?"

"For however long we agree. We'd sign a contract."

I wasn't ready to sign anything, not until he answered all my questions. "You don't seem that old. How long have you been a manager? Who are your other clients?"

"You are asking all the right questions. It proves you're smart."

"And you're evading them, which proves you have something to hide."

"I don't have anything to hide. There are no other clients. You'd be my first."

My jaw dropped open. "You've never done this before? Yet you hear me sing and you're struck with inspiration for a brand-new career? That's ludicrous."

"Not ludicrous in the least. You're exceptionally talented.

And I am basically in sales, so it's no different if I'm selling you or shoes or hats."

"I don't want to be sold."

"Metaphorically, I meant." His hands were neatly folded on the table, his demeanor open and friendly. "I would promote you, talk you up. Sell your ability to get you work."

The waiter returned with our ice cream, which arrived in fancy silver dishes. I quickly took a bite. Rich and creamy, the vanilla ice cream was the best thing I'd ever tasted. I couldn't wait to tell Pip about this when I got home. "How do I know you can actually help me? You say you know these owners, but you could be swindling me."

"I could be, but I'm not."

"Which is what a swindler would say."

He gave me a broad smile, one I didn't trust. It was forced, with too much teeth, and it never reached his eyes. "How about this? In a show of good faith, I'll get you a meeting with an owner of one of the local theaters. I know several of them, like Mr. B. F. Keith and the Vincents, the Kimballs. If you feel good about our arrangement following that, then we'll discuss a contract."

Those were names I knew from the newspapers. Maybe he was telling the truth? "A contract allowing you twenty percent of my earnings."

"Yes."

"Fifteen." I held my breath, unsure if this was wise or not. However, if we were going to work together, he had to understand I wasn't a fool. And I still didn't trust him. "But you have to get me that meeting first. You have to prove that you're legitimate."

He stroked his jaw, his long fingers smoothing over golden skin while he stared at me. Finally, he stuck out his hand. "Deal."

Reaching out, I placed my palm in his, our gloved fingers brushing. "Deal."

When he tried to release me, I tightened my grip and held on to him. Then I leaned in; our eyes locked. Flecks of gray lurked in his irises, little bits of silver to break up the bright blue. For some reason I found this reassuring, like I'd discovered a chink in his perfect armor.

He was merely a man, and I wouldn't let him take advantage of me.

I lowered my voice to my most serious tone. "Hear this, Leo Hardy. I'll allow you one opportunity. But if you're swindling me, I'll kick you in your credentials so hard that you'll feel it into the next century."

The smile disappeared as he sobered and nodded. "I understand perfectly, Miss Smith."

"Good." I let him go and eased back in my chair. "And I suppose you may call me Josie."

I SLAMMED THE apartment door closed. "Pips! Where are you?"

"Back here," I heard my friend call out from the bedroom we shared. "I'm coming."

I tossed my bag and hat on the worn kitchen table, then began stripping off my gloves. "Hurry!"

There wasn't far to go. Our place was small, but we took very good care of it. The floors were clean, the wood polished. We never left a dirty stocking or used dish lying about. Also, Pippa was easy to live with. The two of us were more like sisters, considering we grew up together since we were babies. I knew all her foibles and she knew mine.

Pippa emerged from the back, running a brush through her damp brown hair. "This had better be important for all the ruckus."

"Of course it's important!"

"Then let's hear it."

"I met a man," I started.

"Forget it." Pippa turned on her heel and started for the bedroom.

"Wait, wait, wait." I lunged to grab her shoulders. "It's not that sort of story."

She turned and narrowed her eyes at me. "Is he handsome?"

I hated lying, always had. Pippa was well aware of it, too, which explained why she asked. "Yes." She started to walk away again, so I tugged on her hair. "Give me a chance, Pip. This isn't romantic, I swear."

Pippa sighed as she came back toward our small kitchen table. "All right. But you better not be falling for some sweet-talker."

"I'm not, I'm not." We lowered ourselves into opposite seats. "A man heard me singing in the square today. He took me for ice cream—"

"Holy Christmas, Josie. You said this wasn't romantic!"

"If you don't let me get this story out, I swear I will cut your hair when you're asleep." Pip loved her hair more than anything else.

"If you do that, I'll tell the nuns at the asylum that you're the one who broke the Jesus statue in Sister Mary's office."

"Cruel, Pippa. Exceedingly cruel. Are you fixing to be quiet and let me finish?"

She nodded once and continued brushing her hair.

"This man wants to help my singing career. He heard me sing in the square and thinks I could end up on Broadway."

"Anyone who hears you would think so, but how can he actually help you?" I opened my mouth to answer, but Pippa held up a hand. "Wait. Recite the whole conversation for me."

It had been this way my whole life. Words, like a conversation or song lyrics, never left my brain. Ever. The ability was mostly a blessing, but there were times that I wished I could forget something. Unfortunately, my memory wasn't selective at all.

I closed my eyes and began recalling the conversation with Leo from the moment he approached me in the square. Pippa made noises of agreement along the way and snorted when I ordered vanilla ice cream. Ignoring her, I continued, going through Leo's proposal and how I haggled with him for fifteen percent.

When I repeated the part about kicking him in his credentials, she laughed. "Good! I'm glad you put a dose of fear into the man. Does he seem honest? Trustworthy?"

I thought about his wide smile that tried to say too much, while his eyes said nothing at all. "Hard to say. Time will tell, I suppose. He has to live up to his promises first."

"Do you honestly think he knows anyone in the theater business?"

Pippa and I were as suspicious as they came. We'd worked and struggled our whole lives, receiving very little in return. Two unwanted orphans who never had a thing handed to us.

But weren't we due for some good luck?

"I don't know," I said. "But I have to try. Why else am I singing on the street and at the saloon, if not to make something of this gift I've been given?"

"Understandable." She reached over, grabbed my hand, and squeezed. "But I don't want you hurt or taken advantage of by some huckster."

"I'm too smart for that." I squeezed her fingers back. "And when I become rich and famous I'm taking you with me."

"Hell yes, you are, Josie Smith. We're going to live in a big mansion on Beacon Hill."

"And we'll be old ladies together, with handsome footmen who fulfill our every need."

"Every need?" Pippa waggled her eyebrows suggestively as she let go of my hand.

I couldn't help it—I chuckled. "Get your mind out of the muck, young lady. We're not taking advantage of our footmen."

"Then we must find handsome young lovers to live with us. I'm not cut out for a life of celibacy."

"I'm well aware, based on the late nights at the saloon recently. Who have you been messing about with?"

"The new bartender," she said, eyes turning dreamy as she brushed her hair. "I like the way he kisses."

I tried not to feel envious, but it wasn't easy. I missed kissing and touching. There had been a few experiences since we left the asylum two years ago, but I refused to let myself grow serious about a man. My future came first. Most young men didn't mind; they weren't interested in sticking around, anyway. "Maybe I'll come by tonight and see if there's someone who catches my eye."

"You should," Pippa encouraged. "In fact, that dockworker, Stevie? He's been asking about you."

Stevie had been nice enough, but he smelled like trout. "Not interested, but thanks."

Pippa glanced at the tiny clock we kept on the counter. "Shit, I need to hurry. I have to be across town in less than an hour." She stood up, then came around the table and hugged me with one arm. "Josie, I'm happy for you. I hope it's the beginning for you."

"The beginning for *us*," I corrected. "Never leave a friend behind, remember?"

"Never leave a friend behind," Pippa echoed our motto, then straightened. "A word of warning, though. Don't pay this Leo character anything up front."

"I won't. He only gets a portion of my earnings from future performances."

"Good. Keep an eye on him—a suspicious eye. Not a lascivious one, trying to see what's underneath his fancy suit."

I picked at the scarred wooden top of our kitchen table. "How did you know he had on a fancy suit?"

"Please. Your head always turns at the fancy ones."

"I can't help it. Maybe I was a queen in a former life."

"Sure," Pippa said with a laugh as she walked toward our bedroom. "You were a princess and your mother left you on the asylum's doorstep. By the way, it's your turn for laundry, Your Majesty."

Ugh. I hated scrubbing and rolling out our clothes. "Didn't I do it last time?"

"No, I did it. You were singing in the square."

"Fine. I'll do it tonight—after I practice a little." I was too excited, too hopeful, to sit in a quiet apartment all night.

"Good idea. And wash your stuffed rabbit. It's beginning to stink."

I stuck my tongue out at her, even though she couldn't see me. The small stuffed rabbit was the only thing I had left from my childhood. The nuns said the bunny was with me when I arrived at the asylum, and it was more precious to me than anything else on earth.

"Though I'm not sure what *Leo* would think of his prized client keeping a stuffed toy," she said.

The way she exaggerated his name, like he was someone important, had me rolling my eyes. "You would like him. He's very charming."

"I bet he is," she said from inside our bedroom. "Handsome men usually are. But they aren't used to hearing the word no, Josie. Be careful."

"Don't worry about Leo," I called out. "I'll stick to him like flypaper."

"That, my dear, is precisely what I'm worried about."

Frowning at the empty room, I considered telling her she was wrong, that I wasn't at risk of falling for a man like Leo. But it was a waste of breath. We worried about each other because we had no one else. In fact, I'd give Pip the exact same warning if some man was making her big promises.

In this case, however, I was going into it clear-eyed. I was a fighter, a scrapper, like the city of Boston itself, which had been at the forefront of the Revolution more than a hundred years ago. I could handle Leo Hardy.

And if he wasn't telling the truth? Then I would sing of his misdeeds on every corner in this city and make him suffer.

Right after I kicked him in his credentials.

Chapter Four

LEO

I wedged a toe in the door to prevent it from slamming in my face. "Listen, Roy. You have to do this for me. You *owe* me." Roy was the doorman at the Park Theatre, a playhouse on Washington Street. He and I went back a long time.

Except Roy wasn't being helpful at the moment. I was determined, though, so I pushed my way inside the tiny corridor. "Come on. Let me meet Mr. Abbey. Five minutes is all I need."

"I told you, he ain't here. Now get lost before you get me into trouble."

"Then what about Mr. Frohman or Mr. Harris?"

After my meeting with Josie, I spent quite a lot of time researching Boston theater owners. Then I remembered my connection to Roy and decided to concentrate my efforts here. This had to work.

Roy scowled at me. "You're gonna get me fired. I need this job."

I put up my hands. "I swear, I won't cause trouble. Just point me in the direction of someone's office and I'll take care of the rest."

"No one's here," Roy said. "You're wasting your time."

A door down the hall opened and a gorgeous woman appeared. Brown hair fell in waves around her head, a robe covering her slight frame. She wore a deep frown as she examined me from head to toe. "What's the commotion out here?"

Recognition hit me and my jaw dropped open. "You're Lotta Crabtree."

Charlotte "Lotta" Crabtree was one of the most famous performers in the country. At least, she had been at one time. Her brother was a partner in this theater, but I hadn't expected to see his famous sister here.

The edge of Lotta's mouth kicked up. "Hello, handsome. Any reason you're out here interrupting my nap?"

Sensing my opening, I pushed by Roy, removed my derby, and closed the distance between me and the petite woman. "I sincerely beg your pardon, Miss Crabtree. Though I do have to say, you look perfectly refreshed to my eye."

She pursed her lips and gave me another once-over. "A smooth talker. Why am I not surprised?"

First rule of being a confidence man: the confidence.

My mentor, St. Elmer, drummed ten important rules for a confidence man into my head as a boy. He wasn't a real saint, of course, but all the Back Bay kids idolized him then. Thanks to his tutelage, by the age of fifteen I knew how to pickpocket, how to work a crowd. As I got older, he showed me how to use my looks to put people at ease, especially women.

St. Elmer always said I was his prize pupil.

"I'm honest to a fault," I lied with a wink. "I suspect we're alike in that manner, Miss Crabtree."

"Not a far reach, but you're right. I do tend to say what's on my mind. And on my mind right now is that I'd like you to leave so I can rest before the evening show."

"May I have five minutes of your time? I have a proposition for you."

"Honey," she said with a laugh. "I'm a little tired of those sorts of propositions from men."

"It's not that, I swear."

"Sure, but this is my nap time. Send your proposal to my agent and I'll consider it."

She started to turn away, but I knew I'd never have another chance like this. Her agent would toss my proposal in the garbage.

I quickly blurted, "If I guess something about you, something not everyone knows, will you give me five minutes of your time?"

Lotta paused and threw me an exasperated glance over her shoulder. "You are pushy, aren't you?"

"Ambitious," I corrected. I suspected we had this in common and she'd appreciate the trait.

"All right, Mr. . . . ?"

"Hardy. Leo Hardy, ma'am."

"Leo, then. Go on. Guess something about me."

Though it had been many years since I used my cold reading skills—too many widows and grieving parents for my liking—I remembered the basics. Any confidence man worth his salt could read a mark's cues and make broad enough statements to apply to most anyone.

I pretended to study her as I sifted through what I knew of the famous actress. "Though you are disciplined and controlled in your career, you are quite insecure inside."

"Aren't we all?" she muttered. "You'll have to do better than that, honey."

I kept going like she hadn't interrupted. "Your father wasn't as supportive of your choices as you'd hoped, and you've been attempting to prove your talent to him your entire life."

Lotta's mother had managed the actress's entire career, so my guess about Lotta's father wasn't a difficult one to make. And most people in this world had one parent, deceased or living, they were still trying to impress. God knew I did.

The air in the corridor grew thick as I awaited her response. She blinked several times, and I could feel sweat building between my shoulder blades. But I never let my worry show, not once.

Finally, she spoke. "I like you. Come inside and sit for a spell. Tell me what you're doing in my theater."

Roy sighed heavily, but I ignored him and trailed Lotta into the dressing room. I expected costumes and cosmetics, but this was more like an office, with a desk, divan, and metal cabinets.

She reclined on the divan and gestured to an armchair. "Have a seat, Leo."

"Thank you, Miss Crabtree."

"Call me Lotta. Would you like a drink?"

There was a sideboard, so I took the hint and went over to make her a drink. "Allow me. What would you prefer?"

"Bourbon and water. Light on the water."

"A woman after my own heart," I murmured and poured two.

When we were settled with our drinks, she asked, "So tell me what you were arguing with poor Roy about."

"I have a singer that I manage—"

Lotta rolled her eyes. "Goodness, I should've known. Let me guess, your sweetheart?"

"No, nothing like that. I mean, it is a woman, but we're not involved. It's all strictly aboveboard."

"Hmm." She studied me, her eyes inscrutable. "Is she any good?"

"Not as talented as you, of course, but yes. She's quite good."

"Pretty?"

"Gorgeous," I said without thinking.

She sipped her drink and watched me over the rim. I couldn't tell what she was thinking, so I hurried to explain. "Josie is . . . unique. She's honest and raw, a girl raised on the streets. But she's tough. I heard her singing on the corner one day and knew I had to help her."

"Out of the goodness of your heart, no doubt," Lotta drawled.

I shrugged and added a small chuckle that I hoped came across as endearing. "She talked me down from twenty percent to fifteen. But I think she's worth it. The girl's destined to be a star." *Not for singing, though. The world would soon know her as the lost Pendelton heiress.*

Lotta sipped her drink. "Raised on the streets, you say?"

I nodded solemnly, latching onto Lotta's interest in Josie's humble background. "She was orphaned as a baby, then raised by the nuns at the Children's Asylum until she grew too old. Now she performs on the street for money."

"No family?"

"None. She lives with a friend."

"And now she has you?"

"Yes, but I only have her best interests at heart."

"Oh, honey." The famous woman threw her head back and laughed, giving me a peek at her famous dimples. "No man ever has a woman's best interests at heart, especially when money is involved."

"I swear—"

She held up her hand. "Save it. I want to meet her."

"Really?" Triumph raced through me, making my heart thump.

"Yes. If nothing else, I have to warn her away from men like you."

My excitement dimmed considerably. "Wait a moment. I thought you could give her career advice and some such. Tell us how to break into the business."

"You don't ask for much, do you?" Lotta took another long sip of her drink. "Bring her here tomorrow afternoon and have her sing. If I like her, then I'll talk to her—alone—and give her some advice."

Would Lotta try to talk Josie out of working with me? I couldn't let that happen. I had to convince both of them that I was a straight arrow.

I gave Lotta my most charming smile, the one I used to disarm a mark. "You don't trust me."

"You're too handsome to trust. Pretty men know they can get away with whatever they want."

"I can't decide whether to be flattered or offended."

"Both, probably."

"Aw, now you've hurt my feelings."

Shaking her head, she put down her drink and reached for a box on the table. Surprisingly, she pulled out a cigar and cut it.

Then she lit the cut end and puffed a few times, filling the room with fragrant smoke. "I've performed across the country and I've met all kinds. You might be able to roll over some people with that face, but not me. Still, I'd like to help her if she's really as good as you say."

"You won't be disappointed."

"I hope not, but the chance that you've discovered a star out on the streets of Boston is slim. Lucky for you I'm restless. If nothing else, you've given me something to look forward to."

A knock on the door sounded. "Yeah?" Lotta called.

A well-dressed man appeared, his age not much older than mine. I saw the way his eyes found Lotta first, expression softening, then he saw me sitting in the chair and sobered. "Oh," he said. "I will return later."

"No need, darling. Leo was just leaving."

That was my cue. Downing the rest of my drink, I set the glass on the table. Then I stood and shook her hand. "Thank you for the drink, Miss Crabtree. I look forward to surprising you tomorrow afternoon."

"It'll be a first, handsome."

I passed by the man in the doorway and closed the door. Jamming my derby on my head, I started for the exit. I practically whistled as I went, flush with my success. Roy was seated at the back door, and he scowled when I approached.

I clapped him on the shoulder. "Now, don't frown at me, Roy. It all went fine."

He shrugged off my hand. "You're going to get me sacked, Hardy. You can't come back here."

"Too bad. Miss Crabtree has invited me back tomorrow."

"Oh, Christ. What for? She's already got a man." He hooked his thumb in the direction of Lotta's dressing room.

"I'm bringing a singer. Lotta said she'd give the girl a shot, see if she's got any talent."

"And what, you give up confidence schemes? I don't believe it."

"Shut it," I snapped. "No one knows about that—and this isn't a scheme. It's legitimate." *Sort of.*

"I ain't buyin' it. You don't do anything on the level."

Roy and I had known each other for years, though he went straight a while ago when he met his wife. After checking to make sure we were alone, I lowered my voice. "Look, don't ruin this for me. The girl is talented and I'm going to manage her career."

Roy shrugged. "Whatever you say, Leo. Just leave me out of it. I need this job."

Roy was safe from me—as long as he didn't get in my way. "Consider yourself uninvolved. I'm bringing Josie here tomorrow to sing for Lotta. Once she hears this girl, big things are going to happen."

"With you that could mean any number of things and god knows I don't need a brush with the law." Roy pushed open the door. "Get lost, Hardy. Forget we know each other."

I stepped into the alley, my mood too jubilant for anyone to ruin. "Already forgotten. See you tomorrow, stranger."

JOSIE

My leg bounced as nerves twisted inside me. Leo had insisted on taking a hack over to the theater, which was absurd. I would've been fine walking or riding a streetcar. Now all I could do was sit and think.

This could go wrong in a hundred different ways. Maybe my voice would crack. Maybe Miss Crabtree changed her mind. Maybe our hack overturned and we were killed on the way over—

"Will you please relax?" Leo said. He sat across from me, looking as cool as a block of ice.

"You're not the one who has to get up and sing. I'll be calm when it's over."

"Take a deep breath. This will go well, I promise."

He was just telling me what I wanted to hear, but I didn't care at this point. I inhaled and exhaled a few times, trying to stave off the panic. Part of me still couldn't believe this was happening. In one day Leo had landed me an audition with Lotta Crabtree. It was unbelievable. Everyone with a pulse had heard of the actress.

Now I was going to sing in front of her.

Black dots appeared in my vision, so I bent over and tried to put my head between my legs. Damn corset made it impossible. Why had I laced it so tight today?

Sitting up, I dragged in a breath. Strong fingers suddenly wrapped around my hands. Leo's voice broke through the chaos in my mind. "Look at me, Josie."

I peered over at his serene gaze and some of the tension left my shoulders. "I'm nervous."

"Good. That means you're alive. I'd be concerned if you weren't." His mouth lifted in an adorable half smile and I found myself smiling back. "There you go," he said quietly, his deep voice soothing. "You can do this. You have an incredible voice. This is merely the first step toward the rest of your life, sweetheart."

His eyes were the color of the ocean on a sunny day, with streaks of lighter blue and gray running toward the center. They reminded me of the time Pippa and I went out to Wollaston Beach. It had been the best day of my life, up until today. If this audition went well, I supposed this would take top prize.

He called me sweetheart.

I licked my dry lips. "Thank you. That helped."

He leaned back, releasing me. "That's what I'm here for."

Maybe having a manager wasn't as bad as I feared. At least I'd give Leo today. I had nothing to lose, except a few hours of my time.

Soon we were pulling up to the theater. Leo paid the fare, then helped me down to the walk. I could hardly stand, my knees were knocking so fiercely, but I refused to take his arm. If I was going to do this, it would be on my own.

We walked to the stage door and Leo rapped twice. The heavy metal parted and a man's face appeared. "Oh, it's you," he said, frowning at Leo. "Come in, I guess."

"Thank you, Roy." Leo swept his arm out for me to go first. "After you."

When we were inside the man named Roy said, "Miss Crabtree wants you out onstage. Through there." He pointed to a corridor. "Third door on the left and keep going. You'll see the steps."

I lifted my chin and forced my legs to move. The small amount of food in my stomach threatened to come back up, but I took more deep breaths and kept going. Before I knew it, I was at the edge of the stage. A single light shone overhead.

Lord, I was scared.

"Josie, wait."

Leo grabbed my arm as I started to move forward, stopping me. Turning, I tried to stem my rising panic. "What is it?"

He put his hands on my shoulders, but maintained a respectable distance. "Repeat after me: I'm going to be one of the greats."

"I'm going to be one of the greats," I whispered.

"Now say it like you mean it."

"I'm going to be one of the greats," I said with more conviction than I felt.

He nodded once. "Good. Now you're ready."

Was I? At least he'd distracted me from my terror for a brief second. Was that what managers did? Calmed down singers who were on the verge of hysteria?

Releasing me, he folded his arms but didn't move. I motioned to the stage behind me. "Aren't you coming with me?"

"I'll be right here. I'll be watching the whole time."

It was now or never. I'd sing on street corners forever if I didn't take a risk sooner or later.

Exhaling, I hurried out onto the stage. My boot heels thumped on the wooden floorboards, the sound echoing as I walked. When I was under the light, I gazed out at the audience.

Sakes alive, this place was huge.

Rows and rows of empty seats surrounded me, the details indiscernible thanks to the light in my face. But I could make out the loge and mezzanine, up to the balcony, as well as the surrounding boxes. What was it like to have all those eyes on you? Everyone's attention solely focused on the sounds coming out of your mouth?

My knees started knocking again and I took a tiny step back. Maybe I couldn't—

"There you are," a woman's voice called from the darkness below. "I was beginning to wonder if you'd changed your mind. Do you need to warm up your voice?"

I frowned. Warm up? "No, ma'am. I'm ready."

The tip of a cigar glowed in the audience. Who was out there with Miss Crabtree? "Well, so am I," the woman said. "Let's hear it."

I had decided to sing songs I knew well, the ones I thought best showcased my vocal range. Inhaling, I stared off into the distance and delivered my first note. The sound startled me, it was so loud and clear, like the vibrations were reverberated back at me. I stopped and cleared my throat. "My apologies. I'll start again, if that is all right."

"Of course, honey."

I began singing a light and bubbling piece from Gilbert and Sullivan's *The Gondoliers*. The theater was silent when the final notes finished and I wasn't sure what to do. I hadn't expected applause, but perhaps some sort of reaction would be nice. Hadn't Miss Crabtree liked it?

Panic started to swell in my chest, but I beat it back. I couldn't fail. Maybe she preferred more popular tunes?

I quickly began singing Sousa's "You'll Miss Lots of Fun When You're Married." I lost myself in the rousing tune, one that always pleased the saloon crowd. It was better with a piano, but I made sure to sing dramatically.

More silence ensued when I finished. I resisted the urge to fidget.

Broadway. Of course! Miss Crabtree was known for her work in Broadway shows, so I should sing one of those. I quickly began a song from *The Shop Girl*, a very popular musical comedy from London that had been on Broadway last year. Surely, Miss Crabtree would know it.

In the middle of the second chorus, the woman called out, "No need for more, honey. Leo, are you there?"

"I'm here, Miss Crabtree," he said, stepping out onto the stage.

"Bring her to my dressing room, will you?"

"Will do!" He motioned to me. "Come on."

"Was I any good?" I whispered when I reached him. "I can't tell whether she liked it or not."

"You were dashed fantastic." He grinned at me. "I have a feeling she liked it."

Excitement thrummed through my veins as he led me backstage. I felt numb, like my brain was spinning, and I couldn't focus on anything. What if Leo was wrong? What if I'd blown my only chance?

He stopped at a door and knocked. "Enter," the voice called, and then I was standing in front of Lotta Crabtree. Should I curtsy?

"Hello," I said, dipping my knees awkwardly.

"Oh, aren't you the cutest?" Lotta came forward and stuck out her hand. "I'd rather shake hands than bow."

I shook the other woman's hand. "It's an honor to meet you, Miss Crabtree."

"Thank you, honey. Have a seat." She glanced over my shoulder. "Leo, wait in the hall, will you?"

Leo tipped his hat and withdrew, closing the door behind him. Lotta sat on the divan opposite from me. "Forgive me," the famous performer said, "but I wanted to talk to you alone, without your manager listening in."

"Because it's bad news?"

"No, nothing like that. You are very talented, Miss Smith."

"Thank you—and please, call me Josie."

"You are talented, Josie, but unpolished. You're a little rough around the edges."

My stomach sank, my chest caving in on itself. I'd muffed it. "Oh."

"Now, don't let that give you frown lines. What I mean is you're young and you haven't any experience performing. It's clear you need some training. But with the right guidance, you'll go far in this business."

"That makes sense. I mostly sing on the street. I'm not used to being onstage."

"I can tell. Now, from what I understand you don't have anyone looking out for you."

"Well, there's my friend Pippa. And Mr. Hardy, of course."

"A man like Leo is not on your side, honey. He's on his side. Never forget it." She reached and lifted the lit cigar from the dish on the table, then took a few puffs. "Forty years I've been in this business and without my mother watching out for me, I never would've made it half that long. She made certain I was paid and she invested my money. Never let anyone cheat me. Do you understand my meaning?"

"You don't trust him."

"I'm warning you to be careful. He's handsome and charming, but how much do you truly know about him? Maybe I'm wrong, but I've seen it happen too many times. Some talented young woman led astray by pretty words and a slick smile."

I nodded, though I knew better. I wasn't some sheltered girl who sat at home, working on my needlepoint. I'd been raised by no one but myself. Right now, I was keeping one eye on Leo and the other on my future. Nothing would stand in my way. "I understand."

"Good girl. Come by tomorrow morning and I'll show you some things. Does that sound all right?"

My jaw fell open, my brain scrambling to make sense of the offer. "It sounds amazing! Holy Christmas!"

Lotta chuckled. "I suspect we're going to get along just fine. I should mention that I'm leaving in two days, so unfortunately tomorrow is all I can give you."

I lunged out of my chair and thrust out my hand. "That's more than I ever dreamed. Thank you."

Lotta took my hand in hers. "You're welcome. We all need a break in this business, and I'd prefer to help you do it the right way. But I predict your name will be on everyone's lips before the year is out."

I left Lotta's dressing room in a daze, my skin buzzing with possibility. Leo straightened off the wall, his eyes searching my face. "Well?"

"She asked me to return tomorrow morning. Offered to show me some things to help my performance."

His face broke out in a wide grin. "Josie, that's wonderful. Congratulations."

I nearly skipped toward the exit. "I can't believe it. This is like a dream. Thank you for this!"

"I told you I'd get you a meeting," he said. "Does this mean I am your official manager?"

"Yes, I believe it does."

He stopped and held out his hand. "Let's shake on it, then."

I clasped his palm and pumped his hand eagerly. "I look forward to doing business with you, manager."

The light bounced off his sparkling blue eyes and formed a golden halo around his dark hair. He seemed almost magical in that moment, a guardian angel who'd dropped out of the sky to help me achieve my dreams. He leaned closer, still holding on to my hand. "You and me, Josie? I guarantee we'll make headlines together."

Chapter Five

LEO

For three hours the next morning, I sat in the front row and watched the stage. Lotta was leading Josie through some tips on performing. Where to stand, how to best project her voice. Where the lights should be positioned. Never had I dreamed any of this was so complicated.

Maybe because I know nothing about singing or acting.

True, but I was fixing to learn a whole lot in the next few weeks. I had no choice. This plan had to work.

Goddamn, but Josie was beautiful up there. More than that, though, Lotta's advice had poured confidence into my little fake heiress. It was like watching a flower bloom under the sun. She stood taller, stared at the audience as if she owned it. New York would have to take notice of her now.

Earlier, I went to a friend's newspaper office to do some light digging. Turned out the Pendeltons still lived in their big Fifth Avenue mansion, the same one my father toiled at for years. Mrs. Pendelton was notoriously reclusive since the disappearance of her daughter, but Mr. Pendelton remained a public figure, keeping up with his business interests. There hadn't been any more children, and the reward was still unclaimed.

All that money sitting there, just waiting for me.

I didn't feel bad, not in the least. Once we succeeded, Josie would live as Joséphine Pendelton, one of the richest young women in the world. At which point she could build her own theater in the middle of Central Park, if she wished. We'd both be living easy.

Lotta began fussing with Josie's skirts. "Leo?" the star called, shielding her eyes to stare into the seats. "Where are you?"

"Here," I called.

"Wrong. What that means is you are supposed to be here." She pointed at her side. "And hurry."

I smothered a smile at her bossiness. I liked women who weren't afraid to speak their own minds. A result of having five sisters, I supposed.

I bounded up the steps and strode across the stage. "Yes, Miss Crabtree?"

"What are you doing about her wardrobe?" Lotta swept her hand to indicate Josie's drab brown dress. "This won't do."

"We'll have some dresses made, of course." I said it with conviction, as if I'd been planning this all along.

"Don't forget handbags and shoes," Lotta said, walking a circle around Josie. "That is the mark of whether a woman has herself put together. There's no fibbing with a handbag or shoes. And please, for god's sake, no brown."

"I like this dress!" Josie stared down at herself. "It's only been mended twice."

"Yes, love. And it's the color of Boylston at three in the afternoon after the horses come through."

"Shit brown. Is that what you're saying?" Josie's shoulders tightened like she might be ready to argue.

I decided to smooth things over. "It doesn't do much for your skin tone. Brighter colors would be better. Right, Lotta?"

"Exactly." Lotta patted my shoulder. "He knows clothes, Josie. You should listen to him."

Yes, I knew clothes. Except I didn't know who was *paying* for Josie's new clothes. My mother made all my clothes, but I couldn't ask her to sew for Josie, too. She already had enough to do every day.

Josie dragged her gaze over my cream-colored suit. I didn't

miss how her gaze lingered on my shoulders and chest, either. Was that . . . interest? I stood a bit taller as an unexpected heat sparked in my belly.

"He dresses nicely," Josie said. "But that color is as bland as day-old bread."

Lotta wrapped an arm around Josie's shoulders and they both faced me. "Darling, when a man looks like this"—she gestured to my face—"he could wear a flour sack and have women swooning. And we are not discussing men. We're discussing you, a woman. For good or bad, we're held to a different standard."

"That's not entirely true," I protested. In my experience, no one trusted a stranger in shabby clothing.

"Quiet," Lotta told me. "Women are talking."

Josie folded her arms across her chest, a stubborn tilt to her chin. "Next you'll tell me I need a better corset to lift my bosom higher and fancy French lingerie."

Lotta snapped her fingers in my direction. "Leo, darling."

I didn't pretend to misunderstand. "Got it." Jesus, this was going to cost me a fortune—and we hadn't even reached New York yet.

"New Yorkers are a cut above, darling," Lotta was saying to Josie. "You want to impress them, not elicit their pity."

"I thought my voice was going to impress them." Josie's gaze narrowed as it darted between Lotta and me. "Or are you both lying to me? In cahoots in some kind of swindle?"

That hit a little too close to home, so I did my best to appear outraged. "Josie!"

Lotta merely laughed. "What on earth would I swindle you for? The motes of dust under your bed? Honey, I'm leaving for San Francisco tomorrow. There's a theater with my name over the marquee. Still, it's good to remain suspicious of those who offer up good deeds. Don't forget it."

I purposely kept my expression clear of any guilt.

"Josie, go to my dressing room and I'll have some tea sent in. Relax for a spell. I want to bend Leo's ear a bit."

Josie looked between me and Lotta, clearly torn between staying and obeying this woman who'd done so much for her. I nodded once. "It's all right. Just a few minutes, then I'll come find you."

"Bobby!" Lotta called into thin air. "Tea to my dressing room for Miss Smith!"

"You got it, Lotta," a disembodied voice shouted back.

Josie walked off the stage and disappeared into the wings. Lotta took my arm. "Let's sit. My feet are killing me."

I led her to the chairs in the audience and got her settled. Then I sat next to her. "Thank you again for this."

Lotta waved away the gratitude. "I'm doing this for her, not for you. And I'm happy to help. She's a real diamond in the rough. It's nice to see that genuine talent still exists out there."

"She'll take Broadway by storm."

"No doubt, but that's not what I want to talk to you about."

"Oh?" I angled toward her and crossed my legs. "Let me guess. Another warning."

"I doubted you once, so I won't do it again without cause. But I will say this: do not fuck her."

I hadn't expected such a thing to come out of her mouth, so I couldn't hide my surprise. A denial sprang to my lips. "You don't need—"

"You heard me," she interrupted. "I can see it brewing, and you're about to spend a lot of time together. Don't do it, Leo."

"I have no intention of letting things turn in that direction."

"A fancy way of avoiding a promise." She sighed and pursed her lips. "She's young and vulnerable. Relying on you to keep your word and help her achieve her dreams. Let her stand on her own. Don't play on her inexperience to get under her skirts and manipulate her."

"I won't."

"If you do, I'll know. Somehow I'll know and I'll return from San Francisco to make your life a living hell. That is my promise to you."

I believed it. "Understood."

"Good." She reached into her bodice and took out a small card. Passing the card to me, she said, "Here. This is the man to see in New York. We go way back. He'll give her a fair shake. And it'll keep you away from the confidence men and mashers that prey on those unfamiliar with how Broadway works."

There was a name and an address embossed on the front. "Is this a producer?"

"Melvin is a bit more than that, but you'll see. Tell him I sent you."

"Will he believe me?"

She made a motion with her finger and I flipped the card over. Lotta had jotted a note on the back. "He will when he sees that."

"Thank you, Lotta. This is more than either of us could've dreamed."

"Again, I'm doing this for her. You have a girl?"

I was having trouble keeping up. "A girl? No."

"A friend you meet to let off steam now and then?"

Ah. We were back to this. "Occasionally."

"See her before you leave for New York. Get it all out of your system. Then take Josie to Broadway and focus on her career—and only on her career. Are we clear?"

This was the strangest conversation I'd ever had. "Yes, ma'am."

"Good. Now, go and see her home. I'm sure she's exhausted."

I rose and held out my hand toward Lotta. She didn't take it, so I let my arm drop. "Are you coming?"

"No," she said. "Goodbyes aren't my speciality. Tell her I said good luck and I'll be watching for any notice of her."

"I will. Safe travels, Lotta. And thanks again."

She waved me off. "I just told you goodbyes aren't my thing. Get lost, Leo."

Unable to help myself, I grabbed her hand where it rested on the armrest and brought it to my lips. "Until later, then." I kissed her knuckles and released her hand. Then I turned and walked backstage.

I didn't bother knocking on Lotta's door before going in. Josie was reclined on the divan in the corner, sipping tea. She already looked the part of a Broadway star. Or wealthy heiress. "Shall we go?"

"Where's Lotta?"

"She stayed behind to rehearse. Though she did say to tell you good luck and she'll be looking for notice of you in the newspapers."

"Oh." Josie's eyes flashed with something—Annoyance? Hurt?—before she set the cup on the saucer and rose. "That's that, then. It was nice while it lasted."

I held the door open for her. The scent of vanilla teased the air as she went by. "What was nice?"

"Feeling like I made a new friend."

I trailed her along the corridor, wondering over her dour attitude when the day had been so positive. "Josie, the two of you are still friends. She said goodbyes aren't her speciality."

"That makes sense, I suppose. She travels a considerable amount."

"Yes, which means it's not about you. Don't be so quick to write off other people."

She frowned at me, the lines of her brow deepening. "Maybe that's how you navigate the world. But I learned a long time ago it's easier to let people go first rather than to try to hold on. You get hurt less that way."

I frowned at the back of her head as we pushed through the exit, but kept quiet. Who was I to tell her how to live her life? She was an orphan. No doubt she'd taken some knocks during her time on earth. And we all had to get by somehow. Christ, I was a confidence man. What did I know?

I flagged a hansom and handed her up. After I gave the driver Josie's address, I followed her inside. She barely waited for me to sit before demanding, "Tell me what you and Lotta talked about."

"You." I settled my derby on my lap. "She gave me the card of a man in New York to see."

Josie's shoulders relaxed. Had she been worried? My suspicion was confirmed when she said, "Good. I thought she was telling you I was terrible or that I'd never make it on Broadway."

"No, none of those things. She's a great believer in your talent."

"So that's all? Just the card?" I hesitated and Josie pounced. "I knew it! There's more. Tell me what she said."

There was no reason for me to lie, not about this. "She warned me to keep our relationship entirely platonic."

Josie's mouth fell open. "As opposed to what? Us sleeping together?"

"Yes."

I expected outrage or embarrassment. Instead, she threw her head back and laughed. "Imagine, me and you in bed!"

I could, actually. Josie was beautiful and bold, and I could see luscious curves under her drab dresses. I'd have no objections to stripping her naked, wrapping her legs around my hips, and feeding my cock inside her. Most healthy men I knew wouldn't.

Still chuckling, she nudged my foot with the toe of her boot. "Come on. You don't think that's funny?"

This was veering into dangerous territory. I tried to brush it aside with a casual grin. "You certainly know how to bruise a man's pride."

That quieted her down. A flush worked its way up her neck as the moment stretched. "Are you saying you *want* to sleep together?"

JOSIE

L eo wore a strange expression and didn't meet my gaze. "Of course I don't want to sleep with you."

I didn't believe him. His shoulders were stiff, like he was a statue sitting across from me. Granted, I hadn't spent much time around men, but Leo was smooth and easy. Good-looking, a real people person. He was tea with lots of sugar and cream. I bet everyone liked him.

Stood to reason he didn't get turned down much by the ladies.

But I was careful, more distrustful and wary. I watched out for myself. Twice I'd been intimate with a man, but nothing serious. I had big dreams and men only got in the way.

Would I like to get into bed with Leo? Maybe, if he wasn't my manager. I bet he could show a girl a good time, with those long limbs and lean, strong hips. But things were too tangled up now. My future rested in this man's hands. He could easily derail it, if he chose.

"So that's settled then," I announced. "When do we leave for New York?"

"I don't know." His gaze remained on the passing street through the window.

"Well, what's your plan?"

"I'm not sure yet."

I pursed my lips and stared at his hard jaw. A muscle jumped under the skin, like he was clenching his teeth. I was never one to keep quiet, so I said, "You're bothered by it, me not being interested in you physically."

"Please," he scoffed, his upper lip curling ever so slightly.

Oh, yes. Bothered, indeed.

Well, too bad. Even if it wounded his pride, I wasn't interested in him that way. At least, I hadn't been until a few minutes ago.

Now I was thinking about it, wondering if all that charm and smooth talk extended to his bedroom skills.

Damn it.

"Are you tired?" he asked after a few moments.

Tired? My blood was humming with excitement, the day more than I'd ever dreamed. Lotta's instruction—already committed to memory—had been invaluable. Not only had she provided valuable insight into performing onstage, she'd passed along the name of a man to see in New York. I wanted to run through the city streets, swim the length of the St. Charles River, then go jump into the harbor. I felt like I might never fall asleep again.

"Hardly," I answered. "I feel like celebrating. This has been the best day of my life."

"I'm glad, but let's not celebrate yet. Instead, I want to take you to see a friend of mine."

A friend? That deflated my happiness a tiny bit. "What for?"

"Polish."

"What does that mean?"

He cracked the knuckles on his right hand, one by one. "You'll see."

Did he mean clothes, like Lotta suggested? And why was he so surly and quiet all of a sudden? "Can't we eat first?"

"We'll have food there." Leaning up, he pulled open the tiny window to speak to the driver. Leo gave the man an address on Queensberry Street, which seemed odd. That was a nice neighborhood.

He didn't say anything when he resettled. Instead, he proceeded to crack the knuckles on his other hand. I tried not to react, but the popping sound grated on my nerves. Who knew men could be so annoying?

I closed my eyes and remembered Lotta's lessons. I couldn't wait to recount the entire day for Pippa.

"What are you doing?"

I didn't look at Leo as I answered his question. "Remembering."

"Remembering what?"

"Everything Lotta said today."

"Ah. I could get you a journal. Then you could write it all down."

I lifted my eyelids and met his gaze. "I don't need to write it down. After I repeat it to myself, it's locked inside my brain."

He nodded, his lips pursing like he approved. "But you'd remember more if you wrote it down."

"You don't understand. I can recall every word of a conversation once it's committed to memory."

His eyebrows flew up and his mouth fell open. "That can't be true. Surely you can't . . . You can remember every word Lotta spoke today?"

"Yes."

"Is this something you do often?"

"Every time I think there's something worth remembering, yes."

"Have you always been able to do this?"

I lifted a shoulder. "I suppose. The nuns used to test me by reading long passages to see if I could recall every word."

"And could you?"

"Yes, but it isn't hard for me. The nuns said I must have more space in my brain to memorize things because I had no family memories."

A strange expression skimmed over his face, so quick I almost missed it. Did he feel sorry for me?

I kept talking, unwilling to accept anyone's pity. "It's a useful skill. And annoying because there are often things I can't forget but wish I could."

"As in?"

"Like platitudes and false compliments. Phrases people say to ease their conscience but don't mean. When they give you false hope."

For years the nuns said the right family would come along eventually and adopt me. I just had to remain patient, be a good girl. I could still hear Sister Catherine telling me, *A family will want you someday, Josie. Believe in God's plan, child.*

But the family never came.

And I stopped believing.

I swallowed the old bitter memories. "It's devastating when you realize the words are nothing but a lie."

Leo put his elbows on his knees and studied his shoes for a long time. "I've tried to always be square with you—"

"I wasn't talking about you. I'm not a rosy-cheeked kid who believes in the goodness of mankind anymore. That naivete was sucked out of me eons ago."

"Yeah, me too." His glance slid toward me. "What about me? Are you able to remember every word I've said to you?"

"Pretty much."

I could tell he didn't believe me by the way the lines around his mouth deepened. "You remember everything I said at the ice cream saloon?" When I nodded, he ordered, "Repeat it back."

"Why?"

"Because I'm curious."

"I'm not one of Barnum's oddities, Leo."

"I never implied that you were. Come on, for me." He nudged his boot against the toe of my shoe, as I'd done earlier to him.

Closing my eyes again, I repeated every word he said that day, from the offer to buy me ice cream and purging Boston from his voice, to his five sisters and our discussion of vanilla. Top to bottom, I recited it like a play, deepening my voice to perform Leo.

At the end, I exhaled and folded my hands.

He was staring at me as if I had two heads. "Holy shit, Josie."

"I know." I couldn't help but grin. "It's quite all right if you find me amazing."

"Amazing doesn't cover it."

"Aw, go on." I pushed his knee with mine. "Seriously, do go on."

He chuckled. "I see humility is not one of your best qualities."

"Says the very handsome man who uses his looks to get whatever he wants."

His shoulders jerked. He opened his mouth, then promptly closed it.

"I know I'm right," I told him. "So don't bother denying it."

"Have you tried to use your memorization skill to make money?"

I allowed him to change the subject from himself to me. "Isn't that what we are doing? How do you think I memorize song lyrics? Soon I'll memorize parts for plays and musicals, too."

As the carriage slowly turned up Queensberry Street, Leo said softly, "You are nothing like I assumed, Josie Smith."

God only knew what he'd first thought of me, then. I was pretty much an open book. Easy to read, nothing to hide. I spoke my mind and didn't lie.

When the wheels stopped, Leo pushed out the carriage door. "Wait here. I'll return in a moment."

After he gave directions for the driver to hold at the curb, Leo strode up the walk of a charming three-story town house. Petunias bloomed in a box on the windowsill and a small plant rested on the stoop. The residence looked nice and comfortable, a decent place on a fancy street. This was where his friend lived?

He rang the bell and a woman answered the door. At the sight of Leo, the woman's face broke out into a wide grin and she reached to embrace him. There was something intimate and familiar about the way he leaned in to kiss her cheek.

Warning bells went off inside my head. Was this . . . ? No, he wouldn't bring me to his paramour.

Would he?

They spent a few minutes chatting, but I couldn't hear what was being said. The woman was beautiful and well dressed.

Probably in her late twenties. No wedding ring that I could see. I liked her hair, the way it was swept up in a soft bouffant with curls. Gibson Girls, they called the ladies who styled their hair in such a fashion. And her dress was fancy, probably expensive.

The two of them continued to go back and forth, with Leo laughing at one point. His expression was relaxed, easy. Genuine. He liked her.

So, this was the type of woman Leo bedded. It made sense, actually. No doubt I was as appealing as spoiled porridge to a man like him—which was fine and dandy with me. I liked to know where I stood with people, and seeing this woman with him helped make it clear.

Leo bounded back to the carriage and opened the door. "I have a friend I want you to meet. I think you'll like her."

"Why?" He'd said "polish" earlier, but I had no interest in meeting the women he slept with.

"She's agreed to show you a few things."

Now I was definitely on edge. I folded my arms across my chest. "Like what?"

Confusion wrinkled his brow. "Tea, dresses, society rules. That sort of thing." Then he cocked his head. "What did you think I meant?"

I didn't want to answer that, so I pushed out of the carriage and he helped me to the walk. "Sounds good to me. Let's go."

I started up the walk without waiting for his arm. I didn't need his help, not for this. I'd been looking after myself for a long time. A pretty face wouldn't fool me into changing that fact.

Chapter Six

LEO

I followed Josie to the door. Martha waited patiently for us, her demeanor polite yet welcoming. I owed her big for this favor. I stood between the two women. "Miss Josie Smith, I'd like to present Mrs. Stockwell. Martha, this is Josie."

Martha held out her hand toward my singer. "How do you do, Miss Smith?"

Josie grabbed the other woman's hand and pumped twice. "Nice to meet you. Call me Josie."

I could see Martha struggling not to wince under Josie's firm grip. I took Josie's elbow and began leading her into the vestibule. "Let's go inside, shall we?"

Josie edged away from me as soon as we were in the entry. "What a place." Whistling, she took in the chandelier overhead, the fine paintings on the walls. "It's like a palace in here."

Martha looked at me quizzically. I put my hands up, trying to reassure her that letting us in wasn't a mistake. With a genial smile, my friend swept her arm out toward the parlor. "Shall we sit? I'll ring for tea."

Josie nodded. "And food, please. Leo promised."

"Ringing for tea is a polite way of saying she'll provide refreshments," I told Josie quietly.

"Oh, right. I knew that," she said, though it was clear she hadn't.

I followed Josie to the sofa and we both sat, careful to maintain a respectful distance. After asking a footman for tea, Martha settled in an armchair. "I understand from Leo that you will soon be traveling to New York," Martha said. "He asked if I could show you a few tips on how to interact in polite society."

Josie wrinkled her nose. "I don't see why I need to know about things like tea and polite society. I want to work in theater."

Martha handled this easily. "The world revolves around social customs, my dear. To succeed, we must adapt and conform. You may break the rules, of course, but you must first learn them."

"And," I put in, "there may be times when you're required to interact with members of high society." Like Mrs. Pendelton.

"I suppose." Josie didn't appear convinced.

One of Martha's girls came in and crossed the floor. Bending, she whispered in Martha's ear. Martha's face paled. "Goodness, I'd best come straightaway. Leo, Miss Smith. If you'll excuse me a moment."

The two women left and I relaxed into the plush sofa. I'd spent a fair amount of time here over the last two years. Martha and I went way back.

"Was that her daughter?"

I looked over at Josie. "Daughter? Oh, no." I chuckled. "That was one of the women who works for Martha. This is a high-end bordello."

"Bordello?" A grin split Josie's face, like this was the most exciting thing she'd ever heard. "You brought me to a bordello to learn polish."

I felt the need to defend my choice. "For your information, this is one of the best bordellos in the city. It caters to the posh Beacon Hill crowd. Second, I've known Martha forever." As someone else who'd adapted and transformed herself into someone new, Martha and I understood each other.

"Do you have intimate relations with her?"

The question surprised me. I hadn't expected it, though I truly should have with Josie. Anything could come out of this woman's mouth. "Occasionally, yes."

"And the other girls here?"

"If the mood strikes, yes."

Josie's head swiveled as she looked around. "I'm friends with some of the working girls in my neighborhood. Never been in a place as nice as this, though. How do you afford it?"

I shifted on the sofa, uncomfortable with this line of questioning. "I manage."

"Really? I know what some of my friends earn and it's a pretty penny. These girls must be expensive. Except you said you weren't rich."

"I'm not."

"Then how often are you here? Weekly? Monthly?"

I couldn't believe this. Frustration caused me to snap, "Do you wish to hear about the frequency of my climaxes? My preferred positions? Jesus, Josie."

I expected shock or outrage, but Josie merely shrugged. "Sure, if you're willing to discuss it."

Thankfully, Martha returned before I could say anything else. A footman trailed behind her, a tea tray in his hands. "I apologize. There was a matter upstairs that required my attention."

The footman placed the tray on a table, but Martha made no effort to begin serving. Instead, she addressed Josie. "Miss Smith, tell me what you know of preparing tea for guests."

"Not a thing," Josie answered unapologetically. "Pippa and I don't have guests all that regular. And we don't serve tea when we do."

Was she referring to men? I nearly slapped my forehead. Damn, I was an idiot. The prospect of a man in her life hadn't occurred to me. But of course a beautiful woman like Josie, so brash and outspoken, would attract men wherever she went. Why hadn't I asked?

The uncomfortable feeling skittered down to my stomach. I didn't like it. A man could intervene in what I was trying to do, prevent Josie from following my lead. Sow seeds of mistrust and whatnot.

Josie and Martha stared at the tea set, with Martha explaining the various pieces and their purpose. "Is there a man in your life?" I blurted, not even caring if I seemed half cracked.

Josie's mouth flattened. "How's that any of your concern?"

"As your manager, I need to know if some boy will insert himself into your career."

"Now he's a boy?" She straightened to glower at me. "What is wrong with you?"

I didn't back down. This was too important. "Just answer the question."

"I'll answer your question when you answer mine from earlier."

About how I afforded to patronize a place like this.

Christ, this woman. I pressed my lips together, and the two of us engaged in a staredown, each waiting for the other to break first. Did she think I was so easy? I'd faced down street toughs and coppers. Gangsters. Never had I willingly revealed more about myself than necessary.

A good con man had to remain a mystery—especially to his mark.

Except Josie's green eyes gave no hint that she would bend anytime soon. She stared at me, truly *stared*, and it was as if she saw every part of me, even the parts I kept hidden just for myself. I didn't care for the sensation. It felt like layers of tender skin were being slowly stripped away to expose everything underneath. I shifted in my seat.

When another half minute went by I couldn't take her stare a second more. "Fine," I growled from behind clenched teeth. "When necessary, I provide entertainment during parties for house credit."

"Entertainment?"

The one word conveyed her disbelief and suspicion, as if the entertainment I provided was salacious in nature. I saw no reason to correct her assumption, even though I'd meant sleight of hand card tricks. "Yes."

Josie lowered her gaze. "I see. No, there isn't a beau in my life."

A shockingly strong wave of relief went through me at this news. "Carry on," I snapped at Martha, annoyed at myself and everyone else.

I would need to be more careful with Josie. She had a strange power to make me confess things, apparently.

"Please excuse him," Josie said in a terrible stage whisper. "Leo's been in a rotten mood ever since we left the theater."

Martha's brow lifted as she turned in my direction. "Is that so?"

I didn't like how either of them was looking at me. "Are we done here?"

"We've barely begun," Martha said, then she added, "We need to let Josie practice her serving skills on you."

Perhaps it was our location, but the words conjured up an image in my head that had nothing to do with tea—Josie on her knees, serving me, attending to my cock. Plump lips taking me deep while those green eyes stared up at me . . .

A wave of unexpected heat curled through my groin, the second one today. Shit.

Horrified, I attempted to collect myself as Martha droned on about proper tea service. The way to serve, how to hold the saucer and not the cup. Adding the milk first to preserve the porcelain. Lips moving ever so slightly as Martha spoke, Josie was clearly repeating the instructions to memorize them. Indeed, what a fascinating talent.

When we first met, I assumed her to be a rube, a simple orphan who wouldn't give me any trouble. I could take her to New York under false pretenses, parade her in front of Mrs. Pendelton, collect my reward money, and come back to Boston a wealthy man.

But Josie was no rube. She was smart, and had a quick mind. Intelligence like mine, not learned from books but rather the streets.

This could pose a problem if I didn't remain sharp.

"Leo? Are you listening?"

I lifted my head. "Yes, of course."

"How do you take your tea, sir?" Josie asked in an exaggerated British voice.

"With bourbon."

"Plain it is," Josie said and handed me the saucer and cup.

Soon the three of us were sipping bland tea, my leg bouncing in irritation. I wanted to leave, go somewhere to collect my thoughts. First the carriage ride, now this conversation at Martha's. Josie was like a sliver under my skin, and this cordial scene was more than I could handle at the moment. I'd much rather yell at her instead.

What was happening to me?

I reached into my coat pocket and pulled out my flask.

"Leo," Martha admonished as I unscrewed the cap. "It's one o'clock in the afternoon."

"Sorry, Martha." I topped my tea off with a healthy dash of Kentucky's finest. "Can't be helped." I put my flask away and took a drink of my bourbon-laced tea. The burn went all the way to my stomach. Much fucking better.

"How did you learn all this?" Josie asked Martha. "The tea and how to be a lady."

"My mother. She used to work as a maid in one of the Brahmin households."

I hadn't known this, but it made sense. The Boston Brahmins were a very exclusive social set, like the Knickerbockers of New York City. That influence explained why Martha's bordello was so genteel and why she dressed like a society lady.

When Josie excused herself for the facilities, Martha frowned at me. "What on earth has gotten into you today?"

"I don't know what you mean."

"Yes, you do. What are you doing with this girl?"

"As I told you earlier, I'm planning to help her become rich and famous." Just not as a singer.

"And that's all?"

I gulped the rest of my drink in one go and set the cup on the table. "Of course."

"I saw the way you looked at her."

"Like she's a pain in my ass?" I muttered.

"No, and do not be so crude. You looked at her like you wanted her. In the biblical sense."

"Balderdash—"

"Don't lie to me. You think I haven't seen that look in your eye once or twice myself? I know what it means."

"It means I need new friends."

Martha laughed and shook her head. "Fine. Enjoy your denial. But don't hurt her, Leo."

"Why does everyone keep saying that to me?" I stretched one arm along the sofa back and crossed my legs. "You've met her. Josie can hold her own."

"Does she know what you do for a living?"

"No, and don't tell her. I'm turning over a new leaf with her."

"Oh, darling." Martha lifted her cup and sipped her tea, her gaze holding mine over the rim. "Men don't turn over new leaves. They just find new pots with fresh dirt to ruin."

"You're wrong, but I don't have time to argue. I still need another favor."

Martha's lips parted as her eyebrows soared. "My goodness, you are bold today."

"I know, but she needs a few things to wear in New York. I'd be grateful if you could see fit to helping us."

"You are mounting quite the large debt with me, Leo Hardy."

I let my voice drop. "I'm happy to work it off however you see fit."

She pursed her lips, then exhaled heavily. "I shall hold you to that. But fine, I'll lend her clothing."

"Thank you, Martha. I appreciate it."

"Speaking of your debt, do you plan to stay after?"

JOSIE

Speaking of your debt, do you plan to stay after?

I stood near the edge of the doorway, out of sight, as I eavesdropped, awaiting Leo's answer. Would he stay? I nibbled a broken fingernail, my stomach churning. Either those two tea sandwiches were spoiled or I hated the idea of Leo with another woman. Even one he paid for.

I shouldn't care. But now, thanks to our earlier conversation about sleeping together, I couldn't stop thinking about it. Hot sweaty bodies, rolling around in bed together. Eager kisses and rough hands. What it would feel like to run my fingers through his thick dark hair . . .

"You lonely today, sweetheart?" Leo asked in the other room, his voice deepening into a sensual purr—and heat exploded under my skin.

I fanned my face, suddenly parched. No man had ever talked to me in such a way, like he was seducing me. I'd initiated my few intimate encounters myself, mostly out of curiosity and boredom, but none of them had been particularly exciting. I never felt hot and cold at the same time, not like this.

I put a hand on the doorjamb and took a deep breath. I couldn't walk back in there with lust in my eyes and sweat running down my face.

"No," Martha said. "I'm far too busy for you this afternoon. But I'm sure one of the other girls would be happy to entertain you for a bit."

"Sadly, I must decline," Leo replied. "I'm broke."

I exhaled, relieved. So that was that. Good. He could focus on me and our upcoming trip to New York . . .

Wait, how did he plan to manage it without any funds?

He's lying to me. He can't help me.

The words, dark and poisonous, crept through my mind, and I could feel my natural skepticism coloring what had been an amazing day.

True, Leo admitted he wasn't rich, but that was different than being *broke*. He definitely hadn't mentioned that. I had some money saved, but not enough to float a trip for two to New York.

Stupid, stupid, stupid. Why had I blindly followed his lead and believed whatever came out of his mouth? Didn't I know better? At an early age I had learned not to count on anyone other than myself. Maybe Pip, but definitely not a stranger.

Yet for a few hours today, I'd forgotten. Between Leo's pretty face, Lotta's attention, and Martha's tea, I'd started to think there might be goodness out in the world. That some people really were angels here on earth.

But angels weren't real, and the world was mostly full of devils who used others for their own gain. I needed to stop relying on Leo for everything. My fate rested in my own hands, no one else's, which meant I needed to take more of an active role in the planning.

Leo owed me answers.

Head high, I strode into the sitting room and retook my seat. Martha was sitting with her hands folded in her lap, her ankles crossed under her chair, so I tried to emulate her even though my limbs felt awkward. *Play the part, Josie.*

"Josie," Martha said with a smile, "I have some gowns upstairs that might fit you. This would save you the time and expense of visiting a dressmaker. Would you like to see them?"

"That is incredibly generous of you, thank you. And I insist on paying you for whatever I take."

Leo leaned forward, his brows pulling low like this comment confused him. "That isn't necessary. I'll settle up with Martha."

"I prefer to settle with her myself," I explained, my voice leaving no room for argument.

But of course, Leo started one. Jaw tight, he asked, "Do you have such funds on hand?"

"Consider the dresses a loan," Martha interjected. "All I ask is that you bring them back in decent shape."

"I swear that I will," I said, putting my hand over my heart. "Thank you. May I see them now?"

"Direct and to the point. I approve, Josie." Martha rose and smoothed her skirts, shaking them out a little.

I did the same, mimicking her. My dress wasn't nearly as fancy, though, and her sleeves were puffier, which was all the rage these days.

Someday I'll own expensive gowns and wear them in my own sitting room.

"Leo," Martha said, "you may go to the kitchen and wait, if you prefer. There's some ham and more bourbon there."

He rubbed his jaw and didn't respond, his expression inscrutable. Was he unhappy with me? Tough. I had a mind of my own and if we were doing this, we needed to be partners.

"Ready?" I gestured toward the door.

Martha nodded and led me out of the sitting room. I didn't look back at Leo, even though I swore I could feel the weight of his stare on my back.

I followed Martha upstairs. When we were alone, I couldn't help but ask, "You and Leo. You go way back?"

"Oh, yes. I've known him a long time."

"And?"

She paused outside an ornately carved wooden door. "You want to know if he's paid me for services."

"No, I don't care about that. I want to know if he's on the up-and-up."

Unlocking the door, she pushed inside. We entered a bedchamber and Martha placed her keys on a small round table. "Leo is Leo, Josie. And he's not the kind of man you keep."

"Oh, I don't—"

"Pray, hear me out." She strode to a wardrobe and pulled open the latch. "He's not a man who sticks. Do you understand? He's interested in Leo, nothing more. My grandmother would have said he's like a puddle, shallow and small. You don't want a man like that. You want an ocean, deep and infinite. A man who will love you without limits."

"I'm not interested in him that way."

"Good. See that it remains so." She took out a dress of golden silk. "This is the right shade for your coloring. Here, hold this up in the glass."

The evening dress was so magical that I was almost afraid to touch it. The embroidery was delicate, the fabric smooth and shiny. It would hug my body, giving me a true hourglass shape. "It's beautiful," I whispered. "I couldn't possibly borrow it."

"Nonsense. You need something to wear at night and that will fit you perfectly. I don't have a ball gown, but I'll lend you a tea gown and a few day dresses. They're new and I've hardly worn them."

I was overwhelmed by her generosity. "Thank you. I'll take very good care of them."

Martha gave me a kind smile. "I know you will. I could tell the moment I saw you."

"How?"

"Your shoes." She gestured to my boots. "They're old, but polished with new heels."

I lifted up my skirts to show her. "I believe in having things that last."

"Precisely why I'm warning you away from romantic notions surrounding Leo Hardy."

"I swear—"

All of a sudden, there was a scream and loud thumps down the hall. Was a customer getting rowdy with one of Martha's girls?

"I was afraid of this," Martha said as she dashed toward the door. "Excuse me, Josie!"

I wasn't about to let her face that ruckus alone, so I hurried into the corridor. Martha was faster, though, having already flung open one of the doors and disappeared inside. Before I could close the distance to see for myself, Leo came flying up the stairs two at a time, a blur as he bounded into the open room.

I skidded to a stop in the doorway just as Leo pulled his arm back and cracked a half-naked man across the jaw. The man stumbled, his big body off-kilter as he tried to stay on his feet. When he righted he launched himself at Leo, his face mottled with fury. "How dare you hit me, you fucking—"

Quick as a flash, Leo punched the man in the face and twice in the stomach. Just like a bare-knuckle fighter. I gaped at him.

The man dropped to the ground, curling in on himself. "She owes me," he wheezed. "You have no right to intervene."

Even though the other man had at least fifty pounds on him, Leo showed no fear, leaning down to snarl, "The hell she does. Now, stay down or I'll hit you again."

"Sir," Martha said, her arm around a sobbing young girl on the bed, "we already discussed this. Your payment is nonnegotiable. Ariella and I both told you what your money would buy, nothing more."

"She's a whore, and she'll take it anywhere I say!"

Leo snatched the man's hair and somehow got him up on his feet. Then Leo was holding a blade to the man's throat. The man sputtered and attempted to break free, but Leo held him fast, his expression menacing and fierce. "You're going to apologize and get the hell out of here," Leo snarled, "or I'm going to spill your blood all over the floor. Understand?"

I watched, gobsmacked. Gone was the smooth-talking charmer, the handsome man-about-town. In his place was a dangerous ruffian, a man who wasn't afraid to slice off the tip of an ear here and there. This was a side to Leo that I hadn't imagined.

I was impressed.

"You get one last chance," Leo said with deadly intent as he squeezed the man's throat. "Apologize and leave, or I'll make you regret it."

"My apologies," the man rasped.

Spinning, Leo marched the customer in the direction of the doorway where I was standing. I couldn't believe it was over. That was it? This man deserved worse than a few punches.

When the unruly customer was right in front of me, I couldn't help myself. I lifted my skirts and delivered a swift kick directly between his legs. I used the toe of my boot, too, making sure to hit all the pertinent spots. "That's for making her cry."

The man slumped in Leo's hold, groaning as he cupped himself, and Leo struggled to keep them both upright. "Goddamn it, Josie! Was that necessary?"

"Only a man would ask such an inane question," I said.

"Move." I stepped aside and Leo shoved the larger man out the doorway then down the carpeted stairs. We all rushed to watch, clutching the railing, as the scene played out.

"Wait, my clothes! I need my clothes!" the man said.

Martha disappeared, then returned with the customer's coat, shirt, and collar. She threw them over the banister, where they floated down to the first floor. "Nicely done with the kick," she said to me under her breath.

"We were all thinking it," I returned with a shrug.

Leo shoved the clothes toward the front door with his foot, never releasing his hold on the larger man. "You'll get dressed on the stoop. Keep moving."

We stayed glued to the banister as Leo threw open the front door and shoved the man outside. Next went the clothes, thanks to the footman standing nearby. Leo pointed in the customer's face. "Don't ever come back here. You hear me?"

The disheveled man was too busy collecting his things from the ground to put up a fuss, so Leo slammed the door closed. Then he spun toward the stairs, his face twisted with irritation. "Josie, I swear to God!" he snarled. "Get down here this instant."

"I'm not a dog, Leo," I said. "Stop ordering me around."

Putting his hands on his hips, he tilted his head back to glare at me. "You could've been seriously hurt! Are you cracked?"

Martha muttered, "Oh, dear," before going down the steps. Unwilling to bend to Leo's demands, I took my time and shook hands with Ariella. She also thanked me for the kick and I wished her well. Then, at a leisurely pace, I descended the steps, my head high.

Martha and Leo were having a heated exchange, but I couldn't hear what they were discussing. It was past time to leave, however. Martha had more important things to do than give me lessons and gowns. I found my hat on the side table and affixed it on my head using the hallway mirror. "Leo, let's go."

He stalked over and snatched up his derby. Martha promised to pack up the gowns and have them sent to my apartment. I thanked her profusely and said goodbye. Then Leo and I were outside.

There was no sign of the unruly customer.

Waves of anger radiated off Leo as he jammed his hat on his head. I didn't pay him any mind and started walking south.

He caught up to me. "Do you ever think before you act or speak, woman?"

"He deserved it. You should've sliced his ear off."

"You could've been hurt."

"As could've you, tearing up the stairs like a banshee before you knew what was happening. And he had almost fifty pounds on you."

"Josie, wait." He grabbed my arm and pulled us both to a stop. "Will you listen to me?"

I didn't want to have this conversation. We had bigger issues than what happened at Martha's. "Why didn't you tell me you're broke?"

His lips parted and he searched my face. "What are you talking about?"

"I heard you tell Martha you couldn't stay today because you can't afford it."

"You shouldn't eavesdrop, Josie." He stared off into the street, his arms folded across his wide chest. "It's rude."

Not in my book. Sometimes eavesdropping was the only way to learn the truth.

"Look, Leo," I told him. "We're either partners in this or the deal's off. I need you to be honest with me. How are we getting to New York?"

Oh, that jaw grew so solid, so tense. He didn't care for this conversation one bit. "I told you I wasn't rich."

"Yeah, but you're buying me ice cream, hailing hansoms, and talking about Broadway. I'm not some silly empty-headed ninny. I might not know my exact age, but I've been looking after myself for at least nineteen years. So, tell it to me straight or get lost."

Head bent, Leo studied the ground. "You want the truth? Here it is. No, I don't have much money." He looked up and his steady gaze met mine. "But I believe in you, Josie. I believe in your voice, your presence. You can be famous. I know it deep in my soul."

If he was lying, I couldn't tell. There was nothing but sincerity looking down at me, no hesitation in his voice whatsoever. Either he was the best actor in Boston, or he believed what he was saying.

Still, I wasn't ready to declare him 100 percent trustworthy.

I folded my arms over my chest. "If we're going to muddle through together, then we need to be totally honest with each other. Right? I don't like liars and I never forget the lies. Are you telling me the truth?"

"Yes." He relaxed and nodded once. "Absolutely."

"And everything with Lotta, that was legit?"

"Are you under the impression I paid her to say those things to you?"

I started walking again. I thought best when I was moving around. Leo caught up with me in two long strides. He nudged my arm. "Come now. You don't really think I'd do something like that, do you?"

I thought about the man who'd held a knife to an unruly customer's throat a few moments ago. "Considering I don't know anything about you, maybe."

"Everything Lotta said was legitimate." When I said nothing, Leo held out his hands. "What do you want to know? I'm an open book."

"Why do you carry a switchblade?"

"You grew up near Tremont Street, so you know why. The city's dangerous."

That was fair. Pippa carried a pistol for her walk home at night after the saloon. I dodged a woman carrying a basket of flowers, then asked, "How are you planning to afford a trip to New York?"

"I have some money saved," Leo said. "Enough for two third-class tickets. We're staying at a friend's place there."

"What friend?"

"Someone I used to know here. But don't worry, he's out of town. It'll just be you and me."

Me and Leo, alone in a room? I didn't find that news entirely reassuring, not when I considered my reaction to overhearing him and Martha.

I lowered my voice as we crossed the street. "You said you don't want to get me into bed. So why do you care if there's a man in my life or not?"

"Damn it, Josie."

"Answer the question, Leo."

We continued to walk, yet he remained silent. Evading my question again? This man was truly trying my patience.

After we stepped onto the walk, I grabbed his arm and pulled him to a stop. "Why does it matter if I have a beau? You and I aren't romantic. What difference would it make to you?"

He stared off at the carts and horses in the street. The brim of his hat shaded his eyes from me, but I could see the tight set of his mouth. "Drop it. I never should've asked."

"I won't drop it. Not until you give me an answer."

"There's no reason. Curiosity, is all."

"That's bull and you know it. Just tell me." The skin of his throat turned a dull red and he actually growled. Did he think that would scare me? "Spit it out—"

"Because if I were lucky enough to call you mine, I'd never let you out of my sight. I certainly wouldn't let you go to New York with another man."

He blurted the words like they were unwillingly pulled from his throat.

Neither one of us moved, the words falling between us like a stone. I sucked in a surprised breath and held it.

If I were lucky enough to call you mine . . .

Mine.

An indescribable rush of longing went through me, a tiny earthquake so strong that my knees actually shook. I couldn't imagine belonging to anyone or having anyone love me that much, let alone a man. After all, my parents hadn't wanted me. Not one family had inquired about adopting me from the asylum. Besides Pippa, I had no one.

What would it be like to belong to a man? To Leo?

Quickly, I repeated his words to myself. I never, ever wanted to forget them.

He's not a man who sticks.

Good thing Leo wasn't interested in me like that. At the moment all my focus needed to remain on me and my singing career. Nothing more.

I patted his lapel. "See you tomorrow, Leo."

"Wait, where are you going?"

"Home to pack." I waved and disappeared into the crowded street.

Chapter Seven

New York City

LEO

This city held nothing but bad memories for me.

Having lived in Boston since the age of ten, that was a place I knew well. From the ins and outs, to the people who mattered and those best to avoid, Boston was a big city that felt small. Busy and loud in certain moments, then calm and quiet when so desired.

New York City was the opposite.

Though I hadn't been here in sixteen years, I remembered the vastness, the stunning expanse of the crowded island. Dirty and huge, always under construction with the new replacing the old. A city with no loyalty, no sense of fairness. It was every man for himself here, a place that would crush you if you weren't careful.

We'd only arrived and I was already itching to leave.

"Where to?" Josie shouted above the noise of the busy train depot.

"This way." I gestured to the right as if I knew the direction in which we needed to go. *First rule of being a confidence man: the confidence.*

I held open the door to the street. Josie came through, and I started for the row of hansoms waiting at the Forty-Second Street curb in a neat line.

"Hold up," she said, grabbing my arm. "We should walk."

The morning light bounced off her features and her simple beauty struck me like an electric charge. I'd avoided looking at Josie today because I didn't like how she was affecting me. Already I spent a lot of time thinking about bright green eyes and a wide, lush mouth. Too much time, actually.

I looked away. "Let's treat ourselves. Once we learn the city, we can take the elevated or ankle it."

"Only if you're sure."

"I'm sure," I said with no hint of hesitation.

Soon we were in a hansom and traveling west on Forty-Second Street toward Broadway. Josie kept her face pressed to the carriage window. "How long will it take us to get to your friend's place?"

"I would imagine thirty minutes or so, depending on traffic."

"How do you know this friend?"

While I debated my answer, I took a playing card out of my coat pocket and began threading it through my fingers. An old habit to keep my hands busy. "I've known Ambrose forever. We met as young men in Boston with similar interests." *Conning people.* "He moved to New York about three years ago to work in finance." *Wall Street stock schemes.* "At the moment he's in Saratoga Springs." *Selling phony elixirs to the racetrack visitors.*

"So I won't meet him?"

"No, he'll be gone for a few weeks." Which would allow me enough time to get Josie in front of Mrs. Pendelton without Ambrose asking a hundred questions—or trying to take a cut of the reward money. "By the time he returns we'll have made our connections and established ourselves."

"Oh, look! It's Longacre Square!"

We were approaching Broadway, exactly where many of the theaters and clubs were located. Advertisements and colorful posters adorned the short buildings, large signs that told us where to visit, what to see. *Castle Square Opera Company. Lyceum Theatre. Bergen Beach.* A sanitation worker cleaned out the gutters, while another brushed horse leavings off the stone street.

"It's grand, isn't it, Leo?"

I grimaced. "Yeah, grand." And crowded. And flat. What was so great about this city, anyway?

Josie cast a quick glance at me over her shoulder. "You're not even looking."

I flicked the card over my knuckles. "New York's not so hot. Boston's better."

"You're a Boston snob." She returned to her window. "I love it here."

"That's good, considering we're aiming to get you a job in New York."

"Look at all these buildings going up."

Looked like buildings being torn *down*. But mostly what I saw was money, gobs of it. Shops, jewelry, fancy buildings, and new carriages. This city was crawling with sawbucks for the taking.

And I had the ultimate prize sitting next to me.

At least I didn't have to worry about running into the Pendel-tons down here. They lived a considerable ways uptown at Fifth Avenue and Seventieth Street. I didn't recall much of the interior, but I sure remembered the gardens in the back. Were they still the same?

I lowered my hat over my face and leaned my head against the seat back. "Wake me up when we get to Eighteenth Street."

"Why don't you care? Have you visited New York before?"

"I was born here. Lived in the city until I was ten."

Suddenly, my hat disappeared off my face. Josie's bewildered expression filled my vision. "What on earth? You didn't tell me any of this before."

"Not really worth talking about." I took my hat back and smoothed the brim. "I was a boy. And it wasn't like we had the money for operas and musicals."

She angled toward me, her eyes big and curious. "Tell me everything you're able to remember, no matter how small."

"I already told you—"

"Balderdash. I know you remember *something*."

Mostly I recalled trailing my father around on the Pendelton estate, a small boy running amuck on the grounds. The dirt on my father's hands. The small west side apartment where the entire family lived. My mother's laughter. It had been cramped, but full of love.

Josie wouldn't want to hear any of that, so I went with broader memories. "The noise. The windows were always open. You could hear what was happening on the street at all hours."

"What else?"

"Hot corn on the street. We used to beg our mother to buy us some." I searched my mind for anything else I could tell her. "They say you can be anyone here. It's a city where dreams are made and lost. I used to dream of living in one of those big Fifth Avenue mansions."

"What happened? How did all of you end up in Boston?"

Swallowing my bitterness, I said, "My father lost his position. We moved in with my grandmother in Back Bay before moving to Tremont Street."

Her face fell, the lines deepening around her eyes as she studied me. "That's terrible. What did he do, your father?"

"He was a gardener."

"I bet he brought lovely flowers home for your mother."

I froze as the memories resurfaced. Yes, my father always had flowers for my mother, big bouquets of whatever was being cut from the Pendelton estate. Clippings and leavings, blooms and branches, it didn't matter. Papa always made it look beautiful for her. How had I forgotten?

I cleared my throat and returned to flipping the playing card in my hand. "He did, actually. He was good at caring for things."

A responsibility that fell to me after he died.

"You must miss him."

I did, terribly. Losing him had been a crushing blow to all of us. "I shouldn't complain, especially to you."

"Why? Because I have no family?" Her green eyes were understanding, not the least bit haunted, as she shook her head. "While my experience was different, it doesn't negate yours. Everyone's pain feels awful to them."

"You're right and I beg your pardon." We exchanged a slight smile, but she quickly turned her attention to the street.

"Where are we?"

"Around Twenty-Eighth Street, I think," I said after a quick check of the area.

"When will we see Lotta's friend?"

"A few days or so."

"Why wait? I'm ready now." Josie bounced a little on the seat, almost like a small child. "I've been ready for this my whole life."

I needed her in New York for an extended period of time. We had to work our way up Fifth Avenue and manage to put her in front of the Pendeltons. Under no circumstances could this be rushed. "Let's get you settled, see a bit of the city. We can rest up and talk about it tomorrow."

"Will you take me to see Central Park at some point?"

Eventually she'd be living right on the edge of it, overlooking the whole damn thing. I fixed my eyes on the street and imagined what I was going to do with all that reward money. "Sure, sweetheart. Whatever you want."

JOSIE

Leo went out to find a grocer as soon as we arrived at his friend's apartment. He told me to stay put until he returned. I offered to go with him, but he said it was best if he went alone.

He'd been acting squirrelly all day, ever since we left Boston. Hardly looking at me, barely talking. A chill had developed between us seemingly overnight, and he'd taken the first opportunity possible to escape my company today.

I tried not to take it personally, but what other way could I take it?

Because if I were lucky enough to call you mine, I'd never let you out of my sight.

Was he off to visit a lady friend first? That would explain why he didn't want me tagging along. That would also explain why he'd been in such a hurry, paying for a hansom when I knew he didn't have the funds.

I unpacked a little, then explored the place. The apartment was small but nice. Leo had offered to sleep on the sofa and allow me the bedroom, which I wasn't stupid enough to argue over. The sofa looked dashed uncomfortable.

Bored, I wondered what to do. I didn't have any books and it felt wrong to snoop through a stranger's belongings. I glanced out the window. It was windy, but a nice day. Children scampered up and down the walk, chasing one another and having fun. Maybe I could go for a stroll and see some of the neighborhood.

Leo certainly couldn't complain, as he'd gone out to do the same. Besides, I wouldn't go far.

I found the extra key, then went out and locked the door behind me. Pocketing the key, I descended the three flights of stairs until I reached the stoop. The street was busy, with the hustle and bustle of carts and horses and pedestrians all intermingled. I loved it.

I sat down, content to watch the activity on the street. No one paid me a bit of attention as they went about their day. A heavily mustached iceman guided his horse and wagon up the street, while two mothers chatted while walking their prams side by side. A fancy-looking man strode along in a hurry—until he bumped into a small child. The youngster fell down but instead of helping the child up, the man cursed and continued on like he found the whole incident a nuisance.

I was off the stoop in a flash. "You bounder!" I yelled after the man as I hurried to the child's side. It was a young boy. He couldn't have been more than six or seven years old. "Are you hurt?"

He grinned and held up a fancy gold watch.

My mouth dropped open. "Tell me you didn't pinch a watch from that man."

"I didn't pinch a watch from that man."

He was clearly lying. "You little scamp." Straightening, I put my hands on my hips. "And here I thought you were hurt."

"I am hurt," the boy said as he scrambled to his feet. "My ass'll be sore all week!"

"That's not a very nice word for someone so young."

After he slipped the watch into his pocket, he dusted off his dirty and torn trousers. "I'm not young. I'm nine."

Goodness, he was small for his age. Something tugged at my heart. "I'm Josie," I said, thrusting my hand out.

"They call me Sticks." He gave me a hearty pump of his hand.

"Why Sticks?"

"Because when I follow someone, I don't lose 'em. What's your story?"

"I'm here from Boston. Going to be a Broadway singer."

He squinted up at me. "Can you sing?"

"I should hope so, if I hope to make it to Broadway."

"Then sing already."

I frowned down at him. "As easy as that?"

"What, you need an invitation?"

Did he think I hadn't sung on the street before? That I was shy? I strode over to the apartment building's steps and turned to face the street. Then I drew in a deep breath, opened my mouth, and sang. It was one of the songs I performed a lot on the street back in Boston. An attention grabber, this tune used to get me a lot of money.

People stopped to watch as I went on. I didn't give it my all, not like I would if I were collecting tips, but I sang clearly and well. It felt nice to be outside, singing in front of strangers. I liked the attention and hoped I might bring a bit of happiness to one person's dreary day, similar to when the nuns sang at the Children's Asylum. It always used to make me feel better.

When I finished, the crowd applauded and I took a little bow. Several people asked where I performed, but I told them to ask me again in a few weeks. "For right now, only here," I said with a tiny shrug.

A man shoved his way through the crowd, a deep scowl on his face.

Leo.

He was carrying two sacks, one in each arm. They looked heavy. He charged right up to me. "What do you think you're doing?"

"Making friends." I gestured toward where Sticks had been standing a second ago, but saw that he'd disappeared. Huh.

"You can't sing on the street anymore," Leo snapped. "We're not giving the goods away for free."

"The goods?"

"Your voice. Your talent. Come inside and help me put all this away." He indicated the sacks in his arms. Without waiting to see whether I agreed or not, he started up the steps. When I wasn't right behind him, he hollered, "Josie!"

I hurried to open the door for him, then trailed him inside. "Why are you so cranky?"

"Because these sacks are heavy and you didn't listen to me."

He jerked his chin, indicating I should proceed him up the stairs. I tried to explain. "I was bored, and I didn't see the problem with getting some fresh air."

"Fresh air! You were giving a show out there."

"Would you feel better if I put a jar down for tips?"

"No." He ascended the next flight. "I'd feel better if you didn't get lost or taken advantage of here. I would feel better if you stayed inside, where I said."

"I'm not a dog, Leo."

"I'm well aware," he muttered under his breath.

"What does that mean?"

"Nothing. Listen, this is a big city full of unscrupulous people. Stay safe and don't deliberately cause trouble."

"God forbid I have any fun or meet anyone new," I grumbled.

He was breathing hard outside our door. "Unlock it, please, Your Majesty."

I took out my key and fit it into the lock. When the door was open, Leo went in and dropped the bags on the table. He leaned over, exhaled, and shook out his arms. I strolled closer and peered into the sacks. "What did you buy?"

"Food."

"I offered to go with you. I don't know why you're so mad. I figured you'd be gone awhile."

"Why would I be gone any longer than necessary?"

"Because you were in such a hurry to get away from me. I thought you were going—"

I clamped my mouth shut. There was no reason to admit what I'd really thought. Leo might get the wrong idea.

He studied me carefully from under the brim of his hat before slipping it off his head. "Where did you think I went?"

I waved my hand in a vague gesture. "Around."

He leaned on the chair back with one hand, his expression turning stormy. I could almost hear the clap of thunder due any moment. "Around where, Josie?"

"Hither. You know, yon. Nowhere in particular."

"Did you think I went to a saloon? That I was planning to have fun all afternoon while you waited here?"

"Are you saying you wouldn't?"

He shook his head, threw his hat on a chair, and dug into the bags. "You are unbelievable."

My wayward thoughts kept spilling right out of my mouth. "Though you don't strike me as a drunk. More like a—" I pressed my lips together, but it was too late.

Something heavy dropped onto the table. He spun to face me. "Go on, finish that sentence."

Why couldn't I just be quiet? I turned to put the food away, but Leo was suddenly right in front of me, holding gently on to my arm. "Josie. Sweetheart. Finish that sentence."

I wasn't deceived by his endearment. His voice was as sweet as vinegar. "Let me go, Leo."

"Not until I hear what you were going to say."

He wasn't wearing gloves and the heat of his grip sank into my skin. My stomach started doing flips and swirls under the intensity of his furious glare, which seemed to bore right through my flesh and bones, right down to my lonely soul. He was so close, the clean masculine scent of him flooding my nostrils, and I had to moisten my dry lips. He squinted in response and the gray flecks in his blue gaze sharpened.

The air turned charged, the oxygen disappearing from the room, and I could scarcely draw in a deep breath.

What was happening? Were we fighting . . . Or something else?

"I don't think I want to tell you," I whispered.

The anger leached out of his expression, and his mouth hitched into a lopsided smile. It was a flirtatious look, one that seared through every part of me. He could melt ice with that look. I had no defense against it, not at this close range. I was caught, like a spider in a web.

That was when his thumb started a slow, deliberate back-and-forth over my arm. A simple up and down of one digit, but I could feel the caress in every part of my body—my breasts, my toes. My ears. Between my legs. Heat unwound in my belly and my knees trembled.

His tone dipped. "Come on, honey. Tell me what you really think of me."

Like he'd mesmerized me, the truth tumbled from my lips. "More like a degenerate tomcat."

I expected anger at the insult. Instead, he slid closer and gently brushed a loose strand of hair behind my ear. "You thought I went out to find a woman to fuck?"

I hadn't expected him to say the word. I'd heard it over the years, of course, but never in such close quarters by a man. It was dirty and illicit. Forbidden. And tantalizing.

My mouth was too dry to speak, so I merely nodded.

He tilted his head. "Were you jealous?"

I wanted to lie. Badly. But I believed in telling the truth, so I nodded once more. A muscle jumped in his jaw as his expression wiped clean. I waited for him to do something, say something, but the moment stretched, and my nerves wound tighter and tighter. I was good at reading people, but I couldn't figure him out.

Was he going to kiss me?

Did I want him to?

Leo was normally charismatic and cheerful. Right now, he was a statue—flat expression, with secrets lurking behind those brilliant eyes. Without warning, he dropped his arms and stepped back. "You know, a night of debauchery is just what this degenerate tomcat needs. Don't wait up."

He was nearly to the door by the time my brain restarted. "It's four in the afternoon!"

"Never hurts to start early," he called on his way into the hall. The door closed behind him with a snap.

Silence descended and I felt like the world's biggest fool. Why had I admitted to being jealous? Now Leo would think I had feelings for him. Which I didn't. I just didn't want him out with other women while we were here.

I was supposed to be his focus, no one else.

I stared at the door. Perhaps he'd come back, rethink his hasty decision. We'd have a good laugh over this, eat dinner, and then walk around the neighborhood a bit.

Except the door remained closed.

A sick feeling bloomed behind my ribs. Was he really going out to find a woman? I rubbed my sternum and tried to ease the growing ache there. For a moment or two when he returned from shopping it seemed as if he cared about me, about my safety. Now he was gone and had left me to fend for myself.

Soon it would be dark. Men were able to roam about on their own, but the second a woman was alone, every man in the vicinity thought she was fair game—especially at night. Pippa often asked a bartender from the saloon to walk her home, if it was late. It was too dangerous otherwise.

Leo would know that I couldn't leave at night without an escort. This meant I was stuck inside until he returned.

I drew myself up straight. This was how he wanted to play it? Fine. I could be cordial business partners, nothing more, nothing less. We owed each other nothing but a handshake on a dream.

And one way or another he would make good on his part of that deal.

Chapter Eight

LEO

For a few moments after leaving Ambrose's place, I actually considered a brothel. My skin was crawling, itching, as something dark and dangerous threatened to undo all my hard work. I should purge the feeling out of my system. Regain my equilibrium. Focus on the task ahead.

It had been a close call.

She'd been beautiful, staring up at me with her gorgeous eyes and angelic features. Except Josie was no angel. She was feisty and stubborn, bold and clever, unafraid to push me. Everything I liked in a woman. No doubt she'd be fantastic in bed.

But those thoughts would only land me in trouble.

Second rule of being a confidence man: never lose sight of the endgame.

St. Elmer had drilled this into our heads, as young boys are notoriously unfocused. The moment you take your eye off the goal, the instant you ease up or grow lazy, the game is over. You want the money? Then you have to put in the work.

Best to return after Josie was asleep and couldn't tempt me anymore. With no destination in mind, I hopped on a late-night omnibus headed north and cleared my mind of all things related to Josie.

When I raised my head, I was surprised to find myself on the corner of Fifth Avenue and Seventieth Street. The block where the Pendeltons lived. It felt like fate.

I hopped off and stared across the street at the massive mansion. It hadn't changed much in all these years. The fading light bathed the Gothic limestone structure in a burnt orange color, making it appear otherworldly, almost hellish. Which was fitting, I supposed, considering who lived there.

The home was every bit as imposing as I remembered. To a boy, it had been a palace. But now, sixteen years later, it was nothing but a symbol of greed and decadence at the expense of good hardworking people.

People like Steven Hardy.

Many of the servants were let go or quit after the kidnapping, but not my father. He continued to work on the estate for two more years while the investigation wore on. Then, without warning, the Pendeltons sacked him, leaving a family of seven without income.

My father never talked about it after that, even going so far as to forbid the family's name from ever being spoken in our home. Being kicked out so abruptly turned him bitter and angry, a drunk. The fun-loving man who'd let me trail him through the gardens here disappeared overnight. What had he ever done to this family to deserve such shabby treatment?

I hated the Pendeltons with everything inside me. I couldn't wait for Josie to fool them and then I could collect that reward money.

My father had poured his blood and sweat into the grounds here. He had overseen a team of men, but he'd personally obsessed over every tree, every bush. Each tiny flower. Had the Pendeltons torn those up, too, like they tore up our family?

I had to know.

I started around the block, toward the rear of the estate. The gate off the mews was still there, so as if I'd last done it yesterday, I reached over and felt for the latch on the other side, flicked open the catch, and pushed inside. I closed the gate softly behind me.

No one was around, so I eased deeper into the gardens, careful not to make any noise.

It was like stepping back in time.

The landscaping was much the same, except the trees were bigger, the bushes thicker. The flowers were different colors and sparser, however, as if the gardeners had reduced the number of blooms. A shame.

Funny how it seemed like a jungle when I was a kid. Now it was a nicely manicured, albeit boring, garden. I stopped by a row of arborvitae trees that my father had planted. They used to be tiny shrubs. Now they were tall points, forming a hedge along the path. He would have loved seeing the fruit of his labor.

They look good, Papa. Sorry you didn't get to see them.

"Ho! Who goes there? What are you doing here, mister?"

I flinched at the booming voice. An older man in faded trousers and a coat was coming toward me, so I held up my hands and tried to appear nonthreatening. "I beg your pardon, sir. I wanted to look around a bit."

"You can't wander about in here," he snapped. "Go on. Get out."

I made a living as a confidence man because I could read people. And I could tell this man wasn't angry with me—he was nervous. It was obvious by the way his eyes kept darting toward the house. He didn't want to get into trouble.

I spoke softly, palms out. "I mean no harm. My father used to work here in the gardens."

He drew to a halt and peered at me. "Your father?"

"Yes. He was a gardener for the Pendeltons, way back in the day."

"How long ago?"

"Sixteen years."

The man scratched his head under his cap. "I've only been here three. They can't keep good help around." He jerked his head toward the house. "Head gardener before me only lasted sixteen months."

Interesting. My father had lasted twenty years. "Why's that, do you suppose?"

"Can't keep anyone around, not since their girl was taken. You know, the baby." He shook his head. "Sad thing, it was."

"Indeed. They never found her?" I pretended not to know.

"You didn't hear?" After I shook my head, he continued. "Offered a big reward. Hired Pinkertons. No sign of her anywhere. Disappeared without a trace."

"How sad." I put a great deal of sympathy in my voice. "And the family? You said they can't keep good help."

He glanced over his shoulder. "I shouldn't be speaking ill of Mr. and Mrs. Pendelton."

"Don't worry. I won't say anything." I stuck out my hand and adopted an affable smile. "Robbie. Robbie Youngblood."

"Nice to meet you, Mr. Youngblood. I'm George Richards. Everyone calls me Georgie, though."

"A pleasure, Georgie. Would you show me around a bit? Is the old fountain still running?"

"No, sir. They removed that years ago. Come on. I'll show you."

We wandered away from the big house deeper into the gardens. "You've done a marvelous job here, Georgie."

"Thank you. We do what we can. It's down to just me and two other men. I'm the only one here full-time."

"And you live on the property?"

"In the stables. There's plenty of room in there, since they only keep the two grooms now."

Two grooms? I remember six or seven men in the stables, along with almost a dozen horses. "We never lived on the property when my father was here. We had a house downtown, but he let me tag along with him."

"I imagine much of this was his work, then." Georgie pointed to the rosebushes.

"Oh, yes. I remember helping him with those." We continued along the path. "The carriage house . . . is it still a smaller replica of the mansion?"

"It is, though it's fallen into some disrepair. We can't get them to fix the leaky roof."

"They have the money. Why not fix it?"

"Mr. Pendelton, he's busy with his company. Mrs. Pendelton, we don't see her much. Rumor has it she hardly leaves her room."

I shoved my hands in my pockets and considered this. If true, it would make getting Josie and Mrs. Pendelton in the same room together a challenge. "That so?"

"The estate manager and the butler, they do what they can for the place. But it seems she's given up over the years."

A minuscule twinge of sympathy tightened in my chest. I resolutely pushed it aside. What happened with their daughter was a tragedy, but they'd been callous and cruel to my family. If I swindled a buck or two from these people to put the Hardys back on their feet, I wasn't going to lose sleep over it.

"She never leaves at all?" I asked.

"Once or twice a month. The opera. Never anywhere else. I hear the grooms talking about it."

This was excellent news. The opera meant she loved singing. And knowing she attended the performances gave me something to work with. I'd need to think on it.

We stopped by a patch of dirt. I stood in this spot for long hours as a child. "This was the fountain at one time, am I right?"

"Indeed, sir. It was right here. I can't get anything to grow in its place. A shame."

"There used to be big fish and frogs."

"I'm told the fish developed some disease and all died. That's when they tore the fountain out."

Christ almighty. The place really was cursed. "Well, I should be on my way." I held out my hand again. "Georgie, I appreciate your time. Keep up the good work."

"It was nice to meet you, young man. What do you do now?"

I puffed out my chest. "I'm a manager. Actors and actresses on Broadway."

Fourth rule of being a confidence man: keep your lies as close to the truth as possible.

Georgie's face broke out in a big smile as he slid his cap higher on his forehead. "Sakes alive, that's impressive! I never see any musicals or plays."

"That's too bad. Maybe I'll send over some tickets one of these days. The next time we have a show opening."

He looked thrilled at the offer. I didn't know if I could ever make good on it, but I sounded as if I might.

Slapping my shoulder, he said, "That's very generous of you, Mr. Youngblood."

"Please, call me Robbie."

We spoke a few more minutes and then I bid him farewell. I hurried from the gardens, a spring in my step. I'd learned quite a bit from Georgie. Now I just had to come up with a plan to put Josie into Mrs. Pendelton's path.

JOSIE

I woke up the next morning in a foul mood. I'd tossed and turned all night, hardly sleeping as I listened for Leo's return. He finally stumbled in around two o'clock. I heard cursing and a loud thump, as if he'd hit his leg or head on the furniture.

The whole time I imagined him in bed with some woman, laughing and having a grand time without me. I was sick to my stomach over it.

I feel as if a night of debauchery is just what this degenerate tomcat needs.

I hated it. I hated his attractive face and boyish smile. His long legs and lean body. And I absolutely loathed that he was able to go out and have fun while I stayed home. It wasn't fair.

I didn't bother trying to keep quiet when I came out to make breakfast. There was Leo, flat on the sofa, still in the suit he'd worn yesterday. Mouth parted, he snored softly. I sniffed, searching for hints of perfume. I couldn't detect any, but that didn't mean he hadn't visited a lady. Or two.

Ignoring the ache in the pit of my stomach, I made tea and eggs. I would not ask him about his night or hint that I cared. Because I didn't.

As I was eating at the table, I heard him groan. Clothing rustled as he shifted. "Too loud," he murmured.

I banged my cup on the wood as I sat it down.

"Damn it, Josie." He was facing away from me, toward the back of the sofa. "Let me sleep."

"It's half past nine, tomcat. Get moving."

"I didn't get to bed until three."

"Not sure why that's my problem. And you need to shake a leg. We have a Broadway producer to see."

"*Christ.*" He rolled over and pinned me with a hard stare. Dark circles rimmed his eyes. "Is this what I have to look forward to every morning?"

"I don't know. Are you planning on going out every night?"

The irritation disappeared from his expression, quickly replaced with an annoying smirk as he sat up. "You're jealous."

I let out a derisive sound. "You are delusional."

"No, you are. You are jealous I went out alone last night."

"That would mean I cared about you and your whereabouts. Which I don't. But I don't wish to be awakened at two o'clock by your drunken stumbling."

"I wasn't drunk." He dragged a hand through his hair. "I couldn't see."

"But you did go out drinking." While I was here. Alone.

He leaned over and put his elbows on his knees. Leo was

usually so polished and put together. Slick and guarded. I liked this version better, the one with whiskers on his jaw and wrinkled clothing. His hair was a delightful mess.

He stood and stretched, throwing his arms over his head. I dragged my gaze off him. I needed to remember this was a business arrangement, nothing more. Leo had no problem keeping it straight.

He doesn't want me as a friend or lover. It's about money for both of us.

"Do you want to hear where I went?" he asked.

"Nope."

"I wasn't with a woman."

"Bully for you."

He sighed, but I concentrated on my food. I heard him digging around in his case. "Any chance you made some breakfast for me?"

Unbelievable. I went to the sink to clean my dishes. "I'm not your wife or your housekeeper, Leo. Make your own damn breakfast."

"Cold, woman. Very cold." I heard the door open. "I'm off to get cleaned up down the hall. Try not to miss me."

I didn't say a word. I had a problem letting my mouth get away from me, so better to keep quiet than risk saying too much. Like yesterday.

When he finally returned, Leo was back to his usual fancy self. I flipped through the magazine in my lap and tried not to lament the transformation. He fixed a cup of coffee, then leaned against the counter and fixed his eyes on me.

I pretended to read the magazine. "Do I meet with your approval?"

"Of course. However, I am curious why you are upset with me."

I shut the magazine with a snap. "If I can't go out at night, then neither can you. It's not fair."

His lips parted slightly, the cup paused halfway to his mouth. "You know it isn't safe for you out at night alone."

"Then I guess we'll be going out together, partner."

He set his cup carefully on the counter. "Josie, I need to go out at night for business meetings and the like. You should stay in and rest your voice."

"Oh, so you had a business meeting last night?"

"No, but I will at some point while we're here."

"If you have a meeting that concerns me and my career, I expect to be present."

After all, this was what Lotta had stressed. *A man like Leo is not on your side, honey. He's on his side. Never forget it.*

Leo's back stiffened as he frowned, little lines of unhappiness emerging to bracket his mouth. "That won't always be practical. It'll be easier to talk candidly with producers and directors without you there."

"Then I'm going back to Boston." I tossed the magazine onto the tea table and stood. "We are either in this together or we're not. Partners or nothing. You promised me we would work as a team. That you have my best interests at heart. Prove it. Let me attend these meetings."

"That isn't how it's done."

"I don't care, Leo. I've got to look out for myself."

Head down, he fixed his gaze on his shoes. "I see what's going on. You don't trust me."

Was he trying to guilt me into allowing his selfish behavior? If so, he wouldn't succeed. I wasn't giving him license to do as he wished without me when it pertained to my career. "I trust you well enough . . . when I'm able to keep an eye on you."

"Fine." He threw his hands up. "You want to stick? We'll stick. You'll stay by my side except for sleeping. Happy?"

"Yes." I was oddly relieved. I thought he'd fight me harder on the issue.

"Thank god. Now, what would you like to do today?"

"Go see Mr. Birdman."

He picked up his teacup. "I thought we said we would wait a few days, get accustomed to the city first."

"No, *you* said that. I want to pay the visit today."

"You're a real peach in the morning, you know that?"

"If you think I'm insulted, guess again. Are you ready to leave?"

"Any chance that I might convince you to postpone this outing?"

"None." I collected my hat and gloves. "Now, do you know where we're going and how to get there?"

"Of course."

I squinted at him skeptically. "How?"

Sighing heavily, he picked his derby up off a side table. "While you thought I was out tomcatting, I was walking around. Getting reacquainted with the city."

He had? This surprised me. It was very responsible of him, not at all what I thought he'd been doing.

He leaned against the wall near the door. "Care to retract your earlier statement about not trusting me?"

His blue eyes twinkled with amusement and I felt myself nearly falling into his trap again. It would be too easy to forget my wits around this man.

I was tough, though, tougher than most gave me credit for. Merely to torture him, I moved in close. I let him think maybe he'd affected me, like maybe we were more than friends. I ran my fingertip over the gold stud he wore to keep his tie in place. "No, I don't," I whispered.

His throat worked as he swallowed. I gave him a victorious smile and opened the door. As I sailed into the corridor, I heard him chuckle. "I am going to change your mind about that, Josie Smith, if it's the last thing I do."

Chapter Nine

JOSIE

The uptown trolley moved slowly, stopping often to let passengers on and off. I couldn't stop fidgeting. In my head I went over what I planned to say and sing, if given the chance. A lot was riding on this visit.

"Stop," Leo said, placing his hand atop mine. "Just breathe. We have no appointment, so we might not even see him today."

I was certain that wouldn't happen, not with Lotta's introduction. "What if he doesn't like me?"

Leo smoothly crossed one leg over the other. "Then we find someone who does. This city is crawling with opportunity—and we'll catch one. Don't worry."

"I wish I shared your confidence."

"You could, if you tried," he said. "The first step to having confidence is projecting it. Then one day you find the mask fits well enough that it's no longer a mask. Understand?"

I wrinkled my nose. "I don't want to wear a mask."

"It's a metaphor, sweetheart. Pretend until it becomes real."

"That feels wrong. And deceitful."

"The world is based on deceit. The stock market, cosmetics, perfume. Corsets." He gestured toward a large sign on the side of a building hawking cigars. "Advertising. If you don't participate in the game, how do you expect to win?"

I considered this as we rolled along. Maybe Leo was right. I'd lived my entire life in a ten-block radius in Boston. *Sophisticated* and *worldly* were not words I associated with myself. But I always hoped being me would be enough.

I shook my head. Who was I fooling? When had I ever been enough? In my whole life, no one had wanted me.

"You're right," I told him. "It's all acting, anyway."

"That's the spirit. Think about who Josie Smith should be. What impression do you want to leave behind? Then create that persona in your mind and act it out."

"Is that what you do?"

"Been doing it since the day I was born, sweetheart."

Hmm. I thought back to the smiles that never quite reached his eyes. What was he like under the suit and charm?

Who did I want to be? That was easy—I wanted to be like Lotta, as if I belonged in every room, no matter where I went. Independent and smart. Talented. A strong woman who bent the world to her whim, not the other way around.

Could I do it?

Getting off in Herald Square, Leo and I walked toward the address on Melvin's card. Thank goodness he knew where he was going, because I was too nervous to navigate.

"That building there." Leo pointed to a five-story limestone building. "Are you ready?"

"Yes."

Just as he'd done before I met Lotta, Leo put his hands on my shoulders and looked down at me. "Repeat after me. I'm going to be one of the greats."

The edges of my mouth curled. "I'm going to be one of the greats."

"Good girl. Let's go show this Melvin fellow what he's been missing out on."

We went inside. A marble lobby greeted us, and we discovered that Melvin's office was on the fifth floor. "Lift or stairs?" Leo asked.

"Stairs. I'm too nervous for the lift."

"The stairs it is."

I kept my chin up and tried to look confident as I trailed Leo, who definitely looked confident. He appeared at home, like he belonged in this fancy building and this fancy town. People trailed down the stairs, nodding at him as they passed like he was someone important. I wondered if any of them were singers too.

We stopped in front of a door with block lettering on it.

MR. MELVIN BIRDMAN, THEATRICAL PRODUCTIONS

Leo reached for the knob, paused, and glanced over his shoulder. He gave me a slow wink. I tried to offer up a smile, but my face felt strange, as if my muscles didn't work right.

This had to go well. My whole future was riding on this meeting.

Then we were inside. A secretary sat behind a desk, her fingers flying over the keys of a typewriter. Four other people were waiting in the anteroom. I tugged on Leo's sleeve. "Maybe we should come back later, when Mr. Birdman isn't so busy."

Leo didn't even break stride. He strode right up to the secretary. "Good morning. Miss Josie Smith and Mr. Leo Hardy. We'd like to see Mr. Birdman."

The secretary didn't even glance up. "Mr. Birdman's appointments are all full today."

Undeterred, Leo gave her a grin that would melt cold butter. "Well, how about tomorrow?"

"He is booked through the end of the month."

Oh, heavens. I could feel the disappointment settling in my stomach. This was a waste of time. We couldn't wait a month. I started to leave, but Leo touched my arm, staying me.

"I realize Mr. Birdman is incredibly busy, Miss . . . ?"

"Bryce."

"Miss Bryce. I understand he is busy, but a mutual friend of ours sent us to New York to see Mr. Birdman." Leo presented the card from Lotta to the secretary. "You'll see a note there on the back."

She read the note and her eyes went wide. Pointing to the chairs, she stood. "Please, have a seat."

In a flash Miss Bryce disappeared through the door behind her. Leo gestured to the open chairs. "Let's sit down. Maybe he'll work us in when he has the time."

We picked two chairs and sat down. No sooner had my bustle hit the padding than we heard a booming voice say, "From Lotta!"

The door flew open. A short man with thinning hair and a long mustache barreled into the anteroom. He wore a sharp brown suit, a fancy pocket watch chain dangling off his silk vest. "Which one of you knows Lotta?"

Leo stood, at the same time tugging on my elbow to help me up. "We do."

"Well, good gracious. Get in here already. What are you waiting for?"

"Excuse me, Mr. Birdman!" This was one of the gentlemen waiting in the anteroom. "I've been here an hour already."

"And you'll wait an hour more, Sid. Get comfortable." Mr. Birdman ushered us directly into his office. After he closed the door, he held out his hand. "Melvin Birdman."

We shook and introduced ourselves. At least, I'm fairly certain I did. Words definitely came out of my mouth and Leo appeared pleased, so I must've done something right.

Mr. Birdman pointed at the chairs in front of his desk. "Sit, sit. Tell me, how is my girl?"

"Very well, sir." This was Leo, who spoke calmly, as if having tea with a friend. "She left Boston for San Francisco a few days back."

"Always too busy for me." Mr. Birdman sighed, eyes dancing while a smile tugged at his lips. "I wish I could convince her to come back to Broadway. Few were able to pack in a crowd like Lotta Crabtree back in the day."

"I bet. I remember her shows in Boston were always standing room only."

"Now you're just rubbing my nose in it," Mr. Birdman said with a chuckle. "So, tell me why you are here."

"Lotta was gracious enough to work with Miss Smith before she left town. She sent us to New York to come see you."

"Is that so?" Mr. Birdman's gaze turned to me. "Lotta isn't known for taking baby chicks under her wing. You must be something special."

It was my turn to speak, but I wasn't sure my mouth worked. *Pretend. Wear the mask.* I forced my shoulders back. "I am."

"Confident," Mr. Birdman said. "I like it. Tell me, what do you do. Dance?"

"I sing."

The older man swept his hand out. "Then sing."

I didn't hesitate. I stared at a spot on the wall, pretended it was an audience, and sang like Lotta had instructed. I let the notes and words flow, expressing the emotion of the melody as I always did, but also allowing that emotion to show through my expressions. Lotta said you had to *live* the song, feel it deep in your bones. Then the audience would feel it, too.

No one interrupted. I finished the entire piece, the room reverberating with the final note. I knew I'd done well. Hadn't missed a note or garbled a lyric. As far as a cappella performances went, it was damn good.

So the ensuing silence surprised me.

I risked a glance at Mr. Birdman, but his expression was guarded. Instead of speaking, he stood and began walking to the door—and my stomach dropped into the floor. Failure tasted like spoiled milk in my throat.

He'd hated it.

I started to stand, ready to run and hide, but Leo put a hand on my arm. "Wait," he said under his breath.

Mr. Birdman ripped open his office door. I peeked out into the anteroom, where Miss Bryce and the visitors were staring at Melvin's office, mouths agape. No one moved a muscle, their eyes wide with disbelief.

When Mr. Birdman slowly turned toward me, he was grinning. "It's not often I see Miss Bryce rendered speechless." He closed the door and returned to his desk.

Leo still held on to my arm. Instead of letting go, his thumb began absently stroking my wrist, a slow sweep back and forth, just as he'd done yesterday in the apartment. Once again, the soft brush of that single digit was all I could focus on. His simple caress both soothed and excited me, my skin turning hot.

Was this going to be a regular habit with him? If so, I wasn't complaining.

His hand fell away as soon as Mr. Birdman settled into his chair, facing us. I missed the warmth of Leo's touch so much that it should have embarrassed me.

I cleared my throat and tried to appear professional. "What did you think, Mr. Birdman?"

"I think you should call me Melvin. We are going to be spending a lot of time together."

What did that mean? I wished he would come out and say what he thought instead of dancing around it. My shoulders tightened, my muscles instantly wary. "Doing what, exactly?"

Leo's voice was smooth as he interjected, "I think Miss Smith is asking what you have in mind for her career options."

Melvin held up his palms. "Understandable. I see why Lotta sent you. You have real talent, Miss Smith—a *too-good-for-the-chorus* sort of talent. Any girl with a pretty face is able to harmonize in the background. You are bigger than that. You have . . . gravitas." He paused. "It means—"

"I know what it means," I said. "I learned Latin with the nuns. So, a supporting part in a musical?"

"Think bigger."

"A lead part?"

"Yes, eventually. But first we need to make a name for you. Build up a little mystery and mystique."

"How?" This question was from Leo.

"Let me worry about that. I have some friends at the newspapers." Melvin cocked his head at Leo. "Now, I have to ask, who are you in relation to her? The sweetheart?"

"No, I'm the manager."

Melvin's glance darted to my wrist, the one Leo had been holding a moment ago. "And what experience have you in managing a singer?"

"None," Leo answered, "but I come from sales. I know what it takes to hustle. More important, I'm committed to looking out for Miss Smith's best interests."

"I see." Melvin sounded as if he didn't believe it.

Sakes alive, why did everyone assume Leo and I were sleeping together? "There is nothing romantic between me and Leo," I asserted.

"I should hope not, for everyone's sake." Melvin reached to press a button on his desk and suddenly we heard Miss Bryce's voice.

"Yes, sir?"

"Draw up a standard contract for Miss Smith, will you? I'd like to get her signed right away."

I glanced over at Leo, who was already looking at me, his eyes dancing with excitement. Was this really happening?

"Now," Melvin said and clapped his hands to get our attention. "We need to gain publicity in a short amount of time. I don't like the name Josie, though. It's too boring, too plain. No offense, merely stating facts. Do you have a middle name?"

"None taken," I said with a shrug. "And no, I don't."

"We need something else," Melvin said, stroking his jaw. "Another name. One with panache."

"What about Joséphine?" Leo suggested. "It's similar."

Where had he thought that one up? It sounded too grand, too fancy. "I'm not certain—" I started, but Melvin interrupted me.

"Mysterious, foreign," the producer said. "But close enough to her actual name. I like it. And it helps with the backstory."

"What backstory?"

"You let me worry about that." Melvin rose out of his chair and straightened his vest. "We'll have the whole town talking about you soon."

LEO

After Josie signed her name on the contract, we left Melvin's office. I could tell she was ready to burst with excitement, but she contained herself until we reached the walk outside.

"Oh my god, Leo," she breathed, grabbing my arm. "That was amazing!"

Without thinking, I took her hand and led her into the alley between buildings. The excitement and relief weren't merely on Josie's side. I was grateful that meeting went as well as it did. Melvin would ensure the entire city talked about Josie, which meant I'd be able to get her in front of Mrs. Pendelton that much sooner. Everything was lining up even better than I'd hoped.

When we were away from prying eyes in the alley, I dragged Josie to my chest and hugged her. She went stiff for a brief second, then slowly relaxed. "Bravo, Josie," I said into her ear. "You were dashed perfect in there."

"Thank you. I was so nervous when he got up and went to the door. I thought for certain he was kicking us out."

I squeezed her tighter, my brain overcome with happiness. "You sounded too good for him to kick us out. Did you see their faces when he opened the door?"

Her arms shifted and she gripped me loosely about my waist. *She's hugging me back.*

"I did," she answered into my collar. "I was relieved they seemed to appreciate it."

Her breath tickled my throat, the soft warmth of her body pressed to mine, and my brain finally caught on. Warmth traveled through me to settle in my belly, then moved even lower. It was the closest we'd ever been and I . . . liked it. A lot.

And soon she'd be able to tell how much.

Shit.

Abruptly, I let her go. She stared at my chin, not meeting my eyes, and I used the opportunity to set myself to rights. I straightened my vest and adjusted my cuffs. Keeping my tone light, I inquired, "So tell me. How would you like to celebrate, sweetheart?"

"I want to see Central Park. Will you take me?"

How could I say no? Josie was impossible to resist, with her big eyes brimming with hope and happiness, and a smile that could tempt a bishop. Men waged wars over a beauty like hers, and I had no chance of denying her when she looked up at me like this.

Treat her like an older brother. I could do it. I had to think of her like one of my own sisters—Molly or Hattie, maybe.

Yeah, that could work.

I took her arm and led her out of the alley. "Central Park it is."

We took a northern-bound streetcar. I decided to splurge today in celebration, even though I didn't have a lot of money. As we walked around the park, we ate clams and hot gingerbread. Then I bought her ice cream and took her through the Central Park Menagerie. She gawked over the elephants, camels, and monkeys, every bit as enthusiastic as the children around us.

The sun was low in the sky by the time we headed toward the trolley stop, Josie holding on to my arm as we meandered the paths in the park. An easy silence had fallen between us, and I tried not to think about how much I liked spending time with her. She was good company, funny and bright, and didn't feel the need to fill the silence with empty chatter.

A sister. Think of her like a sister.

"Tell me about growing up here."

Her question caught me by surprise and I hesitated. It wasn't my favorite topic. "Why?"

She nudged my shoulder with her own. "Don't sound so prickly. Your childhood can't be worse than mine. Tell me."

"What do you want to know?"

"Anything. Everything. All you said was your father was a gardener. Who did he work for?"

I debated what to say. Was there a reason not to tell her? I tried to see the problem from all angles, but the silence dragged on too long. I decided to go with the truth. "The Pendeltons. Have you heard of them?"

"I think everyone in the country has heard of them." She let out a low whistle. "Big money."

"Indeed, but I've generally found that more money doesn't mean more character."

"How so?"

"My father worked for them for twenty years. Helped Mr. Olmstead himself design the gardens in the back of the Fifth Avenue estate. Then the Pendeltons let him go with no notice, no reference. When he couldn't find work, we came to Boston to live with my ma's family."

"That is awful. It must've been a shock to your whole family."

I remembered my mother's tears when she packed up our small house here, my father's misery. Everything changed—and not for the better. "It was a rough time. But I learned a valuable lesson: Never rely on anyone other than yourself in this world. Because they'll only let you down."

"I feel the exact same."

I believed it. Life had kicked Josie around too. "How old were you when you arrived at the asylum?"

"You mean when I was left on the doorstep? Around two, I'm told."

"Any clue as to who left you? A note stuck to the swaddling?"

"None." She inhaled and let it out slowly, like trying to clear away unpleasant emotions. "I used to make up all kinds of stories, though. My favorite involved a prince and princess, who left me with the nuns for safekeeping during one of their trips abroad. I imagined them returning for me, showering me with a crown and jewels."

I understood those sorts of childhood dreams. "I imagined the Pendeltons mailing my father a check with an apology letter. Then we would move into one of those big Beacon Hill houses and be happy again."

A man came toward us, but he switched to walk on Josie's side of the path. Then his gaze darted to the coin purse on Josie's waist. I went on alert, my senses tingling. I could be wrong, so I didn't want to worry Josie unnecessarily.

I tightened my grip on her arm, watching the man through my lashes.

When the man bumped into Josie's shoulder, it threw her off-balance and into my side. I knew what was happening, so I grabbed his wrist to stop him before he could lift Josie's coin purse. "Don't try it," I warned.

The man began struggling, as did Josie, who asked, "Leo, what on earth are you doing?"

I tried to hold on to both of them, but it wasn't easy. Just then the man hit me in the cheek with his free hand. Pain exploded and my grip on the thief's arm slipped, my derby tumbling to the ground. He seized the advantage and took off running through the park.

"My purse!" Josie lifted her skirts and instantly gave chase as the man darted into the woods.

"Josie, no!" I called after her, but it was pointless. Panicked, I snatched up my derby and sprinted after them. My cheek throbbed, each beat of my heart echoing in my face, but I kept going, petrified of what could happen to her. Damn that reckless woman.

Branches slapped my legs and chest as I tore into the woods. "Josie!" I called. "Let him go. It's not worth it!"

Where was she? I kept going, pausing every few steps to listen for any sign of her. After a few minutes I heard grunting and cursing off to my right. I jumped over a log and pushed through some bushes. On the other side was Josie, sitting on the thief's back, while he was pinned to the ground. She wrestled her coin purse out of his hands with a mighty tug.

Then she scrambled to her feet and kicked the thief in the ribs with the toe of her boot. "That is for taking a lady's only good purse."

He groaned, rolled to his feet, and disappeared off into the undergrowth. Josie took a step in that direction, but I lunged for her arm to stop her. "That's enough," I said. "No more fighting hooligans."

Emerald fire flashed in her eyes. "But he stole my bag, Leo! We must turn him over to the police."

"He *tried* to steal your purse. He failed. And the police here have more important crimes to worry about."

She lifted her chin and let out a frustrated noise. "Then some other woman will have her bag stolen."

"They are not my concern." Gingerly, I touched my cheek. "You are."

That gained her attention. She gasped when she saw my face. "You're hurt. Oh god, Leo. I'm so sorry."

"I'm fine," I muttered. It hurt, but it wasn't the worst punch I'd ever taken.

Josie didn't listen. She dragged me over to a rock, stripped off her glove, and examined my cheek carefully, pressing gently with her bare fingers. "I'm fine," I grumbled.

"It's my fault you're hurt. Let me ensure that your cheekbone isn't broken."

With nothing to do but sit, I realized how close we were at the moment. She was near enough that I could count each long eyelash, study her high cheekbones and straight nose. The gentle curves of her full lips and her flawless skin. God almighty, she was pretty.

When was the last time someone took care of me like this? Caressed me with such care and tenderness? Normally I was the one looking after everyone else.

Josie's exhales warmed my skin and a surge of nonbrotherly heat rolled through me, sparks that spread south to my groin. I could kiss her so easily. Just lean forward and place my lips on hers. I wanted to, desperately.

I was starving for it, in fact.

I knew it was a terrible idea, but in this secluded section of the park, surrounded by trees, my resolve weakened. It was like we were in our own world in the midst of the most crowded city in the country. Me and Josie, no one else, with the sweet brush of her fingers against my skin.

"Stop staring at me, Leo." Her gaze remained locked on my cheek.

The truth tumbled out. "I can't help it. You're the most beautiful woman I've ever encountered."

Her breath hitched as her eyes flicked to mine. "You're not supposed to say things such as that."

"Why not?"

"You know why."

I did, but those reasons mattered less and less with every passing second.

The hint of a pink tongue emerged as she moistened her lips.

The movement was innocent, yet highly erotic, and I nearly groaned. "Josie," I whispered helplessly, adrift and unsure. I wasn't a man who became tongue-tied very often, but sitting this close to her, alone, I could hardly string two thoughts together.

Her free hand came up to cup my jaw, her palm warm and soft on my skin. Earlier in the apartment, her bold touch had scared and surprised me. Not now. At this moment I longed for her to caress me all over.

"Careful," I warned, my voice husky. "Or I might attempt to corrupt you."

Her mouth twisted slyly, like she had a secret. "Perhaps I'll let you, tomcat."

"A man may dream," I murmured. "But I shouldn't like to take advantage of you."

"What if I wish to take advantage of *you*?" She let her fingers trail up over my temple, down along my hairline, and along my jaw. "I'm curious. Aren't you?"

Yes. In fact, I was dying to know what she tasted like, what she felt like. She was sharp and bold, a fierce lioness with a whole heap of talent. I'd bet my meager life savings that screwing her would be electrifying in the very best way. "Josie . . ." I didn't want to lie, not about this, but I'd promised both myself and others that I wouldn't.

When I remained silent, her hand angled my face toward hers. "I'll take that as a yes."

And then she kissed me.

Chapter Ten

JOSIE

It was reckless to kiss him. We had agreed to keep our association professional. Platonic.

Except there was nothing platonic about this kiss.

I hadn't been able to stop myself. Leo was handsome and charming, and when I read the desire swirling in his gorgeous blue eyes, desire for *me*, it felt like the most natural thing in the world to lean in and seal my mouth to his.

His lips were soft, much softer than I'd imagined, and I moved gently. I carefully brushed my mouth over his once, then again. I liked kissing. Been told I'm decent at it too.

But, after a few seconds, it became clear Leo wasn't kissing me back.

Oh. He wasn't enjoying this. I'd thought . . .

Horrified, I ripped my mouth away from his, all the while my mind racing for an acceptable excuse for my bold behavior. I should apologize. Claim temporary insanity brought on by an exciting day and blue eyes.

Except something remarkable happened. The instant I retreated, Leo suddenly came alive.

In a blink, his mouth latched onto mine as his hands pulled me closer. He didn't ease into it either. This wasn't tentative or unsure in the least. His lips were aggressive, hungry, overwhelming my senses in the very best way. He stole my breath, but I didn't mind. Who needed to breathe?

Not me. Not when I could have this instead.

A deep rumble sounded in his chest as his lips slid eagerly over mine. He tilted his head and flicked his tongue over my lips, so I parted them and he was inside. My head swam with his taste, the slick feel of our tongues dueling, while the wild thump of my heartbeat echoed in my ears and between my legs. I clung to his shoulders, needing to anchor myself as the kiss wore on.

Lord, Leo was good at this. Confident. Skilled. It was clear he had loads of experience. I hadn't expected to lose myself so completely in the moment. I lost my sense of where we were, and the ache inside me intensified, twisted into something undeniable and urgent. At some point he shifted toward me, his hands moving to cup my jaw, and I placed my palms on his chest. The silk fabric of his vest was smooth against the hard planes of his body.

He broke off from my mouth and his lips skimmed my jaw, teasing kisses that sent tingles down my back and along my thighs. I arched my neck and he took the hint, bending to kiss my throat. My eyelids fell shut, my brain buzzing as my limbs grew heavy.

"Sweetheart," he whispered. "What are we doing?"

I hadn't a clue, but I wasn't ready for it to end. "Please," I begged, not even a little ashamed.

Suddenly, it was over.

My overheated skin turned cool and my lids flew open. I found Leo staring off into the trees, his expression one of profound regret. Stomach clenching, I released my hold on his vest, smoothing the silk before backing off.

He exhaled loudly, his shoulders drooping. "We shouldn't—"

When he didn't say more, my back stiffened. For a moment I thought there was something in his eye when he looked at me— a longing, a flare of desire. But I'd obviously been wrong.

My finely honed survival instincts kicked in. Instead of waiting for him to reject me, I would say the words first.

Face scorching hot with embarrassment, I stood and shook out my skirts. "That was a mistake."

"Josie, wait." Out of the corner of my eye I saw him lift a hand as if to touch my arm, but he let it fall to his side. "We should talk about it."

"No need. I threw myself at you, we kissed, it's over. Don't worry. It won't happen again."

"Damn it, woman." Leo shot to his feet. "There are reasons why this is a bad idea. There are things you don't know about me. I'm a terrible choice for you."

I nearly laughed. Altruism? Leo didn't have a charitable bone in his body. This was because he didn't want me—and no way in hell would I let him see how much that hurt. "Obviously. You're my manager. Our interactions should remain strictly professional. Are you ready to return downtown?"

Pushing the sides of his coat back, he put his hands on his hips and stared at the ground. "It wasn't my intention to hurt you. I merely think—"

I tried to wipe my expression of any emotion whatsoever. "Leo, stop. I understand. And I agree with you."

His gaze lifted to mine and we stared at each other for a long moment. Then he drew closer until the tips of his shoes brushed my skirts. I didn't move as his knuckles brushed the underside of my jaw. "You'll thank me one day, I promise. You're destined for greatness, Josie Smith."

Irritation swept through me. I didn't need him to tell me what my future held. And I didn't need him to coddle me.

I shoved down the flutters as a result of his gentle touch, along with the memories of our kiss. I intended to wipe every bit of this encounter from my brain. Stepping away, I gave him a bland smile. "I feel like a walk. No need to wait up for me."

A look of horror broke out on his face as I moved around him. He grabbed my wrist. "Wait, you can't go traipsing around the city alone."

Of course I knew this, but at the moment I didn't care. I'd stick to populated areas after dark and I had enough money for a hansom, if it came to that.

Starting up the path toward the street, I gave a wave over my shoulder. "See you around, tomcat."

"Damn it, Josie!" He was on my heels. "It isn't safe."

"Go away, Leo."

I hurried to rejoin the parkgoers on the promenade. Headed in each direction were fine ladies and gentlemen, bicyclists, and children and their nurses—a variety of ethnicities and races. The park was a fascinating glimpse into the heart of this vibrant city. I could get lost here, which was exactly what I wished for at the moment.

"You're being stubborn," Leo grumbled behind me. "Do you honestly think I will allow you to put yourself in harm's way?"

Allow me? I didn't need Leo's permission to do a dashed thing. "Stop following me."

His jaw was firm as he grasped my elbow. "No. I'm escorting you home."

I tried to pull away, but he was stronger. "Are you harassing me? Do I need to find a roundsman?"

Leo had the gall to snort. "How is attempting to keep you safe harassing you?"

"Let me go." My voice was loud and sharp as I tried to extricate myself from his grip once more.

"Miss?" A tall man stepped up beside me, his brow lowered in concern under the brim of his derby. He had kind brown eyes and a crooked nose. "Have you need of assistance?"

"Yes," I answered instantly and gestured at Leo. "This man won't release my arm."

"Now, see here—" Leo started, but it was too late.

The newcomer grabbed Leo's shirtfront in a tight fist. Leo was tall, but this man had several inches on him. "You picking on a woman?"

Leo released me and put up his hands. "I'm not hurting her. I'm trying to protect her."

"Don't sound like it to me," the other man said. "Sounds like you're a masher."

"I swear, I'm her manager and am merely trying to see her home safely."

"Miss?" The man glanced at me for confirmation.

To be fair, I was the one to kiss Leo first, not the other way around. He honestly didn't deserve a punch in the face for it. And I didn't like to lie.

"Josie!" Leo's eyes were wide with panic when I hesitated. "Tell him the truth."

I touched the stranger's arm. "Sir, he is telling the truth. I'm trying to go off on my own and he thinks he needs to keep me safe."

My rescuer opened his fingers, freeing Leo's shirt. "Apologies. I assumed you were in trouble with this gentleman, miss."

I am, but not the kind you think.

I smiled up at him. "And I appreciate it. What is your name, Good Samaritan?"

"William, but everyone calls me Brick." He continued to stare at Leo, like he was waiting for Leo to try something else.

"Nice to meet you, Brick. I'm Josie. Would you like to walk with me?"

Leo opened his mouth, probably to launch an argument, but I lifted one eyebrow in challenge. *Try it,* I dared.

"I suppose that would be all right," Brick said. "I was on my way home from work."

I put my hand on Brick's arm and led us away from Leo. "Oh? And where are you employed?"

"Construction uptown."

I believed it, considering Brick's size. "That must be hard work. Shall we go and get a drink somewhere? Or must you hurry home to your wife?"

Leo cursed behind us.

Brick shook his head. "No wife, miss. I was going home to my cat. And a drink sounds like a fine idea."

"Excellent! Let's go explore the city together." I looked back over my shoulder to where a fuming Leo stood watching us. "And we won't let anyone tell us what to do."

I didn't wait to see Leo's reaction. I turned around and put him right out of my mind.

LEO

Of course I followed them.

Josie and Brick entered The Hell Cat, a saloon on Eighth Avenue. Damn it, places like this were not fit for young unmarried ladies.

I waited a few moments and then went in. It looked like every other saloon in this city, dingy and dark, with a long bar stretched out on one side and round tables littering the floor. The hour meant it was crowded, men finished with their workday and stopping for a drink before going home. There were a few women as well, but they were working the room, looking for customers.

I pulled my derby low and kept near the back wall. Josie and Brick were seated at a table and appeared to be engaged in an honest-to-God conversation. My hands curled into fists. I tried to tell myself she was retaliating because of our earlier kiss, that this stranger meant nothing to her, but it didn't help.

"Drink or get out, mister," a voice said.

I turned and found the bartender staring at me. "I'm staying."

"Not if you ain't drinking." He motioned toward the rows of bottles. "What'll you have?"

No doubt the liquor was watered down. I ordered the cheapest beer they served, then continued to watch Josie's table. When the bartender returned, I paid and tilted my chin toward Brick. "You know the big fellow?"

"Sure. Everyone knows him around here. Brick's a decent one."

Decent? I frowned. I still didn't like him.

"Listen," the bartender continued, "if you're thinking of starting trouble, I'd advise against it. Brick comes from a long line of bare-knuckle fighters. He'll knock your pretty face into next week."

"I'm not starting anything. I'm watching out for—" I clamped my lips shut. I'd almost said *my girl*.

"Yeah, I get it, pal. But if Brick wants your woman, you'd best let him have her."

Over my dead body.

Sipping my beer, I leaned on the sticky bar and continued to watch the couple. They were drinking beer as well, and I was thankful that Josie sipped hers slowly. Time dragged on, but I wasn't going anywhere. I would stand here all night, if necessary.

Josie drew a lot of attention. She chatted with the men at surrounding tables and the working women, too. She laughed loudly and gestured with her hands, so beautiful she made my teeth ache. Kissing her had been unbelievable, all my fantasies come to life. Her soft lips and wet tongue, not to mention the little noises she made, would haunt me forever.

But I was a terrible man, a liar and a cheat, planning to use Josie as revenge on the Pendelton family. It felt wrong to entertain these feelings for Josie, even if she instigated it. Eventually she would learn the truth of why we were in New York and regret kissing me.

The third rule of a confidence man: you can't feel sorry for your mark.

Safe to say St. Elmer would be quite disappointed in me. I was letting my attraction to Josie color my judgment. All the more reason to keep my hands and mouth to myself. I needed to focus on my scheme, nothing else.

The saloon's front door burst open. A group of men and women marched inside, some carrying lamps and the rest carrying banners. Peering closer, I made out the words *New York Society for the Suppression of Vice* on the cloth.

Oh, shit.

Four policemen followed next, billy clubs in their hands, each taking a strategic position in the room. The hairs on the back of my neck stood up. What was this, a puritanical street mob with police muscle?

"Ho!" the bartender shouted. "You can't come in here. It's a place of business."

"A place of sin," one of the older banner carriers said. "And we are shutting you down, sinner." Like righteous sheep, the other mob members echoed their agreement.

"The hell you are!" a man at a table shouted.

In retaliation, a policeman strolled over and whacked the patron on the side of his head with a club. The man fell out of his chair and slumped onto the floor. He didn't move or make another sound.

The banner carrier pointed at the various women around the saloon. "Arrest these slatterns. They are a plague and a blight on our society, intent on leading decent men astray."

Policemen began rounding up the prostitutes in the room and my jaw dropped open. The women were complaining loudly, but the men at the tables remained silent. Was no one going to do anything about this?

Before I could speak up, an officer approached Josie—and my blood turned cold. I was halfway across the room in a blink.

"Get up, whore," the officer said, the tiniest hint of an Irish brogue in his voice.

"I'm here to have a drink, nothing more," Josie said, trying to rip her arm out of the officer's grip. "Tell him, Brick."

Brick lifted his palms. "I don't want trouble, Officer."

Fine help he was. Evidently, I needed to take matters into my own hands.

Not a problem. I'd fibbed enough to Boston coppers in my day. I could handle these New York City boyos.

In my deepest Irish accent, I called, "Josie, my darlin' wife. Here's your drink." I set my nearly full beer on the table, then looked at the policeman. "Is there a problem, Officer?"

Josie stared at me as if I'd lost my mind, but I concentrated on the officer.

He let go of Josie's arm, but he didn't move away. "This woman is your wife?"

I gave him a proud smile. "Indeed, sir. Married three years now, we are. She's a fine lass, ain't she?"

Still dubious, the officer glanced at Josie. "Do you know this man, ma'am?"

Her eyes were round and confused, like shock had ahold of her tongue. Willing her not to argue, I slid into a chair and pulled her into my lap. "Josie, love. Tell him."

"He's my husband," she muttered, her body stiff against me.

That wouldn't do.

When the officer looked over at Brick, I took the opportunity to whisper "Relax" into Josie's ear. She squirmed a bit on my lap, then went loose into my hold. "Good girl," I said quietly.

The officer was addressing Brick. "And who are you? Do you know these people?"

"No, I don't know them," Brick said. "I came in for a drink."

"Did this woman approach you and offer you favors?"

I spoke up. "Of course not, sir! There weren't enough seats and my wife is increasing." I gestured to Josie's midsection. "I can't have her standing at the bar. This nice gentleman agreed to let us sit at his table."

"You are with child?" the officer asked Josie.

"Positively full with one!" my fake wife said cheerfully. "He wanted to wait, but you know how that goes. I can't get enough of my man." She patted my chest.

The officer squinted at her hand. "Why are you not wearin' a ring, then?"

"Do you think I'm the bleedin' pope?" I snorted. "Been savin' up for one, but then with the baby coming I wanted to take her back to Belfast first."

"You're from Belfast?" The officer broke out into a wide smile. "My parents were from Banbridge."

"A good town, Banbridge," I said with false confidence. "Decent folks."

"I don't remember it," the officer said. "I was a wee babe when we left. Always wanted to go back, though."

"If you do, make sure to stop by The Silver Harp. Tell them Charlie O'Connor says hello."

The officer held out his hand for me to shake. "Nice to meet you, Mr. O'Connor—"

"What is going on here?" The leader of the banner wavers had arrived. "Officer, why haven't you arrested this whore?"

Josie bristled, her muscles tightening, so I stroked her hip to calm her down. "I'll thank you lads to stop callin' my wife names."

As I'd hoped, the officer leapt to my defense. "These are decent people and they've done nothin' wrong. We've done like you asked with the rest."

The older man sneered at Josie. "Decent people? No decent woman would sit on a man's lap in public. It is a shameless display of immorality by a whore."

"You had better—" Josie started, but I squeezed her tight.

"What my wife is tryin' to say is that she's with child and not feeling well. We don't know the city as we've just traveled here from Boston. We stopped so that she can rest."

"In a *saloon*?" the banner waver asked.

"This is a pub, I thought." I looked around dramatically. "The whole town of Belfast gathers at a pub every afternoon."

"Now, let's leave these fine people to their day." The officer motioned for me and Josie to stand. "You'd best go and find your rooms. This place ain't safe for decent folks."

"Thank you, sir." I rose and placed Josie on her feet. Then I wrapped an arm around her shoulder, keeping her close. "We appreciate your consideration."

"Officer! Arrest her this minute!" Now agitated, the banner waver lunged for Josie and grabbed her arm.

He was touching her. Bold as you please, as if he had the right.

A red mist coated my brain.

Before anyone could blink, I snatched the front of the man's shirt in my fist and pulled him close to my face. Voice low, I snarled, "You best release her, boyo, or I'll bleedin' burst ya."

His face paled and he let go of Josie immediately. "He threatened me! Arrest him, Officer."

My new friend on the Metropolitan police force rolled his eyes. "You cannot manhandle another man's wife, Reverend."

I let the reverend go, then reached to shake the officer's hand. "Good to meet you. *Éirinn go Brách*."

"*Éirinn go Brách*," he repeated back. Then he tipped his cap at Josie. "Ma'am."

She placed her hand on her stomach—a little too high for a baby, but who minded?—and said, "Thank you, kind sir. I'll never forget you, Mr. . . . ?"

"Dooley. Name's Daniel Dooley."

"That's a fine name." Josie sighed and looked up at me, her green gaze twinkling with mischief. "If we have a boy, we must name him Daniel."

The officer turned pink. "Well, now. I'd be honored, ma'am."

"Mrs. O'Connor," I said, gently pushing Josie away from the table. "I think it's past time for us to go."

"Fine, Mr. O'Connor. Don't forget, you promised to rub my back," she announced loud enough for the entire room to hear. "It's been so sore with the baby and all."

"I know, love. I'll do that when we get back to our rooms. Keep going."

The officers and Holy Rollers watched us go. I nodded as we passed, trying to keep up the ruse long enough to get Josie to safety. After what seemed like an interminable walk, we reached the door.

Somehow, I sensed Josie wasn't through. I could feel her vibrating, like she was biding her time, building up to something.

Good Christ, I hoped I was wrong.

I yanked on the door and held it open for her. She glanced over her shoulder, a determined glint in her eye. Just as she opened her mouth, I gave her a tiny shove outside. "Don't do it. Let it go."

Instead of listening to me, she started shouting. "No one has committed a crime in there—and you are hypocrites!"

"Damn it, woman. Keep moving before you get us arrested." I tugged her across the walk and toward the street. A hack happened to be rolling by, so I flagged the driver down.

"Stop blaming the women!" she shouted toward the saloon. "The blame belongs with the men!"

I had the door to the hansom open before the wheels stopped moving. Picking Josie up, I practically tossed her into the conveyance. "Let's get out of here."

Chapter Eleven

LEO

The next morning, I sipped my coffee and watched Josie bustle around the tiny kitchen.

How was she so damn chipper?

I barely slept last night, my mind tangled with thoughts of meeting Melvin, the kiss, the saloon . . . I didn't care for the feelings that were emerging when she and I were together.

Lines were not supposed to blur like this. Josie was part of a bigger scheme, nothing more. I'd get the reward money and she'd gain a family, notoriety, wealth, everything her little heart desired. I couldn't let my head—or my cock—get in the way of that.

Yet I couldn't stop thinking about that kiss. Wondering what it would be like to fuck her.

I licked my lips and stared at her while she stood at the stove. Her waist was perfect for my hands, her backside round. I'd caught a glimpse of her long blond locks this morning before she pinned them up. How I'd like to feel those silken strands all over my skin . . .

Shit.

I had to stop this. It wasn't productive in the least.

The persistent ache in my groin needed to be dealt with before we left for the day, however. I had to stroke myself and purge this craving from my veins to prevent myself from doing something stupid. A climax was exactly what the doctor ordered.

Standing, I tugged my coat over my crotch. "I'll be back—"

A knock sounded on the door, startling me. I glanced over at Josie. "You expecting someone?"

"No," she answered, already moving to the door. "You?"

"Of course not."

She cracked the wood and a young boy stood there. It was the same lad Josie had been talking to on the street when we first arrived. Instantly, I recognized something in his world-weary eyes, something familiar from my boyhood. He'd seen too much for his age. I was instantly on edge.

Coming up behind Josie, I stared him down. "What do you want?"

Josie pulled the door wider. "Sticks! What a nice surprise. Come in."

The boy removed his cap and slid past me into the apartment. "Hey, Josie. Delivery boy just dropped this off for you."

It was a parcel wrapped in brown paper. Sticks handed it to her, then tilted his head toward the cups on the table. "Got more coffee?"

"How old are you?" I asked, not bothering to hide the irritation in my voice.

He stared at me like I was something on the bottom of his boot. "Nine, and what's it to you?"

"Yes, there's more coffee," Josie told the boy as she took the parcel to the table. "Go and help yourself."

I frowned as Sticks went toward the stove. He found a cup on the shelf and then poured a healthy amount of my coffee into it. I went to refill my own cup, asking dryly, "Would you like cream and sugar, too?"

"Prefer it black, but thanks." Sticks lifted his cup in a toast and then sipped.

Jaw tight, I sat back down at the table, where Josie was now un-wrapping the brown paper. "How did you know where to find me?"

"I followed you the other day. Watched you from the stairs when you entered this apartment."

The clever bugger. I hadn't even heard him behind us.

Josie took a newspaper out of the parcel, along with a note. She put the newspaper on the table to unfold the note. "It's from Melvin."

I leaned over and reached for the newsprint. "What does the note say?"

"'Dear Miss Smith, Have your manager escort you to the Metropolitan Opera House this evening. Have him ask for your seats inside. It's important you don't speak. See the article and it will all make sense. Big things await. Regards, Melvin.'"

Our gazes met briefly before I opened the newspaper. It was a portion of the prominent society notices. The headline screamed:

MISS JOSÉPHINE SMITH ARRIVES FROM PARIS
SOUGHT-AFTER SINGER MUST REST HER VOICE BEFORE
NEW YORK CITY DEBUT

I whistled. "Clever. Melvin is a genius."

"Is that you?" Sticks asked Josie. "I didn't know you are from Paris."

She wrinkled her nose. "Those are a bunch of lies."

I wasn't surprised she didn't approve, but this was a smart move. The press loved nothing more than a spectacle, as did Manhattan. "Think of it as a way to generate excitement, not to mention a bit of mystery." I skimmed the rest of the article. "It says you'll be in a box at the opera tonight. You've lost your voice and will be performing again as soon as it recovers."

With a huff, she frowned at me. "I hate this."

"Josie, this is good business." And perhaps an opportunity to rub elbows with the Pendeltons and their ilk. I rubbed my hands together. I could hardly wait.

"I don't want to be a sideshow spectacle. And Joséphine? I'll never remember to answer to that name."

"It sounds fancy," Sticks put in as he went for another cup of coffee. "I like it."

Though it was nice to have an ally in the name choice, I was still annoyed at his presence. "And has anyone invited your opinion?"

Sticks stuck his middle finger up at me.

Resisting the urge to kick the lad out, I concentrated on Josie. "You have one of Martha's evening gowns?"

"Yes. Do you have a formal evening suit?"

"No, but Ambrose does."

"Who's Ambrose?" This was from Sticks, who was leaning against the counter and sipping from his cup.

"The person who lives here," I said impatiently. Why was I explaining myself to a nine-year-old?

"Will it fit you?" Josie asked.

"It should." Ambrose and I were of a similar build. If not, I could find a way to fake it enough for one night.

Nibbling her fingernail, Josie studied the newspaper article again. "What should I do with my hair?"

While I hadn't attended a society event myself, I've certainly seen society ladies out on the town over the years. "You should curl it, then pin it up."

"I can't do that. Pippa is the one who's talented with hair."

"My ma'll do it," Sticks said. "She used to be a maid in a big house uptown."

"That would be much appreciated," Josie gushed before I could weigh in. "We'll pay her, of course. Won't we, Leo?"

I saw more of my limited cash disappearing. But how could I refuse? Josie needed to look the part, and I liked seeing that hopeful, excited light in her eyes. "Of course."

Josie clapped her hands. "This is going to be fun. And I needn't worry about saying the wrong thing or lying to anyone, because I'm not allowed to talk."

I had to admit, Josie's silence would make it easier for both of us. One liar in our group was enough.

Staring at the newspaper, I sent up a fervent prayer that Mrs. Pendelton planned to attend the opera tonight. Georgie would know for certain, but I couldn't go all the way uptown to find out for myself without raising Josie's suspicions. After the other day, I promised we'd stay together.

A promise I was now deeply regretting.

Josie started across the floor toward the bedroom. "I should air out the dress. It might have wrinkles."

She closed the door behind her, thankfully, which gave me a moment alone with Sticks. "Was your ma really a ladies' maid?"

He set his cup down in the sink. "What's the difference? She knows how to do hair."

I glared at him, trying to figure him out. "What's your angle, kid?"

"I might ask you the same thing." He jerked a thumb in the direction of the bedroom. "I see the way you stare at her. Like she's your free lunch and ladybird all in one. What gives?"

"Listen, Josie might tolerate you asking questions, but I won't. Go home and stay there."

"If that's the way you want to play it, mister."

"Yeah. That's the way I want to play it."

His tiny mouth flattened, but he didn't argue. He put on his cap and gave me a cocky salute. "What time should I tell my ma?"

"Five o'clock. That should be plenty of time."

"Sure. She'll do it for a sawbuck." He strolled to the door, in no hurry whatsoever. "And we want cash. No bank drafts or promises."

My eyebrows shot up. "That is highway robbery."

"That's my offer, take it or leave it. If you think you can get someone else to do it cheaper on such short notice, be my guest."

I wrapped my hands around the wooden kitchen table and dug my fingers into the wood. "A sawbuck, then."

He grinned widely, his expression victorious. "See you at five, pal."

The door closed behind the young boy, and I stared at the tabletop. Ten dollars to pin up hair? I felt as if I'd been swindled. In fact, I was almost sure of it.

Damn, the kid was good. Maybe I was losing my touch?

I set that aside for later.

Tonight required careful planning. Above all else, Josie needed to meet Mrs. Pendelton at some point. During their introduction I would plant a few well-crafted seeds about Josie's background, then I'd comment on the slight resemblance between the two women. That, along with Josie's new name, should be enough to pique Mrs. Pendelton's interest over the mysterious singer's identity. How could it not?

Also, Melvin's newspaper story gave me a good idea. Maybe I could drop some hints in the press about her upbringing, subtle crumbs to start the town wondering if she might be the lost heiress.

Damn, I was good. The plan was falling into place nicely and we'd barely arrived. Before long I'd have revenge for my family and enough money to set them up for life. No more laundry, no more sewing. No more talk of factories or unwanted marriages. We could finally afford a lung doctor for Tess.

Indeed, everything was about to change for the better.

JOSIE

I peered up at the hulking yellowish brick building on Broadway and Fortieth Street. "Is that it?"

Leo paid the hansom driver through the slat, then opened the door. "That's it. Ugly, wouldn't you agree?"

Not exactly ugly, but I'd expected something far grander.

This building was flat and plain, comparatively. Perhaps the inside would make up for it.

Leo stepped to the walk, and I took a quick moment to appreciate how fine he appeared in his borrowed evening suit. Black wool trousers were paired with a white vest and shirtfront. The topcoat was tailless—a tuxedo it was called, which Leo claimed was all the rage. I didn't know much about fashion, but my heart sped up every time I looked at him.

Holding out his hand, Leo reached in to help me down. I eased out of the carriage carefully, terrified of wrinkling Martha's precious silk gown. It fit perfectly, as if it had been sewn to my frame. Polly, Sticks's mother, had performed a miracle on my hair and I felt like a true princess as I stepped to the walk.

Leo's gaze traveled up and down my frame. "You look perfect, Josie."

My stomach warmed, some of my nerves dissipating. The compliment wrapped around all the cold and empty places inside me, the aches of a little girl who'd never been right for anyone. It was exactly what I needed to hear. "Thank you."

We started across the street. The opera house entrance, with its huge rounded arches, loomed ahead. I drew in a deep breath and let it out slowly.

"Are you ready?" he asked.

"I think so. My only task is to remain silent."

"That's right. I'll lead you around at the intermission and introduce you to various people. You'll smile and say nothing."

"Feels strange, not to talk."

He chuckled. "For you, I believe it. But this will ensure everyone's interest in you. Melvin's quite brilliant."

I knew this was true, but lying to people didn't sit right with me. For Melvin, though, I would do it.

Streams of operagoers hurried all around us. The gowns were gorgeous, with ostrich feathers and silk top hats bouncing in every direction. I clung to Leo's arm and allowed him to lead me through the crush, while I concentrated on not tripping in my borrowed evening slippers.

"Slow down," I finally whispered. "These shoes are not easy to walk in."

He frowned at me. "Quiet, remember."

"Then don't walk so quickly."

We entered the opera house on the Broadway side. I couldn't see much, due to the crush, but Leo was taller than most of the other patrons. He dodged and weaved until we reached the ticket window.

"Miss Joséphine Smith," he told the man at the window. "There should be two tickets waiting."

The man checked his list. "I don't have them, sir. Best to check around the corner at the Thirty-Ninth Street entrance."

Leo tipped his top hat. "Thank you."

We pushed through everyone trying to come in, but it wasn't easy. I feared for the state of Martha's skirts with how people were jostling me. When we reached the walk, I breathed a sigh of relief. "Why are they making us use a back entrance?" I asked Leo.

"No idea, and keep quiet."

I hadn't forgotten, but it was hard not to use my voice. I pressed my lips together tightly and gave Leo's arm a squeeze.

Shockingly, the people entering on Thirty-Ninth Street were even fancier. Under their fur-edged capes, ladies were draped in elaborate silk gowns, the intricate beadwork sparkling in the yellow gaslight. Gentlemen, fashioned in black and white, wore serious expressions as they escorted their women along a long red carpet, while perfectly polished black carriages lined the curb, their matching horses standing proudly. It was a dizzying glimpse into a world I'd only heard about: New York's High Society.

This couldn't be the right place for Leo and me. I tried to pull on his arm, but he kept moving forward, like he'd done this a hundred times. "Leo," I tried quietly.

"Come on," he said and approached the door.

A staff member held up his hand, looking us up and down. "May I help you, sir?"

"The ticket man on the other side told us to enter here," Leo said. "On Thirty-Ninth Street."

"Ah, I see. Follow me."

We trailed the staff member inside to a small window and Leo gave my name. Our tickets were produced and we were shown to the stairs. "Miss Smith," another staff member said after checking our tickets. "Please, follow me to your box."

Box? I was prepared to sit in the top balcony. Perhaps stand on the floor. But a box?

This had to be a mistake.

As if he could feel me about to speak, Leo squeezed my arm in a silent message. To the staff member, he said assuredly, "Very good. Lead the way."

We climbed a set of ornate marble stairs, complete with brass fixtures and a plush carpet. Never had I been inside a building this grand. The back of my neck twitched as uneasiness crawled along my skin. Would everyone spot me as a fraud? How could I ever appear as if I belonged here?

"Relax," Leo whispered. "Confidence, remember?"

Right. I needed to show confidence before I could feel it. Pushing my shoulders back, I kept my head high. My mouth was bone-dry, so it was a good thing I wasn't supposed to speak tonight.

After another flight, we started down a narrow corridor. To the left were salons and retiring rooms, while on the right were open doors. There were brass plaques with numbers hanging above each doorway, and we kept walking toward the middle. Finally, we stopped and the young man waved his arm. "Here you are. Programs and champagne are inside the salon. The seats are through the curtain. Enjoy the performance."

Leo produced a coin from somewhere and handed it to the attendant. "Thank you."

I couldn't wait a moment more. We had a box at the opera

house, something I'd never dreamed possible. I hurried into the tiny salon, but kept going. I needed to see the inside and the stage.

On the other side of the curtain a glittering golden fantasy greeted my eyes. Holy smokes! This place was *beautiful*. I sucked in a breath and tried not to swoon.

Gaslights flickered overhead to illuminate rows and rows of seats and boxes that faced a huge stage. A towering proscenium framed the closed curtain, while patrons milled about on the floor below. Most of the other boxes were empty, but I couldn't take my eyes off the stage. What would it feel like to perform at a place like this, to have all these people staring at you?

Someday I'll find out.

"What do you think?"

I turned at the sound of Leo's soft voice. When I opened my mouth to speak, he held up his hand. "No talking, remember."

I frowned. How was I supposed to share what I was feeling if I couldn't talk?

But Leo was perceptive. His lips twisted into a fond smile. "I can tell you love it. It's breathtaking, isn't it?"

I nodded vigorously and looked around, wishing to memorize every detail. Who knew when I'd return?

Leo touched my arm. "Come. Let's have a glass of champagne before the performance starts. We can speak freely in there."

I didn't want to leave yet, but privacy meant I could ask all the questions burning my tongue. Once in the salon, I blurted, "Christ, did you see it? I've never imagined a place so grand. How did we get this box? Does it belong to Melvin, do you think? Have we the funds to pay for this champagne?"

Leo handed me a full glass. "Drink and try to calm down. You're a famous singer from Paris, Josie. When we return to our seats out there, you need to appear as if this is old hat to you."

I knew he was right, but it wasn't going to be easy. I was a singer, not an actress.

Lowering myself onto the sofa, I brought the glass to my lips and swallowed half the bubbly. It burned as it went down, but it wasn't often I had the opportunity to drink champagne.

Leo sat next to me, a glass cradled in his elegant fingers. If he felt out of place, I certainly couldn't tell.

"To answer your many questions," he said, "I did see it and it is indeed grand. According to the plaque by the door, the box belongs to a shareholder, Mr. Wetmore. I assume Melvin is friendly with Wetmore, who loaned out the box for the night. And the champagne is complimentary."

"You think I'm silly."

"No. I think you're adorable."

He was staring at me with affectionate amusement, like I was an annoying younger sister. It didn't help. I felt out of place, a fraud. As if I'd be kicked out at any moment and exposed as a liar to the entire world.

There was every chance I could ruin everything before we even began.

I swallowed more champagne, hardly noticing the burn this time. I had to find my spine. This crowd had to believe I was one of them—worldly and experienced, beautiful and rich. But how?

I needed confidence. My eyes slid to Leo again. I needed him to distract me and make me feel wanted, like he had in the park.

I didn't stop to think if it was a good idea or not. Putting my glass down, I blurted, "I need you to kiss me."

His amusement died, his expression turning blank. "What?"

"I'm too nervous and I don't want to drink too much champagne. I know kissing isn't professional and you don't want me like that. But I'm about to jump out of my skin, Leo. Help me."

"Take a few deep breaths," he advised, though his gaze darted to my mouth.

"It won't work. I'm telling you, a quick kiss will distract me."

He shook his head. "We shouldn't. What happened in the park was a bad idea. Besides, what if someone walks in?"

Those were valid points, but I was too anxious to care. My corset felt too tight, the lighting too bright. My heart was racing like a rabbit in my chest. We would be the topic of conversation and speculation tonight, all those fancy people judging me, and I needed to quiet my thoughts.

I placed my glass on the side table and edged closer to him. He froze. "What are you doing?"

Being careful not to wrinkle my dress or ruin my hair, I put my hand on his chest and leaned in. Our faces were close and I could feel his heart thundering beneath my hand. "I know it's madness. Yes, you're a scoundrel, a terrible choice for me, but you're here and I'm desperate. Kiss me, Leo. Please."

He still didn't move, though our mouths were only inches apart. "If I kiss you, everyone will know what we've been doing in here. Your lips will be swollen and I'll be as hard as wood."

Hard as wood? Did that mean he desired me too? Maybe a tiny bit?

Encouraged, I boldly placed my other hand on his thigh. "Help me, Leo. Make me feel beautiful, like I belong here. *Please.*"

Finally—finally!—he closed the distance between our mouths. He brushed his lips across mine and the familiar electricity jumped between us, heat and sparks that went bone-deep, and I sighed with satisfaction. Before I knew it his tongue was in my mouth—or maybe mine was in his?—and he tasted like champagne and secrets and man. Like Leo. I had a brief thought that the intoxicating combination should be bottled like elixir for lonely people everywhere.

My plan worked, because I soon forgot about our surroundings, why we were here. Everything fell away, leaving Leo and me in our own little haven. As our tongues slid together, flicking and dancing, I clung to him, desperate for more. More kisses, more touching. I wanted to feast on this man.

It was foolish, my craving for him. I'd determined this morning never to repeat what happened yesterday, to keep our interactions professional, and yet I'd asked for this kiss. Needed it like air.

I angled my head as he shifted to drop kisses along my jaw, then I gasped when he sank his teeth into my throat. "You are wanted. You are beautiful. Never doubt it for a single second in my presence."

The words wrapped around my heart, knitting together a few of the fragments of doubt and slivers of uncertainty. "Don't stop."

"This is madness." He dragged his tongue over the sensitive skin of my collarbone, his breath hot. "Your dress will be ruined."

Who cared about ruined dresses?

Not me. Not while his mouth was working magic on my skin. I wanted to feel him everywhere, to explore and be explored, and to allow these dizzying sensations to spiral out of control. My breasts were heavy, aching, while my nipples were tight against the corset, and the pounding beat between my legs was almost unbearable.

"Please, Leo. Touch me."

Nimble fingers began lifting the layers of cloth covering my legs. He put his mouth near my ear to whisper, "Are you wet for me, sweetheart? Let me—"

The lights flickered overhead.

"Shit," Leo hissed. Panting, we broke apart, our breathing harsh in the relative quiet. Without a word, he rose from the sofa and faced away as he adjusted himself in his clothing. Smoothed his hair and coat. "We should take our seats," he said after a beat. "The performance will begin soon."

Indeed, the performance. The reason we were here.

The fever in my blood cooled significantly. *Be professional, Josie. He didn't want to kiss you, but he did you this favor.*

At least I wasn't as nervous now. Bully for me. And I had no reason to be cross or hurt. Leo hadn't lied about his feelings for me, not once. He didn't want anything other than a working relationship, so I should be grateful he'd bent the rules this one time.

Standing, I shook out my skirts. Ignoring the way he tensed when I approached, I patted his chest. "Thank you, Leo. I admit, it's nice having a tomcat around for moments like this. Your skills do come in handy."

Instead of grinning at my attempt at humor, he frowned, his eyebrows low as he stared at me. I couldn't read his thoughts, the cheerful blue of his eyes mostly swallowed up by stormy gray. Was he unhappy?

Before I could ask, his expression cleared and his practiced, happy-go-lucky smile returned. "At your service, sweetheart. Now, let's get out there and give New York City a real show."

I walked to our seats in the box, hating that smile of his.

Chapter Twelve

LEO

It's nice having a tomcat around for moments like this.

The words still stung as we took our seats in the box. The entire tier watched as we sat down, curious stares and whispers trailing our movements, but I hardly noticed. Yes, my pride was a bit bruised.

I'd lost myself in that kiss, my desire burning hotter than at any time in recent memory. Yet Josie's comment made the whole thing feel tawdry, as if I kissed every woman like I kissed her. As if the partner didn't matter to me. Did she believe that I indiscriminately fucked my way across Boston, without any care for where or whom?

She calls me tomcat. Of course she thinks that.

Had the partner mattered to her, or would any man have sufficed a moment ago?

I shook my head and tried to concentrate on the moment at hand. This woman was turning me inside out. She caused me to doubt myself like no one else ever had before, and tonight was too important for hand-wringing.

Josie studied the program as if she were memorizing it, so I said under my breath, "Look up and let them see you."

She lifted her face and focused on the stage, a playful smile on her lips. God, those lips. They were magic. No, heaven. Heavenly magic. I lost my head whenever I kissed them.

The opening notes boomed from the orchestra and the house-lights lowered. Josie bit her lip and clasped her hands tightly in her lap. Her excitement was palpable, and like a desperate fool, I moved my leg closer until our thighs touched.

I'm becoming attached to her.

I shoved that idea ruthlessly aside. I was doing this for *her*, trying to keep her calm and confident. She was the focus here, the only person who mattered.

The performance began and though I didn't know much about opera, I tried to appear interested. While the singers were talented and the costumes elaborate, the whole bit was too stuffy for me. Give me a good saloon singer and a beer and I was a happy man.

Josie, on the other hand, was enraptured by the happenings onstage. She gasped and smiled, cried and laughed. I more enjoyed watching her as opposed to the actors.

Finally, she shoved my leg. "Stop staring," she said under her breath. "People will notice."

But she didn't ease away, our thighs still pressed tight. I counted that as a win.

I focused on the crowd, looking for one person. Was Mrs. Pendelton here? I intended to find out during the second intermission.

Except I couldn't see all the boxes, I could only see those in our tier. Mrs. Pendelton might be above or below us, and time was too precious to waste on guessing.

"Excuse me," I whispered to Josie, then slid out of my chair and went into the back of our box. Opening the door to the corridor, I looked left and right. An usher was standing by the entrance to the smoking room.

He straightened as I approached. "May I help you, sir?"

"I need a favor." Reaching into my inner coat pocket, I withdrew a sawbuck. "Do you know where the Pendelton box is located?"

The man eyed the ten-dollar bill. "I shouldn't . . ."

But it was clear he wanted the money, his eyes gazing at the bill longingly. I spotted my opening and gave him a wide, reassuring smile. "Mrs. Pendelton is an old acquaintance. I wish to say hello and introduce her to my friend. It won't take but a few moments, and I'll never tell anyone we had this conversation."

Once more he snuck a peek at the money, then checked our surroundings to make sure we weren't overheard. "Tier above, two left of center." Quick fingers darted out and removed the bill from my hand.

"Much appreciated," I said with a nod. "And mum's the word."

I returned to our box, my veins vibrating with anticipation. During the second intermission, I would lead Josie up and get her in front of Mrs. Pendelton. It wouldn't be easy without a proper introduction, but I had a plan for that.

All I needed was a little buzz, tongues wagging about the Parisian singer in their midst. Once these Knickerbockers realized they had a star here—according to Melvin's newspaper article, at least—everyone would be eager to meet her. This was what the first intermission was for. I'd ensure that everyone in our tier knew Joséphine Smith.

Josie cast me a worried glance as I retook my seat. Her thigh touched mine, almost as if she'd missed me. "Everything all right?"

"Dandy," I whispered back.

By the time the first act ended, I wasn't paying much attention to the stage. My mind was racing ahead toward intermission and my plans. As the lights came back up, I stood and noticed the older woman from the neighboring box staring at me and Josie. Her expression was a mix of disapproval and curiosity. I didn't like it. We needed to win this crowd over, fast.

I gave her the boyish and flirtatious smile that worked best on older women. "Excellent beginning, wouldn't you say, ma'am?"

She tilted her head and opened her fan. "I cannot say that I have seen you here before. Are you an acquaintance of the Wetmores?"

"They are friends with Miss Smith's producer. Perhaps you've heard of him? Mr. Melvin Birdman."

"Oh, goodness." Recognition dawned in her expression as she tried to peer around me at Josie. "He is very well known. I saw his production of *The Shop Girl* last year."

"That's him." I reached for Josie's arm and helped her to her feet. "This is Miss Joséphine Smith. We've just arrived from—"

"From Paris," the woman finished, her gaze growing wide. "You are the woman mentioned in the newspaper today."

Josie smiled and inclined her head. Then she pointed to her throat.

"She must rest her voice, you see," I explained.

"I remember," our neighbor said. "You poor dear. I do hope you recover soon. I am Mrs. Thomas Nyland. This is my husband, Mr. Nyland."

I eased closer and bowed over her hand, then shook her husband's hand. "Mr. Leo Hardy. A pleasure, ma'am. Sir."

Whispers in the adjoining boxes reached my ears. It was the sweetest music, sweeter than the performance onstage. At this very moment eavesdroppers were spreading news of Miss Joséphine Smith's appearance throughout the tier.

"We are great supporters of the theater," Mrs. Nyland explained. "Which is how I know of Mr. Birdman and Miss Smith. Will she be performing soon?" This question was posed to me.

"When her voice is strong enough. We have been in discussions with Mr. Carnegie's Hall, as well as some of the Broadway shows." Josie tried to elbow me for the lie, but I ignored her. "It won't be long before audiences here are cheering every bit as loud as they did in France."

Mr. Nyland leaned in to ask, "Where in Paris did you say she has performed?"

"We've been to many theaters there," Mrs. Nyland added. "Perhaps we caught one of her earlier productions."

I played along. "Perhaps you did. When was the last time you were in Paris?"

"Eighteen months ago," Mr. Nyland answered.

"What a shame," I said. "Miss Smith didn't begin performing there until a little over a year ago. You must have just missed her debut at the Paris Opera House."

Other patrons began crowding into the Nyland box, edging forward with hope shining in their gazes. New Yorkers loved to brush elbows with anyone who possessed a bit of notoriety. I didn't mind. I needed news of Joséphine Smith to reach the Pendelton box.

The next few moments were a blur, with a stream of theatergoers coming forward to meet Miss Joséphine Smith. Josie was regal and beautiful and silent. She fit the part perfectly, and her demeanor only added to the hum of excitement surrounding us.

"You look so familiar," one older man said to Josie as he studied her face. "I cannot put my finger on it, but I feel as though I've seen you before."

"In Paris, perhaps?" The suggestion came from another woman in the box.

"I haven't been to Paris in thirty years. No, this is more recent. Do you have family in New York, Miss Smith?"

Josie shook her head ruefully. I rushed to shut this line of inquiry down. I couldn't allow anyone else to collect that Pendelton reward money—it belonged to me. "Her family is deceased, but they hailed from Boston. Are you acquainted with anyone there?"

"Not too many people, no." He scratched his jaw, but he was soon edged out of the way by another patron.

We were peppered with the same questions over and over and I could feel Josie growing restless at my side. It was easy for me to fib, but I knew she wasn't comfortable with dishonesty. But she didn't complain, thank goodness, and dazzled the crowd with her ephemeral beauty.

The lights flickered, so everyone slowly returned to their seats. Josie tugged on my sleeve and tilted her head toward the salon. I followed her in and shut the curtain behind me. "All good?"

"That was awful," she whispered, making a face. "None of that was the truth."

It was smart of Melvin to give her an ailment that prevented her from lying tonight. She never would've lasted. "Don't worry. It'll all work out in the end, I promise." We'd both become rich when this was over.

"I know." She pinched the bridge of her nose between her thumb and forefinger, then exhaled. "I need a break. I'll return in a few moments."

"I'll escort you."

I started forward, but she quickly held up her hand. "No need. I'm visiting the ladies' retiring room and I'll be fine on my own. I won't speak, I promise."

Uneasiness crept through me. Her eyes were flat, missing their usual mischievous sparkle. I didn't like it, but rule three prohibited me from insisting.

You can't feel sorry for your mark.

I shoved down my protective instincts. *Keep it together, Hardy.* This was no time for personal feelings. I wasn't allowed to care about anyone without the same last name as mine.

I picked up my champagne glass and refilled it. "If you're certain, then I'll wait here."

"How was that so easy for you?"

The question caught me off guard. I paused with the coupe halfway to my mouth and thought of an excuse Josie would swallow. She had to believe me honest and trustworthy, not an accomplished liar.

For once, the words weren't easy to force out. "I did that for you. Because it's what Melvin wanted, what will help your career. I felt awful lying to those people too."

Her shoulders relaxed, clearly relieved at my answer. "Good.

I started to worry for a minute or two. You sounded so believable that even I started to think I was a famous Parisian singer."

I laughed like this was a big joke. "I want this to work. And, Josie, it will. You were perfect out there. Lotta would be very proud."

She started for the door to the corridor, her skirts rustling as she moved. "Lies are nothing to be proud of, Leo." She disappeared through the door and I was alone.

I threw back the contents of my glass. The champagne tasted like ash in my mouth.

JOSIE

If I didn't take a moment to breathe, I would scream.

All those people and their incessant questions . . . They stared at me like I was one of the animals in the Central Park Menagerie. Curiously, as if waiting for me to do or say something outrageous. I hadn't liked lying to them.

Leo, on the other hand, had lied so smoothly. Too smoothly.

It shouldn't bother me. He was good with people, always knew what to say. His cocksure demeanor exuded confidence and people relaxed around him—including me. Seeing him tonight, hearing the lies fall so easily from his mouth, reminded me of Lotta's warning about him. And Martha's warning. Hell, even Melvin had seemed suspicious of Leo.

It was all overwhelming. I needed a break.

Thankfully the corridor was empty. I started toward the retiring room, but stopped. I'd met nearly this entire tier during intermission—*lied* to nearly the entire tier during intermission. I couldn't face any of them right now.

I made my way toward the stairs.

An usher opened the door for me. I smiled and pointed up, a

question in my eyes. "Retiring room?" I whispered, hating the charade of having no voice.

"Yes, miss. There is one for ladies at either end of the tier."

I thanked him and continued on, careful of my skirts. This wasn't how I ever dreamed of attending the Metropolitan Opera, unable to speak and pretending to be someone I'm not.

Someday I'll be on that stage. And I'll not pretend to be anyone else.

As I entered the next tier, I felt my shoulders relax. No one knew me up here. I was a stranger, just another theatergoer enjoying a night out. When I reached the ladies' retiring room at the far end, I glanced around, certain I was lost. This was a retiring room? The space was every bit as opulent as the rest of the theater, with a crystal chandelier, velvet sofas and chairs, and brass fixtures.

"It is far too much, wouldn't you say?"

A woman was seated on a sofa. Her beaded evening gown was elegant, but she wore little jewelry and her dull blond hair was pulled into a simple style. A haunted weariness shone in her eyes, much like the nuns at the asylum. It was the look of a person who'd seen too much heartache and tragedy to be cheerful.

I gave her a polite smile. "I beg your pardon?"

Shit. I wasn't supposed to talk. Five minutes away from Leo and I'd already screwed up.

"The room," she said. "A tad gaudy, wouldn't you say?"

With my silence already broken, I saw little use in continuing the pretense. I drew closer to where she was sitting. "It's not relaxing, at least not for me. I'm worried I'll break something."

"Are you particularly clumsy?"

"Yes. No." I shrugged and offered a tiny chuckle. "Maybe? With all this fancy glass and crystal around, I feel like a donkey at a debutante ball."

That caused her lips to twitch like she might laugh. "One would never know it. You are a beautiful young woman."

I could feel my skin heating. I wasn't used to compliments from strangers. "Thank you." The older woman didn't move, and I found myself curious about her. I lowered myself into a nearby bench. "Are you escaping the performance? Or all those people out there?"

"What makes you think I'm escaping?"

I tapped my temple. "Like recognizes like, ma'am."

"You are very perceptive. I know my excuse. However, I can't understand why you would need to escape. Is your escort misbehaving?"

I thought of Leo and his lies. "No, it's not him. I feel like a camel out there, with everyone staring at me."

"A donkey and a camel? Goodness, you have quite the imagination."

Pippa always said the same growing up. What else could an unwanted orphan do but make up fun stories to ease the loneliness? "Guilty. You're probably used to these fancy crowds, but it's new for me."

"Not used to them, no. Learned to tolerate them, yes. I used to love it, but then—" She shook her head. "The key is to smile and never let them inside your head or your heart."

"That is decent advice."

"Unfortunately, I have experience in this area. Are you new to Manhattan?"

"First trip. I've recently arrived from . . . Paris." I caught myself just in time.

"Ah. It is the perfect city for someone young and pretty like you. Full of excitement and fun. But there are dangerous elements as well. Be careful."

"Oh, thank you. I'll be fine." I've been taking care of myself nearly my whole life, after all. "But I appreciate the warning. Have you lived here long?"

If my invasive question bothered her, she gave no indication. "All of my forty-five years."

"You must love it, then."

I expected her to agree, but the lines in her forehead deepened thoughtfully. "I both love and hate this city. It's my home, but there are many bad memories. I keep telling myself I should move away."

"So why don't you?"

"Hope." She lowered her gaze to stare at her hands clasped in her lap. "It's a terrible thing, hope. It's a prison without walls." Without warning, she rose and straightened her skirts. "I should return to my seat. My husband is no doubt wondering where I am. It's been very nice chatting with you, Miss . . . ?"

"Smith." I stood and offered my hand. "Nice to meet you, ma'am."

She touched my hand lightly, as if unused to the concept of a handshake. "Likewise. Enjoy the rest of the performance and your time in New York."

"I will. Good evening."

Regal and calm, she floated to the door and disappeared through it. It was then I realized she didn't return the introduction. I was slightly disappointed. For a moment I thought I'd made a friend here.

An attendant hovered inside, ready to offer assistance, so I asked, "Do you know the name of that nice older woman who was in the outer room a moment ago?"

A worried expression came over the attendant's face, a pinch to her lips as if the question distressed her. Maybe she was hard of hearing or didn't speak English. Whatever the reason, my question rattled her. I smiled and put my palms up in apology. "Never mind. I shouldn't have asked. Have a lovely night."

I left and returned to the corridor, where muted sounds of the orchestra filled the space. Violins swelled, signaling a dramatic point in the story, and I suddenly regretted missing the performance. Who knew when I'd return here? I needed to soak in every minute.

If life has taught me anything, it was to make the most of each opportunity.

I hurried down to the lower tier and our box. When I emerged from the curtain I swore I saw relief on Leo's face. Had he been worried about me?

Of course he had. He was worried I would ruin the evening by talking or telling someone my real name.

After I retook my seat, Leo leaned over. "Where were you?" When I opened my mouth to answer, he put up his hand. "Wait, tell me later. Save your voice."

I watched the performance, my chin high. I felt better. Perhaps it was meeting that woman in the retiring room, but I suddenly felt as if I could do this. I could pretend to be someone else, dazzle and charm the snobbish Knickerbocker crowd. All I had to do was smile and not let them in my head or my heart.

And that included Leo as well.

Chapter Thirteen

LEO

I stared through the window of the hansom, disappointment throbbing, pounding in my temples. No, not exactly disappointment.

Failure.

I'd failed tonight. This had been my best opportunity to put Josie in front of Mrs. Pendelton . . . and I'd failed.

A crowd packed into our tiny box during the second intermission, preventing our opportunity to visit the other tier and Mrs. Pendelton. One after another, nearly everyone in the opera house pushed in to meet the famous Parisian singer—everyone save the person I most needed her to meet.

The entire night had been a waste. Now I needed to come up with another plot to get the two in the same room together.

Goddamn it.

"Why are you such a sour face?" Josie asked as we turned a sharp corner. "I thought it went exceedingly well."

No, it hadn't. And I couldn't tell her why. "You certainly caused a stir. Melvin will be very happy."

"But you aren't."

"Indeed, I am. Why wouldn't I be?"

"I've no idea, but you've been awfully quiet since the second intermission ended."

"Maybe I'm tired of talking. I did quite a lot of it tonight to maintain our ruse."

"You? Tired of talking?" She made a dismissive sound in her throat. "I'll never believe it."

Fair. In my line of work, I did do quite a lot of talking. Right now, however, I felt too hollow, too mad to carry on a conversation.

Empty. Drained.

Exhausted from failing at such a simple task.

I tapped my fingers on the side of the carriage, restless, as I tried to consider my next move. What was I going to do if I couldn't make this work?

If I failed, Flora would go running to some dangerous man, lured in with big promises and empty kisses.

My mother would work herself into an early grave.

We'd never afford a doctor for Tess, who still had trouble breathing properly.

My other sisters would accept marriages they didn't want, or work factory jobs that would suck out their souls.

Take care of them, Leo, after I'm gone.

I had promised my father that I'd always look after my sisters. Some fine job I was doing of it at the moment.

By the time we reached our street, my head was a mess. Frustration simmered under my skin, and the proximity to Josie wasn't helping one bit. The smell of her perfume had teased me all night, reminding me of the kisses we'd shared. I was craving another taste of her like a drug.

It's nice having a tomcat around for moments like this.

I closed my eyes and struggled for control. Focus was a strength of mine, the one advantage I had over all the other charlatans out there. What good was I without it?

The carriage finally rolled to a stop. I paid the driver, then jumped out to assist Josie down. With ruthless determination, I ignored the soft feel of her small hand in mine.

And I ignored the swish of her skirts, the plump heft of her bosom in the low neckline of her gown. I ignored the way my pulse leapt as she took my arm, the press of her body to mine as I led her inside.

Most of all I ignored the demand in my gut, the yearning to do filthy things to her.

When we reached the vestibule, I dropped her arm as quickly as I could manage. Thankfully, she stayed quiet while we climbed the stairs. Each step brought more dread, more concern that I would cross an irrevocable line with her.

I wasn't sure I cared anymore.

When I unlocked the door, her eyebrows dipped in confusion. "Are you planning on telling me what is the matter with you?" she asked.

"My dear," a voice within the apartment answered. "Leo is a cranky curmudgeon. It can definitely take some gettin' used to."

A man inside the apartment . . . That deep southern twang . . .

No, it couldn't be.

My head swung around. There he was, relaxed on the sofa with his feet propped on the low table.

Ambrose Lee Turner.

Fuck me.

"You're supposed to be in Saratoga," I blurted.

Ambrose unfolded his long limbs from the sofa and stood. "That's a fine way to greet your closest friend in the world." His wool suit had seen better days and his hair was longer than I remembered. The mustache was definitely new.

But the determined, crafty gleam in his gaze? That I well recognized.

Keeping my focus on my friend, I shifted to block Josie from him. "Why are you here?"

"I came back," Ambrose said, lifting his hands in a careless shrug. "You inform me you're comin' to visit—and bringing a woman with you, no less—and you think I don't want to see that for myself? You should know me better than that, Hardy."

"You know the rules." *Ninth rule of being a confidence man: never interfere in another confidence man's scheme.*

"Yes, but you've never brought in a woman before." He leaned around me to see Josie. "Hello, sweetheart."

Josie stepped to the side. "Hello, sir. You must be Ambrose," she said.

"Indeed." He gave a dramatic bow. "Ambrose Lee, at your service."

"What happened to Turner?" I asked.

Ambrose's grin turned sheepish, like a little boy who'd been caught stealing treats behind his mother's back. "Had a little trouble in Scranton. Now, tell me all about yourself, sweetheart. What's your name?"

Josie began peeling off her opera gloves, one finger at a time. "I'm Josie Smith. A singer from Boston."

Ambrose slipped his hands into his trouser pockets, and I clenched my teeth together as he let his eyes travel up and down Josie's body. "Lordy almighty. I can see why he's trying to hide you. What are you doing here in New York City, Miss Josie Smith from Boston?"

I didn't like this. I didn't want Ambrose around Josie. "We're tired. This can all wait until morning—"

"It's all right," Josie said. "I don't mind staying up a bit to talk."

"Yeah, Leo." Ambrose cocked an eyebrow at me. "Do allow the lady to speak."

While Ambrose and I glared at each other, Josie said, "Leo brought me here to help launch my singing career. He's my manager."

Ambrose's jaw fell open as his eyes darted back and forth between Josie and me. Then he burst into laughter, his head thrown back as loud guffaws filled the room. "A *manager*? Oh, this is perfect."

"Shut up," I snarled. The last thing I needed was for Josie to start doubting me again. I couldn't have her pulling out, not yet.

"It's genius." A still laughing Ambrose bent over at the waist, a hand on his stomach. "You don't know a dashed thing about—"

I lunged for him and got a hand on his suit coat, then I began dragging him toward the door. "Josie, excuse us. I need a private word with Ambrose."

Without another word, I tugged my friend out into the corridor. He was still chuckling, not putting up a fight, yet I kept towing him toward the small washroom. I threw him in the empty room and closed the door behind us. "Shut the hell up."

Ambrose wiped his eyes dramatically. "You having trouble getting pussy, Leo? Now you have to pretend to be some poor girl's manager to get under her skirts? As I live and breathe, I never thought I'd see the day."

I advanced on him and shoved his chest with both hands. Hard. His arm knocked a porcelain soap dish off the sink as he went, yet he continued to grin at me. My fingers curled into fists. "I swear, I'm going to hit you. This is on the level." *Sort of.*

Ambrose waved his hand dismissively. "Please. You never do anything on the level. It's why we're such good pals."

"Well, it is this time. So whatever you're thinking of saying to her, stuff it back inside your gob."

"Horseshit." Sobering, Ambrose folded his arms across his chest. "Tell me what you're really doing, or I'm giving that sweet girl a complete recounting of your illustrious history."

"Why?" I ran a palm down my face. "Why are you making this difficult for me?"

"Come now. You haven't been to New York in almost twenty years. Why now? Why her?"

"Just plain curiosity, is that it?"

"Yes, dearest Leo. Who knows? Maybe I can offer advice on whatever con you're running. We've always helped each other in the past."

"This is different."

"Doubtful." He studied his fingernails. "If you aren't going to tell me the truth, then your lady friend has a right to know how we truly know each other."

"Don't you dare. That would ruin everything," I said before I could think better of it.

"Ha!" With a triumphant expression, he pointed a long finger at my face. "I knew it." Then he rubbed his hands together, like a greedy thief. "Allow me to guess. She's paying you to take her to meetings and auditions and whatnot, and you're pocketing the money?"

"Christ, no. I told you, I'm acting as her manager."

"And? Besides fucking her, obviously."

"I'm not fucking her," I hissed, hoping no one could hear us out here. Especially Josie.

"I beg your pardon. I assumed you'd made a claim on the young lady. If not . . ." His lips twisted into a slick smile. "Then indeed, I am pleased as punch to hear it."

My upper lip curled as my muscles tightened again. "She is *not* available for your depravity."

"I see."

I didn't care for the way he said it, as if I were as transparent as glass. But I didn't have time for this conversation. I needed to return to the apartment and deal with Josie.

"Just keep quiet." I straightened my vest and smoothed my hair. "I need to get back in there and make sure she's all right."

"For now, I'll go along. But I expect answers tomorrow, Leo, or else . . ."

"Or else? Jesus, Ambrose. Is this how you treat a man you've known for over a decade? What about the ninth rule?"

"I'm not going to interfere. You know you can trust me."

"Do I?"

"Now you're hurting my feelings. Perhaps I merely wish to learn from you. You always were St. Elmer's favorite."

Sighing, I stared at the sink. I couldn't fool Ambrose. We were cut from the same cloth. We'd grown up together, run schemes together. And if he was living in the apartment with us, I needed him on my side.

I nodded once. "Fine. Let me see to her tonight and we'll talk tomorrow."

"Fine." Ambrose swept his hand toward the door. "After you, sir."

I pushed on the latch and went into the hall, my borrowed shoes pinching my toes as I hurried to Ambrose's door. When I twisted the knob, the door didn't budge. I tried again—but only met resistance. What the hell?

"What's the delay?" Ambrose said behind me. "Go inside already."

"I'm trying." I slapped my palm on the wood a few times. "Josie, the door is locked."

"I know," she called from the other side. "That's because I locked it."

I rested my forehead on the rough wood, closing my eyes as frustration stole through me. "Any reason you locked the door?"

"I heard you two arguing down the hall. I know it's about me."

Like he was settling in for a show, Ambrose leaned against the wall, arms folded, his grin wide.

I focused on the closed door. "Ambrose and I go way back. I just needed to have a private word with him."

"About me," she said.

"Ambrose doesn't have a great reputation with ladies, Josie. I needed to ensure your safety."

My friend shoved my shoulder, his face stormy. *Fuck you*, he mouthed.

I glared at him, then returned my attention to the door. "Let us in. Please."

She was quiet for several seconds. Finally, she said, "No. My gut is telling me something is off with you two. I'd rather be alone for a little while."

Goddamn it.

Though I was angry, I couldn't let on with her. I kept my voice light and reasonable. "Josie, I'll explain everything when you let us in."

"I'd rather not. When you talk, I get distracted by your face. I like having the door between us."

"I don't want to have this conversation in the hall."

"I told you, I want to be alone for a while. Go away, Leo."

Shit. I stabbed my fingers in my hair and pulled on the strands. This was a disaster. "Josie, please—"

"I mean it. The two of you can go and argue elsewhere."

I knew better than to push now. Tonight had been bad enough; I didn't need her even more suspicious about me. Maybe a little time and distance would help her regain her perspective over our association. "Sure, take some time for yourself. We'll see you tomorrow."

"Tomorrow!" Ambrose hissed. "That's my goddamn apartment!"

I grabbed his collar and began dragging him down the hall. "Shut up and come along, Ambrose *Lee*."

HEAD POUNDING, I stomped down the stairs. Why had Ambrose returned to New York? Why hadn't he kept his mouth shut? Why wouldn't Josie let me explain?

Why, why, why?

"Slow down," Ambrose grumbled behind me.

"Fuck off."

"Aw, there is no need to be sore at me, Leo. You'd have done the exact same in my shoes."

Whirling on the last step, I narrowed my eyes at him. "The hell I would. I wouldn't ask so many questions and give anyone reason to doubt you."

"How was I to know that would happen?"

"It's as obvious as the large nose on your face."

"My friend, you brought a girl here, to my apartment, and you're clearly up to something—"

"Keep your voice down," I snarled.

This was pointless. Turning, I continued down the steps and out onto the stoop. Where was I going to go? A saloon?

I started north.

"I see what's going on." Ambrose had caught up and was now at my side. "I see it clear as day. You have feelings for this girl. You like her."

"Don't be ridiculous."

"No, you do. You are head over heels for her."

"I'm five seconds away from punching you, Ambrose."

"Leo, we've been friends forever and a day, which is how I know two things. One, you can't punch worth a damn. And two, you are smitten with this girl."

"I told you, I'm her manager. It's a professional relationship."

"I don't believe a word of that. I saw the way you looked at her. She has you tied up in itty-bitty knots. Not to mention the second she told you to leave, you practically sprinted out of the building."

We passed a saloon, so I dragged him toward the door. "Come along. You're going to buy me a drink while we figure out where we are sleeping tonight."

"While I cannot speak for you, I intend to sleep on my sofa."

"The hell you are. You're not sleeping in that apartment alone with Josie."

"Once more, dear sir," he said in his deepest drawl. "I must reiterate that it is *my* apartment."

"Which you lent to me, you ass. And if it weren't for your mouth, we'd still be inside it."

We went in and claimed one of the empty tables. After we ordered, I rubbed my eyes tiredly. "Your timing couldn't have been worse, Ambrose."

"I disagree. It seems that I arrived just in time. You never did your best work alone. Remember the scheme we pulled in Philadelphia? The—"

I cut him off with a slash of my hand. "This is not helpful. I'm not reminiscing with you tonight."

He held up his palms and leaned back in his chair. "Fine. Tell me, then. What is your plan with Josie? Because I know it's more than it seems."

That was the thing about confidence artists: we could smell a scheme from a mile away. Also, we were constantly searching for new ways to swindle people, and the way we learned was by talking to other confidence men. We were like a small group of zealots, passing on secrets, except it wasn't about scripture or salvation. Our holy grail was the almighty dollar.

At least if I told him, he'd leave me alone.

But I also wasn't stupid.

There was no reason to give him the truth right now. While we never interfered with another's scheme, I couldn't risk Ambrose's big mouth. The three of us in a tiny apartment meant conversations could be overheard. God forbid Ambrose said something about the Pendeltons that Josie picked up on.

I'd come clean after Josie was safely secure in the Pendeltons' mansion and I had that reward check.

Our drinks arrived and I took a long sip of lager, then carefully set my glass on the table. "If I tell you, will you promise to keep quiet and stop agitating? I need her to trust me."

Eyes glittering with interest, he put his hand on his heart. "I do so solemnly swear, Your Honor."

"You were right. I'm squiring her around town to look for work in exchange for a hefty fee."

Ambrose's glass hit the table with a thump. "I knew it!"

"It's good, right? The best part? She can really sing. The girl is very talented."

"Then you should be rolling in the bucks."

Every confidence man's dream. "Not quite. She has an agent now—Melvin Birdman. He sent us to the opera tonight to set tongues wagging among the high society types."

Ambrose swallowed a mouthful of beer. "You will be paying to have my evening suit cleaned, by the way."

"I had no choice but to borrow it. There wasn't time to get one of my own."

"So, back to this manager swindle. Sounds like you'll have to split the profits with this Birdman character."

I swallowed more beer, then licked my lips. "Yes, but Birdman wants to turn her into a star. She's going to make buckets full of money."

"With you taking a cut, of course."

"Yep. Though I won't do this forever. As soon as she signs her first big check, I'm cashing out and heading back to Boston."

"I like this." Ambrose smoothed his mustache with his fingers thoughtfully. "It's low risk. Coppers won't care, and there's likely hundreds of singers and actresses out there hoping for a big break. You're not doing anything grossly immoral or illegal, merely playing into their ignorance."

"Exactly," I said, though I didn't like that Ambrose would consider Josie ignorant.

"How many other times have you run this scheme?"

"Never. Josie is the first."

The light in Ambrose's eyes dimmed, his smile falling. "I don't understand. You're not making any money yet and this is the first time you've tried it. How do you know it'll work?"

"Talked to other guys in Boston."

"Who?"

We knew most of the same people, so I had to lie. "No one you'd know. Guy passing through town."

"Ah." He lifted his glass in a toast. "I wish you much success, friend."

"Thank you." I touched my glass to his. "Tell me about Saratoga."

"Not much to tell. My cart tipped over one afternoon and spilled most of the damn elixir all over the place. I only sold about a quarter of what I had."

"That's bad luck. What was in it?"

"Wine laced with a little bit of cocaine. The ladies are especially fond of it."

"I bet."

Ambrose took a long drink from his glass, studying me the whole time. When he finished he asked, "Sooo . . . Josie. Are you telling me nothing romantic is going on between you and this girl?"

Flashes of the park and the opera went through my mind.

What if I wish to take advantage of you?

Perhaps I'll be the one to corrupt you, tomcat.

It's nice having a tomcat around for moments like this.

Ambrose rapped his knuckles on the wooden table. "Hello? Leo? Are you planning to answer?"

"Sorry," I mumbled. "We've agreed to keep our relationship professional."

"Oh, I see. This means that there has been discussion regarding propriety. Interesting."

"It's nothing sordid. She calls me a tomcat. She thinks I'm out chasing pussy half the time."

"And aren't you?"

"Fuck off," I said, shoving the table a bit in his direction. "I don't have the time or money for that. And don't act like you're a choirboy."

"I know I'm a scoundrel. Never claimed otherwise." Ambrose pulled out his gold pocket watch and checked the time. "You know, there is a little house not far from here where the girls—"

"No," I said quickly. His lips twisted in apparent amusement and I realized my mistake. "It's not because I have feelings for her, Ambrose. I can't afford it."

"What if it's my treat?"

I stared at him, willing myself to say yes. Willing the knot of dread to leave my chest. I should want to bed another woman tonight. After all, I hadn't been with one since I ran from O'Toole back in Boston. Shouldn't I have the itch to find release with a partner?

Say yes. There are thousands of women in this city. Say yes.

Why wouldn't the words leave my lips?

Because I could still remember.

I could still remember what it was like to kiss Josie, those little noises she made when I sank my teeth in her skin. The hitch in her breath when I pulled her closer. I haven't forgotten the sweet smell of her soap or the taste of her mouth.

My thoughts were a tangled mess when it came to this woman. I wanted to protect her and ravish her and use her all at the same time. My cock twitched whenever she brushed against me, which turned any carriage ride into pure torture. And worst of all, I was staying with her in that tiny apartment, listening to her, surrounded by her. I never wanted to leave her side.

Yet I couldn't soften toward Josie. I had to see this Pendelton scheme through. There was no alternative and I'd come too far already.

The seventh rule of being a confidence man: never change for a woman.

I opened my mouth to agree to a night of debauchery . . . then promptly closed it.

Shit. My shoulders sank and I heaved out a sigh. Some tomcat.

"Oh, my goodness," Ambrose drawled, his voice threaded with false sympathy. "It's as I thought. Smitten."

"Fuck off," I repeated, finishing my drink. The hops and the barley weren't enough to wash the taste of disappointment out of my mouth. "Buy me another beer and let's talk about something else."

Chapter Fourteen

JOSIE

When I emerged from the bedroom the next morning, I found Ambrose stretched out on the sofa, asleep, with Leo in a chair, his upper half folded over on the kitchen table. He looked uncomfortable and I told myself I didn't care.

They were fortunate that I unlocked the door an hour or so after they left. As suspicious as I was of Leo, I still didn't want him sleeping on the street. Or worse.

As I completed my morning ablutions in the washroom, I avoided looking in the mirror. I knew without checking that I looked tired. I hadn't slept much, my thoughts running like a freight train all night. Ambrose's arrival and their subsequent discussion illustrated one point very clearly: I was right to be suspicious of Leo.

You know the rules.

Yes, but you've never brought in a woman before.

The exchange meant something. The phrasing was odd, a special conversation only Leo and Ambrose understood. But I could feel its importance, like there was a message I should heed in there. I merely needed more time to figure it out.

My instinct had been to push them away, let them go elsewhere while I used the quiet to think. Because when Leo was in the vicinity, my brain turned to mush.

Unfortunately, I hadn't come to any resolution. The confusion and uncertainty were still plaguing me this morning. The only person who could provide answers—Leo—was unlikely to tell me the truth.

I returned to Ambrose's apartment and began fixing my breakfast. I didn't care if I woke them or not. I was here in this city for me—and only me.

"Christ, Josie," Leo grumbled. Out of the corner of my eye, I saw him slowly sit up, then wince. "Ow."

I will not feel bad for him.

I hated to notice the dark whiskers kissing his strong jaw, the rumpled hair. Had a woman run her fingers through those strands last night? I bet he and Ambrose had a grand time out in the city, laughing and drinking with several ladies.

You are wanted. You are beautiful. Never doubt it for a single second in my presence.

I'd believed those words, felt them deep in my bones. Did he say such things to all the women he kissed . . . or only me?

"Have a nice night, tomcat?" I asked.

"No, for your information." Leo yawned and stretched, a hand reaching to clutch his lower back. "I was worried about you."

"Me?"

"You locked us out, Josie."

I lifted a shoulder with more nonchalance than I felt. "Sometimes a girl has to do what a girl has to do, Leo."

"What on earth does that mean?"

I spread a tiny bit of marmalade on a slice of bread and avoided looking at him. "It means I have to look out for myself, not worry over your hurt feelings."

Ambrose's rough voice sounded from the direction of the sofa. "I do wonder if y'all wouldn't mind carrying on this scintillating conversation in another location?"

"Shut it," Leo grumbled. "I slept in a chair last night, so you have no right to complain."

"And as I have stated many times, this is my apartment."

A knock sounded on the door. Ambrose groaned and called out, "Just who in the blue blazes is that at this ungodly hour?"

Leo rose to see who was there. It was Sticks, a newspaper in his hand. "Morning," the boy said and came in, walking toward me. "Thought you might want to see the early papers. You made an impression at that fancy opera."

My breath caught as I took the newsprint from his hand. "Me? In the newspaper?"

"It's you all right."

I went to the table and spread the paper on the wooden surface. Leo was beside me, peering over my shoulder. "What page?" he asked.

The young boy was pouring himself coffee. "Inside somewhere. Keep flipping, genius."

I devoured the letters on each page, searching. When I reached the third to the last page, the headline jumped out.

MYSTERIOUS FRENCH SINGER DAZZLES DIAMOND HORSESHOE AT MET OPERA HOUSE

Gasping, I reached to clutch Leo's arm. No idea why, but I needed to touch him, to anchor myself as I read the story in my head. Leo began reading as well, vocalizing the words to the room:

"The Gotham elite lined up to meet Miss Joséphine Smith during the intermissions of last night's performance of Goldmark's *Merlin* at the Metropolitan Opera House. The French beauty, accompanied by her manager, smiled and nodded, maintaining a regal presence in the effort of the preservation of her voice. Miss Smith is reportedly in talks with several Broadway producers, who are keen for this international celebrité to helm their latest projects."

"I can't believe it," I said, turning to him. "That's me. They called me a beauty. Regal. A celebrité."

"Because it's true," Leo said quietly, and butterflies erupted behind my ribs.

"But y'all have forgotten an important flaw," Ambrose said on his way to the stove. "What happens when she opens her mouth and that dreadful Boston accent comes out?"

"That's a good point," Sticks said after a sip of coffee.

"Don't worry. No one expects you to speak French," Leo said reassuringly, probably in reaction to the panic on my face. "Stop scaring her, you two."

Ambrose leaned against the counter and stared down at Sticks. "And just who are you and why are you in my apartment?"

"I live down the street. I'm friends with Josie."

"That's Sticks," Leo told his friend. "Leave him alone."

Ignoring them, I read the newspaper mention once more. Now that I thought about it, Melvin never said I was French. He told them I had performed in France. I'd be fine.

I could do this. Probably.

Persona, remember?

"So, what?" Ambrose asked me. "You're a Boston singer who went to live in Paris? A bit boring, if you ask me."

"I'd rather be boring than a liar," I said. "It was awful not being able to speak at the opera, having people think I'm famous."

"You have to maintain the ruse." Leo pointed to the newspaper. "We must stick to Melvin's story."

"I know, but I don't like lying. It doesn't come as easy to me as it does to you, apparently." I met his eye squarely, not hiding the mistrust building in my gut toward him, and the moment stretched. His jaw grew tighter and tighter, the lines around his mouth deepening. He wanted to argue, to press me on last night, but we weren't alone, thankfully.

"Am I sensing trouble?" Sticks said. "Let me guess? You found out why he hopped an uptown streetcar the other day."

"He went walking around," I said, repeating what Leo had told me.

Both Sticks and Ambrose snorted. "And you believed that?" Sticks asked, shaking his head as if disappointed in me.

Leo pinned the young boy with a hard glare. "You followed me."

Sticks shrugged his small shoulders. "Not the whole way. I know you went uptown. Is that where your ladybird lives?"

Leo continued to stare daggers at Sticks. "Like she said, I went out to explore the city."

Doubt swirled in my head. Had Leo been merely exploring that day—and night? For more than eight hours? That was a long time to "explore."

I caught a glimpse of Ambrose out of the corner of my eye. He was studying Leo, his expression suspicious. It set off more warning bells inside my brain.

What wasn't Leo saying?

I needed to get an answer. "I don't want lies or evasions. If you want me to trust you, then tell me where you went."

Leo held up his hands, as if he had nothing to hide. "I told you. I was walking around, reacquainting myself with the city."

No one else in the room appeared to believe it, so I pressed. "You didn't stop or talk to anyone else once?"

He huffed and shifted on his feet, his attention on the far wall. I could tell the wheels were turning in his head, evaluating, thinking, but I wanted the plain, unvarnished truth.

My stomach tightened in anticipation of bad news. "Leo, where did you go?" He locked eyes with mine and I could see the hesitation in his blue depths. I wouldn't budge, however. "Trust, remember?"

Throwing up his hands, he said, "I went to the house where my father used to work."

"The Fifth Avenue mansion?"

"Yes." Then he turned to sneer at Sticks. "Satisfied?"

Sticks shrugged, while Ambrose drawled, "Pendeltons? Interesting. I hadn't realized you were still acquainted, Leo."

"I went to see the gardens in the back. For old times' sake.

After that I stopped for a drink and supper, then I came back here."

That was it? Why hadn't he wished for anyone to know?

"Oh, yeah." Sticks snapped his fingers, then pointed at me and Leo. "There's a carriage out front waiting on the two of you. Some bird guy uptown wants to see you."

"Bird*man*? As in Melvin Birdman?" When the boy nodded, I let out a strangled noise of surprise and confusion. "When were you going to tell us?"

"After I had a cup of coffee," the boy replied. "What's the rush?"

I didn't know how to respond to such a question, so I faced Leo. "There's no need for you to come along. I'm fine traveling uptown by myself, seeing as how you aren't ready."

Leo's right eye twitched ever so slightly, then he began closing the distance between us. I couldn't look away. He was sleepy and disheveled, with no collar or necktie, and his shirt was open at the throat. His undergarment peeked out, as well as the hair on his chest, and I found the intimate display of manliness both tantalizing and fascinating.

I suddenly longed to touch him there . . . and discover what other secrets he might be hiding under his clothing.

Heart thumping hard in my chest, I pressed my lips together and held on tightly to the back of the chair. I couldn't allow myself to do anything foolish.

Now at my side, he leaned down, his voice soft yet determined. "I know you're annoyed with me, but under no circumstances am I turning you loose on the streets of New York City. Give me a few moments and I'll escort you."

As he turned and walked out into the hall, I released the breath I'd been holding. I didn't care for the warmth in the pit of my stomach or the heaviness of my breasts. Memories of that kiss at the opera came flooding back, and I wanted *more*. More kisses. More sweet words. Even with all the uncertainty between us.

He was like an itch under my skin that I couldn't scratch.

Pull yourself together, Josie.

As I shoved a bite of bread into my mouth, my gaze locked with Ambrose's—and he was watching me with a thoughtful expression I didn't much care for. The edges of his lips hitched slightly. "I've decided to let you and Leo have the apartment," he said. "There's a friend I can stay with for a few weeks."

I paused midchew. "That isn't necessary. This is your place. We can find somewhere else to go."

"Absolutely not. I won't hear of it. Besides"—he gave me a wink—"this friend is of the female variety. It gives me a good excuse to spend time with her."

"Oh, I see." I supposed that made sense. But after the kiss at the opera, was it wise for Leo and me to be alone here?

Swallowing, I cast a quick glance at the bedroom door. My toes curled inside my leather boots.

Ambrose rose off the sofa, stretching his long arms. "Don't worry, Josie. I'll be gone by the time you and Leo return from your errand."

Precisely what I was worried about.

LEO

"Miss Smith! Finally, you're here!"

Melvin's booming voice greeted us as Josie and I entered the Herald Square Theatre. The interior was everything one would expect from a Broadway house. Rows and rows of seats, a stage, and gold fixtures in abundance. The current production, *The Heart of Maryland*, starred the legendary Mrs. Leslie Carter and Maurice Barrymore. I had no idea why Melvin had us brought here this morning, but I trailed Josie down the aisle toward Melvin and another gentleman.

Josie shook Melvin's hand. "Good morning, Mr. Birdman. I apologize for taking so long."

"I understand. Have a wife at home myself. I know you ladies prefer to take your time in the mornings."

"Actually," Josie said with a tilt of her head in my direction, "it was Mr. Hardy who delayed us today."

I nearly rolled my eyes. Patience wasn't Josie's strong suit. "Mr. Birdman." I stuck out my hand. "My apologies."

"Don't worry, young man. Save your apologies for your sweetheart and your priest. May I introduce Mr. David Belasco?" He gestured toward the man at his side. "David, this is Miss Smith and her manager, Mr. Hardy."

In a somber dark suit, Belasco had unruly hair atop his head and serious eyes. "A pleasure to meet you both," he said flatly.

"Mr. Belasco is the writer, producer, and director of the play being staged here."

No doubt the surprise on my face matched the stunned expression on Josie's. "It's an honor, sir," I said.

Belasco nodded once to acknowledge the compliment. "Why are we here, Melvin?"

"I wanted for you to meet my newest acquisition. Miss Smith is a talented young actress and singer."

"And?" Belasco asked, his expression nonplussed.

"Shall we sit?" Melvin gestured to the theater seats. "Then we may be more comfortable."

Belasco remained standing, while Birdman and I took seats on either side of Josie. Belasco waved his hand impatiently. "Get on with it, Melvin."

Birdman propped his elbows on the armrests and steepled his fingers. "I've heard rumors Mrs. Carter may depart this production. You are undoubtedly exploring other actresses to replace her and I would like you to consider Miss Smith."

"Don't be ridiculous." Belasco held up his palms. "No offense, Miss Smith, but this is a leading Broadway role. Leslie is one of the biggest stars in the country, perhaps the world. You cannot possibly think to suggest an ingenue in here to replace her, Melvin. The show would close in days."

"You're wrong," Melvin said. "You need someone who is bold. Fearless. A woman with the gravitas to swing in a bell tower thirty-five feet off the stage while wearing a tremendous wig. Miss Smith is precisely that woman."

"You are aware that we must sell tickets, enough to fill this place eight shows a week. I don't need bold and fearless. I need a name." Belasco smiled tightly at Josie. "Again, no offense intended."

"Once you hear her sing, you'll see precisely why I am so keen on her for Mrs. Carter's replacement."

"The part has no singing," Belasco said. "And you're wasting my time."

I agreed with Belasco. This was a waste of time and demeaning to Josie.

Before I could put an end to this meeting, Josie spoke up. "Would anyone care to hear what I think?"

Melvin grinned widely. "Of course, Miss Smith. Pray tell us what you think."

"I would like to sing," she said. Belasco rolled his eyes, but Josie continued on, undeterred. "Not for the role. I agree with Mr. Belasco; I'm not the best actress to replace Mrs. Carter. However, I would like to sing one song on a real Broadway stage. Who knows when I may ever have the opportunity again?"

Belasco appeared taken aback, his expression awash in surprise. "A respectable desire, as it's a lovely theater and the acoustics are perfect. Unfortunately, I cannot offer an accompanist as all the musicians arrive much later in the day."

"I can play." Melvin stood up. "It's been a few years, but I still remember the white keys from the black keys. Shall we, Miss Smith?" He offered his arm to Josie.

Carefully, he led her up onto the stage and two stagehands

rolled a piano out at Belasco's request. Belasco dropped into the seat next to me, and we watched Josie and Melvin discuss which song to perform. The producer's leg began to bounce impatiently. Worried he might leave, I called out, "Do the first one you sang for Lotta!"

Josie nodded and whispered to Melvin, who took his place at the piano. At Melvin's direction, Josie ran through a series of scales to warm up her voice, something I hadn't heard her do before. It made sense, however. Her voice was a tool, one that must be cared for and maintained.

Once she was ready, she nodded at Melvin. The producer began playing and when the first note left Josie's mouth, Belasco's leg stilled. As she started singing, she had his full attention and I could barely keep from grinning. The sound bounced off the walls and the floor, the theater enhancing the volume until we were surrounded, drowning in this lively and gorgeous performance.

Enthralled, I couldn't look away. Her voice sank deep in my chest and I *felt* the music, like she was touching my soul. I couldn't describe it, but Josie had the power to make one forget everything else except the notes coming out of her mouth. Fucking hell, she was good.

I'm obsessed with her.

"She's very good," Belasco murmured, echoing my thoughts.

"I know." I paused, then asked, "Are you reconsidering your rejection of her for Mrs. Carter's replacement? You should. Josie is going to be famous one day." Belasco grunted, so I pressed. "You can say you discovered her. They'll give you the credit, as they do with the other actors you've helped to shine. They'll speak of your brilliance, your acumen. It will only cement your status as a legend of Broadway."

The hint of a smile emerged on Belasco's face and he shook his head. "You're clever and I respect the attempt. But I'm a playwright at heart, not a song and dance man. Nevertheless, she is talented. I think you'll have no trouble whatsoever in finding her a lead role."

I hoped so. Josie deserved it.

The song finished and Belasco quickly bade us all goodbye. I could see Josie's disappointment as the famous writer/director left the theater, so I hurried to reassure her. "He was impressed."

"Really?" She perked up a bit. "What did he say?"

"That you were very good and will easily land a leading role somewhere."

"Thank goodness," she breathed and put a hand on her stomach as if to settle it. "He was like a brick wall. I couldn't tell what he was thinking."

Strangely pleased, Melvin checked his pocket watch for the time. "Incidentally, we never cared if Belasco liked you or not."

"We didn't?" Josie blinked. "Why not?"

Today's purpose suddenly clicked into place in my head. Good god. It was so obvious.

Melvin was a swindler after my own heart.

Chuckling, I explained it to Josie, "Mr. Birdman knew you'd never be granted the part, but word will get around that you've auditioned. Everyone will start wondering about you, wondering why Belasco considered you for such a prestigious role."

"Precisely," Melvin said as he tucked his pocket watch into his vest pocket. "This is part of building up your name, dear girl. All Broadway is able to talk about these days is who will replace Mrs. Carter. Getting you in the soup was important, and a nice bonus is earning Belasco's respect. He's well regarded around town and his opinion carries considerable weight."

Josie bit her lip. "I don't understand this city at all."

Melvin took her arm and began leading her up the aisle toward the exit. "That's perfectly all right because I understand it. And I'm going to help you succeed here."

I shoved my hands into my pockets and followed them, barely able to conceal a grin. Josie might not understand how to play games such as this, but I did. I've been running schemes since I was a boy, using my wits to earn money. What Melvin did wasn't much different . . . and it was entirely legal.

I had to respect it.

Maybe in a different life I could've tried a new vocation, one like Melvin's. But now I was committed to this Pendelton scheme and there was no backing out of it. I would deal with the repercussions down the road, even if it meant disappearing.

Even if it meant Josie hated me.

A heavy weight settled in my stomach. Undoubtedly she would hate me, but she would end up an heiress or famous as a near heiress. Then she could use that notoriety to pack theaters from Broadway to Birmingham. In both cases she would be wildly wealthy.

So why wouldn't that weight leave my stomach?

Lies are nothing to be proud of, Leo.

She wanted honesty and trust between us as we grew closer, and it was increasingly hard to hide my true intentions. For half a second this morning, as I stared into her green eyes, I'd considered coming clean. Lying came easy to me—except to Josie, apparently. When it came to her, my conscience had decided to make an inopportune appearance.

I had to ignore it and remain strong. Josie would never agree to trick the Pendelton family, and if she learned of what I was doing, she'd never speak to me again. I'd go back to bunco on the Boston streets, the small schemes and evading O'Toole. Keeping the family afloat by the thinnest of margins.

No, I had to see this through, even if it ate me up inside.

Josie stopped on the walk under the marquee. "Thank you for everything, Mr. Birdman."

After giving her a list of things to accomplish today, Melvin took Josie's gloved hand and kissed it. "Let the driver help you into your carriage. I must speak with Leo for a moment."

Josie's gaze flicked between me and Melvin, then she nodded. "See you soon, Mr. Birdman."

When she was in the carriage, Melvin faced me and tilted his head toward the street. "Walk with me a bit, Hardy."

I kept my face impassive as we started up the walk. It was obvious that whatever Melvin wished to say was not good news, and in situations such as this, it was generally better to remain quiet and let it play out.

"She did well last night," Melvin eventually said. "You, too, from what I understand."

"Thank you."

Sighing, he stopped and slipped his hands into his trouser pockets. "Leo, I've been doing this a long time and I'm not fond of surprises. Generally, I find it's best to know who I'm working with." He paused and stared at me. "I did some digging with a friend in Boston."

Shit. Though my muscles went on alert, I forced myself to relax and appear unbothered. "Oh?"

He waited for me to say more, his sharp eyes assessing my face. I stood five or six inches taller than Melvin, but right now it felt like he towered over me. I tried not to squirm. *Confidence, Leo.*

Melvin continued. "You have quite a reputation with the law."

With no idea how much he'd learned about me, I adopted a sheepish smile and leaned in like we shared a secret. "I was a bit of a rascal in my younger days."

"From what I understand, it wasn't only in your youth."

Damn those chatty roundsmen. "Is a man not allowed to change?"

"Yes, of course. But I get nervous when I hear that a small-time confidence man has appeared on my doorstep, acting as a manager for the very first time. Are you truly trying to help her—or just help yourself?"

"You heard her sing. She's a true talent."

An evasion—and we both knew it. Melvin pressed me, saying, "I want your word that you have only her best interests at heart."

I held his gaze steady and gathered up every bit of my experience as a practiced liar. "I give you my word that I have Josie's best interests at heart."

He watched me carefully, then nodded once. "Good. See that it stays that way." He offered his hand and I shook it. Then he added, "I gave her a list of tasks for the day. See they're all completed, will you? That girl is going to be a star before we know it."

I promised him we'd see to the errands, then headed to the carriage.

I hadn't lied. I did have Josie's best interests at heart.

But I also had *my* best interests at heart, as well as my mother's and sisters' interests. And those were the ones that mattered most.

Chapter Fifteen

JOSIE

Leo and I spent the next few hours on errands as dictated by Melvin. At the dressmaker I was measured and inspected, poked and prodded for much longer than was comfortable. Then I sat for a photographer, which felt interminable, with different poses and expressions. Finally, Leo and I stopped for a late luncheon at a small hotel restaurant, also paid for by Melvin.

After we ordered and our meals arrived, an easy silence fell between us. I sipped my tea and looked around, marveling at the fancy women dining here. I couldn't wait to be independent and wealthy, able to travel about luxuriously and perform. Where everyone recognized me. Like Lotta.

Except Leo seemed to be receiving most of the attention during our lunch. The ladies lunching in the vicinity of our table were admiring him quite openly. He was the youngest man here and definitely the best looking, but that didn't give them the right to ogle him, especially while I was sitting with him. I directed a pointed glare at our neighbor—and she looked away guiltily.

"What has you frowning?" Leo asked as he added a splash of cream to his tea.

"Do you not even notice anymore?"

One eyebrow shot up. "Notice what?"

I leaned in and lowered my voice. "The women staring at you."

The edges of his mouth twisted into a boyish grin, and his handsomeness struck me like an arrow to the gut. "Jealous?"

"No—and answer the question."

"I don't believe you."

With a huff, I sat back and looked away. "Forget it."

"Come now, I'm teasing. And the answer is I try to ignore it for the most part."

"Why?"

He lifted his broad shoulders in a tiny shrug. "Because it's just a face. I didn't earn it."

"But you said 'for the most part.' That implies there are times when you don't ignore the attention."

"Yes, when I use it to get what I want."

"A woman to warm your bed, you mean."

He set his silver spoon on the table carefully, lining it up with the other flatware. "Or a woman from whom I need a favor."

"Like Lotta. And Martha." I remembered the intimate way he'd smiled at them, like he knew a wicked secret. Part of me wished he would smile at me that way.

I watched his lips hug the porcelain as he took a sip. Those lips were dangerous. I couldn't stop thinking about that kiss at the opera, the feel of him holding me, touching me. He was some kind of sorcerer with the ability to turn my bones to jelly.

Are you wet for me?

A tiny shiver worked its way down my spine. I didn't know if this was how all lovers spoke, so real and raw, but I liked it. And it made me realize that I knew next to nothing about his history. "Have you ever had a sweetheart?"

He blinked twice, teacup paused halfway to his mouth. "I don't have time for that sort of thing."

"What are you busy with? Your sales job?"

"Yes, as well as my family."

The five sisters and his mother. "Tell me about Ambrose."

"What would you like to know?"

"Let's begin with how you met and how long you've known him."

He looked down at the table, his fingers smoothing the white cloth carefully. "I've known him over ten years. We met through mutual friends in Boston growing up, and with similar interests we immediately hit it off."

"What similar interests?"

"You're asking a lot of questions today. Why the sudden curiosity?"

"Because I hardly know anything about you."

"Well, I don't know much about you, either," he grumbled. "But I'm not peppering you with a dozen questions about your past."

Why was he so surly? Did he never talk about himself with anyone? "You told me you were an open book."

"When on earth did I say that?"

"When we left Martha's. You said—"

"I get it." He waved his hand. "You don't need to recount the entire conversation. I told you my father died when I was young, right?" I nodded, so he continued. "Ambrose had no family, so the two of us were apprentices of a sort with a salesman around town."

"You weren't in school?"

Looking down, his eyes remained on the table. "There was no time for that. I had to earn money with my father out of the picture."

"That must've been hard."

"Life is hard, sweetheart." He lifted his head and focused on my face. "But you already know that."

Yes, I did. But I refused to be bitter about my past. I couldn't change it, and I was more interested in the future. "I could've had it worse. The nuns looked after Pippa and me. They were strict, but kind."

"You must've given them headaches," he said, his smile soft, almost affectionate. And it reached his eyes this time.

Butterflies erupted in my chest and for a second I almost forgot what we were talking about. Which was certainly strange.

That never happened to me. I cleared my throat and focused on the plate of food in front of me instead. "I didn't make it easy on them, that's for sure. 'Ladies do not argue, Josie. Ladies do not interrupt when a person is speaking, Josie,'" I mimicked. "They weren't sorry to see me go."

"The nuns sound a lot like my sisters," he muttered.

Though he sounded annoyed, I could tell he didn't mean it. Not when he'd worked since a young age to take care of them. "Tell me about them."

"Oh, you don't want to hear—"

"I do, I do. *Please*, Leo."

He inhaled a deep breath through his nose, then exhaled out his mouth. "Let's see. There's the oldest, Flora. She's a wild one. Carolyn is next and she's the most honest, trusting person I know. Hattie is in the middle, then Molly and Tess are the twins."

"Goodness. Your house must be loud."

"It is." He considered me, his pale blue eyes clear and bright. "They would most definitely like you."

"Why?"

"Because you're real and unpretentious. Unafraid of anything. And you never hesitate to take me to task."

I picked at my fried fish and tried not show how much his observations pleased me. No one had ever spoken so highly of me before. Except Pippa, maybe, but we were family. "I don't think Pippa would like you."

"Because I dragged you away to New York?"

"She doesn't trust handsome men."

"Aw, you think I'm handsome."

I ignored him. The man was well aware of his good looks. "*And* she worries that you're taking advantage of me."

Leaning in, he gave me a half grin. "You said in the park that you were going to take advantage of me."

That voice. It was his low seductive purr, the same one he used with Martha, and I didn't stand a chance. Flames licked my insides as heat raced to every part of my body. I struggled to breathe, the air in the room suddenly weighted with longing and desperation. I stared into his eyes, my brain trying to make sense of what was happening.

Was he flirting with me?

No, it couldn't be.

He'd been reluctant to kiss at the opera, not to mention he pulled away in Central Park. Leo didn't harbor those sorts of feelings for me.

You are wanted. You are beautiful. Never doubt it for a single second in my presence.

I assumed the words were hyperbole, meant to bolster my spirits before we ventured out into the opera box.

But what if they weren't?

I had to ask Pippa's opinion. She was the only person I trusted to tell it to me straight.

"I need to send a letter to my friend, Pippa," I blurted.

Leo sat back in his chair, his expression shuttering. "Sure. We can pick up materials today, if you like. What's the rush?"

I couldn't tell him the truth, that I needed advice about *him,* so I said, "I want to update her on Melvin and the Metropolitan Opera House. While it's still fresh in my mind."

"But I thought you never forgot anything."

This was why I hated lying. I could never fool a soul with the simplest of fibs. "True, but I promised to tell her I arrived safely. Otherwise, she's likely to come here and track me down. By the way, are you ever going to tell me what you and Ambrose were fighting about last night?"

Using his knife and fork, he cut a bite of chicken very carefully. "How much did you hear?"

"You're answering a question with another question again."

He took the time to chew and swallow the chicken before speaking. "He doesn't believe I'm truly your manager."

"Then what does he think we're doing together."

"Something inappropriate and unrelated to your singing career."

"That's ridiculous." I said the words quickly, loudly, as if to convince both him and myself that the idea was preposterous.

But was it?

What would've happened at the opera if the show hadn't started? And would those things have continued if Ambrose hadn't arrived?

Had Leo been flirting with me a moment ago?

Men were so confusing.

"Don't worry," Leo was saying. "I set him straight. And when he hears you sing, he'll understand."

He didn't say more, just concentrated on eating, but there were still too many unanswered questions rattling around in my brain. And he couldn't very well dodge the questions while trapped at lunch with me, could he? "Why did you go to where your father used to work? The Pendelton mansion?"

Annoyance flashed over his expression, a muscle jumping in his jaw. "Curiosity."

"About what?"

"Why does it matter?"

So prickly, which was entirely unlike Leo. Had I touched a nerve? "Question with a question once more. That's two in one conversation. Indeed, for a loquacious man, you are being exceedingly difficult over this."

"It was nothing. I wanted . . ." He exhaled and rubbed his eyes. "I *needed* to see everything my father worked so hard to accomplish. Those gardens are his legacy."

"And what did you discover?"

"Not as lush, but still beautiful. It made me feel, I don't know, connected to him in a tiny way. Seeing everything he'd planted still growing there, thriving? It's proof that he didn't fail, even though they let him go. I was proud of him again, and I haven't felt that way in a long time."

The emotion in his voice, sad and wistful, wound around my heart and squeezed. This was the real man underneath the fancy suit and slick words. The one who felt deeply and carried the responsibility for his family, the one who still hurt from losing his father.

I understood.

I longed for a similar connection to my lost family, a place where I belonged. A sense of *roots*. The asylum had been a building in which to live, but it wasn't a home. I didn't care if I ever went back there.

But Leo had this marvelous memorial of his father, tangible evidence of the care and love his father had provided to the world. He must've been a wonderful, remarkable man.

"Does that make any sense?" Leo asked, looking up from his plate.

"Perfect sense." He didn't say anything more, but the haunted expression remained. It tore me up inside, so I blurted, "Will you take me there?"

Startled, he rocked back in his chair slightly. "Where?"

"To see the gardens."

"Why?"

Because I want to learn about you. Because I want to see more of the real you.

I couldn't tell him as much, so I lifted a shoulder. "Why not? It'll be fun."

"It's just a bunch of flowers and plants, Josie."

"No, it's not. As you said, it's your father's legacy. Show me what he worked so hard to create, what he lost when he was let go."

I could tell Leo didn't care for the idea. A war raged behind that bright gaze, now gray with his thoughts. He studied my face as if searching for a weakness, an opening upon which to refuse my request. "They might not let us in," he tried. "And it's a long way uptown."

"We have the time *and* we have Melvin's carriage for the day.

It's the perfect opportunity for such an excursion. If they don't let us in, who cares?"

"Josie . . ."

He sighed heavily and I could feel him wavering. *"Please,* Leo." I put as much feeling as I could muster behind those two words.

His mouth curved, as if I'd pleased him, while his hooded blue gaze burned across the table from me. The moment stretched and I felt both heavy and light at the same time. Cold and sweaty. Dizzy, but unable to move.

Abruptly, he pushed his plate away and signaled for the waiter. "Let's go."

LEO

I stared at the Pendelton mansion, a silent Josie by my side. I tried to see it as she did in the dying afternoon light, with the peeling paint, chips, and stains. The once grand structure, though still imposing, had fallen into disrepair.

According to Georgie, the Pendeltons had trouble keeping good help around. Looking at the mansion, I wasn't surprised. The family's knack for destruction was unsurprising to me. My chest ached with what might've been, the future of which our family had been robbed.

Josie sighed and folded her hands. "I bet it was beautiful once, back in the day."

"Yeah, it was."

"Come on. Let's go around back."

Grabbing my elbow, she towed me across the street. When we reached the other side, I led her to the garden entrance. I slid open the latch and held the gate for Josie to pass through, then followed her inside.

"It's nice," she said, looking around.

"They've pared it down quite a bit over the years. When my father was here, the place was overflowing with greenery and blooms. Here, let's walk." I took her arm again and we stepped onto the path.

"Did your father plant all these trees and bushes?"

"A lot of them, yes. The original landscape designer outlined the entire space, then my father was hired. He was here a few years before becoming head gardener. After he took over, he worked closely with Mrs. Pendelton and Mr. Olmstead to enhance the gardens. But this is a fraction of what the space used to look like."

Lifting her skirts, Josie stepped over a fallen branch. "You spent a lot of time here."

"I did. I loved coming to work with him. My favorite part was the fish pond. It's gone now."

We continued around the path, and I pointed out all the things I remembered. I told stories about my childhood, about the games I invented and the adventures I undertook.

"It sounds lovely," she finally said. "And you spent a lot of time around your father. Most children aren't so fortunate. It's an extraordinary gift you were given."

I supposed that was true. I never thought of it in such a way, but then of course Josie would, seeing as how she'd never had a family of her own.

I guided her to the left. "Come this way. I want to show you something."

She didn't argue but asked, "What is it?"

"Hush, it's a surprise."

We wound along the path, past boxwoods and small trees, toward the rear of the property. Then, through a clearing, it came into view.

This had been my favorite spot as a child. Something told me Josie would love it just as much.

Josie sucked in a sharp breath. "Sakes alive, it's a tiny replica of the main house."

"It's the carriage house," I said as we approached the two-story Gothic building. "A replica of the main house down to the tiniest detail. The stables are directly behind it."

Like the main building it was modeled after, the carriage house was in disrepair, dirty and surrounded by weeds. Cracked stone and peeling paint. It felt forgotten back here, uncared for and unloved. For some reason this saddened me more than anything else.

"It is adorable, like a doll's house," Josie said as we stopped to take it in. "I bet it was your favorite place as a boy."

A small smile broke free. "Indeed, it was. I hid on the second floor and watched the grooms and horses for hours."

"Let's go in."

"We can't. The grooms will—"

Josie started toward the carriage house, not bothering to wait for me. It took me a second to recover before I hurried after her. "Hey, wait up!"

She didn't slow in the slightest, her shoulders back like she had the right to be here. Like she owned the place.

Except I preferred not to encounter anyone, if at all possible. They would ask questions that I didn't care to answer, especially in front of her. "Josie!"

Damn, it was too late. She was already inside.

I darted through the door, hoping to find the carriage house empty.

It wasn't. Three men sat around a stump, playing cards. One of them was Georgie, the head gardener, and they all gaped at Josie.

"Afternoon, miss," one of the men said, standing. "May we help you?"

"Afternoon, sirs," she said. "We're looking around at your magnificent gardens. Is one of you responsible?"

"I'm the head gardener, miss," Georgie said as he rose. His gaze shifted to me as I stepped closer. "Oh, it's you again. Youngblood, wasn't it?"

"Good memory." I tipped my hat. "Yes, sir, that's me."

Josie's face registered her confusion, but she didn't contradict my lie.

The oldest man frowned at us. "You folks can't wander about here. This is private property." He was older, probably in his early sixties, with graying sand-colored hair. Was he a groom?

"It's all right," Georgie said to the other men. "His father used to work here."

"I don't remember no Youngblood," the older groom said. "And I've been here nearly twenty-five years."

Before I could stop her, Josie blurted, "What about a Hardy?"

I held my breath. Maybe he wouldn't remember.

He stilled, then his gaze swung to me. Recognition dawned in his expression and my stomach dropped. "You're Steven's boy?" he asked.

Shit. I hadn't wanted anyone here to know my real name or my connection to the place.

With no choice but to admit it, I nodded once.

"Well, now." The man looked me over. "Leopold, wasn't it?"

I couldn't recall this man specifically—there'd been countless workers on the estate in those days—but I must've met him at some point. "Yes, sir. Good memory."

"I thought you said your name was Robbie," Georgie said, eyebrows pinched in confusion as all three men retook their seats.

"Robbie is my middle name," I answered smoothly. "Robbie Youngblood is what I use in my professional life."

"Ah." The confusion left Georgie's face. "He's a manager on Broadway," the gardener explained to the other men.

The old groom's eyebrows rose at this news. "You trailed after your father everywhere in those days, a little wee sprite running about. I'm Freddie, though you probably don't remember me. How's your father these days?"

"He's dead." My voice was flat, unemotional.

"Sorry to hear that, son."

A lump lodged in my throat, bad memories sitting in my stomach like spoiled milk. I looked at Josie. "Ready to go?"

"No, not yet," she said absently, then asked the groom, "Are you the only staff member from that time still working here?"

"Yes, miss, I am. The others were all let go either directly after the episode or within a few years."

"The episode?"

"The missing little girl. You know, the kidnapped heiress." He scratched his jaw. "I thought the whole world knew about that."

"Why the difference in time," Josie asked, "in letting the staff go?"

"Josie," I said quietly, not wanting to dredge up the past. It was bad enough standing here.

"No, wait, Leo. I'm curious. Why let some of the staff stay, only to sack them later?"

The groom tilted his head toward the mansion. "After a while the police weren't making progress, so the family hired a Pinkerton. The investigator uncovered new details and Hardy was sacked as a result a couple years after the kidnapping."

That got my attention. I frowned at the older man. "What new details?"

"I couldn't say. Your father wouldn't tell us nothing, other than it weren't true."

Wasn't true? New information? I hadn't heard about this.

Josie flicked a glance at me, then returned her attention to Freddie. "But you never heard what he discovered?"

"Well, now." He shifted on his feet. "There were rumors, but they're not exactly fit for a lady's ears."

I blinked several times, sure I misheard. "What does this mean? What are you implying?"

"You can say it in front of me," Josie encouraged. "I'm no Fifth Avenue princess. I've heard it all. So, what were the rumors?"

Freddie shook his head. "I'm the epitome of a God-fearing man," he said, though he mispronounced *epitome*, rhyming it with "home." "And I don't like to speak ill of the dead. That poor little girl was never found, and there's no use trying to blame anyone for it now."

Disbelief and anger poured through me, so much so that my muscles began shaking. Had the Pinkerton insinuated my father was involved in the kidnapping? It was patently absurd. I *knew* my father. He'd loved working here, had taken pride in every square inch, and the man hadn't a nefarious or cruel bone in his body. As a boy, I took an apple off a cart without paying and when my father learned of it, he marched me back there the next day and forced me to apologize to the owner, as well as pay for the apple from my own savings.

Under no circumstances would he participate in a kidnapping scheme for anyone, let alone a baby.

I swallowed the fury gripping my tongue. "My father would never have involved himself in something as terrible as kidnapping a little girl."

"Now, I'm not claiming he did." The groom put out his palms toward me. "I'm merely repeating what happened at the time."

"And this was why Steven Hardy was let go?" Josie asked.

"Yes, miss."

"Why weren't you fired?"

Freddie scratched the back of his neck at her question. "I don't rightly know. I kept my head down, I suppose. Did my work and never bothered no one."

I was hardly paying attention. The edges of the room wavered. I couldn't speak. Couldn't think. That anyone would even suspect my father was absolutely infuriating. What was this new evidence that revealed itself two years after the kidnapping?

Josie touched my arm. "Leo—"

The sound of hooves and carriage wheels thundered nearby, drawing closer. The men in the carriage house began scrambling to clean up the evidence of their card game.

The younger groom waved us toward the back. "You two can't

be here when the mister comes in. Hide in one of those side rooms until he goes inside."

The mister? Did he mean Mr. Pendelton? Good. I had a thing or two to say to that man. How dare the Pendeltons think my father capable of such a heinous act? I straightened my cuffs, preparing for battle.

Josie grabbed my hand and tugged, but I didn't move. She tugged harder. "Come on, Leo. Let's get out of sight."

"No." I ground my back teeth together, frustration clawing at the nape of my neck. "I want to speak to him."

"Are you cracked? You can't do that. He'll have you arrested for trespassing."

I didn't care. I needed to set the record straight and clear my father's name.

"Go, go!" The grooms were waving for us to hide, while the sounds of a carriage thundered along the mews.

"Leo, look at me," Josie whispered. Then she was in front of me, her beautiful face all I could see. Her palm cupped my jaw and she stared into my eyes. "This is not the time. I promise, we'll fix this. But we can't do it now. You'll get these men in trouble. And we might get arrested."

Part of me wanted to stay and fight, but I supposed this made sense. I wasn't in the frame of mind to have a rational conversation with Mr. Pendelton. But I would soon.

Eighth rule of being a confidence man: keep a cool head at all times.

Numbly, I nodded and followed Josie to a side room. I heard her close the door behind us, but it was too dark to see anything inside. As soon as my eyes adjusted, I discovered a large sleigh, dusty and forgotten. I remembered this room from my time here as a boy. I would sit in the seat and pretend I was an explorer at the South Pole, driving the sleigh over frozen tundra.

Christ, I hadn't thought about that in years.

A small hand grabbed mine. "Climb in. We'll wait together until the coast is clear."

Chapter Sixteen

JOSIE

Never had Leo been so quiet.

As we sat in the sleigh together, he remained still and stiff. There was no life in him, his usual vibrant and charismatic personality buried under his shock. Not far away, horses snorted and stamped at the ground, the grooms shouting as they tried to calm the animals, but Leo was unmoving, a statue staring at the front of the sleigh.

I nibbled my lip and tried to think of what to say. I couldn't stomach his pain. I hated it. Could I bring Leo out of wherever he'd gone to in his head?

When I couldn't take the tension any longer, I said, "Leo, I'm sure he wasn't involved."

"Of course he wasn't involved." He let out a bitter chuckle. "Though I suppose this explains why he was sacked without notice and refused a reference."

"At least you know. It's unfair and horrible, but you have answers as to why he was let go."

"Except I don't." He rubbed his eyes with his fingers. "What did that Pinkerton uncover to point the finger in my father's direction?"

"Who knows? But it cannot be credible. Otherwise, he would've been arrested. It's probably just a rumor among gossip-loving servants." Leo still wouldn't look at me, the haunted glaze of his eyes trained downward. He appeared so lost, so hurt, and my heart squeezed. "I learned a long time ago that you can't rewrite the past. And you know he had nothing to do with the kidnapping."

His throat worked as he swallowed, then his voice turned rough. "After we moved to Boston, he just gave up. He was never the same, and it nearly destroyed our family. He drank himself to death, Josie."

Oh, no. For once, I had nothing to say.

The outcome was too terrible for platitudes, and I wasn't one for lies. "I'm so sorry."

"Thanks."

I've been jealous of people with families my entire life, envious of their relationships and shared history, wishing I had the same. But Leo proved this could also be a source of immense pain, something I hadn't truly considered before. Apparently, families were also complicated, tangled with heartbreak and tragedy.

My upbringing hadn't been perfect, but perhaps it wasn't all bad, either.

Seconds ticked by in awful silence. Leo was usually the one calming me down, helping me to focus when I was about to faint. Could I make him feel better?

What should I do? Hug him? Pippa was the only person I'd ever hugged, except Leo in the alley after we left Melvin's office.

Would he even want a hug?

Indecision gripped me, and I nibbled on my lip.

He sighed and angled toward me. "What is it? You're wringing your hands like an elderly aunt."

"I want to make you feel better, but I'm unsure how to do so."

His hands lifted to gently cup my face and his thumbs swept over my jaw. We stared at each other for a long moment. The room disappeared, and even in the dim light his eyes were captivating, burning with intensity. I couldn't tell what he was thinking, but at least he was here, focused on me instead of his father.

"You are making me feel better, merely by being here with me."

I could feel the surface of my skin heat at his compliment. "I can't see how. I hardly know what to say."

"There's no need to say anything. I like hearing you breathe next to me, the shift of your legs under your skirts. Feeling the warmth of your skin against me. You're so bright and beautiful, Josie, so *alive*. It's what comes through when you sing, this joy that you bring to the world around you."

This was what he thought of me? My bones turned to jelly, the fluttering in my chest like a swarm of bees. I couldn't comprehend it. No one had ever said such nice things to me before.

I had no words.

His thumbs continued to work their magic on my skin, sending tingles along my spine and down to my toes. "I want to kiss you right now," he murmured. "I want to kiss you and never stop."

My hopeful heart skipped in my chest. *Yes, yes, yes.* God, I wanted that, too. "What happened to keeping our relationship professional?"

The edge of his mouth curled wickedly. "I think that went out the window a long time ago, certainly before I almost devoured you at the opera."

"Yes, but I had to push you to devour me."

"Merely because I've been trying to do the right thing by you. But it's a lost cause. I want you too damn badly."

"You do?"

"Are you fucking kidding?" Hints of Boston crept into his deep voice, and it caused more fluttering in my chest. I liked knowing that I affected him, that I could uncover the real man underneath the polish. "I'm dying to touch you and make you come."

I appreciated this approach. Direct, no sugarcoating. It meant more somehow, especially coming from him. His honesty turned me reckless, and my desire clouded any sound judgment.

I began lifting my skirts.

With a tiny growl, Leo closed the distance between us and

pressed his lips to mine. Instantly, this kiss was different, with less exploration and far more hunger. Desperation exploded between us. It was like we picked up exactly where we left off at the opera, with deep, thorough kisses and his tongue wrapped around mine, flicking and rubbing. I moaned into his mouth, and he gave a groan of satisfaction deep in his chest, like he'd found something precious. Suddenly, I needed to hear him make that noise again every day for the rest of my life.

He broke off and his lips and teeth set to work on my neck. I sucked in deep breaths as sparks radiated through my core and settled between my legs, pulsing behind my clitoris. He bit me and I gasped, my hand yanking my skirts up past my knees. "Hurry," I whispered.

"Shh," he crooned, resting his forehead against my cheek as blunt fingers swept along my inner thigh. "I'm going to take such good care of you, sweetheart."

He found the part in my drawers and the rough pads of his fingers brushed my folds. I closed my eyes as a burst of pleasure coasted under my skin. "Goddamn," he said. "You are so wet for me. Just soaking. My poor girl."

His touch was frustratingly light at first as he explored. I worried for a moment that he was similar to the other men with whom I'd dallied—tentative and incapable of improving upon my own ministrations. But then . . . *Oh, thank god.* Leo's fingers grew more certain, firmer, concentrating on precisely where I needed him most. Dipping to my center, he spread my slickness up to my clitoris, where his fingers circled over the swollen nub. I swear, I saw stars.

How had I ever doubted him?

I closed my eyes and held on to his shoulders, and he bit my earlobe between his front teeth. "Do you ache inside? Want to feel my fingers there?"

I did feel empty, like I was craving his thickness and strength. Incapable of speech, I nodded, so he circled my entrance with a fingertip, then slowly pushed in. My back bowed at the delicious fullness. "Leo," I whined.

"I'm here. I've got you. Ride my hand, beautiful."

"I don't know what that means. I'm dying. Please, help me."

The scoundrel had the nerve to chuckle. "Rock your hips against my palm."

I tried it—and my eyes nearly rolled back in my head. Pleasure arrowed through my lower half, the friction exactly what I needed. "Oh god, Leo. Why does that feel so good?"

"Keep going. Don't stop until you finish."

I did it again, and the resulting wave of pleasure was the best reward, so I kept moving, churning my hips, surrounded by Leo's scent as he kissed me. The hard knot of flesh between my legs brushed across his palm, each scrape sending me higher and higher. I didn't want this to end. My body was chasing, climbing toward something monumental. A race I had no choice but to win.

He withdrew his finger and I gripped his shirtfront. "What are you doing?" I panted.

Easing away from me, he slid off the bench and knelt between my thighs. "Tasting you."

Now I was well and truly lost. "What does that mean?"

His eyes flicked to me as he angled my body slightly sideways. "No one has licked your pussy before?"

Licked my . . . ? "That's something you wish to do?"

"Yes." Opening my thighs as wide as they would go, he moved in and inhaled deeply right above my mound. Was he smelling me? He groaned, saying, "Trust me, sweetheart. I definitely wish to do this—and you do too. You just don't know it yet."

Without any other warning, before I could ask for more clarity, he pressed his mouth to my center and dragged his tongue through my folds. "Fuck, yes," he breathed.

It was like being jolted with an electric wire.

Then he did it again. And again. *Oh my god.*

I stared at the dark ceiling, awestruck, as his lips and tongue went to work on my intimate flesh with hot, open-mouth kisses. My mind couldn't comprehend it. All I could do was *feel*, my senses overwhelmed, sparks coursing through me. His tongue was divine, laving and swirling, and his lips ate at me like I was a delicacy. He knew precisely the spot I liked, and very quickly I was trembling, shaking as lust compounded inside me.

"Do you hate it?" he whispered, his voice seductive and raspy, like smoke. "Shall I stop?"

Chest heaving, I sucked in breath, and my fingers slid into his hair. I needed to hold on to something. "It's too good. I'm burning alive."

With a deep rumble in his chest, he doubled his efforts, using more pressure, and I squeezed my eyelids tight. My muscles coiled, readying, the only thoughts in my head a string of curse words and blasphemy the nuns would've scolded me for.

Oh shit.

Oh god.

Christ almighty.

Then Leo sucked on the little bud atop my sex—and I was thrown to the heavens, shot to the stars. Broken apart into a million pieces. My body convulsed, inner muscles clenching, as the orgasm went on and on, stronger than I'd ever dreamed possible. Leo didn't let up, his attentions continuing until I pushed him away, too sensitive to bear more.

"Holy smokes," I wheezed as the little aftershocks rolled through my loose limbs.

Eyes closed, I tried to gather my wits. This experience was like nothing I'd ever dreamed. He'd turned me inside out.

I felt Leo's forehead resting on my thigh and the glide of his warm palms over my stocking-clad legs. It was nice, this quiet affection, the care he showed after the fact. Finally, he straightened and I blinked several times before I could focus on him. His expression was taut, his skin flushed.

I said the first thing that came to mind. "Where did you learn that particular trick?"

He braced his forearms on my knees and licked his lips, which bore the evidence of my arousal. "Impressed you, have I?"

"Very much so."

His eyebrows lowered as he asked, "You've been with men before, yes?"

"Two."

Something passed over his face, but it was too fast for me to discern the reaction. Then he moved onto the bench next to me and slipped my legs onto his lap. "Then those two men failed you. Your pleasure should've been paramount, not theirs."

I hadn't missed the way he shifted the obvious erection in his trousers when he sat down. Curiosity scratched at my skin. "May I touch you?"

"I don't think it's a good idea." He cast a glance over his shoulder at the door. "We should go."

He started to slide away, but I put my hand on his arm. "Wait. Tell me why it isn't a good idea, because I very much want to do this for you."

"Why?"

"Nope. You answer first."

"Because I don't want you to feel obligated. I enjoyed pleasuring you and don't expect anything in return."

"But you told me you never do anything purely altruistic."

"When did I say that?"

"When we had ice cream back in Boston. The day we met."

Groaning through a low chuckle, he threw his head back. "Christ, you're impossible. Stop recalling everything I say during disagreements."

"I can't help it." I knew I sounded defensive, but I didn't like being criticized for something I couldn't control.

"Josie, I apologize. I meant it in jest." Reaching out, he clasped my face in his palms and pressed a soft kiss to my lips. He smelled like me. "You're perfect, dashed perfect. Don't let anyone ever convince you otherwise."

I put my hand on his chest. "Tell the truth for once. Do you want me to touch you?"

He exhaled heavily, still holding on to my face. "I've been dreaming about your hands on me since we kissed in the park."

Leo dreamed of me touching him?

With a newly acquired burst of confidence, I moved closer, then I slid my hand down to stroke the thick ridge over his clothing. Leo's eyelids fluttered closed and he sighed, almost in grateful relief. I wasn't an expert by any means, but I took this as an encouraging sign. "Let me, then."

"Are you sure?"

Yes. I was very, very sure.

Instead of answering, I reached to unfasten his trousers.

He watched, silent, as I peeled open the placket, then popped the tiny buttons of his undergarment one by one. I felt bold and adventurous, high on my recent climax, determined to give him more pleasure than he'd ever experienced.

"You're driving me out of my skull," he said softly. "Hurry, Josie."

I bit my lip to trap the smile threatening to burst free. I liked torturing Leo.

I soon freed his erection from his clothing. His cock was long and thick, as beautiful as the rest of him, and I gripped it gently, my fingers barely meeting around the width. Leo leaned back against the seat, his legs sprawled, glazed eyes focused on where I held him. "Grip it hard, sweetheart," he whispered. "I like a rough tug."

I tightened my grip at the base and pulled up toward the tip. I repeated this again and he grunted, his hips jerking. "Yes, exactly like that. Shit, Josie."

Though I'd been with men before, I hadn't really touched

them, not like this. I loved the smooth yet firm feel of Leo's cock. The skin was so soft, but there was steel underneath. What a fascinating appendage. I wondered what he would feel like inside me, whether the stretch would be too much or not enough. "Do you think we would fit?" I asked him as I pumped him.

He grimaced, his face twisting in pain. "Jesus, don't ask me that. You'll have me climaxing too soon, if I think about fucking you."

His chest rose and fell rapidly as I continued to work him with my hand. I could feel heat gathering between my legs once more, my pulse an insistent throb behind my clitoris. Now all I could think about was taking him inside me. My walls fitting around him, letting him in deep. Thrusting. Grunting . . .

Excitement thrummed under my skin and my hand worked faster. "I want to try. Can we, Leo?"

He was panting now, his eyes closed tight. Then his lips curled into something akin to a snarl. "Oh shit. Stop talking about it. I'm going to come."

A bead of moisture escaped the tip of his cock and I watched it roll over the crown. What did he taste like? "I can't help it," I murmured, concentrating on this mysterious part of his body. "I'm curious how it would feel to have you inside me. I bet you're good at it, too."

His thigh and stomach muscles bunched. He gritted out "Oh god. Fuck!" as his cock twitched in my hand. Then long jets of spend erupted from his tip, liquid coating both my fingers and his lap in a beautiful mess. His shout echoed off the ceiling, and I couldn't look away from his face while in the throes of his pleasure.

He was even more handsome, if such a thing were possible.

His entire body trembled and I gave him a few more gentle strokes, the slickness easing the way as his erection deflated. "Jesus Christ," he wheezed. "Come here."

He lunged for my mouth, kissing me deeply while he tried to

catch his breath. His tongue mated with mine, the smell of our pleasure mixed in the air. I normally escaped from intimate encounters as quickly as they concluded, but not this time.

I never wanted this to end.

Eventually, he pulled back to rest his forehead against mine. "We should get cleaned up. I made a mess all over both of us." He reached into his coat pocket and withdrew a handkerchief, which he used to clean my hand.

"I like it. You can't hide your reaction to what I did."

"True, though I'm not sure it will make for a comfortable ride back downtown." Finished with my hand, he began cleaning himself and his clothing as best he could. "This will have to do for now. Thankfully, we're returning to the apartment."

"Well, I would've used my mouth instead, if I were capable of bending in this corset."

Leo closed his eyes and swallowed. "For god's sake, woman. We'll never leave this sleigh if you keep saying things such as that."

I shrugged. "Merely being honest."

He looked at me then, his expression soft with an emotion I didn't understand. "I know. Promise me you won't ever change, not even when you're rich and famous."

"I won't, I promise. We're going to keep each other sane during the whole ride to the top."

Leo didn't answer, his smile fading. Before I could ask what was wrong, he stood up. "Let's go home and clean up, sweetheart."

Chapter Seventeen

LEO

What had I done?

I was a liar by trade, a scoundrel. My moral code was shiftier than a mirage in the desert.

But carrying on a physical relationship with Josie while also using her to get revenge on the Pendeltons? This felt a bridge too far—even for me.

I never should've tongued her pussy. Now the taste of her had invaded my senses, burned into my brain, and turned me starving for her. How was I supposed to resist her, when all I could think about was tasting her again?

I told myself this needed to remain impersonal. Professional. Manager and singer. Revenge seeker and the instrument of said revenge. I even repeated St. Elmer's second rule over and over.

Never lose sight of the endgame.

Yet when we disembarked from the carriage, I took hold of Josie's hand and set it on my arm. And I didn't let go.

I couldn't.

I wanted more, everything she was willing to give me. And I wanted it to last all night.

At least Ambrose would be in the apartment to keep me in check. Josie and I wouldn't be alone, and I could resist the temptation of her for another day. Tomorrow, I would be stronger.

"You're awfully quiet again," she said as we crossed the street leading to Ambrose's apartment. "Are you thinking about your father again?"

No, I wasn't. Indeed, I hadn't thought of my father at all, not since Josie lifted her skirts.

A lie formed on my tongue, slick words that meant nothing. It was second nature to me—but for some reason I stopped myself. I didn't want to lie to her. I would rather tell her the truth.

Before I could think better of it, I went with my gut. "I was thinking about you."

"Me?"

"You and the sleigh, to be more precise. Specifically, the filthy and terribly erotic things I would have done to you there if we had more space."

"Oh." The single word was a husky rush of breath. "Like what?"

I liked that she was curious. "Do you honestly wish to have this conversation on the street?"

"Why not? No one can hear us. And even if they could, who cares?"

I shook my head. If I started telling her, there was no stopping it. I'd reveal every wicked thought in my head in regard to this woman. It was bad enough that I could still smell her arousal on my skin.

We needed to go inside and retreat upstairs to our separate spaces. Where Ambrose would play chaperone. Maybe then I could regain some of my self-control.

I unlocked the building's door and held it open for her. She moved past me—and my cock twitched in my trousers, the randy thing by no means satisfied.

Just a few more steps.

As we climbed the stairs silently, I planned the entire night in my head. I would see her inside, leave her to Ambrose's care, and retreat to the washroom. Once there I would stroke my cock until I climaxed. Then I would feel more like myself. Then I would be able share the apartment with her and Ambrose and return to my original plans with the Pendeltons.

She stopped at Ambrose's door, but waited for me to unlock it.

Odd. *Why not just walk in?* Though I supposed Ambrose might be out and about.

Christ, I hoped not.

Patience, Leo. You can do it.

I disengaged the lock and we went in. Sure enough, the apartment was dark. Damn Ambrose. Now that I needed him around, he was nowhere to be found.

He'd best return soon or I was bound to do something stupid.

I switched on the overhead light, allowing me to watch as Josie stripped off her gloves and removed her hat. Several strands of wheat-colored hair had escaped and rested on her shoulder blade. I gripped the chair back to keep from going over to touch it.

I would've used my mouth instead, if I were capable of bending in this corset.

A rush of lust uncoiled in my belly and a small groan escaped my throat. I coughed to cover it up, which caused her to glance over sharply at me, confused green eyes sizing me up. "Are you all right?"

No, not in the least. I was burning, aching. Trembling with a weakness I barely understood.

Where was fucking Ambrose?

"Go to bed," I croaked, my fingers digging into the wood. "I'll see you in the morning."

"It's still early." Her mouth flattened as she watched me. "And you are acting quite strangely. Is this about the sleigh again?"

"No," I lied. "And we shouldn't discuss such things, not when Ambrose will return at any moment."

"He's gone to stay with a friend for a few days." I froze, stunned, which caused Josie to ask, "Did he not tell you?"

No, he most definitely had not.

The implications sat in my stomach like a stone. Ambrose wasn't here. Josie and I were alone.

Alone. All night. And tomorrow.

My heart drummed in my chest, my breath coming faster

now as blood rushed south to my groin, thickening my cock. My balls drew tight and heavy, like I hadn't climaxed in days. Weeks. *Years.*

We were alone in this godforsaken apartment and I wasn't certain I'd survive it. "When did he inform you of this?" I forced out.

"This morning, before we left. While you were in the washroom. Didn't he tell you?"

No, he hadn't. Fuck. This was a disaster.

Escape, my mind whispered.

"I should go clean up," I wheezed, but my feet didn't move.

As if to torture me, Josie's gaze darted to my crotch. Could she see the state I was in? I hoped the chair blocked my thickening erection.

She started toward me. A slight breeze from the open windows brushed my overheated skin, and a shiver raced down my spine. The heels of her boots thumped on the worn floorboards, and my muscles wound tighter and tighter as she came closer.

By the time the hem of her skirts met my shoes, a sweat had broken out on my brow. Her body was less than an arm's length away and my cock responded by stiffening further, until the pulse at the base matched the frantic beat inside my chest.

The air around us crackled with expectation. I swallowed.

Josie swept the pad of her finger along the edge of my jaw, a simple touch I felt all the way down to my toes. "These filthy and terribly erotic things you would have done in the sleigh? Tell me more."

Shit. I closed my eyes and tried to shake the prurient thoughts from my brain. "Josie, please."

"I want to know." Her fingertip brushed over my bottom lip. "Because maybe I want those things too."

A switch flipped inside me.

My mind went dark, logic and reason disappearing as lust took over. There was one purpose flooding my senses—and Josie was the only woman who would do. I lunged for her, wrapping my hands around her waist to pull her flush to my body. Up close I could see every detail on her gorgeous face, every freckle. Every eyelash. The slope of her graceful nose. She was flawless perfection—and for one night she would be mine.

I didn't hold back. "You want to know? I would do outrageous things, carnal immoral things. I would make your body melt with pleasure as I fucked you all night long."

She licked her lips. "I want that, too."

I rocked my erection against her hip, letting her feel the thick proof of my desire. "Yeah?"

She placed her palms on my chest. "Please, Leo."

A snarl I barely recognized as mine emerged from my throat as my mouth crashed into hers. I wasn't polite or sweet as I attacked her lips. I ate at her mouth like a starving man, my tongue thrusting past her lips to find hers. I felt unhinged, unmoored. Adrift as craving crashed over me, all my good sense washed away.

Her nails dug into my shoulders through my coat—and I needed to feel them on my bare skin. I stripped off my coat without breaking free of her mouth, then dragged off my necktie and collar. My clothing couldn't disappear quickly enough.

Panting, Josie broke off from our kiss and stepped back. I used the opportunity to remove my vest, while she began gathering her skirts, lifting them. I thought she was removing her undergarments, but she surprised me by going over to the table. Once there she bent over the wood, held her skirts up, and presented me with her backside.

When she widened her thighs, I could see her pussy through the part in her drawers, and the pink flesh glistened with her arousal. I stood there, unmoving, taking it in. Mesmerized.

Christ, that sight.

But it wasn't enough. I needed her naked, writhing underneath me on a bed. I had to feel her against every part of me where I could take my time and savor her, worship her.

She peered over her shoulder. "Hurry. I need you, Leo."

I gave her a devious, wicked smile. "You think this will be fast? That I'll toss up your skirts and rut you like a beast?"

"Isn't that . . . ?" She braced herself on her elbows, confusion etched in her expression. "I don't understand. Don't you do it this way?"

Had this been her only experience, taken from behind, fully clothed? Had no man ever taken care with her?

This explained her surprise over what happened in the Pendeltons' carriage house. *And I rushed her, pleasured her in a sleigh, for fuck's sake.*

Anger at those other two men—as well as at myself—flared deep and hot, but I shoved it down. This was not the time. "No, my beautiful girl," I said, easing her off the table and dragging her back to my chest. I nipped her earlobe with my teeth. "I plan to take my time with you. I want you to feel me between your thighs for days."

She trembled in my arms, from what I hoped was an equal amount of desire. Clutching my wrists, she asked, "So where do you want me to stand?"

Stand?

I spun her around to face me. "I can't tell if you're serious or not."

"About what?"

"How this transpires. Josie, I'm taking you to the bed."

"Oh." She cast a glance at the bedroom. "Of course. I knew that."

It was clearly not the truth. Josie was a terrible liar, and I suddenly needed the names of the men she'd been with in the past. They deserved the swiftest of beatings.

Putting my hands on her shoulders, I studied her. "Sweetheart, please tell me those men were careful with you, that you enjoyed it every time."

"They didn't hurt me, if that's what you're asking. It was nice."

I felt my frown deepen. Nice? Again, I would be finding these men when I returned to Boston. "Will you let me show you a better method?"

She nodded. "You weren't lying about what your mouth could do, so I'm apt to believe you in regards to this, too."

I wanted to laugh, but I didn't dare. "Thank you for your tentative trust. I swear, you won't regret it."

Bending, I scooped her into my arms. She clung to my neck as I carried her into the bedroom. Once there I placed her on the bed, where I saw a small stuffed rabbit buried in the bedclothes. It struck me as sweet. I lifted up the toy and placed it on the nightstand.

"Don't laugh at me," she warned. "It's all I have left from my real parents."

"I wouldn't dare. May I remove my clothes?"

"God, yes. Please do so," she said emphatically, and I chuckled. Quickly, I removed the rest of my clothing, leaving on my undergarment. Josie said nothing, merely watched, two bright spots of color on her cheeks.

I reached down and unlaced her boots, then slipped them off her feet. "Now may I take off your clothes?"

She nibbled her lip. Was this uncertainty? The last time I saw this expression on her face was directly before singing for Lotta. My heart softened, a strange emotion filling my chest. I wanted to both protect her and fuck her senseless, which was unsettling. I couldn't remember ever feeling this way about a woman in the past.

I put my hand on my heart. "I swear on my life, I'll take excellent care of you tonight. You will feel like a goddamn princess when I'm through with you."

Instead of answering, she sat up and began popping the fastenings on her shirtwaist. She started at her throat, loosening the buttons, then continued lower, flashing a hint of pale pink undergarments as she went. My fingers curled into fists at my sides, my mind warning me to keep calm. I didn't want to rush her or frighten her. This had to be the best experience of her life.

Finally, she shrugged out of the shirtwaist, and my gaze feasted on her bare arms and sharp collarbones, creamy skin and delicate shoulders. My god, she was lovely.

"Do you want my help?" I asked when she rose up on her knees.

"It will go faster with four hands."

That was all the invitation I needed. As she untied her skirts, I went to work on the tiny buttons of her corset cover. My usually dexterous fingers felt clumsy, shaky, as I pushed the tiny pearls through the openings one by one. The mounds of her breasts, pushed up by her corset, rose and fell with her breathing, nearly bursting out of her chemise. I couldn't wait to see them, touch them. Lick them.

She peered up at me, our eyes meeting as I continued. There was no hesitation in her green depths, only trust and desire, like she truly saw me in a way that no one else ever had. It made me feel like the world's wealthiest and most powerful man. I never wanted to lose this feeling.

Unable to wait any longer, I bent and kissed her. She met me eagerly, her mouth warm, her lips insistent, and I lost track of what I'd been doing. All I cared about was kissing her and breathing in her scent.

"Wait," she said against my lips.

I paused and dragged in air, hoping it would cool me off a bit. Josie shifted and I watched her skirts pool at her knees. Then she fell back on the bed and kicked the layers of cotton and lace completely off, leaving on her drawers and stockings. "There."

"You're having an easier time of this than me." I reached for the tiny buttons once more. "May I finish the rest?"

"If you like." She bit her bottom lip in the most adorable manner. "But I don't know why it matters."

I stretched out on the mattress next to her. I'd dreamed of this so often that it was hard to believe it was actually happening. "I'll tell you why it matters, but you need to roll over first."

She did as I asked, presenting me with her back and the corset laces. I rose up on one elbow and pressed a kiss to the bare skin above her chemise. Goose bumps rose up in response, so I did it again. Then I trailed open-mouthed kisses along every part of her back that I could reach.

"There are things that can be rushed," I whispered, "like a meal or a cup of coffee." *Another kiss.* "Buying something you don't truly need." I scraped the skin behind her neck with my teeth. "A conversation."

"Oh god. *Leo.*"

I loved the sound of my name, a frustrated plea, on her lips. I wanted to hear it again.

Coming up, I threw my leg over one of her thighs and moved to cover her, with my elbows resting on the mattress beside her ribs. I wedged my knees between her legs, the thinnest of cloth separating us. My erection nestled into the curve of her buttocks and a rush of need cramped in my gut.

Soon. Very soon.

I began kissing her other shoulder, the one I hadn't been able to reach before, letting her feel my breath. "But you, my dear Josie, are to be savored."

Kiss.

"I want to suck on your nipples for hours."

Kiss.

"I want to tongue your pussy for days."

A bite, then a lick.

"I'm going to fuck you so slow, sweetheart. And you're going to feel me inside your cunt for *weeks.*"

"*Leo.*" She rocked her hips, dragging the sweet cleft of her arse along my length. "Oh god. Please, please, please."

Clenching my back teeth, I closed my eyes and waited for the sparks to leave my groin. My cock was already leaking, my body straining to get inside her.

Patience, man.

"Not yet," I said. "I don't think you're quite ready."

"I'm ready," she panted. "Get me out of this dashed corset so I can breathe."

Balancing on one arm, I plucked at the strings to loosen them. As soon as I made enough space to release the pins, Josie flipped onto her back beneath me. Her hair had fallen down, wild blond strands streaking across the mattress, her gaze hooded and dark. The position put my erection directly against her pubic bone, and her legs widened to make room for my hips. I was momentarily stunned by the overload of sensation. "Wait," I said, helplessly.

She didn't wait for me, instead popping the corset open with a speed that should've surprised me.

Instead, I was distracted by watching all that glorious flesh set free.

Her tits were perfect, straining against the thin cotton of her chemise. I dragged my palm over her ribs to cup one mound, then pinched the nipple through the cloth, and her eyelids swept closed. "Christ, you are beautiful," I murmured.

"More," was her response, so I lowered the sleeve of her chemise to free one of her breasts. Angling my head, I took the tip into my mouth, her nipple hard and smooth on my tongue, and I alternated between licking and drawing on it.

Her hands came up to clamp around my head, holding me in place, as her hips rolled slightly, seeking. "You're driving me out of my mind. I can't take it."

I moaned around her flesh, more fluid leaking from the tip of my cock. I didn't know how much longer I could hold out. I didn't usually get so frantic while in bed with a woman.

She twisted beneath me, more wriggling to drive me to the brink, so I pulled back. "What are you—"

Her chemise went over her head, leaving her in only drawers and stockings. I stared at her bare breasts, mesmerized. Full and ripe, they had rose-colored nipples and dark areoles. They would fill my palms and a bit more, and I couldn't wait to see them shift and bounce as I rode her to orgasm.

"Leo." She snapped her fingers in front of my face. "You're wasting time."

I shook myself and eased down on top of her, so our fronts were flush. Then I gave her a deep kiss with lots of tongue. "Looking at your body is never a waste of time." I rocked my hips to drag my length over her slit. "Feel how hard you make me?"

She slid her palms over my chest, my shoulders. Then she started to unbutton my union suit. "I'm dying. I need you."

"Are you certain?"

"Very certain."

Her fingers worked fast. She had it halfway down my chest before I sat up on my knees. I pulled my arms free and shoved the cloth to my hips, then all the way off my legs. I let her look her fill at me as I untied her drawers. The scent of her arousal hung heavy in the air between us, and I inhaled it like a drug. Maneuvering her legs, I removed her drawers, leaving her lower half clad only in silk stockings.

I dragged my hands over her knees, up her thighs, spreading her wide so I could see every inch of her. The folds glistened, slick with her arousal, and I couldn't help but bend down to swipe my tongue over her intimate flesh, desperate to taste her again.

Her back arched. "Oh god!"

I slid a finger inside her, stretching her, while I circled her clitoris with my tongue. Fuck, she was tight. It was going to feel so good when these velvet walls strangled my cock.

She rocked her hips, pumping herself on me, so I slipped in another finger, pumping my hand, giving her friction, as I sucked her tiny nub into my mouth.

It happened quickly. She tensed, her fingers curling into my hair, and then her pussy convulsed around my fingers. "Shit!" she hissed, her limbs twitching. "Shit, oh god! *Leo.*"

When it was over I gave her clitoris a soft kiss, but I didn't remove my fingers. I crawled up her body and drew the tip of her breast into my mouth, sucking hard. Slowly, I eased my fingers in and out of her channel, stretching her, preparing her. I didn't wish to hurt her.

"Leo," she said through harsh breaths. "Put yourself inside me. I need you. *Please.*"

Those words . . . I exhaled, unable to take anymore. I lost the battle.

It was time to make her mine.

JOSIE

He was torturing me.

Death by slow and steady pleasure.

No wonder he had women eating out of the palm of his hand everywhere he went. He was very good at this, knowing exactly what to say, what to do. Having him on top of me, pressed against my skin, surrounding me, was everything I'd hoped for. I felt cherished, adored. Wanted.

Why hadn't any other man cared this much?

I couldn't think about that now. My body was on fire, desire like flames under my skin, behind my clitoris. My patience had worn out.

I needed every bit of him—and I needed it *now.*

"Touch me," he whispered against my mouth as he removed his fingers from inside me. "Put me inside you."

I was too far gone to complain. Anything to move this along. Besides, I was dying to touch him again. The sleigh hadn't been nearly enough.

I moved my hand between us and squeezed his shaft, hard. His big body shuddered, his eyes slamming closed. "Damn, but you're a fast learner."

I took this as a good sign. I gave him a rough stroke, making sure to maintain the pressure. He gasped and threw his head back. Then he reached down to clutch my wrist. "No more, or this will end too soon."

"I like teasing you." I gave him another squeeze. "You're usually so calm. It's nice to see you lose your head now and then."

"Except I want to take my time with you." He shifted on his knees and together we aimed his tip toward my entrance. "So hot, so wet," he murmured into my throat.

He nudged my opening with his crown, dragging it through the slick gathered there. Before I could order him to hurry, he pushed inside. We both sucked in a sharp breath and I clutched his shoulder. No pain, but I did feel an intense pressure. All my attention and sensation became centered in the spot where we were joined.

He paused. "Did I hurt you?"

"No." I appreciated his concern, but I was desperate for him. Angling up slightly, I caught his lips with mine, kissing him to let him know without words that I was with him in this.

His muscles relaxed, then his hips began rocking, bringing him deeper with each tiny movement. Little ripples of pleasure stole through me and I widened my thighs, urging him on, as our mouths continued to sweep and meld together.

Finally, his hips met mine, the entire length of him seated inside me. It was . . . a lot. I panted, waiting for my body to adjust.

Then he withdrew entirely.

My eyes flew open as my fingers dug into the smooth muscle of his back. "Don't stop."

He was studying my face. "There's no rush. I want you to be comfortable."

"I'm fine."

"Sweetheart, you're wincing."

"You're a lot to take."

A spot of color hit his cheeks. "Which is why we don't need to—"

"Oh, you're such a man. Never listening to a woman and making decisions for her." I shoved at his shoulder, annoyed.

He surprised me by rolling us over, so he was on the bottom. I stared down at him and pushed errant strands of hair off my face. "Are we stopping?"

"We can, if you like. But some women find being on top is easier. You can control how much or little you take."

Me, on top? I wouldn't have the first idea what to do.

But I also wasn't one to give up easily.

"All right," I said. "Show me."

The edge of his mouth hitched, his bright eyes glittering up at me. "Just straddle my hips, sit up, and slide down on my shaft."

"That's it?"

"That's it."

I adjusted my legs and braced myself on my knees. Then I used his hard chest to push up and balance myself. I felt . . . exposed. On display. No man had seen me fully naked before.

I started to cover my breasts with my hands, but Leo caught my wrist. "Please, don't. I fear I'll cry if you hide them from me."

That made me smile. "You'll cry?"

"Like a baby." He threaded our fingers together. "You are beautiful, Josie. Every bit."

My heart turned over, warmth spreading through my veins. If I wasn't careful, I could become used to this. Worse, I could fall in love with him.

"Raise up," he said, patting my thigh.

I lifted on my knees and Leo angled his shaft between my legs. When I started to lower myself, the crown slipped inside my entrance again, easier this time. He kept his hand between my legs, his thumb brushing over my clitoris to send pulses of heat through my core. I kept at it, sinking down, slow and steady, with Leo rubbing me the whole time. His other hand cupped one of my breasts and molded it, squeezing.

"Look at you," he crooned, watching between my legs, "taking me so well. Fuck, that is a sight."

That helped too. I liked when he talked to me.

I kept working lower, letting him fill me up. He was right, this was easier. The tiny circles he gave the bud atop my sex distracted me, and I let my eyelids fall closed, sensation guiding me. Soon our hips met once again. This was pure pleasure, no discomfort.

When I looked at him, a muscle was jumping in his jaw, his eyes screwed tight. His chest rose and fell like he'd run a race, his hand falling away from my body. "Are you all right?" I asked.

"I will be," he said from behind clenched teeth. "Just don't move for a moment."

"Why?"

A pained sound escaped his lips. "Josie, I'm hanging on by a thread here."

Oh. "Well, can you keep rubbing between my legs while you're hanging on?" I wanted those little shocks again, especially now that he was inside me.

He smiled, one of his genuine, full-mouth grins, the kind he rarely gave, right before his fingers found my intimate flesh once more. "You need me, sweetheart?"

I jerked as pleasure streaked through me. "Yes," I breathed.

"Then start rolling your hips. Work yourself on me."

I began with small movements, trying to find what felt best. Leo's free hand cupped my hip to guide me, his encouraging grunts picking up when I found a rhythm. His thick shaft dragged along my sensitive walls as I worked, his pubic bone hitting the perfect spot with every down stroke.

Leaning up, he wrapped an arm around my back to bring me

closer, then sucked one of my nipples into his mouth. These were long draws of his lips that echoed directly between my legs. I moaned and rocked faster, needing more.

I lost track of time. We were two sweaty bodies working together, straining and grasping, frenzied in our movements. His hands were everywhere, his lips alternating between my breast and my mouth, and I was lost in a haze of intense bliss.

"God, Leo," I gasped. "It's so good."

"Fuck, I know. Can I get on top?"

I nodded and before I knew it, I was on my back, Leo hovering over me. He parted my thighs and reentered me, his long thickness filling all the emptiness inside me.

He withdrew slightly, then slammed his hips into mine—and my eyes nearly rolled back in my head. "Oh! God, yes. Please, more."

"Don't worry, sweetheart." He did it again. "I'm never going to stop."

I grabbed onto him, holding him close, as he rode between my thighs, his body driving into mine. We kissed occasionally, but mostly we breathed each other in as we both panted like wild beasts. I hadn't felt closer to another person in my life. We were our own world, a perfect little haven of ecstasy, and I never wanted it to end.

"You feel so good," he whispered. "So hot and tight. I want to stay inside you for days."

"You feel good, too. I'm so full of you."

"Shit." He hissed through his teeth and froze, his cock buried inside me. "I'm too close."

"No, don't stop." I clawed at his skin, writhing beneath him. "Leo, *please*."

"Oh god. Wait—"

"I can't. I'm burning up."

"Fuck," he groaned, then his hips began pumping. "Fuck, fuck, *fuck*!"

Abruptly, he pulled out and rose on his knees. His hand flew over his shaft, stroking, his muscles taut, then warm jets of fluid shot out onto my belly, my sex, my chest. It went on and on, his body trembling, his head thrown back as the tendons in his neck strained. Lord, he was beautiful.

By the time he finally sagged, spent, I was already rubbing between my legs. "That was unbelievably arousing," I told him.

"Yeah?" The side of his mouth hitched as he focused on my hand. "I like watching you pet yourself."

"You do?"

"God, yes. You look so perfect, using your hand and covered in my come."

He slipped two fingers inside me, and the added stimulation caused my back to arch, my muscles to tighten. It was so good, so easy between us. How was he so in tune with what I needed? We were like a perfect melody paired with the perfect lyrics.

My fingers circled faster. "Oh god. Leo. I'm so close."

He sucked my nipple into his mouth, and I couldn't hold back any longer. The pleasure crested and I started to orgasm, my body squeezing around his fingers. I never wanted it to end. I wanted to stay here, in bed with Leo, enjoying his touch and kisses, for the rest of my life.

When I finally came down to earth, Leo kissed my temple and stretched out next to me, pulling me close. I bit my lip to hold back a grin. Holy Christmas, what an experience. Lotta would be disappointed in me. Melvin as well.

But it was hard to regret getting into bed with Leo when my body was swimming in a blissful haze.

I hadn't imagined anything of the sort before. Sleeping with Leo had been intimate, wonderful. Revolutionary, as if he'd shown me something I'd been missing my whole life. Like he'd turned me inside out and upside down.

I should feel self-conscious, unclothed here with a man, his spend drying on my stomach. But I didn't. Leo always found a way to make me feel comfortable, to believe in myself. His confidence was beginning to rub off on me.

"What are you thinking?" he asked, rubbing my back.

"I'm thinking how good that was."

"Yeah, it was." His lips twitched. "Not sure it was a wise idea, but I don't regret it."

"Neither do I."

Shifting, he rolled onto his side to face me. He drew a fingertip through the drying remains of his orgasm on my breast. "I'm pleased to hear it, because I plan on doing that again. Soon."

"You didn't finish inside me."

"Of course not. We didn't have a method to prevent any consequences." His expression darkened as he leaned back to better see my face. "Are you saying those other men did?"

Yes, they had. I thought that was the way of it. "Never mind. I was only making an observation."

Leo shook his head and blew out a long, exasperated breath. "I want names, Josie."

"Names?"

"The men you were with before me. Because coming inside you was reckless, unless we are trying to conceive a child. So yes, I want their names."

I didn't wish to discuss those others. It was clear my wellbeing hadn't mattered in the least to either previous lover. "They aren't important."

"That is where you are wrong. They are important to me—very important. I need to have a long chat with both when I return to Boston."

His choice in words was not lost on me. When *he* returned—not when *we* returned.

Oh.

Indeed, that cleared things up nicely. *We are temporary to each other.*

It shouldn't have surprised me. Leo's family was in Boston, while my future was here in New York City. Then maybe London or Paris. Who knew where my voice and Melvin's connections would take me?

He's not a man who sticks. He's interested in Leo, nothing more.

So, how long would he stay? Until the first big bank draft? The second? I had no idea when he would decide to leave me.

Precisely why I couldn't allow myself to get attached.

The warmth in my chest cooled considerably, my senses returning. I was better off looking out for myself, like always. I didn't need a man. Pippa was all the family I needed. And just as soon as I had my own place here, I'd send for her.

Leo was a temporary diversion, a bit of fun to pass the time. Nothing more.

I swallowed hard and studied the ceiling, unsure why my chest felt so hollow. I was used to being alone and Leo hadn't made any promises beyond my singing career.

"Let's go and take a bath."

I looked over at him, shoving aside my dark thoughts. "A bath? Together?"

He slid off the mattress and reached for my hand. "Yes. Plus, getting clean means we'll be able to come back here and get dirty again."

Temporary, Josie.

All the more reason to enjoy him while he was still here.

I placed my hand in his and let him pull me to my feet. "Sure, sounds like a good idea."

Chapter Eighteen

LEO

I never thought I'd willingly walk into a police station, let alone New York City Police Headquarters.

But here I was, strolling inside the great stone building, the center of Gotham's law and order, of my own free volition. In broad daylight. All by myself.

There was no choice. This morning I had stopped by the local Pinkerton office to inquire, under the ruse of writing a newspaper article, as to the identity of the last investigator on the Pendelton case. I was informed it was a William Porter, who'd gone to work as a police detective several years back.

Therefore, I had to speak with Porter. I had to find out what accusation this man made all those years ago against my father and do whatever I could to restore his reputation. Because Steven Hardy was neither a kidnapper nor an accomplice to a kidnapper. It may not matter to anyone anymore, but it mattered to me and my family.

Once I dealt with my father's legacy, I needed to come clean with Josie. Last night had changed something between us. It was more than screwing—I'd screwed plenty of women. No, this had to do with how I felt about her. I wanted her, and not for a few hours or a few days. I wanted her forever.

She was mine.

That meant I had to tell her the truth about my background, as well as the reason I brought her here.

A cold sweat broke out between my shoulder blades. I wasn't used to confessing the truth. But perhaps it wouldn't be so bad? Now that she knew about my father, I was mostly confident she would understand and forgive me.

Fairly confident.

I hoped, anyway.

I couldn't lose her—and not because of the money I knew she was going to earn one day. It was because I was lost without her, just a man with no moral compass or direction, no foundation upon which to build something meaningful. Josie helped me discover that I have an ability to handle people, to open doors for her. I was able to negotiate on her behalf. Who better to know when she was being swindled than me?

All that combined with her talent? The two of us could take over the world.

This wasn't about the Pendeltons any longer. This was about Josie. She deserved a good man, a decent man. The man I knew I could be, if given a fair chance.

And it started just as soon as I cleared my father's name.

Bounding up the steps, I strode inside police headquarters, where an officer sat behind the entrance desk, scribbling in a book. A heavy beard hung over his collar, bushy brows peeking atop his spectacles. He didn't even glance up at my approach. "What is it?"

"Good morning, Officer. I wish to see a Detective Porter."

"What for?"

"To inquire about the old Pendelton kidnapping."

"Son, that case is more than a decade old. What business is it of yours?"

I could tell my straightforward approach wasn't going to work with this old-timer. I leaned against the desk and relaxed, merely two men having a friendly conversation, my smile wide. "I bet you were just starting out in those days, a brand-new patrolman. Cracking heads, arresting drunks and gangsters. It must've been exciting, the days before Commissioner Roosevelt got involved."

Most of the old guard resented Roosevelt and his reforms. I hoped this man was one of them.

The officer finally looked up at me and shook his head sadly. "You don't know the half of it. All these new rules? They take away the power we had, give it right to the hopheads and thieves. A damn shame, if you ask me."

"Well, what can you expect? Fancy boy from Upper Fifth Avenue. What does he know about walking the streets, putting his life in danger every day?"

"Exactly!" The officer slapped his palm on the desk. "And if we take a little somethin' extra on the side every now and again, who's to blame us?"

"Not me. Not all of us were born on a gilded blanket in a gold bassinet."

The officer chuckled. "I like that. Gilded blanket in a gold bassinet." His mouth hitched as he looked me over. "You an officer, too?"

I smelled an opportunity, so the lie fell out of my mouth easily. "Patrolman in Boston. I'm here for a short visit, but I remember the old Pendelton case from when I lived here as a boy. I was hoping to get a sense of where the investigation stalled."

"I know some boys in Boston. Where are you stationed?"

I was familiar enough with the police back home to say, "Station House No. 3, over on Joy Street. You know it?"

"Can't say that I do. My cousin is at No. 4, on Lagrange."

"Ah, not far. I'm friendly with a few of the patrolmen there. They have the Commons, not an easy assignment."

"That's what my cousin tells me. Vagrants and hoodlums all hours of the day, guys running bunco games. It's a real mess." He knocked the wooden desk a few times with his knuckles. "Let me see what I can do about finding Porter."

"I'd really appreciate that, sir."

He stuck out his hand. "Call me Gilly. Last name's Gilbert, but everyone calls me Gilly."

"How do you do?" I said as I shook his hand. "Hugh Wright."

"Pleasure, Wright. Have a seat. Give me a few moments."

Gilly returned shortly with another man and waved me forward. "Detective Porter, this is Officer Wright."

A slight man in a rumpled suit, Porter ignored the hand I offered. "What's a patrolman from Boston doing here, asking questions about our old cases?"

I tried to keep my expression as friendly as possible. "How do you do, Detective? It's unusual, I know—and my apologies for catching you unaware. I'm in town for only a few days, but I lived here at the time of the kidnapping. My cousin was friends with one of the old Pendelton grooms, and we heard quite a bit about the investigation growing up. I wondered where it had stalled."

"It has not *stalled*," Porter said, annoyed. "I've worked the case on and off for the last six years as a detective, but I started back when I was a Pinkerton."

There were lots of eyes and ears around us. Doubtful Porter would offer any true insight into the case out here. "Is there a place we can sit? I took a knife in the leg from a pickpocket a few years ago and it still bothers me from time to time."

Porter grimaced and rolled his right shoulder. "Got one in Central Park twelve years ago. Still gives me fits every time the weather turns. Come on. We'll go to my office."

I followed him through the corridors, trying not to meet anyone's eye. Old habit, even though no one here would likely recognize me.

Once we were in a small office, Porter closed the door. I took the chair opposite his desk, while Porter dropped into the leather chair on the other side. "I only have a few minutes. What do you want to know?"

"Any new leads on the person or persons responsible for the kidnapping?"

"I can't comment on that," Porter said.

"Not even to another policeman?" I leaned in. "Look at it as confiding in a colleague. I can offer my insight, maybe break the case open."

"Doesn't matter. The man who likely orchestrated it is dead, anyway."

My throat dried out, so I swallowed. "Oh? Who's that?"

"The old gardener. Guy named Hardy."

It was a struggle, but I smothered any reaction. "How do you know it was him?"

"After I was hired, I found love letters between Hardy and the child's nurse. The two were having an affair."

I squeezed the wooden armrest so hard I worried it might break. Then I coughed to mask the rage punching through my gut. My father *never* would've cheated on my mother. The two had been wildly in love.

But this explained a few things: one, why my father was abruptly let go from his position and not provided a reference. And two, why he never wished to discuss any of this once we moved to Boston.

I hid my feelings behind a curious frown. "An affair, you say? But wasn't he married?"

"Man like that? They'll screw anything that moves." Porter eased back and studied me. "How did you know Hardy was married?"

I waved this off with a flick of my wrist. "Like I said, my cousin knew one of the servants on the estate. We were fascinated with the case." I paused, as if I were considering this new information. "So why wasn't the nurse arrested?"

"The police questioned her, of course, but she disappeared a few days after the kidnapping. She's always been my main suspect."

Interesting that he said "my" and not "the." But Porter wouldn't be the first detective to let his personal opinions cloud an investigation. "No one ever found her?"

"Nope. Never seen or heard from again. But she must've had help getting the baby out the window and down the ladder. No woman is strong enough to do it alone."

"So you discovered these letters between Hardy and the nurse some time later, after the kidnapping? Isn't that a tad suspicious?"

Porter frowned, his brows lowering over his eyes. "The letters were found because I conducted a more thorough search of the estate than the police did at the time. Hardy had a shed containing a few personal belongings. Inside that shed, under a loose floorboard, was a packet of letters."

Which could've been planted by anyone.

"Do you happen to have one of these letters? I'd love to see it." I hoped I sounded casual enough to be believable.

"I can't show an outsider any evidence."

"Understandable, but I'm an officer, too. I know the rules concerning ongoing investigations. I won't tell a soul. And as I said, I'm familiar with the old Pendelton staff from when I was a boy. Perhaps I can glean some clue from the letters."

"I suppose there's no harm in letting you see one." Porter rose from his chair and went to the tall cabinet in the corner, which he unlocked and opened. He withdrew a thick packet from inside and brought it over to the desk.

After some searching, he produced a few sheafs of paper. "These are addressed from her to him. You can have a quick peek."

I took the letters from his hand, noting he hadn't counted the number of pages he'd given me.

I read the words quickly, never believing for a second that they'd been directed at my father. Who had been the true recipient?

I would need to study one of these letters carefully, out from under Porter's watchful eye.

Distraction. Dip. Departure.

The pickpocket's mantra.

"Oh, look here." I leaned across the desk with one of the papers in my hand. I set it on the desk and pointed. "See, this sentence. What does this mean?"

Porter leaned forward to read it—and that split second was all I needed to fold one of the letters in my other hand and tuck it into my pocket.

The detective quoted, "'You are my golden light, my reason for existing.'" He glanced up at me. "Seems pretty straightforward to me."

"Golden light?" I stroked my chin. "Does she mean someone with blond hair? What color hair did Hardy have?" I knew the answer—dark, like mine.

"That's a metaphor. Something one lover says to another."

Possibly, but possibly not. "And you don't have the letters Hardy wrote back?"

"No, those were never found. The nurse probably took 'em with her when she left."

I handed over the remaining letters and sat back. "What did Hardy say when you questioned him?"

"Denied it, of course. We leaned on him fairly rough, but he stuck to his story. Wasn't having an affair and wasn't involved in the kidnapping plot."

"Does the nurse mention the kidnapping in the letters?" I gestured to the file on his desk.

"Not directly, but she would've known better than to write it down."

"So, other than the alleged affair, you don't possess evidence that points to either of them?"

Porter appeared genuinely annoyed at my question. "Baby nurse and gardener are having an affair. Neither have much in the matter of funds, so they hatch the kidnapping plot as a way to start over somewhere new, together. Baby nurse has access to the little girl. The ladder used in the kidnapping belongs to the estate and is stored in the gardener's equipment shed. Baby nurse disappears, and the gardener sticks around to steer the investigation away from them."

"But they didn't end up together. The gardener moved to Boston and died."

"Only because the kidnapping went sour. They never had a chance to demand a ransom for the little girl."

This theory was a stretch, based on very little evidence. And the evidence Porter had—the love letters—only involved one of his suspects. "It sounds like you've given this a lot of thought. I'm surprised you couldn't arrest Hardy."

Porter shifted in his chair and straightened the papers on his desk. "The detectives at the time said there wasn't enough evidence to convict him. So I went to Tammany and got myself appointed to the department. Then I took over the case when the others gave up."

"Smart of you." I slapped my thighs and rose out of the chair. "Indeed, thank you, Detective, for indulging me. I've taken up enough of your time."

We shook hands. Porter walked with me to the door. "Incidentally, who did you say you knew who worked on the estate?"

"The old groom. Freddie."

"Ah, I remember him. Good man. He was very helpful every time I came by."

"Yes, he does like to chat," I said with a chuckle. "Quite the old storyteller, from what I recall."

We walked into the corridor. I put my hat on and gave him a nod. "I'll see myself out. Thank you again, Detective. If you're ever in Boston, stop by Station House No. 3."

"I will. Take care."

"Take care."

I walked out, choking on bitterness and resentment. And I swore right there, as I exited for Mulberry Street, that I would find the answers myself.

I would clear my father's name all on my own.

JOSIE

Late-morning light filled the bedroom by the time I woke up, my exhausted muscles heavy and sore. Leo and I had stayed up much too late, a blur of sensation and sweat. I couldn't remember the number of orgasms he'd given me—I lost count after five—but it was a night I'd never forget.

I dressed slowly, wondering what Leo was doing while I slept the day away. Except when I finally emerged from the bedroom it wasn't Leo I found.

Ambrose was at the kitchen table. He was reading the newspaper, sipping from a teacup. There was no one else around.

"Good morning," I said as I went to the stove. Was there any coffee left? "I wasn't expecting to see you."

"Good morning, Miss Smith. I beg your pardon for the intrusion. I needed to collect some clean clothing."

After I started heating water, I took a seat at the table. Ambrose folded the newsprint, angled in his chair, and crossed his legs. "You and Leo are having fun, I gather."

I tried to keep a blank expression, though it wasn't easy. "I suppose so, yes."

"You have a discoloration on your neck." He peered closer. "And it looks to be about mouth-size."

Leo had left a mark? My hand flew up to cover my neck, but Ambrose merely laughed. "Now, don't get all shy with me. It's the reason I left the two of you alone, after all."

"Don't be crass, Ambrose." I ignored the heat crawling up my face. "Where's Leo?"

"Left a few hours ago."

"Did he say where he was going?"

"I didn't see him, so I couldn't say. But he left you a note." Ambrose slid a folded piece of paper toward me.

Chest fluttering with anticipation, I opened Leo's note.

Sweetheart,

Went to run an errand. Will return this afternoon. Be ready.

Yours, Leo

I stared down at the words, tracing the loops and swirls of his handwriting while searching for insight. I imagined him sitting down to write it, his hair falling onto his brow as the pen traveled across the paper.

Yours.

One little word, yet it held so much meaning. A lump formed in my throat, a ball of yearning for a dream I'd all but given up on. My whole life I'd only wished for one thing: to belong. To a family, to the nuns. To anyone. All I ever wanted was to be someone worthy of loving.

Maybe Leo and I weren't so temporary, after all.

I refolded the paper, hope bubbling in my chest. A dangerous emotion, hope. I'd avoided it for years, especially when it pertained to other people. In my experience people only let you down if you relied on them.

Yet Leo had somehow worked his way under my skin. And right now I was anxious to see him, touch him. My skin nearly crawled with it, an ache settling low in my belly at the thought of being with him again.

"I can see you are equally smitten."

I shook myself out of my thoughts and returned my attention to Ambrose. "Pardon?"

"You, smitten over Leo. Just as he is smitten over you."

More heat spread under my cheeks. "You think Leo is smitten with me?"

"My dear woman, he is positively over the moon for you."

I bit my lip, wondering about this. If Leo was smitten, why was he talking about what he'd do when he returned to Boston? Shouldn't he plan to stay with me in New York? "Why would you say so?"

"Because I know him. I see the way he looks at you. Not to mention he told you about the Pendelton estate, about his father. That isn't information he shares with just anyone."

There went my hopes even higher. "You know all about it too?"

"Yes, but Leo and I go way back."

"How far back?"

"Ages. Your water is boiling, by the way, and yes, I would love a cup."

I wasn't about to ignore his evasive answer, but I needed to deal with the water for my tea. Once I had two cups ready, I brought them over to the table. "There. Now, tell me how you know Leo."

"It's not an exciting story, I'm afraid. Two young fatherless youths on the streets of Boston. We were both lads, not more than twelve and thirteen. Got into trouble now and then. Those were good times."

I stirred sugar into my tea. "I can only imagine. A terrible thing, what the Pendeltons did to his father."

"Indeed. Leo's always had his mind fixated on revenge against that family."

He had? I quirked an eyebrow in Ambrose's direction. "Revenge? How?"

"Oh, I couldn't say, miss. We used to dream up all kinds of wild schemes as boys. Makes it easier that they never did find out what happened to the missing daughter."

"What do you mean, it makes it easier?"

He sipped his tea, then wiped his mustache delicately. "The schemes. We imagined all number of things, from finding the Pendelton heiress and marrying her, to writing a fake ransom note and running away with the money. Or even convincing a young woman to pose as the heiress and split the reward money with her."

My jaw dropped open as I stared at him in horror. "Those are terrible, awful ideas. I know they mistreated Mr. Hardy, but they suffered a great loss, a misery no parent should be forced to endure. To pile on more is just cruel, Ambrose."

He held up his palms, instantly contrite. "Oh, I realize that now. I would never perpetrate such a thing. I'm merely recalling the ramblings of two young boys with hardly any cash to speak of."

"Shame on both of you for even considering it, though I can understand Leo's side, I suppose. His father's life was destroyed when he was let go."

"Yes, it certainly was. Have you seen where the Hardys live in Boston?"

"No. Why?"

He shook his head sadly. "Quite a small space for seven people. Leo doesn't have an easy time keeping them afloat."

Was Ambrose trying to say I shouldn't have brought Leo to New York? "Well, I certainly hope our trip here will change all that."

"No doubt our dear Leo hopes the same."

We sipped our tea in silence for a few minutes. I got the sense Ambrose was observing me for some reason, though I couldn't say why. Was he worried I was somehow taking advantage of Leo? Or was he trying to see if I was serious about his friend?

Was he waiting for me to confess all my dirty secrets?

I nearly snorted. He'd be waiting a long time, then. Sleeping with Leo was the dirtiest secret I had, and Ambrose already knew about it.

When the silence stretched, I couldn't take it anymore. "Were you waiting for me to say something?"

"No, why?"

He was infuriatingly calm, not to mention impossible to read. "I don't know. I get the sense you're here on a fishing expedition."

"Now, what in the blue blazes would I be fishing for?"

"You tell me."

Ambrose gave me a wide grin, his eyes twinkling. "You are doggedly determined, Miss Smith. I like it. Is it wrong to want to get to know the woman who has stolen the heart of my best friend?"

"Best friend?" I asked skeptically.

"One of them, anyway." Ambrose drained the rest of his tea and stood. "I must be off. Give my regards to Leo, will you?"

Returning to the table, he found my hand and brought it to his lips. He gave me the briefest of kisses, his mustache tickling my skin. "Adieu, dear Miss Smith."

"Goodbye, Mr. Lee."

He slapped his derby on his head and strolled out the front door. I stared at the closed wood and drank my tea. How odd. Ambrose was such a strange fellow. Stopping by and not even waiting for Leo's return.

Suddenly, I realized that he hadn't carried any clothes with him when he left.

LEO

I was nearly bursting with anticipation when I came through the door of Ambrose's apartment. I'd held off on reading the letter the baby nurse supposedly wrote my father until Josie and I could look at it together.

I found her at the kitchen table, with a stack of newspapers in front of her. She glanced up as I came in, her lips curling into a welcoming smile. Everything inside me calmed at the sight of her here, and I couldn't prevent the grin as I removed my hat. "Hello, sweetheart. How was your day?"

"Strange."

She rose and came over to me. Before I could ask why, she threw her arms around my neck and kissed me on the mouth. She met my tongue with hers, boldly invading, and I couldn't remember the last time I'd enjoyed returning to a place this much.

Probably never.

I kissed her hard, forgetting everything else except her taste and the feel of her breath on my skin. I held her close, my hands at her waist, and her palms landed on my chest. My head swam, my body responding as the seconds expanded, and I tilted my head to deepen the angle. She rewarded me by sighing into my mouth, and I stroked her tongue with flicks and swirls. I hoped to be doing the same to her pussy shortly . . .

When she pulled away, her breath was labored. "Goodness. You are happy to return, it seems."

"I'm happy to see *you*. And I have something to show you."

"I also have something to show." She angled toward the table and cast out her arm. "Melvin sent me these shows to review."

"Review?" I drew closer to the newsprint to see. "Why?"

"These are the shows either about to open or recasting a major role. He wants me to see what strikes my fancy."

"He must feel confident about getting you whichever part you decide on."

She shrugged. "I couldn't say. His note didn't elaborate." She lowered herself into one of the chairs. "Now tell me what has you in such a tizzy."

"Let me sit first. Would you like a drink? We could open one of Ambrose's bottles of wine."

"Yes, please. Speaking of Ambrose, he stopped by today."

"What did he want? To see me?"

A little divot formed between her eyebrows. "It was strange. He said he stopped by for fresh clothes, but he didn't carry any out with him when he left. Instead, he sat and talked with me."

The back of my neck tightened with warning. Ambrose hadn't stopped by to see me or to pick up clothes. He'd visited with Josie instead.

To hide my growing concern, I turned and went for the wine. "What did the two of you discuss?"

"You, mostly."

I opened the wine and smelled the contents to make certain it hadn't turned to vinegar. With Ambrose, one never knew. It smelled fine, so I poured two glasses and carried them to the table. "And what about me were you discussing?"

"Would you like for me to recite the entire conversation?"

I did, actually, but I didn't think it was fair to Josie. Handing her a glass, I said, "No, that's unnecessary. Your general recollections will do."

"Let's see, there was your family. Your father. How the two of you met. How you've always wanted revenge on the Pendeltons. He said the two of you discussed it quite a bit."

Now, why had Ambrose said that?

"Also," she continued, "he thinks you're smitten with me."

She spoke shyly, as if she couldn't believe such a thing might be true, and lying never occurred to me. She deserved the truth about this—and so much more.

Leaning over, I kissed her cheek. "That's because I am."

Her expression softened, and she stared at me like I was a frozen ice treat on a blistering summer day. "Good, because I'm equally smitten."

A wave of relief went through me. "I'm glad to hear it."

When I started to pull back, she grabbed my arm. "But you were talking about returning to Boston."

I was? I didn't remember making any plans. "When?"

She drank her wine, then licked her lips. "Last night. You said you needed to have a long chat with the two men from my past when you returned to Boston."

"That doesn't mean I'm planning to leave tomorrow."

"Martha said you're not a man who sticks."

I blinked several times in surprise. Damn it. I knew I shouldn't have let Martha and Josie go off alone that day. But it didn't matter. It was time to tell Josie how I knew Martha, what my life in Boston was like.

It was time to tell her how I knew Ambrose.

I took a long drink of wine to bolster my courage. I wasn't used to the telling the truth; lies were so much easier. But Josie deserved to hear it. Confessing was the right thing to do, even if I wasn't comfortable with saying the words.

I drained my glass. Fuck, I needed more wine for this.

I went to the counter, retrieved the bottle, and brought it to the table with me. When I refilled our glasses, I took another swallow before saying, "I have to tell you something. And you're probably not going to like it."

Josie's green gaze anxiously searched my face. "Are you married?"

"No! Jesus, no. I'm not married."

"Phew!" She wiped her brow dramatically. "That's a relief. So what is it?"

"It's about how I earned a living back in Boston. It was similar to sales, but it wasn't exactly sales."

She froze with the glass halfway to her mouth. "Similar to sales? What does that mean?"

I drew in a deep breath, then let it out. There was no more putting off the truth. "I worked on the street. Mostly as a confidence man."

Carefully, she placed her glass on the table. "Mostly a confidence man. What about the rest of the time?"

"I have other skills." I waved my hands. "Abilities that I may call upon to—"

"Spit it out, Leo!" She straightened. "You're starting to worry me."

"I was a pickpocket."

The air left her lungs in a rush. "You're a thief."

"I prefer 'dipper.'"

"Thief."

She pushed out of her chair and began pacing. I clasped my hands together and waited for her to absorb the news.

"You steal," she said. "From other people. Their belongings and whatnot. Like the man in Central Park, which was how you knew what he was about to do."

"I *stole*, past tense. But yes, all of that is true."

"Stealing is wrong, Leo."

"I didn't have a choice." I needed her to understand, so I gestured to her chair. "Sit down and I'll tell you."

Warily, she lowered herself into her chair. "I hope you aren't going to try to excuse it."

"I'm not. It was wrong. But there aren't many honest opportunities available to a thirteen-year-old boy who has a family to support. The factories don't pay enough, and what else was I qualified for? Some boys I knew sold their bodies—there are always people willing to pay for that sort of thing—but I couldn't do it. So I was on the street, considering joining one of the gangs, when I met a man named St. Elmer. He had a group of young men he mentored, teaching them how to pinch and run schemes on unsuspecting citizens. It seemed so easy—and the money?" I whistled. "More than I could make in a month in a factory. I didn't have the luxury of turning it down. My father was dying, drinking himself to death, and my mother couldn't afford food. We were desperate, Josie. There wasn't time for right and wrong."

Her lips flattened, but at least she didn't look away in disgust. Instead, she continued to stare at me. "This is how you know Ambrose."

I nodded once. "This is how I know Ambrose."

"That makes what he said today slightly more sensible, at least."

The same tightness returned to the back of my neck. "What did he say?"

"How you dreamed of getting revenge on the Pendeltons by writing a fake ransom note and taking the money. Things such as that."

I stared at the liquid in my glass and wondered over this. Why was Ambrose discussing the Pendeltons with Josie? I made a mental note to find him tomorrow and demand an answer.

"Are you . . . ?" She reached for her wine and took a long draught. "Are you going to keep working as a pickpocket?"

"No, of course not. I'm a manager now, remember?" I paused. "That is, if you'll still have me."

"But what if we never make any money? What if my voice gives out? What if everyone hates—"

"Stop." I couldn't stand to hear her doubt herself. Not when she was so dashed talented. I grabbed her hand on the table and squeezed. "Sweetheart, it's all going to work out. I know it."

"So . . . Martha? Was she mentored by this St. Elmer character too?"

"Nothing like that. But I performed at parties for her, card tricks and other sleight of hand. Which brings me to this." I held up the love letter in my fingers. "This is a letter the Pendelton baby nurse supposedly wrote to my father, her lover."

Josie's eyes went huge. "Your father was sleeping with—"

"No, definitely not. But someone was and they tried to pin that, as well as the kidnapping, on my father." I told Josie everything I'd learned from Detective Porter this morning. "So, we have to use this letter to figure out who tried to frame my father."

She pointed to the paper in my hand. "You stole evidence from the police."

"Borrowed," I corrected. "I'll return it when I'm done."

Josie cast her eyes toward the ceiling, like she was looking for divine intervention. "Leo! Stealing is wrong. Did we not just have this conversation?"

"This is the last time, I swear. What was I supposed to do? They accused my father of something terrible, Josie. His name deserves to be cleared."

"There are proper methods for these things. You can't go about making up names and stories and stealing evidence!"

"And I won't, I promise. Not after this. You don't have to worry."

She crossed her arms over her chest and glared at me. "We will discuss this later. For now, let's read the damn thing and see if it proves your father innocent."

Grateful for the temporary reprieve in the topic, I opened the letter. Flowery script flowed over the page. I spread the paper on the table so we both could read the words:

My dearest—

Your affectionate letter, though brief, was most touching. I keep it hidden, of course, but I dare say it resides close to my heart. I do so look forward to the day when we may share our feelings publicly, not in secret as we have done for these many months. As you say, the wait will be worthwhile, but it pains me to be apart from you.

Do not think as I walk by that I am not thinking of you, pining for you. Be assured, my golden angel, that I am forever holding you in my heart most ardently.

"Golden angel?" Josie snorted.

"You wouldn't like it if I used that endearment for you?"

"Be serious." She elbowed my arm. "Now, be quiet. Let me read the rest."

The day rapidly approaches. I do hope we are not caught, as much hinges on our success. I cannot know the epitome of happiness until this business concludes and we are sharing our lives in a distant place. From student and tutor to man and wife, I remain—

Your still constant, faithful, and devoted love,
Annie

"It's dated five weeks before the kidnapping," I noted. "This must be the event to which she refers."

"Student and tutor." Josie eased back in the chair with her wine. "What an odd thing to say."

"My father never tutored anyone."

"No, Annie is the tutor. Man and wife, so man matches up with student."

That made sense. "These were definitely between two members of the Pendelton staff. She talks about walking by."

"Too bad we can't find his letters, too. Then we would know his identity."

Frustrated, I dragged my hands through my hair. "This only raises more questions."

"There are clues here." She patted my arm, her smile teasing. "Do not despair, my golden angel. We will—"

I lunged for her, lifting her over my shoulder and tickling her ribs. Squealing, she wriggled and laughed, but I held steady as I carried her into the bedroom. "Let's go and put your smart mouth to better use."

Chapter Nineteen

JOSIE

Maillard's confectionary shop, located in a hotel, was a feast for the eyes, with bright colors and glass cases full of candy. Looking around, I took in the patrons enjoying tea and sandwiches. The women here were well dressed, with expensive hats and finely made dresses. I tried not to feel frumpy in comparison.

"Ah, there you are."

Turning at the familiar male drawl, I saw Ambrose approaching. That was odd. Why was he here? Only yesterday Leo had confessed his background to me, and knowing the truth made me wary regarding Ambrose.

Especially when I wasn't expecting to see him. Earlier, Leo sent me a cable to meet him here this afternoon after his suit fitting, per Melvin. I hadn't realized Ambrose would be joining us as well. "Mr. Lee. This is a surprise."

"Miss Smith." He bowed over my hand. "How lovely you look today."

"I don't understand. Where's Leo?"

"He'll be along, don't worry. In the meantime, I have someone I'd like for you to meet."

I didn't care for this, not one bit. Was he taking me to meet one of his friends? Considering his and Leo's background, it could mean almost anything. "I'd rather wait for Leo, if you don't mind," I said, digging in my heels when Ambrose took my arm.

"He'll be along. We might as well sit and be comfortable while we wait."

That was sensible, I supposed. Besides, the confectionary shop was crowded and I didn't wish to be in the way. Sitting for a few minutes wouldn't kill me.

I let him guide me deeper into the room, toward the back. Except he stopped at an occupied table, one with an older woman enjoying her luncheon alone. A green silk afternoon gown, slightly faded, adorned her frame, but she was still elegant in the overhead light. She hardly seemed the type of woman with whom Ambrose would socialize.

Ambrose bowed slightly. "Madam, good afternoon."

The older woman looked up at us—and a jolt of recognition hit me. I knew her. We'd met in the retiring room at the Metropolitan Opera House the other night.

I smiled. "Oh, hello. It's nice to see you again."

She angled toward me and blinked several times. "I . . . I don't understand. It's you?"

That was an odd greeting. "It's me," I said with a shrug. "Strange, I know. I never expected to see you again either."

Ambrose's voice climbed in surprise. "Wait, the two of you have met?"

"Is this some sort of a jest?" the older woman said sharply, her voice dripping with disapproval.

"Not at all, madam." Ambrose sounded cool and confident once more. "May I present Miss Smith? Miss Smith, this is Mrs. William Pendelton."

Pendelton. Oh, goodness. *This* was Mrs. Pendelton, Mr. Hardy's former employer and the woman who lost her child all those years ago? But why were we intruding upon her luncheon?

Mrs. Pendelton placed her serviette on the table. "It's clear you are both wasting my time."

"I don't understand," I said, looking to Ambrose. "Why are you bothering her?"

"Now, wait a moment," Ambrose said, putting up his palms as if to calm us down. "Let's sit and have a reasonable chat together."

"There is little to discuss, young man." Though she was seated, Mrs. Pendelton looked down her nose at Ambrose. "You expect me to believe it's her?"

"It's her." Ambrose's smile was a shade too slick for my liking. "I have verified it myself."

What on earth was happening here?

Before I could ask, Mrs. Pendelton narrowed angry eyes on me. "Is this because of our interaction at the opera? Do you believe me so desperate, so mired in grief as to be ripe for a charlatan?" She let out a bitter chuckle. "People have been lying to me for almost eighteen years. Do you honestly think to succeed when the rest have all failed?"

The back of my neck turned hot under her accusatory stare. "I haven't any idea what this is about. I'm here to meet a friend of mine."

"As if I'd believe that."

I didn't care for any of this. Mrs. Pendelton didn't want us near her, and I had no idea what Ambrose was attempting to do. I started to walk away, but Ambrose put a hand on my arm to stop me. "Release me," I snapped.

Ignoring me, he addressed Mrs. Pendelton. "Madam, are you saying that you cannot see it for yourself? The hair, the eyes . . . She looks exactly like you."

"What is going on here?"

The familiar deep voice cut across the room. Leo was storming toward our table, his long stride eating up the distance easily. My shoulders instantly relaxed. Thank goodness. He would set Ambrose straight.

"Leo," Ambrose said. "You've arrived! Perfect timing."

Perfect timing?

Before I could ponder what might be happening, Leo stepped closer to Ambrose, his mouth flat and angry. "Let go of her immediately." Ambrose released me and held up his hands, which prompted Leo to demand quietly, "Explain yourself. What is this about?"

"Who are you, young man?" Mrs. Pendelton said sharply. "Why are you here?"

"I'm with her." Leo gestured to me. "I'm her manager."

"Manager of what, exactly?" Mrs. Pendelton gave me a look that could wither a freshly bloomed flower.

But I was made of stronger stuff than that. I didn't wither. Instead, I straightened my shoulders and answered with all the confidence I could muster. "I'm a singer, ma'am. Miss Joséphine Smith from Paris. Perhaps you've read of me in the newspapers?"

Mrs. Pendelton froze, her body going very still. "What name did you say?"

"Miss Joséphine Smith. I'm quite famous."

"Is that your real name?"

Why would she ask me such a thing? "As far as the newspapers are concerned, yes."

"How old are you, girl?" the older woman asked.

It was always a difficult question to answer, and this time was no different. Through the tightness in my throat, I said, "It's hard to say exactly, but I think I'm almost twenty."

"And why is it hard to say exactly?"

Frustrated, I glanced at Leo. His face was pale, his expression worried. I said, "Leo, I'd like to leave."

"Of course," Leo said and started forward.

But Ambrose put his arm out, preventing Leo from reaching me. "Now, now. Let's not be too hasty. I think we are finally getting to the truth of it."

"Both of you boys, get out." Mrs. Pendelton waved her hand at the two men. "I wish to speak to Miss Smith alone."

"I beg your pardon," Leo said. "But I won't leave without her."

"Then you may wait outside. But I'll not have you two interfering any longer."

Those words. They reminded me of the conversation between Ambrose and Leo after the opera.

We've never interfered before.

You've never brought in a woman before.

This all felt planned. Contrived. Clearly, Leo and Ambrose were up to something. And it involved me and Mrs. Pendelton.

But Leo wouldn't involve me in one of his confidence schemes. He'd given all that up. Hadn't he?

My head spun with doubts and recollections. I needed a moment to think. I knew the answer was in the conversations stored in my brain.

Before I could do that, however, I needed to apologize to Mrs. Pendelton. "Please, wait outside," I told Leo. "Give me a moment."

"Josie, I think you should come with me. Now." Leo moved closer, his blue eyes switching between pleading with me and glaring at Ambrose. He almost seemed nervous. Was he worried about leaving me alone?

"I'll be fine," I reassured him. "And I won't be long."

"You heard the lady," Ambrose said, putting a hand on Leo's arm. "Let's wait outside, Leo."

Still, he hesitated.

Mrs. Pendelton sighed heavily. "Go, both of you. Or I'll ask the manager to show you out."

I didn't want trouble, so I motioned for Leo to go. Apologizing to Mrs. Pendelton wouldn't take long, and it was something I had to do for my own peace of mind. *Just wait outside,* I mouthed to him.

Leo started to speak, then stopped. Nodding once, he turned on his heel and strode toward the door. Ambrose, looking strangely pleased, gave us an elaborate bow as he backed away, then slipped his derby onto his head. He trailed Leo to the exit.

Clasping my hands together, I met the older woman's stare directly. "I beg your pardon, madam. We have clearly wasted your time. I'll leave you to your day and we may forget this ever happened."

"Sit down." She pointed to the empty seat across from her. "I wish to speak with you."

Mrs. Pendelton's words were commanding, laced with the attitude of someone used to being obeyed. She reminded me of the nuns at the asylum. I didn't dare disagree.

I sat.

LEO

A haze of panic and anger clouded my vision as I stepped outside. This was a goddamn disaster—and one person was to blame.

"You son of a bitch!" I shoved Ambrose's chest when he arrived outside on the walk. "What do you think you're doing?"

Unrepentant, Ambrose put his palms up. His smile was slick and satisfied, and I wanted to punch him. Badly. "Now, Leo. Have you forgotten rule number five?"

Fifth rule of being a confidence man: always look out for yourself.

"Fuck the rules," I snapped—and a woman walking by gasped at my language. Scowling, I grabbed Ambrose's arm and led him away from the pedestrians. When we reached an alcove near the corner of the hotel, I pushed him against the brick wall and Ambrose's derby fell to the ground. I snarled, "You had no right to use Josie like that."

Ambrose bent to collect his hat from the ground, then brushed the brim with the sleeve of his coat. "Now, Leo. There's no reason to hate me because I pulled this off before you had the chance."

"I changed my—"

"Aha! I knew it." He pointed at me. "You were planning to get

Josie in front of Mrs. Pendelton and convince the old woman that Josie was her daughter, then skip with the reward money."

Another outraged gasp sounded behind my shoulder. I turned, ready to tell the busybody to get lost—except I found Josie.

Oh, shit.

I froze. Her eyes were wide with hurt, her face slack as she gaped at me. She'd clearly overheard our conversation, and my stomach dropped to the ground.

Say something.

I needed to smooth this over, reassure her that everything was fine, but for the first time in my life I couldn't speak. The words wouldn't come. My mouth was too dry, my tongue too thick with regret. I literally didn't know what to say. How much had she heard?

"Is it true?" she croaked. "Is that what you were planning to do?"

I stood silent, my mind racing. I couldn't deny it, nor could I tell her the truth. I was caught and no escape plan came to mind. All my abilities—reading a mark and saying what they needed to hear—deserted me. Josie wasn't a mark, and she hadn't been for a long time.

Her eyebrows lowered as her gaze chilled. "You're lying. You and Ambrose, this was a scheme to acquire the Pendeltons' money. To finally get your revenge."

Inhaling, I closed my eyes and tried to think of what to say. Unfortunately, what came out was, "Ambrose and I are not working together."

"Oh my god," she whispered and wrapped her arms around her waist. "You were doing this alone? I knew there was something off about your sudden interest in me. But I let you—"

Her bottom lip trembled slightly. I'd never seen her look so small. It tore at my heart. "Wait. Josie, please. I can explain."

"This is what you were planning all along, why you brought me to New York, isn't it?"

"At first, yes. But not now. Josie, you have to believe me—"

"So it was never about my singing or our relationship. Everything since the moment we met has been a lie."

"No! Your voice is a gift, unlike any I've heard. And the rest? The sleigh and what happened after? That was real, too."

"Stop lying. Soon you'll claim that finding me on the street in Boston was a coincidence."

"It was a coincidence. But when I saw you, you reminded me of someone. It took a moment, but then I recalled Mrs. Pendelton. Your hair and eyes are the same color. I used the manager angle to get close to you."

"To get close to me," she repeated, her voice raising. "Stop talking, Leo. Just . . . stop. You're making it worse and I need to return inside."

"Don't go—"

She talked over me. "I came out to tell you not to wait and I'll meet you downtown later." Though her voice shook, she drew her shoulders back and seemed to regain herself. "Though I won't be doing that now."

I could feel her slipping away from me, like wisps of smoke. I stepped closer, desperate to hold on in any way I could manage. "Josie."

When I tried to grasp her hand, she stepped back. "Don't touch me. Don't wait for me. I don't want to see you again."

Spinning, she walked away, hurrying toward Maillard's. I took a step after her, intending to catch up with her and help her understand, but a hand landed on my arm, stopping me.

"Let her go," Ambrose said smoothly. "No good will come from chasing after her on the street. Give her time to calm down."

My muscles trembled with fury. Rounding on him, I pushed him with both hands and he stumbled backward. "Do not tell me what to do. You've ruined everything, you bastard."

He continued retreating, keeping me at arm's length like he knew I was close to punching him. "You are angry because this was your idea and I stole it."

"Wrong. I didn't want her used like this. Now she thinks I'm involved in your scheme and she'll likely never speak to me again."

"Not sure how that is my problem."

I lunged for him, but he danced out of my reach. "Now, Leo. This is what we do, what we've always done. I don't see a problem. You should be thanking me. I've introduced her to the Pendeltons and you can still marry the girl. You shall be rich beyond your—"

I couldn't help it any longer. I charged at him and sent him flying backward into the brick, his arms flailing as he tried to catch himself from falling.

We grappled for a moment or two, until Ambrose shoved me away. His lip curled into a sneer. "Do not dare claim the high ground with me, Leo Hardy. I know you too well."

No, he didn't. Because I'd changed.

A year ago? Six months ago? Hell, even a week ago I would've jumped at the chance to fleece the Pendeltons out of that reward money.

But now?

I didn't want to use Josie for my own gain, even if it meant getting revenge on the Pendeltons and helping my family. Josie didn't deserve it, and I cared for her. A lot. "We are different people now, Ambrose."

"Horseshit," Ambrose spat, straightening to his full height. "I know you better than anyone else on this earth, even your own mother. And you'd sell your soul to make a quick buck. Just like me."

"No, I wouldn't. Some things are worth more than money."

Never thought I'd say the words, but there they were, falling out of my mouth and onto the dirty streets I used to hate.

But they were true. Josie was worth more than money to me. She was worth *everything*.

He snorted and brushed his coat sleeves. "Nothing is worth more than money—and anyone who believes such nonsense is a fool."

"Nevertheless, this idea, this scheme stops now."

"Oh, is that what you believe?" He poked me in the chest with one finger. "Hear me now, Hardy. I am fixing to collect that reward money and nothing and no one will stop me."

I shoved his hand away from me. "I will do everything in my power to ensure it doesn't happen."

Ambrose thrust his fists into his trouser pockets, a grin tugging at his mouth. "I do wish you luck, my friend. Because once I have that money, I'm never letting go of it."

He eased around me and started off down the walk. Heat simmered inside me, but I let him go. I would deal with Ambrose later.

First, I needed to wait for Josie.

Chapter Twenty

JOSIE

Y ou are pale." Mrs. Pendelton's sharp gaze examined my face upon my return. "Has something happened outside?"

"It's not important." I retook my seat, grateful to have a moment to absorb what I'd learned a moment ago. My knees were still shaking.

I used the manager angle to get close to you.

I put a hand on my stomach, as if to ease the nausea and heartache, but it was pointless. More than a few deep breaths would be required to get over this betrayal.

Never trust anyone.

Hadn't I always known it? Yet somehow, I'd allowed Leo to worm his way under my defenses. Indeed, I supposed that was what all good confidence men did.

"I cannot stay long," I told the older woman. There were now a whole slew of tasks awaiting me today, including finding somewhere to live.

"You'll stay as long as I like," Mrs. Pendelton said in a no-nonsense tone. "I demand answers."

"Oh, yes. I suppose that's fair. You see, those two men—"

"I needn't hear anything more regarding those two hooligans. I meant *you*, my dear. I want answers regarding you."

Hooligan was an apt description. I straightened the flatware on the table, avoiding her shrewd gaze. "About what, exactly?"

"Let us start at the beginning. You are from Boston, obviously. It is plain in your voice."

"Yes, that's true. Lived there all my life." I was fairly certain, anyway.

"With your parents?"

"No, ma'am. I was raised at the Boston Children's Asylum until I was eighteen."

A small divot formed between her eyebrows as she frowned. "And your age when you were deposited at this children's asylum?"

"The nuns believe seventeen or eighteen months. More than a year but less than two." I shrugged. "No one really knows for certain."

"The person who dropped you off left no information regarding your background? What of your birth parents?"

I shifted uncomfortably on the tiny seat. Why was she asking so many questions? God knew this was my least favorite topic to discuss. "No information, and I haven't a clue as to who they were."

"And no other set of parents adopted you or took you in?"

On top of Leo's betrayal this was too much. I couldn't withstand dredging up more memories or emotion at the moment. "If it's all the same to you, ma'am, I'd rather go and not answer any more questions."

"Why?"

I nearly gaped at her. Was she so oblivious, then? I could feel my control slipping, the anger taking over. "Because you are delving into my past, which I'd like to forget. Not to mention that it's been a miserable damn day."

Mrs. Pendelton drew herself up and peered down her nose at me. "There is no need to be rude, young lady. And kindly refrain from using profanities in my presence."

I shrank in my chair, small and inferior, like I'd disappointed her. Which was silly, considering we were strangers. "I beg your pardon, ma'am. Though I must say, you were much nicer in the ladies' retiring room."

"That was before three charlatans attempted to swindle me."

I exhaled and rubbed my eyes. "I am no charlatan, but I suppose you won't believe anything I say at this point."

"How do you know those two men?"

"I met Leo in Boston and we came here together. Ambrose is Leo's friend. For some reason they thought . . ." I swallowed hard in an attempt to clear the bitterness. "They wanted you to believe I'm your missing daughter. Then they planned to collect the reward."

She lifted her teacup and sipped, each movement precise and perfect. "Many have certainly tried. That young man called you Josie, but your stage name is Joséphine?"

"That's right."

"Is Josie your given name?"

"I assume so. It's the only name the nuns ever used for me."

"And who thought up Joséphine?"

Suddenly, this was too much. Pain exploded behind my temples, all my emotions crashing into my skull with the subtlety of a steam engine.

I rubbed my head. I hadn't experienced a migraine in years. I used to get them as a young girl, when the prospective adoptive parents would leave the asylum with another child. Each time had devastated me, but I never allowed myself to cry over it. Pippa always said the headaches were my brain's way of coping with emotions that overwhelmed me.

Nevertheless, I hated them. They made me feel weak and helpless.

Maybe if I could lie down, alone, it would go away. Then I could wallow and cry, scream and curse, let everything out that I was holding inside. Afterward, I might feel a tiny bit better.

But where can I go?

I stared at the table, no good answer forthcoming.

"You've gone pale once again," Mrs. Pendelton said. "When was the last time you ate something?"

I pressed on my temples, hoping to stop the incessant pounding. "I don't know. I should leave, though. I don't feel up to answering any more questions."

"Are you ill?"

I rose with the intention to quickly get fresh air. Then I would wander the city until I figured out what to do. "I apologize for upsetting you. Ignore those two men should they approach you again. Goodbye, ma'am."

"Wait, where are you going?"

I didn't owe her an explanation. Putting one foot in front of the other, I moved toward the door. Each step was agony, however, like slogging through heavy mud. When I reached the door, the bright sunlight stabbed through my skull like a lance. I froze for a long second, needing a moment to gather myself lest I throw up.

Squinting, I forced myself outside and dragged in a big lungful of air. Pedestrians crowded the walk in front of the hotel, so I started off in the opposite direction. I'd find a bench and sit for a spell, wait until I felt better before deciding where to go. Perhaps Melvin—

"Josie!"

My stomach roiled, both from the pain and the sound of Leo's voice. Why was he still here? I didn't stop, merely kept walking.

"Josie, wait!"

Before I could cross the street, he was there, standing in front of me, his features etched with uncertainty and panic. I had no choice but to stop, else I'd slam into him. "Out of my way, Leo."

"No, please. Hear me out. Come, let's go sit somewhere and I'll explain."

"I've heard enough. You used me. This was all about your scheme with Ambrose. None of it was real."

"That's not true." He shifted to block my path as I tried to go around him. "Wait, you have to let me explain."

I shoved his shoulder to move him. "Explain how you intended to convince Mrs. Pendelton that I'm her missing daughter? God, Leo. That's awful, even for a confidence man. How can you live with yourself?"

He shook his head. "It may have started out as revenge against the Pendeltons, but I changed my mind. I decided I couldn't use you in such a fashion."

"That hardly excuses your behavior. You selfish, manipulative man. How dare you lie to me? How dare you use me for one single—" Fresh pain burst inside my skull. I closed my eyes and bent over slightly, waiting for the nausea to pass.

"Are you all right?" He clasped my arm, but his touch infuriated me.

"Let go." I gave a weak tug of my arm to break free, but failed.

"Josie, come with me. You're pale and sweaty. Let me take care of you."

"I already told you. I don't want to ever see you again—"

"Release her at once, young man."

Mrs. Pendelton was now beside us, flanked by a hotel doorman. Her disapproving gaze was focused on where Leo gripped my arm. "Or I shall have you arrested for assault."

Leo let go and held up his hands. "I only wish to speak with her, ma'am."

The doorman stepped between Leo and me. "Get lost. If I have to say it again, it'll be a roundsman for you."

Leo began arguing with the doorman, but I paid no attention. Instead, I turned and started in the opposite direction, intent on getting away from there, even though the pain in my head was excruciating. I bumped into a large man and nearly went tumbling to the walk.

A woman's hand grabbed my arm, stabilizing me.

"Come with me." Mrs. Pendelton began guiding me toward the street. I winced at the jostling, every tiny movement like a hammer to my skull.

"This isn't necessary," I protested. "I'll be fine."

"Nonsense. I fear you shall keel over on the walk."

Through the haze of pain, I saw a large black carriage ahead, with a liveried footman lowering the step. I felt too weak to resist. Fine, she could drop me off at Melvin's office. He'd help me find somewhere to stay.

I climbed in, grateful for the temporary escape. The pain in my head eased slightly as soon as I was out of the direct path of the sun. Closing my eyes, I relaxed against the fine leather seat. I heard Mrs. Pendelton's skirts rustle as she settled across from me.

With all the strength I could muster, I said, "You may drop me at Herald Square."

"I have already instructed my man to take us to my home. I'm not through talking with you."

Christ, would this nightmare never end? "Mrs. Pendelton, I have a terrible ache in my head. I'd like to go lie down and be alone, if you don't mind."

"I do mind," she snapped. "The company you keep is appalling. Who knows what this agent is like? Someone clearly needs to save you from yourself." When I grimaced, she softened her tone. "You may rest at my home until you feel up to talking."

I stopped arguing. My head ached, not to mention that my heart felt as if it had been ripped out of my chest. I closed my eyes and let my head rest against the seat back.

If a wealthy older woman wished to kidnap me, I no longer cared.

I AWOKE WITH a start.

I exhaled and stared up at an unfamiliar ceiling, intricately painted with angels.

Oh, yes. I was inside the Pendelton mansion.

Thankfully, the agony in my head was now reduced to a dull ache. When we arrived earlier, Mrs. Pendelton placed me on their sitting room sofa and ordered me to drink a terrible-tasting tonic.

I hadn't complained. Deep down, a part of me liked being looked after. I wasn't used to such consideration, even from the nuns or Pippa.

Regardless, whatever Mrs. Pendelton gave me helped me sleep off the ache in my head.

I allowed myself another moment to revel in the quiet. This was the privilege of the wealthy—big houses, wide streets, and neighbors that were too far away to hear. Quite the change from life downtown.

I would need to leave soon. I had to find Melvin, arrange for a place to stay, and send for my things. But for now, I supposed I could relax a little while longer and pretend my life hadn't fallen apart.

Pretend that the one man I'd allowed myself to care for hadn't used me or lied to me. Or slept with me.

God, I was pathetic.

Eventually, the need for a washroom overrode my misery, so I rose and crossed the long room. I discovered a corridor lined on both sides with giant paintings. I knew nothing about art, but these were probably expensive. Three gold chandeliers hung along the ceiling, their teardrop crystals shimmering in the gaslight.

"May I help you, miss?"

Startled, I turned toward the sound. A footman waited nearby. I hadn't heard him approach. "Yes, please. The washroom?"

"The facilities may be found at the end of the hall. Follow me."

I nodded, though I was capable of finding the washroom on my own. But wealthy people were notoriously incompetent, with a legion of staff to do every little thing for them. This footman's only task might very well be showing guests to the washroom. Who was I to deprive him of his only responsibility?

As we walked, I admired his perfectly pressed livery, the polished shoes that hardly made a sound on the marble floor. Even the servants here were better dressed than me.

He showed me the washroom door, but he didn't leave. I frowned. Why was he waiting? To ensure I didn't steal anything? Of course. How utterly stupid of me. They believed I was friends with Leo and Ambrose, who were established thieves.

"There's no need to wait," I said. "I won't take anything, I swear."

His brow creased with confusion. "I will wait here, miss. To show you back to the sitting room."

Oh. That made sense. Couldn't have the riffraff running amuck in the place, could we? I pulled the handle to open the door. "Suit yourself. But after I finish here, I'll be on my way."

The washroom was every bit as elegant as the rest of the house, with not a speck of dirt to be found. I tried to hurry, feeling out of place and awkward. I didn't want to break anything with my clumsiness. The sooner I left here, the better.

I washed my hands at the marble sink. The mirror reflected a woman I barely knew—gaunt, pale. Dark circles under my eyes.

I used the manager angle to get close to you.

Fresh cuts opened around my heart, like thorns strangling my insides. I would never get over those words.

But this was not the time for wallowing. I shoved thoughts of Leo aside and left the washroom.

The footman was still there. "Follow me, miss."

I assumed we were headed to the front door, but he led me back toward the sitting room. "I must be going," I told him. "I've taken up enough of their hospitality."

"Pray, come in here, girl," a feminine voice called. I peeked into the room and found Mrs. Pendelton perched on the sofa.

Sighing, I considered making a run for it. But that was a terrible way to treat her after all she'd done for me today. Furthermore, I supposed there was no use in resisting. If I answered her questions, she'd let me leave.

As I settled at the other end of the sofa, she ordered a tea tray from the same footman who'd escorted me. "That's not necessary," I said when he left. "I won't stay long enough for tea."

"You need to eat. You look terrible."

Well, that was a blunt assessment. "I know. Today has been awful. Thank you, by the way. The tonic worked wonders."

She folded her hands in her lap. "I'm no stranger to migraines myself. That tonic is an old family recipe."

"I haven't experienced one in a long time. I used to get them at the asylum when I was younger."

"Speaking of this asylum, you said you left when you were around eighteen."

"Yes, that's true."

"And what have you been doing since then?"

"Singing on the street and in a saloon. I live with Pippa. She has a job in the saloon where I sing sometimes."

"That must be difficult for you both."

I lifted one shoulder. "We manage. But I have an agent now, and he feels confident that I'll have a successful career as a performer."

Three footmen entered, each carrying a tray. I couldn't believe my eyes as they set the plates out on the low table. In addition to tea, there was a selection of both sandwiches and desserts that made my mouth water.

"Please," Mrs. Pendelton said. "Select whatever you like, Miss Smith."

I felt no shame as I began piling a small plate with as much food as it would hold. "You should call me Josie."

"You *may* call me Josie."

I paused in the process of biting into a small sandwich. "I beg your pardon?"

"Never mind," she said as she fiddled with the tea. "This manager of yours, the man with whom you were arguing outside of Maillard's?"

"Former manager," I corrected.

"Yes, former manager. Why were he and his conspirator so certain you could pass for my daughter?"

I dusted off my fingers, which prompted Mrs. Pendelton to hand me a serviette. "Thank you. Um, let's see. Leo said, 'When I saw you on the street in Boston, you reminded me of someone. It took a moment, but then I remembered Mrs. Pendelton. Your hair and eyes are the same color.' He thought it would be enough to fool you."

She made an elegant sound that would've been a snort coming from anyone else. "Have you any idea the number of women with blond hair and green eyes who have tried to convince us they were Joséphine?"

"I bet a fair amount, ma'am."

"Indeed. So these two characters hoped to pass you off as my missing daughter, collect the reward money, and disappear."

"From what I've learned today, that sounds about right." I knew I had to tell her the rest of it. The woman had suffered enough, and she deserved the truth. "But Leo had good reason to believe the resemblance might work."

"Oh?"

"Yes. His surname is Hardy. Does that name ring any bells?"

The cup rattled on the saucer, tea spilling over the rim, and she carefully set it back on the table. "Goodness," she muttered and dabbed the spilled liquid with a cloth. "He is the son, isn't he? They believe his father—" She pressed her lips together, unable to finish.

"Steven Hardy wasn't responsible," I said gently. "I know some people may think he was involved in your daughter's disappearance, but he wasn't."

"How could you possibly know such a thing? The investigator we hired was sure of it. And there were letters."

While I hated Leo, I couldn't lie. Furthermore, I remembered Leo's genuine horror upon learning his father was a suspect. He'd been devastated. "Steven Hardy took the family to Boston and drank himself to death. They live humbly. There was never any money or any evidence of his involvement."

"His tendency to imbibe could very well be a result of the guilt. And I cannot accept the son's word on his father's innocence, especially when we've established the son is a liar."

She handed me a cup and saucer, which I gratefully accepted. "On this I believe Leo is telling the truth."

"You cannot know for certain, not when the case remains unsolved."

"Well, no one can know for certain. But I do know that Leo's family struggled after their father was let go after twenty years with no reference from you."

"A reference! For a man who may have helped the kidnappers take my child? He was fortunate not to end up behind bars."

"But what if he didn't do it? Then the detectives wasted time and energy chasing after the wrong man." I bit into another soft round cookie, the vanilla flavor like absolute heaven in my mouth. I groaned in happiness. I'd never tasted something this elegant and delicious. "Why are these so good?" I mumbled to myself.

Mrs. Pendelton was quiet for a moment. "It is the uncertainty, the not knowing what happened to her that eats away at me."

I could see the sadness, the hurt she carried every day, and her comments at the opera made much more sense. Quietly, I recited, "'It's a terrible thing, hope. It's a prison without walls.'"

"Yes, that's quite true. How perceptive of you."

"No, those are your words. You said them to me in the retiring room at the opera." I sipped my tea and tried not to think about that night. Specifically, about Leo and his glorious kisses. When Mrs. Pendelton still appeared confused, I explained, "I'm able to remember every conversation word for word if I try."

"That . . ." Suddenly, Mrs. Pendelton covered her mouth with her hand, her eyes going wide. For a second I worried I'd offended her until she said, "How remarkable."

"Sometimes. But it can be awful, too. I'm also able to recall every terrible thing ever said about me."

I used the manager angle to get close to you.

Yes, precisely like that. *Thanks, brain.*

Mrs. Pendelton's expression softened, her smile a bit wistful and sad. "I suppose that is true as well. Are you able to recall our conversation from the retiring room?"

I sensed this was her subtle way of proving I wasn't a liar, but I didn't mind. I wanted her to know that I wasn't out to fleece her, too.

Closing my eyes, I thought back to the ladies' retiring room. I visualized the wallpaper, the carpets. The soft glow of the electric lights.

"You spoke first. *It is far too much, wouldn't you say?*

"*I beg your pardon?*

"*The room. A tad gaudy, wouldn't you say?*

"*It's not relaxing, at least not for me. I'm worried I'll break something.*

"*Are you particularly clumsy?*

"*Yes. No. Maybe? With all this fancy glass and crystal around, I feel like a donkey at a debutante ball.*

"*One would never know it. You are a beautiful young woman.*

"*Thank you. Are you escaping the performance? Or all those people out there?*

"*What makes you think I'm escaping?*

"*Like recognizes like, ma'am.*"

"*You are very perceptive. I know my excuse. However, I can't understand why you would need to escape. Is your escort misbehaving?*

"*No, it's not him. I feel like a camel out there, with everyone staring at me.*

"*A donkey and a camel? Goodness, you have quite the imagination—*"

"That is enough," Mrs. Pendelton whispered, then cleared her throat.

I let out a breath and opened my eyes. She was watching me

with rapt attention, surprise and something else in her expression. I reached for another round cookie, feeling self-conscious. "I apologize. After I start it's often difficult to stop."

"My mother had the same gift. I've never met a single other person who possessed such an ability."

Odd. I hadn't met anyone else with the ability either.

"The nuns didn't like it. They thought it was evil, that I was touched by the devil."

"That's a terrible thing to say to a child."

True, but god knows I'd heard worse. "I tried not to let it bother me. Mostly I use it to recall stories for Pippa."

"The girl you live with?"

"Yes, ma'am. We've been good friends for a long time. We grew up in the asylum together. There's no one I love more than her."

"Not even your Mr. Hardy?" When I choked on a bite of lemon cake, Mrs. Pendelton quickly added, "I apologize. However, I saw the way he stared at you, how desperate he was for you to hear his explanations. It was a romantic relationship, I gather?"

"Not romantic. There was a moment where I thought it could become more . . ." I sighed heavily. "But it turns out he's a scoundrel. I never want to see him again."

"What did Pippa think of him?"

"She was skeptical, but supportive. Though she warned me to keep an eye on him. I suppose we could say I failed in that regard. He sure had me fooled."

"Do not blame yourself for believing in the goodness of others."

That simple phrase lifted my spirits a tiny bit. It was true. I wasn't in the wrong for trusting Leo; he was in the wrong for lying to me. He deserved the blame, not me. "That is sound advice. Thank you. I'll try to keep that in mind."

I glanced at the windows and noticed the sky had darkened. When had it grown so late? I had to get to Melvin's office as quickly as possible.

I set down my cup and saucer, then rose. "I need to be on my way. I must get to Herald Square and speak with Mr. Birdman, my agent."

She came to her feet, but her brow was creased with concern. "It is rather late for a meeting, isn't it? Is it safe?"

"Oh, I'll be fine. I've been looking after myself for a long time. Thank you for tea, ma'am."

"You are most welcome, but I think you should stay. Here, that is. For tonight." She pinched the bridge of her nose with two fingers. "I am tongue-tied, forgive me. I would prefer you stayed here for the night instead of going out into the darkened city streets alone."

"I couldn't possibly do that. I've already imposed with the tonic and the napping on your sofa. Not to mention the tea and food. You've been too kind already."

"Nonsense. We have eight bedrooms in this house. Seven go unused every night. It is hardly an imposition."

Without waiting for my response, she went to the sitting room door and leaned out. "Jacob, have the yellow room prepared, will you? Miss Smith shall be our guest this evening."

"Of course, ma'am," a male voice said. "I'll instruct one of the maids to unpack her things."

"I have no things," I said loud enough for both of them to hear. "I'll need to fetch them from where I was staying downtown."

"I will send a man," Mrs. Pendelton said in that no-nonsense tone of hers. "Write down the address, please."

Chapter Twenty-One

JOSIE

S ilence greeted me on the ground floor the next morning. I hadn't slept well, tossing and turning, thinking about Leo's betrayal, but I couldn't stay in bed once the sun emerged—an old habit from my days at the asylum. I expected to find a flurry of activity, a bevy of staff bustling about while the Pendeltons breakfasted.

Instead, the rooms were empty. Quiet. Like the place was strangely frozen in time.

I didn't know what to do. I considered pulling on the bell to ring for a footman, but that felt . . . presumptuous. Who was I to ring for the staff? Maybe I should leave. The invitation had only been for one night, after all, and I didn't wish to impose. My plan was to say goodbye to Mrs. Pendelton and be on my way. I had a broken heart to mend and a life to build here in New York, and there was no time to lose in feeling sorry for myself.

But it felt rude to leave without thanking her, so I supposed waiting a few more minutes wouldn't hurt. I could always leave a note, if it grew too late.

I wandered the massive rooms, admiring the paintings and decor. While the Pendeltons had suffered an unimaginable loss, they also possessed more than most Americans. What was it like to be surrounded by so much wealth? To never worry about your next meal or having a roof over your head?

I couldn't fathom it.

As I passed a dim doorway, I glanced in and found a large piano. Curiosity piqued, I wandered inside and cracked the drapery for light—and discovered a music room, complete with wood paneling and a bevy of instruments. *Holy Christmas* . . .

My heart gave a happy little skip, the first sign of life in my chest since Leo's departure last night.

I sat on the small piano bench. For the hundredth time I wished I knew how to play. I could only sing, unfortunately. Not that I'd done much of that recently.

There were a few songs I sang when I was sad, but one was my favorite: "I Dreamt I Dwelt in Marble Halls" from *The Bohemian Girl*. It spoke of a life that was never mine, a love I could never possess.

An emptiness I could never fill.

I let my finger slide over the keys until I found the right beginning note. The sound reverberated in the room and lingered. Not bothering to warm up, I began singing, the haunting tune so familiar. My voice built in tenor and pitch as I went, growing stronger and bouncing off the walls, until the end when I reached full volume.

When I stopped my cheeks were wet. I wiped them with my fingers—and someone started clapping behind me.

I spun around, dread clogging my throat as if I'd been caught stealing instead of singing.

An older man stood there.

He wasn't very tall, but he had a commanding presence. Dressed sharply, neat beard. A gold watch chain attached to his silk vest. And keen eyes that watched me carefully. Instantly, I knew this was Mr. Pendelton.

I stood. "Good morning, sir."

"You must be Miss Smith."

"Indeed, I am. You must be Mr. Pendelton. Thank you for allowing me to stay here last night."

He took a few steps into the room and shoved his hands into his trouser pockets. "That was my wife's doing, but you are welcome. She has really taken a shine to you."

"I didn't wish to impose, but she is hard to turn down."

"Yes, well." The edge of his mouth lifted slightly. "She gets what she wants, certainly. Especially from me. You have a lovely voice. She said you were a singer, but I didn't believe it until just now."

"Oh, yes. I have an agent and everything."

"Who is your agent, if I might be so bold as to ask?"

"Mr. Melvin Birdman."

Mr. Pendelton looked impressed. "I know him. He's one of the best, from what I hear." He paused. "May I speak plainly, Miss Smith?"

"Please." I always preferred to know what people really thought, rather than needing to guess.

"I'm aware of how you came to be involved with my wife. If you think to extort money from us—"

"I don't!" I said quickly. "I wouldn't."

"Nevertheless, I feel it needs to be said. I won't have her hopes lifted once again, only to be dashed. Nor will I entertain a reward check for a pair of confidence artists."

"Understood. May I also speak plainly?"

"Of course."

"I was not aware of what the two men were planning. If I had been, I certainly never would've agreed. I've broken ties with them." Misery oozed in my chest, like a festering wound that would take a very long time to heal.

"You knew these men to be hustlers."

"Not exactly."

"Elucidate."

It was obvious why Mr. Pendelton was successful. He didn't strike me as weak or indirect, nor did it seem as if he'd give up without answers.

And there was no reason to hide the truth.

I folded my hands and looked him square in the eye. "I fancied myself in love with one of them, sir. He had a bit of a murky past, but I believed he had my best interests at heart. I wasn't aware he was using me to . . ." A lump formed in my throat, making it hard to say the rest. I waved my hand dismissively as more tears threatened. "It's not an inventive story, I'm afraid, but it's the truth."

"Unfortunately, I have met many of these types over the years and I know how convincing they are. I'm sorry for you, miss."

"I should've known better," I said with a lift of one shoulder. "Someone arriving out of thin air to help me launch a singing career? No one would do such a thing without an ulterior motive."

"Come now, I've heard you sing. You were bound to get discovered sooner or later." He paused, his gaze sweeping over my face and hair. "In addition, I am able to see how your features resemble my wife's."

"That is kind of you to say, considering."

"Considering that you were nearly part of a swindle to capitalize on the most painful experience a parent can endure?"

Indeed, I liked him. There was no pretending, no dancing around a subject. "Exactly."

"The man you were in love with? My wife said he is the son of our former head gardener."

"Yes, that's true. Leo Hardy is Steven Hardy's son. And before you suspect Steven of kidnapping your daughter, he didn't. In fact, bamboozling you out of the reward money was Leo's idea of revenge for the way you let Steven go."

"Our investigator was convinced Mr. Hardy was the co-conspirator. When the police claimed there wasn't enough evidence against Mr. Hardy to prosecute, we terminated his employment. But that doesn't mean he wasn't responsible. It only means we couldn't prove it."

"I can say with full confidence that pursuing Steven Hardy

as an accomplice or the person responsible for the kidnapping is a waste of time."

"How are you so certain?"

I didn't think I was wrong about this. Leo may have lied to me about everything else, but I was with him when he learned of his father's tainted reputation. I saw the devastation, the utter despair. He was capable of love—for his father, his mother and sisters. Not for me, but the affection for his family had been very real. "Because Leo loved his father. I could hear it in every story he told me and when he showed me around the grounds his father planted. He was proud of Mr. Hardy, and what happened after they left here nearly destroyed them all."

He blinked several times. "He showed you around the gardens?"

"Yes, sir. Leo brought me a few days ago." I didn't mention hiding in the sleigh. I never wished to recall that experience, now tarnished with Leo's lies. "I've also read one of the love letters that the baby nurse supposedly wrote to Leo's father."

"How?"

"Leo went to see the detective who was once the investigator on your case."

"Detective Porter?"

"Yes, sir. That was the name. There are things in that letter that point to someone other than Steven Hardy."

"This is all quite . . . unbelievable. I don't know whether to pepper you for answers or throw you out."

"I hope neither, sir. I'd like the chance to give your wife my thanks first."

He stared at his toes and sighed. "I remember the lad. Leopold. He followed Steven around everywhere the gardener went. You said the father has died?"

"He drank himself to death after leaving New York and settling the family in Boston."

Mr. Pendelton shoved his hands into his trouser pockets. "I am sorry to hear that, truly. He wouldn't admit to anything at the time and we had no choice but to let him go."

I wanted to quibble with saying there had been no choice, but it was pointless to try to rewrite the past. "You can still make it right, sir. You can let the world know that Mr. Hardy had nothing to do with the kidnapping."

"I'll consider it." He peered at me curiously. "You are quite bold for such a young lady."

"I grew up in a girls' asylum in Boston." I shrugged my shoulders. "The nuns tried to mold me into a proper lady, but I never learned how to hide my thoughts and feelings very well. Which likely explains why I was never adopted."

"My wife said they told you that you were evil, touched by the devil."

I lifted my shoulders in an attempt at a casual shrug. "Another reason why I was never adopted, I suppose. No one wants a demonic child."

"You hardly seem demonic to me."

I bit my lip in an attempt to smother a smile. "Well, you haven't seen me hungry. I can get fairly demonic then."

Mr. Pendelton laughed, the dark clouds clearing from his eyes. "Have you had breakfast yet?" When I shook my head, he gestured toward the hall. "Then we should see about getting you fed before you sprout horns and a tail."

I felt foolish. There was no reason to linger. I'd intruded enough on their lives, said my piece about Steven Hardy. I needed to sort out my own life, now that I'd tried to sort out Leo's. "I should be on my way. If you'll pass on my gratitude to your wife, I would appreciate it."

He tilted his head and regarded me carefully. "Where will you be going, if you don't mind my asking?"

"To see my agent, Mr. Birdman. He'll help me find somewhere to stay."

His eyebrows lowered as he frowned. "Forgive me for asking, but do you have the funds for a hotel?"

I didn't, but maybe Melvin would give me a loan. An advance on my future earnings. That was a thing, probably. Or I could sleep on the sofa in his office. "I don't, but you needn't worry about me. I've been looking after myself for a long time. I'll be fine."

"Please, while I don't doubt that you can manage it by yourself, there's no reason for you to rush out. We have the room, as you've seen. And my wife has enjoyed having you here. Take the day. Or two. Just until you figure out your next step."

"I couldn't possibly. You've already both been so kind."

He waved that away with a large hand, his lips twisting into a small smile. "Many say that I am never kind. So you should definitely take advantage of this momentary lapse."

"I'd hate to impose."

"If you fill the house with a voice like yours, how could it possibly be an imposition?"

Something about his earnestness struck me. Maybe this house needed a little life after so long—and he wasn't kidding about having the room. What would one or two more days hurt? "All right. I'll stay, but only until I find a place to go."

He nodded once. "Fair enough. Welcome to our home, Josie."

LEO

Growing up on the Pendelton estate had its advantages. I still remembered the ins and outs, the places to hide.

As well as how to sneak into the main house.

I had no choice. It was imperative I speak to Josie. I'd been waiting for her to return to the apartment so that I could explain, but she never came back.

A Pendelton footman arrived to collect most of her things. When I inquired about Josie, he said she was staying with the Pendeltons, but offered up no other information. Ever since, my mind had churned with questions, my stomach roiling with uncertainty.

Had she left me for good? Or was she willing to hear me out?

I needed to speak with her. I had to explain that I had nothing to do with the drama at Maillard's. More importantly I had to tell her how I felt about her.

So when she didn't return to Ambrose's apartment for the second day, I decided to go to her instead.

The library window slid open under my hand, thanks to a loose latch that was still broken all these years later. I had borrowed books from here as a boy, eager to soak in every bit of knowledge possible. After all, the Pendeltons never seemed to use the room, so I had figured there was no harm in taking book or two.

A clock somewhere inside chimed twice as I slid over the sill and into the dark room. The thick carpets muffled the sound of my footsteps and soon I ascended the main stairs.

I knew which bedchamber belonged to the Pendeltons, so I went in the opposite direction. Only one other bedchamber had its door closed. And it had a sliver of light coming from underneath.

Josie.

If I was wrong, the Pendeltons could kick me out, arrest me for trespassing. But I'd keep trying to see her. I wouldn't give up on her. On *us.*

I knocked softly on the wood and waited.

The latch clicked and the door opened. Josie stood there, gorgeous blond hair loose in waves around her shoulders. She wore her old dressing gown that covered her from neck to toe. My stomach jumped. I was so damn happy to see her. "Hello."

She swung the door closed.

Shit! In a flash, I shoved my foot between the wood and jamb, barely catching the door before it closed. "Let me in," I said quietly.

"Get out before I scream the house down."

She shoved the door onto my toe and I winced. "Two minutes. That's all I need. Please."

"I don't want to see you. Go away."

I had to play dirty. "I'm not leaving until you listen to me. I'll sleep outside your door all night if I must. Do you really want them to find me in the hall?"

That did it. She yanked open the door and pulled me inside. "You have two minutes—and I will be watching the clock."

I stepped into the room and she closed the door behind me softly. True to her word, Josie faced the mantel clock and stared at it, so I started speaking. "I had nothing to do with what Ambrose did. I had no idea it was happening. If I had, I would've stopped it, I swear."

"Except it was your idea in the first place. Ambrose beating you to the punch doesn't absolve you in the least."

"I didn't know he was arranging that meeting. I never told him of my plans regarding you and the Pendeltons."

"Indeed, and I suppose that's why you happened to time arriving at Maillard's when you did." Sarcasm dripped from her voice. "Please. Peddle your lies somewhere else, Leo."

Frustrated, I dragged my fingers through my hair. "I understand your anger and suspicion. And it's true I brought you here with the intention of using you to collect the reward money." I swept my arm around the bedchamber, which was fancier than most hotel rooms. "But can you blame me? Look at this place. Jesus, Josie. They have the money! And my family deserves it after the way they treated my father."

"It's still stealing, Leo. And there is no justification that excuses it." Her arms flopped at her sides. "Don't you think these people have suffered enough? They lost their daughter!"

"Don't ask me to feel badly for them, because I can't. Giving up the scheme had nothing to do with the Pendeltons and everything to do with my feelings for you."

"Feelings? You don't have feelings for me. Men who are smitten with a woman do not use her in a confidence scheme."

I took a step closer to her. "Forget the past. Please, listen to what I'm saying *now*. I've never felt this way before. I'm all twisted up inside. I'm more than smitten, Josie. I can't live without you."

If my words affected her, I couldn't tell. Her mouth remained tight and her eyes held none of their usual sparkle. "You know what I think? All you've ever cared about was money. And now you're losing the chance at not only the reward money, but your only 'client' as well. You can't risk walking away with nothing, so now you're trying to convince me you have feelings for me."

"Christ, Josie. You're wrong. I didn't expect this, but it happened. Somewhere along the way I fell for you."

Head shaking, she pressed her lips together. "I don't believe you. I'll never believe you. You're wasting your time."

I could feel her slipping away. I had to do better, tell her everything in my heart. "I would never willingly hurt you. I love—"

"Do not dare say it," she snapped, her expression forbidding. "Do not tell me more lies. God, Leo. You don't know when to quit!"

"It's not a lie. I have feelings for you, deep and lasting feelings. Ambrose knew it and he used us both."

"Do you believe I am so gullible, Leo? So brain-dead as to believe your story?"

"Stop believing the worst of me. I'm telling you the truth."

She stepped closer to me, her body rigid with fury. "Then I want to hear all of it. Tell me everything Ambrose said. Every single thing the two of you discussed the night after the opera."

"I can't remember," I said honestly. "I don't have a memory like yours."

"Try, Leo. I want to know what the two of you talked about in the bathroom, as well as when you went to a saloon. What were the plans?"

I hesitated. She wasn't going to like this. If I was trying to convince her I wasn't a liar and a charlatan, this admission wasn't going to help. "There were no plans. Ambrose suspected I was up to something and I wanted to throw him off the scent, so I said I was pulling the manager scheme with you."

"What is the manager scheme?"

"You pay me to take you on auditions under the guise that I'm a manager. Except I pocket the money and the auditions are fake."

Her mouth dropped open. "That is reprehensible! My god, you two are awful, despicable humans."

I swallowed hard. This was rapidly going awry. Normally, I had people eating out of the palm of my hand. But when it came to Josie, I bumbled and stumbled my way through a conversation.

Maybe it was time to try something else.

I took a step toward her, then another. And another. I needed to touch her, to be close to the woman who'd stolen my heart faster than a finger-smith lifting purses in Copley Square. She didn't back up, so I closed the distance until we were mere inches apart.

Looking down, I used my pinkie finger to lightly touch the back of her hand—and her breath hitched. Encouraged, I dragged the pad of my finger along the fine bones, the delicate knuckles. Her skin was soft, like velvet, and I inhaled her sweet scent deep into my lungs. Whispering, I said, "I fell for you, Josie Smith. You inspire me, make me want to be a better man. A man worthy of you. I haven't done much to be proud of in my life, it's true. But for the first time I want to try with you."

Her eyes searched mine, the seconds ticking by while her face revealed nothing. I couldn't tell what she was thinking, so I linked our pinkie fingers together and waited.

Would she believe me?

Suddenly, her finger slipped from my grip and she wrapped her arms around her waist. "I can't trust you, not after learning your background and what you tried to do to the Pendeltons. To me. I can't tolerate lies, and I'll never know whether you're giving me the truth."

"I have no reason to lie to you. I only want to be together."

"As what? My manager or my lover? Or maybe more?"

"Whatever you'll allow." I slipped my hands into my pockets to keep from touching her again. "Admittedly, though, I'm a selfish man. I want it all."

She snorted. "You are unbelievable."

"But finally honest."

"Then why do I feel as if you're still manipulating me?"

My shoulders sank. I wasn't reaching her. She saw me only as a liar and a charlatan—but I had changed. *She* had changed me. Josie made me want to be better, someone who played on the right side of the law. Someone who could make a difference in this world instead of hurting people.

I couldn't blame her, not really. She would always see the old Leo, the one who hustled and cajoled. The man hunted by the Boston police.

And who was I kidding? Even if I was a better man, I still wasn't good enough for her. Melvin would ensure she became rich and famous, beloved by all. Her life was about to change in ways I couldn't even imagine.

She didn't need me or my nefarious past dragging her down.

I'd bungled this and I had to accept it. I had to let her live her life without me.

Swallowing the lump in my throat, I straightened and gave her a sad, affectionate smile. "I'm sorry for everything. I'm sorry I found you in that square and I'm sorry I ever lied to you. You deserved better."

"Thank you," she said quietly, her eyebrows lowered warily.

There was so much else I wished to say, but none of it mattered. She was on a different path now and she didn't need to associate with men like me. There were parties and yachts and luxurious trips in her future, a life I couldn't comprehend. Better to cut my losses and move on while I still could.

I placed my hand on her jaw, touching her one last time. She held perfectly still as I leaned in and pressed my lips to her forehead, all the while trying to memorize everything about this moment. Her warm flesh, the scent of roses on her skin.

But I couldn't hold on to her forever. She was destined for greater things.

I straightened and hid my true feelings behind a crooked smile. "Have the happiest life imaginable, sweetheart."

Then I let her go and walked out.

Chapter Twenty-Two

LEO

The next afternoon, I was back at the Pendelton mansion, staring at it as I leaned against a light pole, eating an apple. Regret clawed in the pit of my stomach, churning and twisting with a relentless urgency. Even though I'd apologized, wished Josie well, and said my goodbye, everything in me demanded that I seek her out once more, try to win her over.

Failure was a bitter taste in my mouth, but I had to accept my fate. This whole mess was my fault and I had to live with it.

The trick now was not to think about her so much. I had to keep busy by clearing my father's name. I knew he was innocent— I just needed to convince everyone else of that fact. Then I could return home with at least *some* good news for my family.

All morning I'd pored over the baby nurse's letter, dissecting every word, looking for clues. Something was there, I knew it.

Then a particular word had struck me.

Epitome.

The nurse used the word in the letter, and so had Freddie the groom during our conversation. Except Freddie mispronounced it, almost as if he'd never heard it spoken and had only read it.

Could this be the student and tutor?

It explained why Freddie never found work elsewhere. How better to protect your life's biggest secret than by sticking close to the scene of the crime? The proximity would allow you to throw suspicion onto someone else.

Misdirection.

A tactic I knew well.

Tossing away the apple core, I started across the street and went around to the back. The gate was unlocked, so I edged into the gardens. The weather was turning hotter and as a result the plants were blooming, fuller everywhere I looked. My father would've loved to see it, even if it wasn't as grand as his original design.

I trailed a row of boxwood shrubs toward the back of the property. The pebbled path crackled ever so softly beneath my shoes, the only sound in the vast space. No one else was around from what I could see. Were the men in the carriage house? Or maybe back in the stables?

I didn't care how long I had to wait for an opportunity. I was going to search the groom's belongings for any sort of proof tying him to the baby nurse or the kidnapping.

As I drew closer, I could hear laughter and voices coming from the stables, behind the large carriage house. Good. Hopefully, this meant Freddie wasn't in his room.

The bedrooms were on the upper floor, so I slipped quietly through the carriage house and went up the stairs. I moved as silently as the old floorboards would let me, hoping no one was up here. Most of the bedchambers were empty. The first one I came across had a photograph of Georgie and a woman on the small nightstand, so I went on to the next room.

This bedchamber was sparse but clean, with a small bed and a dresser with a basin. There weren't any visible personal effects, so I began investigating, trying to learn who lived here.

A brush and shaving equipment. Clothes in the dresser. A cross. A small dying fern on a metal stand near the windowsill. Boots and livery jackets in the tiny closet, so definitely a groom's bedchamber. Where were the photographs and books?

I quickly checked the other rooms on the floor, easily learning who lived inside. That left the sparse room as Freddie's.

I went back there and closed the door softly. If this were my room, where would I hide something that I didn't want found?

Under the floor was too hackneyed. Any good Pinkerton would look there. Same with under the mattress or a false bottom in a drawer. Any box or container was too risky. It had to be a place where no one would think to look.

My eyes went to the dead fern.

Indeed, that's what any good thief would do.

I went over and began poking the soil. Dry as a bone. No wonder the plant hadn't lived. I began digging underneath, looking for anything that might be hidden in the bottom of the container. Some dirt spilled out of the side, but I didn't stop, getting my hand lower in the pot.

I hit something.

I poked it with my fingers and the object gave slightly, like maybe it was leather or cloth.

Quickly, I held the pot out of the window, removed the fern, and let the dirt fall to the ground. A lump of oiled leather remained in the container.

Hallelujah.

I set the dead fern and pot down and removed the packet, my fingers steady as I unwrapped the leather. It could be nothing.

It might not be the key to clearing my father's name.

Folded papers fell out into my palms. I recognized this paper. It was exactly like the kind I'd taken from Detective Porter.

The letters.

Holy shit.

Of course. Freddie hadn't needed to give all of them away when he framed my father. Just enough to make the affair seem believable. So what did these letters contain?

I began reading.

Like the others, these were written from the baby nurse to Freddie, only with more detailed plans about the kidnapping and the life they'd lead after collecting the ransom. They were addressed to Freddie by name, which explained why he hadn't used them to ruin my father's life.

Goddamn it.

My anger grew as I continued to read. These two were discussing the kidnapping of a baby, a little girl, like she was a diamond bracelet or gold ingot. Like a thing, not a person. They both resented the Pendeltons and their wealth, felt entitled to some of it. Never once did they consider the destruction that would be left behind. . .

I paused and looked out the window. Hadn't Josie said the same to me when I tried to explain my reasons for swindling the Pendeltons?

It's still stealing, Leo. And there is no justification that excuses it. Don't you think these people have suffered enough?

Shame tightened between my shoulder blades. No wonder she wanted me out of her life. I was no better than the kidnappers.

I shoved that aside for now. This was no time for deep personal reflection.

The baby nurse mentioned taking the baby and staying with a distant friend in Boston, somewhere they could avoid detection—

Wood creaked nearby. I waited but didn't hear another sound. I decided I had all I needed, so I took one of the letters and put it in my pocket. Then I wrapped the others in the leather, placed them back in the pot, and replaced the fern. I cleaned up until there was no trace of dirt on the floor and everything looked exactly as it had when I entered.

Listening at the door, I heard only silence. I hurried into the hall and crept toward the stairs. I couldn't tell if anyone was down there or not, so I went slowly, carefully, making no noise. When I reached the ground floor, it was empty.

I darted through the entrance and into the shrubbery. Should I show this letter to the Pendeltons? Something told me Mrs. Pendelton wouldn't be amenable to hearing anything I had to say.

No, I needed to take this letter to Detective Porter. There I would confess where I found it and why, then the police could come here and discover the rest of the letters.

Freddie would be arrested before nightfall.

Chapter Twenty-Three

JOSIE

The police arrived late in the afternoon.

With no small amount of dread, I watched from my bed-chamber window as Mr. Pendelton led the detective through the gardens, toward the back of the estate. Nibbling on a fingernail, I couldn't help but wonder if this was about Leo. Had he tried to sneak onto the estate again? Or worse, had his past caught up with him?

I'm sorry I found you in that square and I'm sorry I ever lied to you. You deserved better.

It was hard to regret meeting Leo when it brought me to New York, to Melvin. Heck, I was staying in a Fifth Avenue mansion. I had nothing to complain about.

Then why did I feel so low?

I knew the answer, of course. I missed Leo. I wish he hadn't tried to use me, that we could've met under different circumstances. But there was no undoing the past.

A knock sounded at my door.

I called over my shoulder, "Come in!"

Mrs. Pendelton appeared. "Have you a moment, dear?"

"Of course. Come sit."

The older woman entered and closed the door behind her. The expression she wore was new, almost giddy, as if she were holding on to a secret. Was this excitement? I hadn't seen her so vivacious before.

She drew closer to the window. "Have you seen the detective?"

She lowered herself into the window seat next to me, and the smell of her perfume—spring flowers—wrapped around me. "Mr. Pendelton is escorting him to the carriage house."

My throat was dry, but I forced the words out. "Why? What's happening?"

Please don't let this be about Leo.

"I cannot believe it, but we may have a new clue in the disappearance of our daughter."

I sucked in a breath. "Oh, ma'am. That is wonderful news. I'm so happy for you."

She wiped the edges of her eyes with her fingertips. "I am too scared to hope, Josie."

"'A prison without walls,'" I repeated from the night we met in the retiring room.

"Indeed. I don't know what I will do if this results in another dead end or false lead."

"You'll survive." I knocked her foot with mine. "It's what we do as women. We survive and get up the next day to keep going."

"You're right. It's only that it's been so long. What if I find out that she's—" Her voice broke off and she dragged in a shaky breath.

I patted her shoulder awkwardly. "At least you will know what happened. You will have answers. I'll never know who my real parents were or why I was dropped off at the asylum. I'd give anything to have the truth, even if it hurt."

She cast me a sideways glance. "You're very wise."

"Not always."

"The man, you mean."

I grimaced. I didn't wish to discuss Leo. Ever. "You didn't elaborate on the new clue regarding your daughter. What is it?"

"The police have come into possession of a letter. They say it proves that one of the grooms was having an affair with Joséphine's baby nurse. The two planned the kidnapping together as a way of collecting the ransom."

My lungs froze and I tried to reconcile this. Had Leo stolen more letters from the police? No, then the police would already know of it.

Did that mean . . . ?

He wouldn't forge letters to implicate someone else, would he? No, no. Leo wouldn't do that. I didn't think so, anyway.

Had someone else found letters? That certainly seemed far-fetched, considering Leo and I had been reading one together the other night. And he was determined to clear his father's name, so it wasn't all that surprising that he was still investigating the kidnapping.

Leo found more letters, but how? Where? In the carriage house?

"Josie, breathe. What on earth is going on in your head?"

I smoothed out my features, dragging air into my lungs. "Merely surprised is all. What else did the letter say?"

"The baby nurse planned to take my daughter to Boston and stay with a friend until the reward was paid. They knew the police would turn New York upside down to find Joséphine."

"No doubt that was true. I hope this detective can find out what happened to your daughter once she arrived in Boston."

"Me, too."

"Do you know which groom was involved?"

"Freddie."

My lips parted on a swift intake of breath as I stared absently at the trees and shrubs down below. *Holy Christmas.* The groom we met the other day was the one responsible for the kidnapping. Why hadn't he left at some point over the last eighteen years? Why stay, when the truth could be discovered at any time?

A good thing he had, though. Now he might be able to tell the Pendeltons what happened to the baby nurse and the little girl. I eased forward in the seat, closer to the window. This could prove to be an exciting development.

Leo, what have you done?

"I'm telling you!" a deep voice boomed in the gardens. "Those ain't mine! I don't know where they came from!"

Mrs. Pendelton reached over and grasped my hand. Surprised, it took me a second or two to relax and squeeze her fingers back.

A man, clearly the police detective, marched Freddie along the garden path, the groom's arms shackled behind his back. Mr. Pendelton walked alongside, speaking rapidly to the detective. Freddie was complaining, loudly, that he didn't know anything about the letters, they were planted there by someone else, and on and on.

My eyes swept back and forth, searching the gardens. Was Leo out there too?

No one else emerged.

I tried not to feel disappointed. How had he managed this?

Mrs. Pendelton released me and stood, clearly planning to leave. I smiled up at her. I'd liked sharing this moment with her.

Then she surprised me by holding out her hand. "Shall we go downstairs and hear what Mr. Pendelton has learned?"

"Me? Are you certain?" I placed my hand in hers and she helped me to my feet. "Wouldn't I be intruding?"

"You are not intruding at all. To be honest, I'm glad to have someone to share this with. And we shouldn't get too excited—it may turn out to be terrible news."

I threaded our arms together. "We must think positively, ma'am. My friend Pippa says—"

"What is that?"

She had stopped abruptly and was now pointing to my bed. I angled to see what she was looking at. "Oh, that's my stuffed rabbit. It was with me when I was dropped off at the asylum."

Letting go of my arm, she drifted toward the bed. I couldn't see her expression, but I frowned. Was Mrs. Pendelton horrified that I still kept such a childish memento around? Heat stung my cheeks, but I wouldn't apologize. "It's all I have left from my family," I added as explanation.

She was now standing by the mattress, her hand covering her mouth. Her face had gone as white as flour.

Why did she care about a fake bunny so much?

"Ma'am?"

Slowly, as if she were reaching toward a wild animal, she bent to pick up the rabbit. Her mouth worked, but no sound came out. Was she having an episode?

"I think I should find Mr. Pendelton," I said, easing toward the door. "Perhaps you should sit down in the meantime."

"Where did you say this came from?"

It was barely a whisper.

I cleared my throat. "The nuns said it was with me when I was brought to the asylum. I assume my mother or father gave it to me."

"Your mother," she croaked. "Your mother gave this to you."

"Probably." I shrugged. "There's no way to know for sure."

"No, Josie. I know for sure." She turned toward me. "I know because *I* gave this to you."

Confused, I tried to make sense of what she was saying. But the suggestion was ludicrous. Impossible. Mrs. Pendelton wasn't my mother.

I let out a laugh. "You almost had me, ma'am. For a moment there, I started to believe you."

She was shaking her head before I even finished. "No, you don't understand. I bought this for my daughter then made the adjustments myself. This little coat he's wearing? I modeled it on one of Mr. Pendelton's coats. See the pearl buttons for eyes? One is slightly lower than the other. That always bothered me."

The poor woman. Thanks to the detective and the discovery of the letters, she was seeing clues in every direction. "Ma'am, I'm sure it seems familiar to you. Undoubtedly there were thousands of these sold at the time. But it is merely a coincidence."

"No, no. It's not a coincidence. I would know this rabbit any-where because I spent hours modifying it for you. Then you carried it everywhere you went for more than a year."

I still couldn't believe it. This rabbit? The Pendeltons? My parents?

It couldn't be.

"Maybe we should find Mr. Pendelton," I suggested. He was a sensible man. Surely, he could help her to see reason.

Mrs. Pendelton's eyes were sparkling at me, brilliant green orbs similar to my own. "This rabbit, combined with your growing up in Boston? And add in your ability for memorization?" She clutched the bunny to her chest and walked toward me. "I'm convinced you're her."

"No, it can't be," I said, my heart racing, pounding inside my chest. I held up my palms as if to stop this boggling conversation. "It can't be."

"You are her." Mrs. Pendelton snagged my hand and squeezed it hard. "You are Joséphine Pendelton."

LEO

This time I rang the bell.

I received a cable from Josie today, asking me to pay a visit to the Pendelton mansion. I wasn't certain the reason, but if she wished to see me, then how could I refuse?

Besides, I had time to spare. The police arrested Freddie yesterday, which meant my father's name had been cleared. And with Josie no longer my client, the only thing left to do was pack up and return to Boston.

A depressing, but unavoidable, consequence.

My family needed me and there was no reason to stay in New York. Melvin would see to Josie's welfare, and I would try to find work back home.

The heavy front door swung open. A silver-haired butler appeared and he immediately frowned in my direction. "May I help you, young man?"

"I'm here to see Miss Smith. Leo Hardy is my name."

"Come in. I will see if Miss Smith is available."

I stepped inside the entry and removed my hat. The butler told me to wait, then disappeared down a long corridor, which left me nothing to do but look around. I hadn't noticed as much in the dark the other night, but the place was impressive. I knew art, and the paintings on the walls were valuable. As were the marble statues and eastern vases. A thief would do pretty well here.

"Sir?" The butler stood a few feet away. "If you'll follow me."

I caught up with him, then followed as he led me into an elegant drawing room. Josie was there, but she wasn't alone. Mr. and Mrs. Pendelton were there as well, their expressions wary as I walked in.

Josie stood and closed the distance between us. I soaked in her appearance like a man dying of thirst. Christ, she looked beautiful, if a bit tired. Hadn't she been sleeping well here?

I shoved it aside; she wasn't mine to worry about any longer.

"Hello, Leo."

"Miss Smith." I gave her a small smile and bowed over her hand.

When I straightened, I saw the tiny divot between her brows, like my behavior confused her. "Leo, come and meet Mr. and Mrs. Pendelton."

Mr. Pendelton, hands clasped behind his back, waited by the sofa. He was older, but just as imposing as I remembered. Mrs. Pendelton was elegantly perched on the edge of the cushion, her hands in her lap. She regarded me like a speck of dirt on the bottom of one's shoe.

Anger sparked in my belly, resentment roiling in my chest. My father's reputation might've been cleared, but I couldn't forgive these people for what they did. Maybe someday I would feel differently, but being in this house only reminded me how unfairly my father had been treated.

I decided not to shake hands but went for a nod instead. "Sir. Ma'am."

Josie said to them, "May I present Mr. Leo Hardy? Son of Steven Hardy, your former head gardener."

No one spoke for several seconds. Josie sighed. "You both promised."

I didn't know what that meant, but Mr. Pendelton said tightly, "Hardy."

Mrs. Pendelton gestured to a chair. "Won't you join us, Mr. Hardy?"

Sit? Here? What was this about? I looked over at Josie. She gave me an encouraging nudge toward the chair. "Sit, Leo."

I walked toward the chair and lowered myself down. Josie reclaimed her seat at the other end of the sofa, which meant the Pendeltons were now staring at me. I let them stare. I had been summoned here, not the other way around. I'd be damned if I let them see me sweat.

I focused on Josie instead.

Her soft green eyes, wisps of blond hair. Creamy skin and full lips. *God, I miss those lips.* A weight sank in my chest, making it hard to breathe. I'd poured my heart out the other night to her, yet it hadn't been enough. She would never forgive me for what I had done.

My god, you two are awful, despicable humans.

Josie's words cut deep, even two days later. Maybe she was right. Maybe it was too late for me to choose another path. A rotten apple, with no hope of redemption.

"Leo, thank you for coming," Josie said. "Mr. Pendelton? Have you something to say?"

The tycoon cleared his throat. "Mrs. Pendelton and I would like to formally apologize, Hardy, for what happened to your father. It has come to my attention in the last twenty-four hours that he was not involved in the kidnapping."

An apology? I blinked several times, trying to make sense of it. I hadn't expected an apology, not even after Freddie's arrest yesterday.

"And?" Josie prompted when Pendelton fell silent.

"And we would like to make good on our error."

"I don't understand." My gaze bounced to Josie before returning to Pendelton. "My father is dead. He drank himself to death after you turned him out with no reference or severance."

"I would like to offer you his severance now, as well as a bit more in restitution."

Ah. They were trying to ease their consciences with money. Except they hadn't done this of their own free will, had they? Josie had arranged this. I wasn't sure why, but for some reason the Pendeltons were indulging her.

I turned my hat over in my hands, watching them for signs of sincerity.

I found none.

Mr. Pendelton appeared reluctant at best, hostile at worst. Mrs. Pendelton's lips were pinched, her expression conveying her disapproval and dismay.

And Josie.

The way Josie looked at me was perhaps the most disappointing of all. She watched me eagerly, happily, as if she'd solved all my problems.

And maybe in the past it would've been true. Money did solve a lot of problems.

But not this time.

Didn't she understand? I wanted her, not a bank roll.

My god, you two are awful, despicable humans.

Mr. Pendelton withdrew a bank check from his inner coat pocket. He held it up with two fingers, like he expected me to leap over the sofa and grab it from him. "I think you'll find this is more than fair."

I didn't move.

"Leo," Josie prompted softly when I continued to sit there. "Take the money."

I sat perfectly still.

The moment stretched and my responsibilities sat like a stone in my stomach. For my mother, I should take the bank draft. For my sisters, my father. The Hardys needed that money, desperately.

But I couldn't do it. Josie was trying to do something noble, but I didn't want her nobility. I wanted her forgiveness.

And I knew if I accepted this money, I'd never receive it.

If I walked out with that check, I was proving correct every terrible thing she thought about me.

I swallowed. Hard. "No, thank you."

Pendelton's arm lowered, while Josie let out a huff of air. "Leo, what are you doing? It's a lot of money. Take it. Take it back to Boston, to your family."

I rose and faced the older couple, my father's former employers. "The apology is enough. I don't need your money."

"Don't be ridiculous," Josie said, also coming to her feet. "You know you do."

"Joséphine, please," Mrs. Pendelton admonished. "If he doesn't wish to accept the money, then we mustn't force it on him."

Joséphine? Were the Pendeltons buying into her stage persona?

Josie angled toward Pendelton. "Sir. Mr. Pendelton. Leo was left to look after his mother and five sisters from a young age. They haven't had an easy time of it. Please, make him accept the money."

"I'm not sure I can, Josie." Then Pendelton narrowed a suspicious gaze on me. "Are you hoping for more? Because I can promise you this is the best I'm prepared to do."

My muscles tightened, my hands nearly crushing the derby in my lap. I'd heard enough.

"Thank you for the apology. I'll pass the sentiments along to my mother." I put my hat on my head. "I bid you all a good afternoon."

With a nod of farewell, I started across the plush carpets toward the door. The sooner I left here, the better. I may be a despicable, awful human, but I was working on changing that. And though it hadn't been easy, my family had survived since leaving New York. We'd find a way to keep going. Somehow, I'd manage it.

I was in the hall when she caught up with me.

"Leo, wait!"

I stopped, unable to refuse her. If all I had were these last few minutes with her, then I wouldn't waste them by storming out.

"Leo." Josie grabbed my arm and towed me into a side room. "Explain to me why you won't take the money."

"You look tired." It wasn't what I'd expected to say, so the comment surprised us both.

She ducked her head and tucked a strand of hair behind her ear. "Such a sweet-talker."

"I'm sorry. I didn't mean you look terrible. Quite the contrary. You're beautiful, Josie."

Her mouth hitched. "Thank you, but I haven't slept much. You wouldn't believe the last twenty-four hours I've had."

If it kept her here, talking to me, I'd believe anything. "Try me."

"First, tell me how you found the letter in the carriage house."

Ah, so she'd put that together. I guess my involvement wasn't so fantastical, considering. "Potted plant. Old thief trick. No one ever checks there."

"Goodness. How clever."

My lips curled upward slightly. "At least my background is good for something. Now, tell me why you can't sleep."

"Tell me why you won't take the money."

"Someone told me it's all I've ever cared about. Maybe I'm trying to be better."

"That's ridiculous. You know I was hurt and angry when I said that. Don't refuse the money to spite me."

"It's not about spite. Maybe I'm trying to prove something to myself."

"Leo, this is not the time for principles. Think of your sisters, your mother."

She was wrong. If this wasn't the time for principles, then when would be? "I have to start somewhere, I suppose. But back to why you can't sleep. Are they not treating you well?"

"Who, the Pendeltons?" She shook her head. "They couldn't be nicer, actually. But do you know what was found in those letters you led the police to?"

"No, but I can imagine, based on the only one I read before going to the police."

"The baby nurse had a friend in Boston. The plan was to take the child out of New York and stay in Boston until the ransom was paid."

"Yes, I read that. It made sense, knowing the Pendeltons would turn this city over to find their daughter."

"But, wait." She pinched the bridge of her nose between her thumb and forefinger, a small laugh escaping her mouth. "You won't believe this."

Was this more about the letters? "What is it?"

"I have that stuffed rabbit, remember? The one from when I was a child."

I nodded. I always thought it was cute, that she still had the memento from her childhood.

"Mrs. Pendelton believes . . . That is, she's sure that toy is the same one she gave her daughter a few months before the kidnapping."

My body jolted, my feet rocking back on my heels. "I beg your pardon?"

"I know. It's positively unbelievable. But she seems certain."

"Mrs. Pendelton believes what? That you are her missing daughter?"

Josie bit her lip and stared up at me. "A shocking turn of events, wouldn't you say?"

My jaw dropped open and all I could do was gape at her.

She gave a little giggle, her arms flopping at her sides like she didn't know what to do or say. "It doesn't seem real. Wouldn't I know if it were true? Wouldn't I feel it in here?" She put her hand on her heart.

"How could you? If it's true, you were taken from here at such a young age. You wouldn't have any memories from that time."

"I suppose. But I still can't believe it."

I stroked my jaw. "It would explain the resemblance. And you were left at an asylum in Boston around the same time, so that also fits. What happened to the baby nurse?"

"We don't know yet. Mr. Pendelton has every Pinkerton in Boston working on finding out."

I had no doubt. This was the biggest development in the case in nearly eighteen years.

Josie, the missing Pendelton heiress. Who would've guessed it?

"You know what this means?" Josie asked. "If it's proven true, you can collect the reward money, since you found me on that street corner in Boston."

My heart sank.

We were back to this, the question of how much money I could pocket.

She'd never see me as anything but a moneygrubbing grifter. A confidence man and thief, out to make a buck.

A despicable, awful human.

I couldn't fault her. Someone as decent and honest as Josie? She knew right from wrong, good from bad. I'd skated over those lines so often they were murky, indistinguishable. Maybe someday I'd be worthy of her, but I knew it wasn't today.

And now she was a fucking heiress.

Who was I kidding? I'd never be worthy of her.

I leaned down and kissed her cheek, my heart squeezing like there was a fist in my chest. She smelled like flowers and sunshine, a life of possibility. A life of wealth and refinement. A life beyond my reach.

"I'm happy for you," I said through the lump in my throat.

She wrinkled her nose, like she didn't understand. "I'm happy for you, too. This will change everything for you and your family."

It changed nothing, but I didn't bother saying it. She wouldn't understand.

While I didn't have her memory, I tried to put every tiny detail into my brain as I studied her. I never wanted to forget her or our time together. She'd given me so much, more than she realized.

Finally, it was time to go. I touched her chin gently. "You're a remarkable woman, Miss Joséphine Pendelton. I wish you every happiness your heart desires."

"Leo—"

She tried to grab my arm, but I stepped away. There was nothing more to say, nothing more between us. Her place was here and I needed to return to Boston.

Before I could do or say anything foolish, I edged around her and left.

Chapter Twenty-Four

JOSIE

The terrace teemed with newspaper reporters and photographers. It seemed every publisher in the country had sent a man to cover the story.

The story of *me*. The return of the Pendelton heiress.

I was that lost heiress, the baby kidnapped from this house all those years ago.

My heart pounded behind my new—and tightly laced—corset. What was I expected to say to the reporters? That I was happy about this turn of events? I was still in shock and disbelief, even though the Pinkertons had confirmed it.

I traced the edge of the windowsill with my fingernail. All my questions, answered. The puzzle of my life finally solved.

So why wasn't I jumping for joy?

Why was I still sad, two days later?

I didn't want to stand in front of all these strangers, answering questions about my life. Would they find me lacking? Would they laugh at the way I talked? What if I said something crass or came across as a fool?

I didn't want to do this.

Heart racing, I edged away from the second-floor window. Perhaps there was a way to escape the house without being seen.

A knock sounded at my door. "Yes?"

My father's face appeared. "May I come in?"

"Of course."

He came in but left the door open behind him. "Thinking of trying to escape?"

"How did you guess?"

"It's pointless. Your mother will find you and bring you back." He moved closer to the window, looking down on the hullabaloo for himself. "She seems to think today is a good idea."

"You don't?"

"I don't care for the attention. We did this once to announce you were born. And look at what happened."

Fair point.

"Speaking of," he said. "I must apologize to you."

I turned toward my father and found him staring intently at me. I shifted, self-conscious under his full attention. These people still felt like strangers. "Apologize? Whatever for?"

"It was my responsibility to keep you safe as a child. And I failed you." He exhaled heavily. "I know you must resent me for it—"

"Resent you! It wasn't your fault."

"Wasn't it? You were taken because of your last name, a name I gave you. And you were taken from this house. I should've better fortified the premises. Properly vetted the staff and their associates."

I understood the regret, but we couldn't change the past. I gave him a small smile. "But people lie. Even if they were vetted, someone could've hidden the truth. And you did the best you could. Who would've ever guessed something like this could happen?"

"I have chastised myself every day for the last eighteen years. You should be cross with me, at the very least."

I wasn't, though. There wasn't one part of me that blamed my father for what happened. "I've learned to never focus too much on the past. It's over and done with. The future is what we can control, which is why I've always set my mind to achieving my goals down the road."

"You know, you have a very level head on your shoulders."

I soaked in the praise eagerly, my battered heart expanding in my chest. "Thank you. That means a lot coming from you, considering."

"Considering I'm your father?"

"Well, yes. But also because you are a self-made man who doesn't suffer fools easily. And I bet you've seen plenty of fools in your time."

"One or two," he said with a crooked smile. "These goals you mentioned. What are they?"

"To become a world-famous singer, adored by crowds everywhere I go."

The smile dropped from his face. "Have you informed your mother of this?"

"I think so, when we were at Maillard's. I've made no secret of it and my agent feels confident that I have the talent."

"I've heard you sing, so I believe it. But no doubt your mother has assumed your plans have changed since the discovery."

"Why would being the missing Pendelton heiress prevent me from pursuing a singing career?"

"Well, I'm not certain it's safe. Women such as you lead a much different life than what you've experienced. You don't need to work."

"Meaning I should get married and start a family."

"Not tomorrow, but yes, eventually. That is generally how it's done among the lobster set."

"Lobster set?"

He made a circle with his hand. "The social elites. The wealthier citizens of New York."

I frowned. "But things are different now. Women can get jobs, like in factories and offices. We don't need to marry the first mangy dog who comes sniffing around."

"You are a Pendelton," he said stiffly. "You will not marry a *mangy dog*. And you will never work in a factory or an office."

"You know what I mean. I don't want to marry anyone right now. I want to travel and sing."

"Indeed, I think it's best if you speak with your mother regarding—"

"Holy smokes, Josie!"

That voice.

No, it couldn't be.

Whirling, I saw my best friend standing in the doorway with Mrs. Pendelton.

Pippa.

"Holy shit!" I exclaimed and started running toward her.

"Joséphine," my mother admonished. She was standing behind Pippa, a disapproving frown on her face. "Must you use those words?"

"I'm sorry, ma'am!" I launched myself at my best friend, who hugged me equally hard. Almost immediately we were laughing and crying, our shoulders shaking as we embraced.

When we pulled apart, I grabbed her hand like a lifeline. "I can't believe you're here."

"Me neither! But I received a cable yesterday morning telling me to get here as quickly as possible. That you needed me."

I looked over my shoulder at my mother. "Your doing, I suppose?"

"No. It wasn't your father, either."

Instantly, I knew.

Leo.

He was the only other person on earth who knew what Pippa meant to me.

I nearly started crying all over again.

"Now, no more tears," Pippa said. "Come sit on the bed and tell me everything."

"Do I have time?" I asked my father, who'd come over to stand next to my mother.

"They may wait as long as you like." He gestured to the gardens. "They aren't going anywhere."

"Shall I send up tea?" my mother asked. "Then you two may visit properly."

Tea, I was learning, was one of the most important things in this house. "Yes, please. Thank you, ma'am. Sir."

When the door closed, Pippa's eyes were huge. "What in the bleedin' hell, Josie!"

"I know. I can hardly believe it myself. But I'm so very glad you're here. You have no idea."

"Let's sit. I need every detail."

I shook my head as I led her to the bed. "I'm not sure I have it in me for every detail. I might start crying and never stop."

We both dropped onto the mattress, wrinkled skirts be damned. "Cry?" She reached to shake my arm. "You can't cry! You are living every orphan's dream right now."

I knew she was right, but I still felt incomplete. Finding my family wasn't the magic fix I always dreamed about, I supposed. So Pippa wouldn't think me ungrateful, I launched into the entire story, including my relationship with Leo. Her face darkened when I told her about Maillard's, but she didn't comment.

A footman delivered tea just as I started recalling the letters. I poured for us and kept talking: the investigation, the carriage house, Leo's visit, and finally the arrest.

"This is unbelievable," she said around a mouthful of lemon cake. "But what happened in Boston once the baby nurse took you there?"

"We went to stay with her friend in Boston, but the friend never knew my last name or where I came from. Probably because the nurse didn't want to risk splitting the reward. Regardless, the nurse left me with her friend one day and never returned, and this woman told the Pinkertons that one more mouth to feed was too much. She dropped me off at the asylum, hoping the nuns would look after me."

"Astounding." Pippa reached for more cake. "So what happened to the baby nurse? Why leave and never come back?"

"They aren't sure, but there was a terrible omnibus accident during that time and several of the deceased were never identified."

"Damn, that is some terrible luck."

"I know." The whole thing had unspooled like a Greek tragedy. I couldn't help but wonder what might have happened if the baby nurse hadn't disappeared, how my life might've been different.

"Now, don't make that face." Pippa took my hand in hers and squeezed. "You're back here, where you belong."

"I don't feel as though I belong. And I miss—" I almost said the name, but stopped myself just in time.

I expected rebuke, but Pippa's expression was gentle with understanding. "You miss Leo."

"Stupid, isn't it?"

"No, not if you love him. You can't switch off your feelings so quickly."

I traced the pattern on the coverlet with my fingernail. "He's dashed confusing. The whole thing was about money from the start, yet he turned down my father's attempt at restitution. When I asked why, Leo said he's trying to prove something to himself."

"It could be that he's changed. The apology might be enough for him."

"Leo, change?" I snorted. "And an apology won't feed his family back in Boston. When in the world will they ever see that much money again?"

"Well, perhaps he wants you to see him as more than a confidence man."

I considered this. Was Leo's change of heart because of me? "I did call him a despicable, awful human."

"Fair, taking into account how he was using you, but there is the possibility that he's telling the truth. Perhaps Leo developed feelings for you and put his plans on hold, as he claimed."

Possibly, but I couldn't forgive him. "It doesn't matter. What's done is done. He's returning to Boston and I'm beginning my life here."

Pippa handed me a pistachio macaron. "Are you saying you wouldn't give him another chance?"

"How could I? I can't tell the Pendeltons—my *parents*—that I've decided to be with a confidence man. They'd regret finding me again."

She rolled her eyes. "You know that won't ever happen. And, Leo might not be an ideal son-in-law at the moment, but people change. Look at you! Who would've thought a Boston orphan singing on the street would end up here." She waved her hand at the room.

"Leave it alone, Pips. He already said goodbye. It's over."

"I'll drop it—*after* I say one more thing. I know you hate to dwell on the past and prefer to keep moving forward. But Leo's the opposite. He's been so mired in the past that he hasn't had a chance to think about his future. Give him a chance to breathe. He might surprise you."

I didn't want any more surprises when it came to Leo. I had my own life to worry about. "Let's stop talking about Leo."

"Not until you tell me about your night in bed." She nudged my leg with her foot. "You, Josie Pendelton, skipped over far too many details for my liking."

THE NEXT MORNING, I arrived in the breakfast room. My father was alone at the table, reading a newspaper. Though he'd been nothing but kind since we met, I still found him intimidating.

"Good morning," I said on my way to the sideboard.

He looked up from his newspaper. "Good morning, Joséphine. I trust you slept well?"

I picked up a plate and contemplated the breakfast selection. Holy Christmas, these people ate well. I'd never seen so much food for such a small number of folks. Today there were eggs, pancakes, muffins, breads, potatoes, and steak—*steak!*—all spread out on various platters.

The Pendeltons ignored more food in one meal than Pippa and I ate in a week.

When I sat down, my father examined me closely. "What is

amiss? Your bedchamber? Your mattress? You would tell me if you didn't like them, I trust. I'll have the walls painted today, if you prefer a different color."

"I'm fine, sir. I promise. All of this is taking some getting used to, is all."

"That's understandable." He waved to a footman. "Please pour Miss Joséphine coffee, will you, Peter?"

"Please, it's Josie, and I can pour my own coff—"

"Nonsense," my father interrupted, motioning for the footman to continue. "That is Peter's responsibility. Let him see to your breakfast."

I waited, useless, as Peter poured coffee for me. It was bizarre having staff around to do every little thing for you. No more scrubbing my own clothes, running my own bathwater. No more fiddling with my hair or lacing my own corset. I didn't even need to pour my own coffee. Some of it was nice, but I wasn't sure what to do with all this free time.

I started eating. Every bite was delicious, but I wasn't hungry. This all felt horribly *wrong*.

"Joséphine." My father set his knife and fork on his plate. "I realize this is an adjustment for you. But you may trust your mother and me to guide you through it."

Adjustment? That was an understatement.

"Guide her through what?" Mrs. Pendelton—my mother—entered the room and lowered herself into the seat opposite me. "Sit up straight, Joséphine. Slouching will ruin your posture."

I thought my posture was fine, but I pushed my shoulders back and tried to sit tall. "I'm sorry, ma'am."

She waved Peter over to pour her coffee. "It is 'I beg your pardon.' And you may call me Mother."

I wrinkled my nose. That felt strange, especially considering they kept calling me Joséphine instead of Josie, but I decided to give in. "I beg your pardon, Mother."

She gave me a brilliant smile—and I felt churlish for my ungrateful thoughts. If it made my parents happy, then who cared what we called one another?

"An elocution instructor will come later today," my mother said. "And we will begin finishing lessons this morning."

Elocution and finishing lessons. For me? "I don't understand. Why do I need those things?"

My parents exchanged a glance before my mother said, "As our daughter, you will interact with a different class of people now. We want you to feel comfortable."

Comfortable? Or were they worried the way I spoke and acted would embarrass them? "It feels a bit soon, doesn't it?"

"Soon! Goodness, you have eighteen years to make up for." My mother sipped her coffee, every movement delicate and graceful.

"Make up for?" I shook my head as if trying to clear it. "I don't mean to argue, but I feel as if you're saying there is something wrong with me."

"Of course there is nothing wrong with you," my father said gently, while at the same time my mother said, "Just small improvements, dear."

"Improvements," I said flatly. "Because I'm not good enough to be a Pendelton, is that it?"

My mother's eyes rounded almost comically, while my father said, "That is enough, Joséphine."

I rubbed my forehead. I should've stayed in bed. Was this what I wanted? Elocution lessons and lectures? I just wanted them to love me and support me. Was that not what parents did?

"And while we are on the subject," my mother said. "We must eliminate those crude words I heard you use when speaking with your friend yesterday. They aren't proper for a lady."

Suddenly, memories of the nuns scolding me as a little girl resurfaced.

Ladies do not argue, Josie. Ladies do not interrupt when a person is speaking.

I hated it now as I'd hated it then.

"Maybe I don't want to be a *lady*," I snapped before I could think better of it.

A shocked silence descended, the room frozen. No one moved, not even the footmen. My parents seemed both hurt and surprised, and I suddenly felt like an ungrateful and spoiled child. After all they had endured, after everything that happened, now I was refusing them?

"Oh god," I rushed out. "I apologize. That was terrible of me. I-I'm not handling this well at all." My throat tightened and I could feel tears gathering.

"Perhaps we should discuss this later," my father said to my mother. "After she's had a bit more time."

I stared at my fancy plate. This was everything I'd ever wanted for as long as I could remember. A loving family. Parents and a nice home. So why wasn't I happier?

Why was I longing for something simpler? Like when Leo and I shared breakfast in the tiny apartment. That had been familiar and comfortable. A class of people I understood. What the Pendeltons had, this life of leisure and excess, was completely foreign to me.

And I wanted them to love me as I was, not mold me into the daughter they thought they should have.

No matter how rich and famous you become, promise me you won't ever change, Josie Smith.

I missed Leo.

It was difficult to reconcile not trusting a man, yet still missing him. But no one ever said emotions were simple, especially when the heart was involved. And Leo had swindled my heart right out from under me when I wasn't looking.

But these were my parents. Shouldn't I try to please them? If I didn't, would they kick me out? Decide I wasn't worthy after all? I wanted them to love me.

Swallowing my hurt feelings, I looked at my mother, who was stirring her coffee vigorously. "I beg your pardon, ma'am.

Of course I'll be happy to have lessons. Might we also include singing lessons, though? I'd like to keep up my voice before Melvin finds me work."

That didn't appear to please either of my parents, if their pinched expressions were anything to go by. Before I could ask what I'd said wrong, the butler appeared. "Mr. Pendelton, sir. A Mr. Ambrose Lee is here to see you. He claims he is expected."

I sucked in a sharp breath. Ambrose was here. To see my father?

It could only be about one thing: money.

I pushed away from the table, gaining my feet. "Sir, I'll handle this. You needn't bother yourself."

"Nonsense." My father was already out of his seat. "Finish your breakfast."

My stomach squeezed around what little I'd eaten this morning. "He merely wants the reward money. You should refuse to see him."

"Joséphine," my mother said gently as my father left the room. "Let your father deal with this man while you eat." She rang a bell on the table and the footmen reemerged. "There you are. May I have more coffee and a plate, please?"

As my mother was served, I tried to return my attention to my food. I couldn't do it, though. Ambrose was somewhere in this house, collecting a healthy check that rightfully didn't belong to him.

It belonged to Leo.

I'm sorry I found you in that square and I'm sorry I ever lied to you. You deserved better.

So why was Ambrose here to collect the reward instead of the man who'd earned it?

I rose. "If you'll excuse me, ma'am."

"Dear, sit down. You're worrying me. You've hardly eaten."

I waved my hand. "Everything is fine. There's no need to worry. I'll be back before the eggs grow cold."

I hurried from the dining room and practically ran down the corridor. My father's office was near the main entrance on Fifth Avenue. He spent most of his time there, so I guessed this was where he would meet with Ambrose.

A sitting room adjoined the office, which should provide a prime location for eavesdropping. I held my skirts as best I could to keep them from making noise and crept into the sitting room. The door into the office was closed, but I hadn't let a closed door stop me from listening in since I was a toddler. A girl desperate for news of adoption learned to get creative when it came to sleuthing.

I located a glass, put the rim against the door, then placed my ear to the bottom. Nothing. Next I tried the walls, but it was the same result. Damn this house's quality construction.

Without the ability to listen in, I would need to catch Ambrose on his way out.

I edged into the entryway and slipped into the tiny coatroom directly across from the office. Almost immediately, a tall figure blocked all the light, scaring me. I jumped and put a hand on my heart.

"Miss Joséphine," the butler, Ronald, said. "May I help you?"

"I, um . . ." I glanced around. "I thought I would step out for a walk, but I couldn't find my coat."

His long face pulled into a frown. "As it is quite warm today, miss, might I suggest forgoing one?"

"Good idea." As if I hadn't been caught in a lie, I left the coatroom with my chin high. "I'll only be out for a short while."

"Wait. I'll send a maid with you."

"That isn't necessary. I've been walking around by myself my whole life."

"Miss, your mother and father have insisted. It would distress them greatly to know you were unaccompanied on the street. Any number of things might happen."

It was hard to fault my parents for worrying, even if it was unnecessary. I was once kidnapped from this very house. More than anything, though, I needed to get rid of Ronald. "Sure, that would be fine. I'll wait here until someone is free."

He nodded once and disappeared into the back part of the house. Just then, the office door opened. Ambrose, dressed in a brown plaid suit, emerged and closed the door behind him. He was looking down, folding a long thin piece of paper in his hands.

A bank draft. Damn it.

"What are you doing here?" I hissed.

He glanced up and a slick smile stretched across his face. "Why, Miss Joséphine. You are looking delightful, if I might say."

I pointed to the paper in his hands. "You don't deserve that."

"Don't I? And here I thought I'd brought you to your mother, reunited you with your parents."

"You did nothing of the sort. Leo found me, so he should get it."

"Leo has relinquished any claim to this reward. And I told your father it was all my doing. So this reward, dear girl, is all mine."

"A liar and a thief, just like always."

"You wound me, Miss Joséphine. And after all I've done for you." He waved his hand around to indicate the house. "I should think a little gratitude might be in order."

"Then you'll be waiting a long damn time. You and Leo used me."

"Indeed, now. That is a shame," Ambrose said in his deep southern drawl as he tucked the check into the pocket of his coat. "I suppose I'll need to dry my tears with all this money."

"I hope you choke on it instead."

Chuckling, he shoved his hat onto his head, then tipped it in my direction. "Good day, miss."

Chapter Twenty-Five

LEO

"Where is this place again?" Ambrose asked as we walked along Twenty-Ninth Street.

I peeled off another section of orange and tossed it into my mouth. I hardly tasted it, but that wasn't the point. My brain needed to be sharp, and skipping meals because I missed Josie wouldn't help me get back to Boston.

Almost there. One more loose end.

"Not far," I said. "A few more blocks."

My friend slapped my back. "Damn glad you came around to seeing things my way."

"Yeah, well." I swallowed another slice of orange. "I didn't have much choice. Not many employers are keen to hire a man like me."

"I can't fathom why you even bothered. Why go straight? We earn the easiest money in the world. I love this life."

I believed it. I became a confidence man because it provided a great deal of money and I had the charm to carry it off. Ambrose, on the other hand, was a born huckster. I couldn't imagine him ever doing anything else.

We crossed the street and I said, "I'll never make that mistake again. Once we finish this meeting today, I'm headed back to Boston. A friend of mine has a pig in a poke idea, so maybe I'll help him out."

"Ah. Undertook one of those myself two months ago. Sold a

fictitious plot of land in Ohio to an elderly couple. Couldn't have been easier."

"Remember the time we sold fake stock that we printed in your cellar?"

"Ha! Yes, indeed I do." He elbowed me. "You and I make a good team. Why would you ever want to give this up?"

"Because I forgot the rule."

"Never give your real name to the coppers?"

"That's always a good one," I said with a grin. "No, I meant the other one. St. Elmer's seventh rule."

"'Never change for a woman,'" Ambrose recited. "They're a waste of time, my friend. A foolish waste of time."

I slipped another slice of orange in my mouth. Foolish, yes—though Josie would've been worth it. I would've done almost anything to keep her. But I had to respect her wishes, and now she had an entirely different life ahead of her. Parties and balls, Newport and operas. Anything money could buy.

Me? I'd stick with what I did best.

After last seeing Josie, I'd been at odds, living in Ambrose's apartment and trying to figure out my future. He and I arrived at a truce. After all, I couldn't blame him for collecting that reward first. Four months ago, I would've done the same.

Ambrose and I crossed another street. The morning was a hot one, and I was already sweating inside my suit. I couldn't wait to get back to Boston and my family. Perhaps I'd leave tonight, after this errand wrapped up.

"There it is." I pointed to the storefront. "I'm told he's the best in all New York. Discreet, too."

"And you've worked with him before?"

"Not me, but friends from Back Bay. They say he's got the highest quality."

Ambrose seemed skeptical, but it was to be expected in our line of work. We trusted very few people or institutions. In fact,

Ambrose trusted banks less than he trusted the police. Which was to say not at all.

"I'll be the judge of that," my friend said as I reached for the door.

A bell tinkled overhead as we entered the unassuming porcelain shop. Figurines and teacups lined the shelves, while silver spoons and platters resided in a glass case. An older man was behind the counter, polishing a silver vase. He looked at the door. "Morning, gentlemen. May I help you?"

I strode forward. "Are you Mr. Mason?"

"Indeed, I am."

I held out my hand. "I am Leo Hardy. My friend, Henrik, cabled you about an appointment today?"

Mason lowered his voice. "Quiet. Give me a moment." He put down his cloth and came around the counter. At the front door, he turned the lock and flipped the hanging shop sign to Closed.

When he started toward the back, he beckoned for us to follow. Ambrose and I trailed him to what turned out to be a sitting area with a small table and chairs. A large black safe resided against the wall.

Mason gestured for us to sit. "Forgive me, but I don't have these meetings in the front. Too risky. And I find my clients prefer privacy."

"Yes, we most certainly appreciate it," I said as I lowered myself into a chair. "This is my good friend, Mr. Ambrose Lee."

"Mr. Lee," Mason greeted him, shaking Ambrose's hand. "A pleasure. Henrik mentioned you are interested in purchasing some items."

"I've recently come into some money," Ambrose said. "I want to spend it, but I can't deposit it in the banks."

"Why not?" Mason asked.

"Don't trust them. First sign of a panic and all the money disappears." Ambrose shook his head. "I'd rather keep it close, if you know what I mean."

Mason nodded like he'd heard this before. "Saw many men lose everything they had back in the panic of '93. It was terrible. On my life, politicians and bankers are the least trustworthy souls alive."

"Amen," Ambrose said. "I was thinking gold bars. Or perhaps silver coins."

Mason rubbed his jaw thoughtfully. "The price of gold fluctuates dramatically these days. And if there is another panic, the politicians will rush to devalue silver."

"I remember when they did that," I said. "Two years ago in that financial crisis. So what does that leave us with?"

"Us?" Ambrose stared down his nose at me. "You forfeited your right to the money days ago, Leo."

I put my palms up. "I know, but I was hoping you might reconsider, especially because I found Mr. Mason here."

Ambrose's lips flattened into an unhappy line, but Mason spoke first. "It's better if I show you what I have." He pushed up out of his chair and went to the huge safe. With a few flicks of his wrist, he turned the dial and opened the heavy steel door. He leaned in and rummaged around for a long minute. Then he produced a thick brown packet.

After he resettled in his chair, he began unwrapping the paper. Soon, large round lumps began taking shape. Ambrose leaned in, so I did as well. We were both eager to see what Mason had bundled so carefully.

A cascade of glittering white-blue fire tumbled out onto the green baize tabletop.

Diamonds.

Ambrose hissed through his teeth and I sucked in a sharp breath. They were gorgeous. There had to be at least twenty of them, fat and round, sparkling even in the low light.

"Good god," Ambrose said. "I've never seen anything so gorgeous in all my days."

I whistled. "Are they real?"

Mason bristled, the flesh of his throat rippling. "Of course they're real. You two came to me. I didn't seek you out. If you don't trust me, then you may show yourselves out." He started to put the diamonds back in the brown paper.

"Wait." Ambrose put a hand on the man's forearm. "We don't mean any harm. But you have to understand our hesitation. We've come across a shady character a time or two. Now, we sure would appreciate it if you could prove these aren't glass."

Mason sighed. "I will fetch a jeweler's loupe. You know how to use one, I assume?"

I looked at Ambrose and shook my head. My friend glanced around the tiny space. "Do you have a mirror handy? Real diamonds will leave a scratch."

"I do, actually." Mason stood and found his way to the sideboard, where he lifted a small mirror and brought it over. Picking up a diamond, he handed it to Ambrose. "Though I cannot believe this is necessary. Scratch away."

Sure enough, the diamond left a scratch on the mirror.

Ambrose handed the gem back, but he left his palm out. "Another, please."

Mason offered up a different diamond and Ambrose repeated the process. Then another. I said nothing during the third test, but at the fourth request I lost my patience. "Ambrose, they're all real. Stop wasting this man's time."

Ambrose sat back, seemingly appeased. "How much are these worth?"

"The whole lot? More money than you have, no doubt. Each one is in the neighborhood of one thousand dollars. Some more, some less depending on the size."

The check Ambrose received from Mr. Pendelton was for a hundred thousand dollars. I could see my friend doing the math in his head. "I would need one hundred."

Mason's eyes rounded as his eyebrows shot up. "One hundred . . . Good heavens!"

Ambrose's expression grew positively smug. "I told you it was a large sum of money."

"I should say so." Mason exhaled heavily and stroked his jaw. "I have something very rare. Very expensive. The only one of its kind." He rose and went back to his safe. This time he returned with a black case. He withdrew a tiny key from inside his pocket, which he then used to unlock the case and retrieve a box from inside.

He placed the box on the table and opened the lid. A fat pink diamond nestled in the silk winked up at us. I whistled again. "Holy shit."

Ambrose examined the gem closer. "How many carats is it?"

"Six-point-four-eight. It's flawless, mined in India and presented to Queen Victoria. Her son, the Prince of Wales, Prince Albert Edward, brought it to North America in 1860 when he came to open Victoria Bridge. He stayed with President Buchanan at the White House, and gifted the diamond to Buchanan's niece, Miss Harriet Lane, who served as the unmarried president's hostess."

I started to reach out and touch the exquisite piece, but Mason shoved my hand away. "Do not dare to touch this without gloves on."

"How did it find its way to you?" Ambrose asked.

"I am not at liberty to say, but the person was in need of money. I agreed to buy the gem."

"Stolen, then."

Mason didn't confirm or deny the statement, which may as well have been a confirmation. Instead, he offered, "Let us say that a museum may come looking for it one day. I would not flash it around, were I you."

"What's it worth?"

"A hundred and fifty thousand dollars."

"So out of your price range," I said to Ambrose.

"Perhaps not," my friend said. "How do I know what you've said is true?"

Mason slowly turned the box over, revealing the official coat of arms of the Prince of Wales embossed in gold underneath. Ambrose eased back in his chair and I could almost see his mind spinning as he studied the feast of diamonds on the table. Finally he said, "I wish to buy that, sir."

Mason closed the box carefully. "You said you had only a hundred thousand."

"I can bring you fifty more tomorrow." Ambrose reached inside his coat pocket, pulled out the check, and flattened it on the table. With two fingers, he pushed it closer to Mason.

Suddenly, Mason began coughing, and he brought a handkerchief to cover his mouth. "I apologize. I'm recovering from a slight cold. Anyway, Mr. Lee, that isn't how this works. I require all the cash up front—"

A crash sounded from the front of the store, the door's bell jangling violently. We all froze, not even daring to breathe. A voice barked, "Come out, all of you. It's the police."

Mason began wrapping the small diamonds up in the brown paper, his fingers flying. Ambrose's panicked gaze met mine. "I can't be caught," he whispered. "They'll send me to the Tombs for certain."

"Go." I pointed toward the back exit. "I'll answer their questions and cover for you. They have nothing on me. Go, Ambrose!"

Mason was already wrapping the diamonds in an effort to hide them. The sound of heavy boots drew closer, and I heard at least two sets of steps. "Shit!" Ambrose exclaimed, then leapt over the table to grab the box with the pink diamond out of Mason's hands. Mason tried to hold on, but Ambrose was too strong.

Mason snarled as Ambrose darted toward the exit. "Return that this instant! You have no right to take it!"

Ambrose pointed at the check on the table. "There's your payment."

"It's not enough!"

"I sympathize, sir, but you never should've shown me this." He shoved the box into his coat pocket.

"Hey!" Two officers, dressed in their caps and blue coats, appeared in the doorway. "Nobody moves until we find out what's going on in here."

Ambrose didn't wait. He lunged for the back door, opened it, and quickly disappeared into the alley. One of the officers gave chase, while the other copper put his hands on his hips. "Now, what exactly is goin' on here, boyos?"

I put my palms on the table. "Nothing, Officer. A friendly chat, is all."

"I don't believe it. We've been watching this place for weeks . . ." He trailed away, then gave a peek at where Ambrose disappeared. "Think he's gone?"

I stood and walked over to the open door. No trace of Ambrose or the other "officer." Turning around, I clapped my hands. "He's gone. Well done, gents."

Mason chuckled, his shoulders relaxing. "It went down as smooth as silk, just like you said it would, Leo."

"I've known Ambrose a long time. He's fairly easy to predict. Mason, you were perfect with the diamonds and knowing which ones to hand him."

Mason, an acquaintance from Philadelphia, slipped the packet of small real diamonds into his pocket. "It helps to know how to spot the real ones from the fakes. Not that hard once you know what you're looking for."

"You did it seamlessly. And the prince's box for the pink diamond was a nice touch," I said. "Where'd you find it?"

"Found it years ago with cuff links inside. I've been waiting for the right time to use it."

I picked up the Pendelton check off the table and slipped it into my coat pocket. The scuffle of shoes sounded outside just before the other "officer" strolled in from the alley door. I paused, asking, "Is he . . . ?"

"Long gone," the man answered with a smirk. "Took off and didn't stop running."

Good. I doubted I'd ever see Ambrose again. He'd take the pink diamond to another city and try to sell it to someone. I hated to see his face when he learned it was glass.

Reaching for my billfold, I withdrew the remaining money I owed my accomplices. After I paid them, I shook their hands. "If you're ever in Boston, come look me up."

"If you decide to stay in New York," one of the fake officers said, "we could find use for you."

"I appreciate the offer, but I'm headed back tonight."

Mason shut the safe and locked it. "What are you fixing to do with that check?"

I shoved my derby onto my head. "Return it to its rightful owner. Afternoon, gents."

JOSIE

Y ou sound beautiful."

My head snapped up. My mother stood in the entryway, a soft smile on her face as she observed me at the piano. Though I couldn't play, I enjoyed standing by the gorgeous instrument to practice singing. "Thank you."

We hadn't revisited the issue of my stage career. While I didn't wish to argue with her, I would stand firm on the issue. Thankfully, my father was in my corner. Privately, he told me he would hire a team of Pinkertons to keep me safe, if need be, should I decide to pursue a public singing career.

"Which song was that?"

"Oh, it's a popular show tune I heard recently."

"And you are recalling it without sheet music? That's remarkable."

I shrugged. "Once I hear a song it's stored up here." I tapped my temple.

"Yes, just like your grandmother." She approached, her green silk skirts rustling softly. "Though no one in my family could sing nearly as well as you do."

"What was she like?"

"Your grandmother?" My mother leaned against the side of the piano, her gaze thoughtful. "Smart. Strong. And she always made us laugh."

"Do I have aunts and uncles? Cousins?"

"Your father was an only child, but I have many relatives in Indiana. Someday I'll take you there to meet them."

"They never visit?"

A shadow passed over her expression. "I haven't seen them in, oh, seven or eight years now. We haven't been exactly welcoming to guests in the last few years."

Another reminder of how much was affected by my kidnapping. "You must miss them."

"I do, yes. But it was me. I grew tired of answering questions about the investigation and how I was faring. I found it easier to stay home and avoid people."

"Understandable, though I suppose it was an attempt on their part to offer care."

"Most definitely, but some days the pain was unbearable. I cannot fathom how I survived it, actually. The house was a constant reminder, too."

"I'm surprised you didn't sell it and move."

"Your father suggested it many, many times. He thought we needed a fresh start." She pressed her lips together and stared through the window that overlooked Fifth Avenue. "Leaving felt as if we were giving up, admitting we would never see you again. I always held out hope that you'd return."

"I would've returned sooner, had I known. I longed for a family growing up, a mother and father who loved me. You have no idea how much."

My mother rubbed my shoulder as her eyes welled with tears. "I hate that you doubted it for one single day."

I could feel my own throat closing with emotion. "Please, ma'am. No more or else I'll start crying."

If she found it strange that I still didn't often call her "Mother" or "Mama," she hadn't mentioned it. I was glad. It didn't feel right to refer to my parents with those terms yet. Someday, perhaps.

But I needed time to grow accustomed to it.

"You're right." She inhaled deeply and exhaled slowly. "Speaking of hurt, I wish that I could have spared you the disaster of that young hooligan from Maillard's. Mr. Hardy's son."

She said it casually, but her gaze remained sharp. I sensed she was fishing for information about my love life, as any mother might. Except Leo was a topic I devoutly wished to avoid. "He's not a hooligan. A bit gray morally, true, but not a bad person. He has his five sisters and a mother to help provide for, so I can't blame him for hustling."

I did blame him for using me to do it, however.

"Did you care for him?"

"Yes." My quick answer startled both of us, so I amended, "At least I thought I did."

"I am surprised, then, that he hasn't tried to see you again."

I trailed my finger over the shiny black lacquer surface of the piano. "I'm sure he's gone back to Boston. There's no reason for him to stick around."

"No, he's still in the city."

I cocked my head at her. "How do you know?"

"Because he's downstairs with your father right now."

I straightened, my chest fluttering with both panic and excitement.

Leo was here? Why?

I moved around the piano to find out for myself. "Why has no one told me?"

My mother caught my arm as I tried to pass. Her grip was firm. "Josie, where are you going?"

"Down to see what Leo wants."

"Let your father handle it. He is seasoned in dealing with undesirables. Let him protect you from whatever this is."

"Whatever this is pertains to me. I'd like to know what is happening." I eased out of her grasp. "And Leo is not an undesirable. He's a fool, but that's all."

I crossed the floor quickly, but my mother followed behind me. "Josie, you cannot go barging into your father's office. It's simply not done."

Thankfully, I didn't know the rules of what was "done" and "not done."

I kept going, my feet flying down the main stairs, and just as I reached the next to the last step, my father's office door opened. Leo and my father shook hands. More confused than ever, I paused on the step.

"I wish you luck, son," my father said.

"Thank you, sir." Leo stepped out of the office and into the hallway—and our eyes locked. He froze, derby dangling in his hand.

I soaked in the sight of him, cataloging every detail. He wore the same dark blue traveling suit as when we arrived from Boston. His hair was oiled and neat, his face clean-shaven, but there were shadows under his eyes. His lips curled into the faintest of smiles then executed a perfectly polite bow. "Miss Pendelton. Mrs. Pendelton. Good afternoon."

Without waiting for a response, he jammed his derby on his head and went for the exit. Ronald waited to assist with the door, so I blurted, "Leo, what are you doing here?"

He didn't answer, merely continued through the now open door. Sunlight swallowed up his tall form as the heat of the city wafted inside. Why hadn't he answered me? Why had he come here, and why had my father wished him luck?

I turned to my father. "What on earth was that about?"

My father held up a piece of paper. It was a bank draft. "He returned the reward money."

Returned it? My jaw fell open. Leo Hardy, giving up such a huge sum? And what of Ambrose? "I don't believe it."

"He said it was wrong to use you in such a scheme and he never meant to hurt anyone. This Ambrose character apparently went behind Hardy's back to arrange the meeting at Maillard's."

My mother descended the rest of the steps and came to stand on the parquet floor. "Yes, but if not for that meeting, we wouldn't have Joséphine back with us."

"Which is the reason I paid Mr. Lee in the first place," my father said. "But Hardy explained the whole story, that he'd found Josie in Boston, planned to use her to trick us. He said he then developed feelings for her and abandoned the plan here in New York."

"He said that?" I asked.

"Yes." My father lifted his head to study me. "He said he fell in love with you."

Leo said the same the other night when he snuck in, yet I hadn't believed him. Was he telling the truth?

"Love! He's a swindler," my mother said. "As if we'd ever allow our only daughter to—"

I couldn't stand to hear anymore. I needed answers from Leo. About the money, about us. About everything.

I ran for the door. Ronald blocked my way, so I called, "Move!"

"Josie! You need a hat and gloves," my mother said. "And an escort!"

I dodged around the butler, propriety be damned. My father's voice trailed after me as I descended the front steps. "Send a footman out after her!" he ordered.

Looking up and down the walk, I searched for Leo. Unfortunately, there were too many people out and about. A maid was sweeping the side stairs. I asked her, "Did you see a tall man leave here? Navy suit, black derby. I need to know which way he went."

"He went that way, miss." She pointed to the left, so I thanked her and started running.

I found him three-quarters of the way up the block. Head down, Leo was staring at the ground as he walked. I grabbed his arm and pulled him to a stop. "Leo, wait."

When he faced me, his blue eyes were polite but flat. He tipped his hat. "Miss Pendelton. Was there something you needed?"

Panting, I tried to catch my breath. "I need to know why."

"Why what?"

"Why you took that check from Ambrose and returned it."

"Ambrose had no right to the money and neither do I. If anyone deserves it, it's you."

This was unbelievable. It went against everything I knew about him. "But your family, your sisters. Making good for your father. How could you give up such an exorbitant amount?"

"Ambrose didn't give it up."

"What does that mean?"

"Never mind," Leo said. "It's not important. In the end neither of us knew you were the real heiress. The credit is yours."

Hardly. Leo had been the one to make the trip happen. Without him, I'd still be singing on street corners in Boston. He'd taken me to see Lotta, to meet with Melvin.

He believed in me.

Me, Josie Smith. An orphan with hardly two cents to scrape together.

I never would've come this far without him. Every time I was nervous, he'd been there to reassure me. True, he used me as part of his swindle, but Leo had bolstered my faith in my abilities, too.

And he hadn't gone through with the swindle. *He returned the money.*

Movement nearby caught my eye. One of our footmen hovered

nearby, watching over me, so I lowered my voice. "I never would've come to New York if not for you."

"Nah," he said, the side of his mouth hitching. "You would've ended up here eventually. With your voice? You were destined for Broadway one way or another. I'm just sorry I let you down."

"You told my father you fell in love with me."

A flash of something crossed his face, the first crack in his calm exterior. But it was gone as quickly as it appeared. "It can hardly come as a surprise. I said the same to you the other night."

"And yet I am surprised."

"You shouldn't be. You're remarkable, Josie. And for what it's worth, I've never uttered those words to anyone outside my family. I've done a lot in my life, but I wouldn't lie about that."

"Then why are you leaving?"

He lifted his arms and let them fall to his sides. "Because this is the right thing to do. You don't trust me and I ruined any chance we had together. And look at where you live! Your dress, your hair." His gaze swept the length of me. "You're too fancy for the likes of me, sweetheart."

"I'm the same person. I haven't changed just because of my parents."

"You're famous now. Haven't you seen the papers? You are all anyone can talk about, a miracle." A muscle jumped in his jaw as he stared out toward the street. "An association with me will only hurt you."

"You're wrong! Don't leave me. Stay and be my manager. Or my friend. Something. I-I miss you."

Leo stared at me, his blue eyes serious as they searched mine. "Do you honestly believe your parents will allow me to remain in your life?"

"If I wish it, yes."

Head shaking, he wore a sad smile as he stared at the street. "Honey, you don't have any idea how your new world works. Men like me don't associate with unmarried women like you."

"You're wrong. All I'm asking is for you to stay. You can be my manager—"

"Josie," he snapped. "I said I love you and you want me to hang about and be your friend? It would crush me, being close to you day after day, yet knowing I can't have you. Watching you marry some uptown swell. I'm not strong enough for that."

Tongue tangled, I wasn't sure of what to do or say. How did I feel about him? I knew I missed him and I liked having him in my life. I wanted to kiss him and touch him, tell him every single thought in my head.

But *love?*

What did I know about love?

I hadn't seen much of it in my life, and even with my parents, love was a fragile undertaking. My heart wasn't used to allowing others in; I'd protected it since I was a child. Perhaps I wasn't capable of love. How would I know? I went so long without it that such pieces inside of me might be permanently broken.

And if they weren't . . .

Was I ready to risk loving someone and then losing them?

Helpless, I stood there as pedestrians and carts passed by, regular people doing everyday, normal things. Time stretched, yet I wasn't ready to lose Leo. I wanted to prolong this as best I could until I figured out what all these feelings meant.

The wind gusted around us, ruffling the edges of his too-long hair under his hat as he said softly, "I should go and let you return inside."

"Wait."

He didn't move, but I could sense his impatience with me. "Josie, I'm trying to be honorable for once in my life."

Wrong. Leo had honor. I'd seen examples of it, from the way he looked after his sisters, to the careful manner in which he'd treated me during our intimacies. And he returned the most money he'd ever see in his life because he didn't deserve it. "So you're giving up on me? On us?"

"There is no us. You're . . ." Trailing off, he shoved his hands in his pockets and lifted a shoulder. "Look around you. This is your world, not mine."

"That isn't true. We're from the same world."

"Hardly. You may have visited mine for a short while, but this is where you belong."

"I belong on a stage. And once upon a time you were going to help me get there."

"Nah." He ran his knuckles under my jaw. "You don't need me for that. Knock 'em dead, sweetheart. I'll be watching from Boston."

When he turned to walk away, I couldn't bear it. I put my hand on his arm. "Leo, wait. You should've kept the money. Let me speak with my father. I'll ask him to write you another check, a different one with your name on it."

He gently removed my hand from his coat, but he lessened the sting by pressing a kiss to my knuckles. His lips were warm and soft, his hot breath tickling my bare skin. "I don't need it. Some things are worth more than money."

I couldn't believe those words had come out of his mouth. "Like what?"

He dropped my hand. "Like you."

His gaze studied my face, carefully, as if memorizing every detail. Then he tipped his hat, turned around, and walked away. I watched his broad shoulders shift as his long legs ate up the walk, his form growing smaller and smaller.

I didn't move. I waited, hoping.

But he never glanced back over his shoulder at me, not even once.

Chapter Twenty-Six

LEO

The Birdman office was crowded, with six men crammed in to see Melvin. Miss Bryce ignored them all as she typed away on her machine behind the desk. I removed my hat and greeted her warmly. "Good afternoon, Miss Bryce."

Her eyes flicked over to me and she paused midstrike. "Well, hello, Mr. Hardy. Surprised to see you here, considering you lost your only client."

I flashed Miss Bryce a smile. "I hoped to see Melvin today, if he's available. I know I don't have an appointment."

"I bet he wants to see you, too. Hold on." Reaching over, she picked up the handset on her desk and flicked a switch. "Mr. Birdman, Mr. Hardy is here to see you."

A deep voice boomed from the inner office, "Send him in!"

Miss Bryce hung up and gestured to the closed door. "Go right in."

"Thank you. Appreciate it."

As I turned the knob, the men in the waiting room began complaining to Miss Bryce, outraged that I'd been let through first. "That's enough!" she snapped. "Pipe down, all of you, or you're out on the street."

Melvin was alone in the office, behind his desk with a large packet of papers in his hands. He dropped the papers onto the desk when I shut the door behind me. "You were holding out on me, Hardy."

There was no use in pretending I didn't know what he meant. "I had no idea, sir. I noticed a resemblance when I first met her, but I never thought she was actually the kidnapped heiress."

"Noticed a resemblance to who?"

"The mother. I practically grew up on the Pendelton estate."

"Now I have even more questions." He pointed at the empty chair in front of his desk. "Sit down and fill me in."

I dropped into the seat and told him everything, from my father's long history with the Pendeltons, to seeing Josie on the street and convincing her to come to New York. I didn't try to polish it up for Melvin. I gave him the plain truth, even though I wasn't proud of it.

"This sales background you spoke of . . ."

"An elaboration."

"A confidence man from the sound of it. You were planning to pass this girl off as a lost heiress, but it turns out she truly was the lost heiress."

"Yes."

Melvin slapped the desktop with his palm and burst out laughing. "Son, that is the plot of a dramatic play if I've ever heard one."

"It seems fantastic, I realize, but it's true."

"How does the singing career figure into all this?"

"It was Josie's dream, and I figured it was an easy way get her in front of the Pendeltons."

"Smart." Melvin rocked back in his chair, the wood and metal squeaking. "But you said you gave up?"

"I couldn't go through with it."

"Fell in love with her, did you?"

I didn't answer. There was no point. "A friend of mine took matters into his own hands. He approached Mrs. Pendelton and arranged a meeting without my knowledge."

"Ah. I bet Josie wasn't happy about that."

"No, she wasn't. She's convinced I had something to do with it." I rubbed the back of my neck, wishing the ache in my chest would dissipate. "You should know that she terminated our partnership."

"I'm sorry to hear it. You know, I could sell out every theater on the East Coast with her name. I plan to speak with her after the press meeting tomorrow."

"Press meeting?"

"You haven't heard?" When I shook my head, he elaborated. "Park Row is salivating over the girl. The family's agreed to one more interview, how she's settling in and the like."

It was to be expected, but I wondered if Josie was nervous. I remembered how she'd paled right before meeting Lotta, not to mention her trepidation in coming to see Melvin. Would someone hold her hand and tell her to breathe?

Probably, but it won't be me.

"No, I hadn't heard." I needed to get to the point. The sooner I left New York, the better. "I'm here about a different matter."

"Oh? And what is that?"

"I want to work for you." Melvin blinked twice, so I rushed to explain. "I respect and understand what you do. I'm good with people. I can read their faces and say what they need to hear."

"I thought you wished to manage singers."

Yes, well . . . that didn't pan out as I'd hoped. "I think producing might be a better fit."

"Why?"

"Because you're the puppet master, pulling the strings. You oversee the whole operation."

Melvin puffed up a bit at that. "It's not easy. I'm part lawyer, part mother hen, part carnival barker."

"Not to mention part confidence artist."

"A bit of that as well," he said with a chuckle. "It's a juggling act, kid."

"I've been juggling my five sisters for years. I understand it. And I've been surviving on my wits for a long time, sir."

"I don't doubt it." Melvin rocked in his chair and pursed his lips. "I've never had an assistant. But you might be able to take some of that"—he pointed to the anteroom—"off my plate. Which would allow me to focus on more important matters."

"Exactly. Except there is one caveat."

"See? I knew it was too good to be true. What are you fixing to ask for? A hundred dollars a week?"

"After I've proven myself, I want to return to Boston. Open an office there."

"I like the sound of it. Birdman Theatrical Productions, New York and Boston."

"Or Birdman-Hardy Theatrical Productions."

"Don't get ahead of yourself, kid." He leaned forward and pointed at me. "You've got chutzpah. Know what that means?"

"No, sir. Is it bad?"

"It's Yiddish for guts. I like that you thought this up and came to me." He narrowed his eyes, examining me for a long moment. Determined not to show weakness, I held his gaze.

Finally, Melvin said, "Let's see how you do in a meeting."

"A meeting? As in one of your meetings?"

"Of course. Who else is taking meetings here today?" He lifted the handset of the phone on his desk and threw a switch. "Miss Bryce, send one of my appointments in. No, he's staying here. Don't worry. No, it doesn't matter which one."

The door opened and a man introduced himself as Mr. David Easton. I sized him up quickly. Thinning hair, weak chin. Terrible sartorial sense, if his mismatched colors were anything to go by. Either he was unmarried or had a wife disinterested in her husband's appearance.

We shook hands, though Melvin didn't say anything about me other than my name.

"Sit down, David, and tell me why you're here."

Easton cast a curious look my way, then focused on Melvin. "I know we settled on the amount for the chorus, but it isn't enough. I need more money to hire the right number of girls."

"David, when you were last here, I told you there was no more money—and I meant it. I've given you all I mean to invest."

"But you don't understand, Mr. Birdman. These girls, they come at a higher price nowadays. It used to be that we could pay them next to nothing and they'd be grateful for the work. Now we have the factories and department stores to compete with, not to mention the higher-end bordellos."

Melvin appeared to consider it. "How much more do you need?"

"Fifty dollars should cover it."

I couldn't help it—I snorted. It was an outrageous sum.

"Something to say, Mr. Hardy?" Melvin asked.

I cleared my throat. "I beg your pardon, Mr. Birdman. Ignore me."

"Actually, I'd like to hear what you're thinking."

No way to avoid it now. If it meant he didn't hire me, so be it.

"Fifty dollars is a staggering amount of money," I said. "One could hire a hundred chorus girls for that amount. Which makes me wonder if the money truly is for chorus girls. Because I see the lip stain on Mr. Easton's collar and the way his necktie clashes with the color of his vest. No wife would approve of such a choice, unless she's given up on the marriage. Instead, I suspect the money is to keep a woman happy. A mistress, most likely."

Melvin pursed his lips. "Well, David. Is this an attempt to use the show's coffers to support a ladybird?"

"Th-That is an absurd accusation!" After shooting daggers at me with his eyes, Easton shifted in his chair. "We have been friends for sixteen years, Melvin. I don't even know this man and you are listening to him over me?"

"I'm awaiting an explanation," Melvin said calmly. "What is the money for, David?"

"I told you the money is for more chorus girls."

"Then I must say no. Make do with what you have."

After a few minutes of arguing, Easton left in a huff with empty pockets. Conversely, Melvin appeared quite pleased with me. He pointed a finger in my direction. "That was clever."

"Does this mean I'm hired?"

"No, not yet. I want to see her first."

"Who? Josie?"

"Yes. I want to see if she's willing to travel the country." He mimed his hand in the air, as if viewing a marquee. "The Lost Pendelton Heiress. With her voice and that billing we'll sell out shows from Poughkeepsie to Albuquerque."

"Then cable her. Ask her to come to the office."

"I have. Repeatedly. I've also paid a call at the family home, but they wouldn't admit me."

"There's your answer, then."

Melvin's expression turned shrewd as he studied me. "I have faith in you, kid. Get her here and I'll give you a shot."

I never even considered it.

I used Josie once. I wouldn't do that to her ever again. She deserved only the truth from now on.

"I won't use her like that."

Melvin tilted his head, surprise etched in his features. "Then I have to assume you don't truly want the job."

"I guess I don't." Slipping my derby on my head, I stood and shook Melvin's hand. "Thank you for seeing me."

"Your newly found principles mean that much to you?"

No, *Josie* meant that much to me. She'd been through enough. She didn't need me in her life, mucking it up with more lies. "I suppose so."

"Then I wish you luck, kid."

Defeated, I left Melvin's office. I'd need to figure something else out.

Boston

I t turned out having principles didn't pay very well.

Since returning home six days ago I hadn't been able to find decent employment. Oh, I could find any number of illicit earnings, but honest work was proving difficult for a man like me. A person with no legitimate experience to speak of, no former employers to vouch on my behalf.

But I was determined.

Acting as Josie's manager showed that I have skills to offer besides dodging the police and running swindles. I merely needed to find a person willing to take a risk on hiring me.

Quickly.

Arriving in Boston empty-handed hadn't made for a pleasant homecoming. Though my mother was disappointed, she tried to put a brave face on it. Molly and Hattie both called me a fool. Carolyn guessed that I'd fallen for Josie, which made it impossible to go through with the plan. Flora laughed upon hearing the news, then disappeared, likely off with the McLaughlin fellow. I'd deal with her later, as soon as I found a job.

Tess, my quietest sister, merely patted my hand, as if to reassure me that my failure wasn't the end of the world. But we both knew the truth: if I didn't earn money soon, it would be the end—at least for the Hardy family.

I trudged up the front steps, my feet aching from all the walking after a long day scouring the city and visiting agencies. When I pushed inside the door, complete silence greeted me.

That was odd. The last thing I needed was to hear my own thoughts, to drown in the regret and rejection I'd suffered both in New York and Boston.

Where was everyone? Had someone died? Concerned, I hurried into the sitting room, not even bothering to remove my hat. The room was crowded, but my gaze locked on one person.

Josie.

Holy shit. Josie was here. In Boston.

In my home.

Frozen in place, I drank in the sight of her like a man dying of thirst. My god, how elegant she looked, with her blond hair neatly styled and a new green dress to match her eyes. Full lips, a delicate nose. Her skin was a pale rose color now, the result of staying indoors—a luxury possessed strictly by the wealthy in this country.

This was Joséphine Pendelton, not the woman I'd met in Post Office Square all those days ago. My Josie might be lurking underneath somewhere, but this was why I'd let her go. She'd transformed into someone else, someone better. Perfectly illustrated by how out of place she appeared in our shabby surroundings.

A man cleared his throat.

Blinking, I saw Mr. Pendelton standing not far from his daughter, his arms crossed over his chest. He was glaring at me. My family were seated around the room as well, their expressions a mix between curiosity and outright amusement.

I was making an ass of myself.

Slowly, I removed my hat. "Mr. Pendelton. Miss Pendelton. This is a surprise."

Josie rose from her seat and clasped her hands. "Leo. Hello."

No one else spoke or moved, but I didn't glance away from her. I had no clue as to what to say or do, my mind clogged with possibilities and questions.

"Girls." My mother rose and began motioning to my sisters. "Let's give Leo and his guest privacy. Come along."

"I don't wanna—" Molly started, until Flora grabbed her arm and tugged Molly from the room.

"Mr. Pendelton," my mother continued, "I have a fresh apple cake in the kitchen. Perhaps you'd care for a slice?"

The older man nodded once. "I'd like that, Mrs. Hardy." He started across the room, but he paused when he reached my side. "I won't be far."

"Yes, sir. I understand."

Then Josie and I were alone. I was desperate to touch her, to hold her once more. Smell her skin and feel the press of her lips on mine. Being this close, yet maintaining a polite distance, scraped against the inside of my chest like a blade.

I swallowed hard. "Why have you come here?"

"I needed to see you."

"I can't imagine why."

"First, I wanted to thank you."

That was odd. I slipped my hands into my trouser pockets and lifted a shoulder. "You don't owe me any gratitude."

"Of course I do. Without you, none of this would've happened."

"I'm glad it's worked out for you. You deserve it."

She nibbled on her bottom lip. "I'm not sure I deserve it, but I'm trying to adjust to my parents and new circumstances."

"They've been treating you well, I trust?"

"Yes. We've been getting on. They're overly protective, but I don't mind."

Yes, I could imagine, considering she'd been stolen from them once. We fell silent and I couldn't help but say, "You look well."

"As do you."

Awkwardness descended like a thick blanket around us. This was the most painful conversation I'd ever endured, and that included speaking to my sisters about men. Finally, I couldn't take it. "Josie, why are you here?"

"To see you."

"Why?"

She searched my face intently, her head angling slightly. "I thought you would be happier to see me."

Was she serious? Anger sparked in my belly. Hadn't the past two weeks been bad enough? Now I needed to suffer more? Why was I so fucking unfortunate?

I put my hands on my hips. "For god's sake, woman. Every day is an uphill battle, and seeing you is breaking my heart all over again. What else do you expect from me?"

She didn't flinch in the face of my anger. Instead, she closed the distance between us, coming to stand in front of me. "I'm here because I needed to confess. I lied in New York."

"But you never lie."

"Not usually, no, but I lied when I said I didn't return your feelings."

Time came to a standstill, the air pausing as I stared down at her face. "You lied?"

She gave me a tiny nod. "I do return your feelings. Very much."

"You . . . love me?" Another nod. My chest squeezed, hope soaring inside me. But I had to be sure. This was too important. "I need the words, Josie."

She inhaled then let the air out slowly. "I love you, Leo. I realized it as soon as I heard you turned Mr. Birdman down, that you wouldn't use me to get a position with him."

"It wasn't right, not after all that's happened."

"But you could've asked me. I might have agreed to the visit, if it meant you were offered a job."

"I won't use you for my personal gain ever again."

"See? That is how I know I love you." She grinned and rocked on her toes, pleased with herself.

Those words on her lips . . . Would I ever tire of hearing them? They sounded better than anything in the world, even her singing voice.

I started to smile, but common sense prevailed. What did this revelation change? She was still an *heiress*. I was still a struggling former confidence man looking to go straight. Furthermore, I had six other people who depended on me here in Boston. Our lives could not be more different.

We were worlds apart.

I shoved down all the premature happiness and hope. "Thank you for telling me. I'm sure your father is anxious to leave."

Her lips parted as deep lines formed in her brow. "This is your response? To thank me?"

"What should I say, Josie?" My arms flapped uselessly at my sides. "Our circumstances are what they are. I cannot change them and neither can you."

"Balderdash. You're pushing me away, using our circumstances as an excuse. Why? Don't you love me enough to fight for me?"

Her voice tightened, the last few words coming out strangled with emotion. They tore at my heart, even when I was determined to let her go.

I cupped her jaw in both of my hands, holding her, and I gazed at her beautiful face. How could she ever doubt my feelings? "I love you enough not to drag you down. You're an heiress now. Probably the richest heiress in the world. I want you to have a new life, one free of the past, sweetheart. You can become whomever you want now."

"I don't want to forget my past, Leo," she said softly and wrapped her fingers around my wrists. "I realized something the last few days. I *like* who I am. I'm not ashamed of growing up in the asylum or earning a living by singing on the street. All those steps brought me here, to this place right now. Without them, I'd never have met you or found my parents."

"But Joséphine Pendelton—"

"Is still Josie Smith underneath. Please, Leo. I don't want to do any of this without you. Because you're not dragging me down; you make me a better version of myself."

I closed my eyes briefly, absorbing the words and letting them sink in. My chest lightened, as if the dark clouds inside me parted to let in the sun. She'd made me a better person—someone with useful skills to offer beyond lying and stealing.

Was it impossible I did the same for her?

Leaning down, I rested my forehead against hers, letting the scent of her fill my lungs. "Once you say it, you cannot take it back."

"Which part?"

"All of it. Because now that I know, I'm never letting you go. It's you and me until the very end, sweetheart."

Her fingers tightened on my hands, holding on. "That's all I want."

"You don't want anything else?"

"Well, I still want to sing and perform. So I'll need my manager back."

"You can ask, but he comes at a very high price."

She stiffened slightly and started to pull away. "Oh? And what price is that?"

I wrapped an arm around her waist and kept her close. "I want to marry you. Soon. Say yes, Josie."

Her body moved closer to mine, hands sliding up my chest. "Yes, I'll marry you."

"Thank Christ." Her lips were right there, plump and perfect. I was dying to kiss her, even though my family was probably eavesdropping in the hall. "I love you so damn much."

"I'm glad to hear it. Because you're going to need to move back to New York."

"I'll go anywhere with you." I couldn't wait any longer. I started to lower my head, but she pressed on my shoulder to stop me. "What is it?"

"Your family will come with us. And Pippa."

"Jesus, fine. May I kiss you now?"

She slid her arms around my neck and sealed her body to mine. "Yes, but make it fast. Your sisters are listening out in the hall."

Chapter Twenty-Seven

JOSIE

The crowd was still cheering.

"I suppose we owe them another curtain call," our director and lead actor, Frank Smithson, called out. "Everyone, places!"

The cast retook our usual spots and the curtain rose once more. The audience clapped louder, a few whistles rising above the hoots and shouts. I clasped hands with the performers on either side of me and we all bowed as one. As we straightened, I looked out at the faces in the seats and marveled at my life.

I was on a Broadway stage with a supporting part in a new musical. Me, Josie Smith, née Josie Pendelton. Now Mrs. Leo Hardy.

The musical, *The Girl from Paris*, had opened only last week to rave reviews. I'd landed a supporting role as Ruth, the servant to one of the main characters, with two musical numbers in the second act. It was more than I'd ever dreamed possible. Night after night, I was singing on a stage in front of New York audiences.

Not only that, but I'd found my parents and met the most amazing man.

I was the luckiest woman alive.

When the curtain fell for the second time, Mr. Smithson turned to me. "Excellent performance tonight," he said in his Irish accent. "I love the slight change you made to the second bridge in our duet."

Pleased, I couldn't help but grin as we started across the stage together. "Thank you. I think it added a little bit of fun."

"Indeed, it did. You are quite talented. It's a pleasure to sing with you for eight shows a week."

"I could say the same, Mr. Smithson. I'm so grateful you chose me for the role."

"Belasco told me I was a fool if I didn't hire you. And you've proved him right time and time again."

I owed Melvin another bottle of his favorite whiskey for that meeting earlier in the year with David Belasco. "It's been a wonderful experience."

"I'm gratified to hear you say as much. Excuse me, I need to speak with our stage manager. Good night, Mrs. Hardy."

I bid him good night then continued into the wings. Before I could blink, a pair of hands grabbed me and pulled me into the darkness.

Instantly, I relaxed. I knew these hands.

"Sweetheart, you were astounding," my husband said as he held on to my waist. "Dazzling. Breathtaking. The most wonderful performer on the stage."

Even though I longed to remove my costume and cosmetics, I wrapped my arms around his neck and moved closer. "As my manager and husband, you are biased. However, I will accept your praise graciously."

"Christ, you're beautiful out there. I'm so damn proud of you." Leo nuzzled my throat, giving my skin a nip with his teeth. "You improve every night. It's both perplexing and impressive."

"Thank you, husband."

He groaned softly as his mouth found the edge of my ear. "Indeed, I am your very fortunate husband. All those men in the audience watching you, salivating over you. Yet you're mine."

I clutched him and sank my nails into the back of his head. "There's only one man I want salivating over me."

"Oh, do not worry. He was most definitely salivating." Leo

pressed his hips to mine, and even through my costume I could feel his thickness. Then he bent and kissed me, not concerned apparently about my lip paint. This was not gentle or sweet; my husband was desperate and greedy, kissing me as if we hadn't seen each other in months.

My bones were jelly by the time he broke off, our breath ragged. He rested his forehead to mine. "I want to fuck you in your dressing room."

"*Leo*," I admonished half-heartedly. "We were almost caught the last time."

"I don't care. I can't wait until we're home. I need you *now*."

Considering I shared a dressing room with another performer, this was too risky. "You'll need to wait, tomcat. Besides, Melvin is here tonight."

"Shit. I forgot." He took a step back and adjusted himself in his trousers. "I need a moment."

I patted his chest. "Collect yourself, Mr. Hardy. I'll see to Melvin until you're presentable."

He pulled me back for another deep kiss, complete with tongue, that was far too brief. Then he let me go. "Thank you, Mrs. Hardy."

Before we got ourselves into trouble, I slipped out from behind the alcove and walked backstage. It was tight quarters, many performers and crew members crammed into tiny rooms, but I didn't mind. We were like a big family and I loved it.

Soon I entered my dressing room. Melvin was there, along with Annie, the actress with whom I shared the room. They were chatting together, but both looked over at me as I pushed through the door. Then they started laughing.

"What is it?" I asked, looking down at my costume. Had it torn?

"You have lip stain," Annie said, motioning all around her mouth. "Everywhere."

"Oh, no." I hurried to my mirror to inspect the damage. Indeed, there was a large red ring around my mouth. I reached for a cloth to wipe it off.

"Ah, young love. I see you've found your husband," Melvin said, still chuckling. Then he pushed off the wall. "I'm only staying long enough to give you the good news."

I paused in opening a jar of cream. "Are we not having supper together?"

"I'm afraid I can't. I have an appointment."

"A woman or a client?" I asked over my shoulder with a teasing smile.

"I'll never tell. Now, would you like to hear the good news or not?"

"Of course. Tell me."

"The show's been extended and they'd like you to stay on. With an increase in your wages, of course."

Turning sideways in my chair, I faced him. "That is fantastic! For how long?"

"Next summer, at least. Congratulations, Josie. You've earned it."

"Thank you, Mr. Birdman. I appreciate all you've done for me."

Before Melvin could respond, Annie chimed in. "I haven't heard anything about an extension. I wonder if they're keeping me."

Melvin shrugged. "You need a better agent, miss." Then he put his derby on his head. "Now I'll see myself out. Good night, ladies."

"Good night, Melvin."

When I left the dressing room moments later, I found Leo talking animatedly with several members of the backstage crew. They were laughing at something my husband was saying, his charm infectious. He did this everywhere we went, no matter the situation. I didn't mind—I couldn't resist him, either.

He looked over when I shut the dressing room door and a grin broke out on his face. "Shall we go, Mrs. Hardy?"

"I'm ready, Mr. Hardy."

"Sorry, gents," Leo said to the crew. "My beautiful wife needs me."

We bid everyone good night, then Leo walked me outside. Our carriage waited at the curb, as usual. This was at my father's insistence, as he didn't want me, "scuttling about the city at night." My parents were still protective of me, which I understood. Occasionally, this caused a bit of friction between us, but I usually indulged them. Like when Leo and I agreed to live in the mansion after our wedding. My parents had been positively thrilled, even giving us our own wing for privacy.

"I'm exhausted," I said as we settled in the carriage. "Will you rub my feet when we are home?"

"Of course, my love." Leo leaned over and kissed my temple. "Would you mind if we stopped for a drink first?"

"Oh, Leo. Must we? I'm hungry and tired."

"But I'll feed you," he promised. "If you agree, I will rub your feet *and* your shoulders when we arrive home."

"One drink?"

"One drink. And food for you."

"Fine, but I want every part of me rubbed at home. And I do mean every part."

My husband laughed and kissed my gloved hand. "As I recall, I offered to do as much in your dressing room tonight."

I closed my eyes, a smile on my face, as we rode uptown. Finally, the carriage began to slow. "Where are we stopping?"

"Sherry's. I know you love their roast duck."

I did. Duck was a luxury I'd never been able to afford until now, and one of my indulgences. "You spoil me," I murmured.

"I try. It's not easy, though. Your parents are always first in line for that task."

The wheels stopped and we both descended. Late-night diners dotted the main dining room inside Sherry's. But instead of a table, we were led toward the private rooms. Surprised, I looked at Leo. "You reserved a private room?"

"I hope you don't mind. I thought we might enjoy some time to ourselves."

Of course I didn't mind, but the extravagance was unnecessary. The dining room would have suited me fine.

Being rich was certainly strange at times.

"Here we are, Mr. and Mrs. Hardy." The maître d'hôtel opened the door of the private room. It was dark inside.

I frowned, hesitating, as Leo said, "Thank you."

"Why is it—"

My words were cut off as the light suddenly switched on. A room full of people were all staring at me, smiling at me. My parents, Leo's family. Even Pippa was here.

What on earth?

"Surprise," Leo said softly in my ear.

I looked over at him. "I don't understand."

"I'll let your parents explain."

He took my hand and led me forward as everyone rushed toward us. Dazed, I ended up face-to-face with my mother. She wrapped her arms around me. "Happy birthday, my sweet girl."

Birthday?

I sucked in a lungful of air. "Is it today?" I whispered.

"It is today," she answered, hugging me tighter.

My eyes welled with tears and my throat burned as I hugged her back. I'd completely forgotten. Months ago, when I first reunited with them, we'd discussed my birthday, but I'd been too busy with the show and the wedding to remember. After all, I hadn't ever looked forward to one before.

Today was my birthday.

"I thought for sure you remembered this morning," my father said, kissing my cheek. "Over breakfast, when you inquired about the date." Impulsively, I threw myself into his chest. He caught me and embraced me. "Happy birthday, my dear."

After that it was a blur of well wishes from Leo's family. His sisters were a fun group and they always made me feel included.

We often banded together in teasing Leo, and I enjoyed showing Molly and Hattie around the city.

When the flurry of salutations died down, Pippa was there to embrace me. "Happy birthday. I'm so grateful we're together to share it."

"Me, too." My parents had taken Pippa in for a short while, helping her get started in the city. Now she was a familiar figure around our Fifth Avenue home, visiting a few times a week for dinner or tea. She was my sister in every way but blood. "I love you."

"I love you, too."

We grinned at each other, deliriously happy. We'd come a long way from two raggedy girls at the Children's Asylum. "Did you plan this?" I asked her.

"Nope. This was your husband's doing."

My chest swelled with emotion, an overflowing of affection for my champion, my guiding star. My reformed scoundrel. I knew why he'd done this for me. On this, the most important day of my year, Leo made certain to surround me with family and friends, to prove I wasn't alone any longer. To ensure I knew that I was loved.

"Excuse me," I told Pippa. "I need to find him."

She chuckled and patted my shoulder, then I searched the room until I spotted the top of his head near the back. Standing alone, he leaned against the wall with his hands in his trouser pockets, a soft smile on his face. It wasn't the practiced huckster's smile. This was the real one, the smile he used only for me. The one that reached his eyes.

"Hello, sweetheart," he said quietly when I closed in on him. "Do you like your surprise?"

"It's perfect. I would ask how you knew I would love it, but . . ."

He wrapped an arm around my waist and kissed my cheek. "First rule of being a husband: anticipate your wife's every need."

I nestled into his side. "I thought that was the first rule of being a manager."

"Close. Except I don't daydream about all the ways I plan to pleasure my clients the instant we're alone."

"Lucky me, then."

Bending, he put his mouth near my ear. "No, lucky *us*."

Acknowledgments

Anastasia is one of my favorite stories. A fake princess who is really the princess? Say no more! So when my editor suggested the idea for this book, I immediately jumped on it. You already know that I love a morally gray hero, and Leo and Josie were a blast to write.

A lot of research into nineteenth-century Broadway went into this book. I've tried to keep as much accuracy here as possible, though I may have adjusted some of the performance dates. Lotta Crabtree is all true, just as fascinating a person as you'd imagine.

Thank you to my editor, Tessa Woodward, at Avon, and the fabulous team at HarperCollins who work to support my books, especially Madelyn Blaney, DJ DeSmyter, and May Chen.

I'm very grateful to Holly Root and the team at Root Literary, who have been the most awesome cheerleaders for me and this book. Thank you!

To Jennifer Prokop, who helped shape so much of what *The Gilded Heiress* became, thank you! I'm so grateful for your thoughts and feedback. I will learn to keep a timeline someday, I swear!

Thank you to Nicole, the queen who keeps things running smoothly in my author life, allowing me to focus on writing. I'm very thankful for all her hard work!

A special shout-out to Diana Quincy, who is my ride or die. I am incredibly lucky to have her in my life.

Thank you to my family, especially my husband. He keeps my crazy life on track, and none of this is possible without him. Love you, babe!

Lastly, thank you to the readers! You make this job worthwhile, and I'm so grateful for all the support. Let's do this again soon!

About the Author

A *USA Today* bestselling author, Joanna Shupe has always loved history, ever since she saw her first *Schoolhouse Rock* cartoon. Her books have appeared on numerous yearly "best of" lists, including *Publishers Weekly*, *The Washington Post*, *Kirkus Reviews*, Kobo, and *BookPage*. She lives in New Jersey with her two spirited daughters and dashing husband.

READ MORE BY
JOANNA SHUPE

THE FOUR HUNDRED SERIES

THE UPTOWN GIRLS SERIES

THE FIFTH AVENUE REBELS SERIES